A is for Apprentice

A Wizard's Order Novel

by Steve DeWinter

Summary

It is said that when the student is ready the teacher will appear.

In Midguard, Spinners are practitioners of innate magic who must learn to control the power that lives inside them before it destroys them.

With the mysterious death of his father, only days before his training is to begin, the knowledge of Van's lineage as a powerful Spinner is hidden from him. Five years later a near-death experience awakens the dangerous powers within.

Halen, a banished Spinner, is the only one willing to teach Van to manage the magic before it consumes him. He must train Van to hone it into the powerful force needed to stop a vindictive Spinner whose personal mission to conquer Midguard would start a war resulting in the deaths of millions.

But how do they save the world, and Van's very life, when both apprentice and master are forbidden from ever crossing paths by the same organization created to bring them together?

A IS FOR APPRENTICE is a fantasy novel from the #1 Bestselling Amazon Action & Adventure Sci-Fi Author, Steve DeWinter. This is his next foray into the genre after releasing *A Tale of Two Cities with Dragons*, a fantasy mashup of the #1 Bestselling Novel of All Time, co-authored with Charles Dickens. Yes! That Charles Dickens. Get your copy of *A is for Apprentice* today to find out what happens!

This book is a work of fiction. References to real people, events, establishments, organization, or locales are intended only to provide a sense of authenticity, and are used fictitiously. All other characters, and all incidents and dialogue, are drawn from the author's imagination and are not to be construed as real.

WIZARD'S ORDER and the Wizard's Order Logo are trademarks of Ramblin' Prose Publishing.

Ramblin' Prose Publishing
Copyright © 2015 Steve DeWinter

eBook Edition
ISBN-10: 1-61978-108-5
ISBN-13: 978-1-61978-108-5

Trade Paperback Edition
ISBN-10: 1-61978-109-3
ISBN-13: 978-1-61978-109-2

Chapter 1

Everywhere he looked was chaos and death. Halen, a Wizard's Order Apprentice, did his best to stay by his Master's side, but as Spinners and Apprentices alike fell before the invading army, it was barely possible to stay alive, let alone work as a team.

For a thousand years, the armies of Aeron forced their way into Midguard through the gate at Devil's Claw on the night of the third moon. And for a thousand years, the Spinners of the Wizard's Order repelled them. But Aeron grew stronger and smarter with each attempt and it looked as if he would win this time. That would result in hundreds of thousands of deaths within the first week as his army rampaged across Midguard. Before Aeron was finished, millions would perish for the greed of one.

Veren, the most powerful Master Spinner in the Wizard's Order, stood from behind the collapsed wall he and Halen took refuge and swirled his hands in the proper configuration to command the element of earth. He lifted a large chunk of fallen wall made from the toughest granite bored from the deepest quarries of the Middle Kingdom and launched it at the approaching army. Ogres and goblins were scattered like bowling pins as the chunk of rock barreled through their ranks.

Veren ducked back down as a fiery bolt of magic seared the air above him. He regarded Halen with a wild look in his eyes. Halen knew that look. He'd seen it a thousand times before; every time Veren was preparing to do something outside the rules. But this time, it was deeper, more profound, and final. The look that normally thrilled him at the unexpected, froze him to the core. "Don't do it, Master."

Veren's shoulders dropped from the weight of his decision. He unpinned the Wizard's Order Crest from the knot of his cloak and held it out to Halen. "When he is ready, give this to my son. Train him for what is coming. But do not let him follow me."

Halen didn't reach for the small pin that was a shiny silver emblem of the letter W in the shape of an O. Normally, the passing of that small crest pin from Master to Apprentice meant the Apprentice was now a Master. Under normal circumstances it was the most desired dream of all apprentices. But Halen knew this was a very different action. With the destruction increasing around them, it signified something else.

Something Halen refused to accept.

Halen shook his head passionately. "You alone are worthy of teaching your son the ways of The Order and your clan."

Veren's eyes darkened. "Take it! I won't need it after this and if I don't succeed, Aeron cannot get his filthy hands on it."

Halen's heart pounded. He couldn't let his Master do what he proposed. "It's suicide, Veren." He risked using his Master's taken name to prove his loyalty went beyond The Order. His heart was with the man who crouched next to him behind the wall in the midst of the smoke and pandemonium.

Halen could smell the acrid air burning with magic and fire. The sounds of screaming mixed with battle cries as the forces of both armies clashed was nearly deafening, but faded away as Veren leaned in closer and unexpectedly smiled. It looked out of place on his bloody and blackened face, and did nothing to warm Halen's heart. "What I do, I do for all of Midguard. But I also do it for my son. This place may have started out as a blockade, but people have made a happy life here. A home. It is a good place. We need to protect that way of life. There needs to be a place for my son to come and learn the skills he was born with, to feel what it is like to help and defend that way of life. To be part of something greater than himself."

Halen fought back the emotion threatening to make him lose control. It was not the time to show weakness in front of his Master. In that moment, he doubted he could do what was asked of him. He wanted to make Veren proud, ease some of the pain behind his eyes, and prove to him he was making the right choice by promoting Halen to Master. But the emptiness that suddenly filled his heart would make it harder on him to be a true Master to Veren's son. Then there was The Order. How would they react to Veren's decision? This was a forbidden act by The Order's formal decree.

Veren's eyes bored deep into Halen's soul and touched him at the core. Halen witnessed the struggle of conflicting emotions in Veren's eyes as he held out the Wizard's Order Crest. "You are ready to accept this. Train my son as I trained you. Protect him as I protected you. Then when he is ready, as you are now, pass the pin on to him."

Halen reluctantly took the crest pin from Veren. He knew, without a doubt, there was nothing he could do or say to stop him. He couldn't meet his eyes but he also couldn't stay silent to the one who gave him everything, including a nurturing home and a father figure he'd grown to love. "I will never forget you, Veren."

Veren patted him on the shoulder. "For what I am about to do, I doubt anyone will forget me." Halen looked up and saw the small smile on Veren's face. Halen knew it might be futile but he had to try to change his master's mind one last time. "Don't do it for the glory!"

Veren's look shifted to a disapproving stare. "You know me better than that, Halen!" Veren flung an arm to the destruction. "Look around! We are losing!" Then he said more softly "We are dying. Aeron is about to come through that gate." He balled his fists. "I can't let this destruction spread across Midguard. Think of all the innocent lives that will be lost!"

With a final plea, Halen whispered, "Please find another way!"

Veren softened one last time and put a hand on Halen's shoulder. "I wish there was time. But we have mere moments before he is through that gate." Veren's hand on Halen's shoulder turned into a vice grip. "I know my son is in capable hands and I do this to ensure there is a safe place for him to come to train."

Before Halen could say another word, Veren jumped up and rushed for the gate. He ducked and spun as he threw elements at the ogres and goblins endeavoring to halt his progress. Halen watched helplessly as Veren made it to the gate and came face-to-face with Aeron just as he stepped through. The look of surprise on Aeron's face was evident as he swirled the elements around him to stop Veren's hastily implemented plan.

But it was too late.

Veren gathered his elements together and pulled them all into the gate at once, unleashing a massive explosion of energy and magic. Halen ducked behind the collapsed wall as the explosion radiated outward, destroying every creature of evil in one fell swoop. The roar of energy assaulted Halen's ears and he pressed his hands against his head to keep from going deaf. The air filled with debris and grit. Breathing became so hard all Halen could do was focus on curling tightly into a ball and praying he didn't suffocate after surviving everything else.

When the sound died down, and the air cleared a bit, Halen slowly released his hands and waited for a second, half expecting the sky itself to fall on him. When nothing happened, he slowly stood and looked over the top of the wall. Death lay all about. But Veren's plan worked.

The gate lay silent.

And closed.

Halen picked his way through the remains of Aeron's army, helping other Master Spinners and Apprentices to their feet. Those who'd witnessed Veren's sacrifice drew quickly away from Halen, as if the atrocities of his master were now a stain upon him. This did not bode well. The sudden change in the other Spinners' demeanors reminded him about Veren's Wizard's Order Crest pin and he quickly hid it. He looked up in surprise as Master Spinners suddenly surrounded him.

Halen clenched his fists in anger as the accusing eyes of his companions fell upon him. Falen, the High Master Spinner of the Wizard's Order stepped forward. Halen looked beseechingly into his angry eyes. He felt compelled to defend his Master's last act. "High Master. He sacrificed everything to save us!"

Falen's unaltered gaze was cold as stone as he held out his hand. "Veren's crest, if you please."

Halen adopted his best confused look. "What?"

Falen's expression never changed as he said, "Before any Spinner, whether Master or Apprentice, makes the forbidden decision to sacrifice himself, he turns over his crest to the one closest to him. You were with him and you are—were his apprentice."

Halen lowered his face to prevent Falen from seeing the secret hiding in his eyes. With angry, accusing glares directed at him from every angle, there was no way he was going to surrender the last thing Veren entrusted to him. He hid his hands inside his cloak to keep them from giving away his fear at how he was unexpectedly defying a thousand years of tradition. He even surprised himself when he steeled himself to look Falen directly in the eye and said, "I don't have it. He never gave it to me."

Falen's eyes barely twitched but his gaze transformed from demanding to threatening as he glowered at Halen. "Do not think that we will allow you to be promoted or his son to receive the training of The Order. Veren has broken the highest decree with his suicide. Add to that his blatant ignorance of tradition if he foolishly held onto his crest unto death. I will ask you only one last time, hand over the crest."

Halen couldn't keep his emotions in check as he yelled at the highest Spinner in all the realms. "He saved your life!" Halen spun around to confront the condemning eyes of those standing in a circle around him. "He saved everyone in Midguard from years of war and bloodshed. He saved all of you." He faced Falen, his upper lip quivering as he let the emotions flood his whole body. "We'd already lost! If Veren failed to do what he did—"

Halen could see the rage building behind the smoldering eyes of Falen as he cut him off. "You will never speak his name again!" Every Spinner reflexively took a step back and a few gasped with a surprised intake of breath. Falen always preserved a foundation of calm and serenity, wise beyond his years and filled with limitless understanding of the follies of man, even in the face of war. To see him raise his voice at an apprentice in anger was something unexpected by everyone; even Halen.

Falen suddenly noticed the shocked crowd of Spinners and quickly grew calm, his face softening back into the usual blank visage he always portrayed. He took a deep breath, ever so slightly cocked an eyebrow, and looked at the frightened faces around him. "Does anyone else feel we were about to lose Midguard to Aeron?"

Nobody said a word. Halen implored silently for someone to forget who asked the question and to answer honestly. But each face turned away as he made eye contact. They were shutting him out.

"A vote," Falen said suddenly.

Halen's heart skipped. He couldn't help it as a "No!" escaped his lips.

Falen continued as if Halen remained silent. "Who here believes Veren's final lesson to his apprentice was in keeping with the traditions of The Order?"

Everybody gave the same response.

Silence.

Halen took a chance. What did he have to lose at this point?

"I do!"

Falen shot him a withering glare. "You are not to speak."

"Maybe that is the problem—"

"Enough!"

This second outburst in as many minutes from the ever stoical leader of The Order stunned Halen to silence a second time. The atmosphere of the group shifted. And it wasn't shifting in Halen's favor, of that he was certain.

Falen stood straight and faced Halen. "The Order does not believe death is the answer to any issue, no matter how dire. The lesson must be given so the message will be remembered."

Halen's throat constricted. He knew what that meant. He was about to lose everything. He was about to fail his master. "Please! Don't do this, Falen!"

That was a mistake, as evidenced by the look of shock on everyone's face. Even Falen's eyes registered a brief moment of surprise that an apprentice would be bold enough to address him in the familiar.

Falen raised his head high and pronounced "It is the decision of this Circle Tribunal that as a lesson to all Spinners, you…" He pointed an accusing finger directly at Halen, "…be separated from The Order for the crimes of your Master. You are not to advance to Master. You will never train another."

Halen squeezed his eyes shut tightly as the words condemned him to banishment and the loss of everything he cared about. After being permanently deprived of the love of his Master, this hit below the belt. He made a solemn promise to Veren to train his son. That was being stripped away along with everything he knew. Everything he was. If he wasn't part of The Order what purpose did he serve?

He felt burning heat sear his chest, opened his eyes, and looked down quickly. He watched helplessly as his shiny silver Wizard's Order Apprentice Level Crest tarnished and blackened. His power to spin the elements was now taken from him. He would never again spin magic. He was no longer allowed to teach another Spinner how to control the elements. No matter how much he wanted to, he could never keep his promise to Veren. Despite his desperate need to stay strong in the face of this ridiculous tribunal, a single tear fell from his eye, rolled down his face and hit the crest, the tiny drop sizzling away from the heat. An audible reminder of his failure.

"It is the further decision that Veren's line be sealed," Falen said.

Halen's head snapped up and he couldn't hold back as the words exploded from his mouth under their own control. "You can't do that!

His son has done nothing wrong!"

Falen's eyes bore into his. "Veren's constant and willful decisions to ignore the teachings of The Order were not something he suffered alone. His father before him couldn't follow the rules. I dare say, most of the rules are in place because of the Maclean lineage of Spinners. It is time to put an end to that line and stop the incessant testing of boundaries."

Halen shook his head repeatedly. "No," he whispered barely louder than an exhale. Then he found his voice and clenched his fists as he challenged the leader of The Order. "His son is due to arrive for training in a week. It's his thirteenth birthday! Please! Do with me what you will, but do not make him pay for that which he has no control!"

"Control. A fitting word, Halen. The Order begrudgingly accepts the fact that the Maclean line has no ability to control their emotions. Every Spinner knows if you cannot control your emotions, you have no control over your actions. Even you dared to shed a tear during this hearing, proving you were improperly trained. Veren's son is a threat to this Order. He is a threat to all of Midguard. He will never apprentice. He will never spin the elements. He is to never know what he is capable of."

Chapter 2

Van Maclean stared out at the ocean through the window of his second story bedroom. He could see all the way to the wall of fog that would achieve landfall by morning. The bustling twenty-four hour city of San Francisco lay behind him. The only source of noise was the Pandora app on his iPad mini playing Spring Love by Stevie B. on a personalized station algorithmically created based on the hits of the 80's and 90's. It was his father's favorite era of music. Van listened to it now with a renewed appreciation.

The funeral for his father was short, but definitely not sweet. He glanced at the funeral notice still in his hand. It stated in a curvy looping script that was printed in gold leaf print, "In Memorial for Paul Maclean." It was the last thing in the world that would bear his father's name. Van refused to believe the dubious story that his father collapsed at work from a heart attack. The funeral took place the very next day with only Van, his mother, and a few quote unquote friends from work in attendance. Missing were their real friends. The other two families who did everything as one big extended family. They inexplicably neglected to attend the funeral. He would have to ask Lance and Nina why they missed it when he saw them.

Further complicating this difficult time was the strange man who came by the house to speak with Van's mom immediately after the funeral. She acted like she'd known him for years despite Van not recognizing him. She didn't seem exactly pleased to see him and abruptly sent Van to his room. There were too many strange things happening all at once. Van should know what was going on. Something was being kept from him and he wanted to know what it was.

He tiptoed down the staircase, straining to hear what the older man was saying. His mother was sitting in a chair next to the couch holding a cup of tea as she listened to the man. As he spoke she slowly leaned farther and farther away from him until whatever he told her made her suddenly drop the cup of tea and collapse in tears. Van was about to come down and say something when the man stood, patted his mother awkwardly on the shoulder, removed his coat from the armrest of the couch, and left on his own.

Van crept to the edge of the room. "Mom?" he said tentatively. He was relieved to see her sit up and wipe away the tears on her reddened face. She held out her arms; wordlessly inviting him to join her. He immediately rushed to her embrace. "What's wrong, Mom?"

She sniffed in the tears and held his face in her hands, brushing the longish hair out of his eyes as she spoke. "We have to move."

Van's eyes widened in unexpected shock. "Move! Why?"

"The... company your father worked for owns this house and we have to give it back to them now that your father..." She struggled to finish, but failed to find the words.

"When?" Van asked.

"Tomorrow."

Van jerked backward out of her hands. "Tomorrow!"

She met his accusing glare and gave him a very tired look "It can't be helped, honey."

He stood up and faced her. "Can't be helped! Where do those bastar—"

"Language," she reprimanded him.

He stopped and gauged the look on her face. Now was not the time to test her patience. He changed his tactic but this was too important to let go. He still wanted to ask the question but softened the words to not upset his mother any further. "Where do those dingle berries think we can go? How can they just kick us out like this?"

He could see her fighting back the tears and doing her best to put on a brave face for his benefit. But he couldn't leave it alone until he had an answer. "What kind of company has someone die on them and then kick out the rest of the family like yesterday's garbage?"

His mother rolled her eyes upward, then looked at the floor as she answered quietly. "We knew the rules when your father was hired."

Van struggled to understand the callousness. "Screw the rules!"

That seemed too much for his mother as she responded loudly, even for her. "Van!"

Then her eyes softened again and she laughed while tears streamed down her cheeks. "You are more like your father than you know. And that is another reason why we have to move." She reached over and took Van's face in her hands and looked directly into his eyes. "Maybe someday I can tell you everything." Then she kissed his forehead.

Van pounced on her statement. "I knew there was something! What they told us doesn't add up. Dad was in perfect health. What really happened to him?"

This was the wrong thing to ask. Her eyes lost their sparkle and she got a faraway look that meant she wasn't going to answer. "There is nothing to tell. Your father is gone and we are moving. End of discussion."

"But, Mom—"

Her eyes darkened with a look he only saw when she was overwhelmed with work. "Enough, Van! I need you to start packing. Now!"

"Please—"

"Pack your things, Van!" she said emphatically. He realized he was unable to push further so he returned to his room. But he couldn't bring himself to do as she asked. Instead he sat at his bedroom window looking out across the vast ocean. Despite the clear blue sky, the sea broiled and kicked up waves angrily as if in direct response to how he felt. The more he fumed about his situation, the harder the waves crashed against the shore. It was almost like he was drawing the ocean to him.

Behind him a large empty cardboard box sat in the middle of the room with the words "Van's Stuff" written on the side in permanent black marker. It was his rebellious mood that kept him from placing even one item in that box. Even though he knew his mother would be furious over his lack of progress, he also knew she would get over it quickly and implore him to do as she asked and he would comply.

He gazed out at the ocean, his eyes losing focus as he wasn't looking at anything in particular. A blurry face suddenly popped up outside the window, startling him and causing him to jump back and fall over the side of his bed. As he twisted to look at the window, his eyes focused on the smiling face of Nina beaming in at him. She was the girl who lived down the street and was from one of the families that should have been at the funeral. Van was immediately upset. Why wasn't she there when he needed her! He glanced at his bedroom door to ensure it was still closed and then pushed up on the window.

"Hey, boogerhead," Nina said as she climbed into the room.

"Why weren't you at the funeral?" Van demanded while she

straddled the ledge.

She gave him a funny look. "Are you kidding? I shouldn't even be here!"

"What's that supposed to mean?!"

She stepped fully in the room. "It means I was told to stay away from the Macleans."

Van was shocked. "Why?"

She shrugged. "I don't know. That's what I came here to ask. What did you do?"

It was his turn to look confused. "I didn't do anything!"

Her eyes narrowed and she pointed a finger at him. "You must have done something. I was threatened with some pretty hefty consequences if I even considered wanting to see you."

Before he could reply, another head poked up outside the window. It was Lance, the boy from the third family on the same street, and Van's other closest friend that made the trio complete. "Is this a private party or can anyone join?"

Nina placed her hands on her hips. "Only boogerheads need apply."

Lance smiled easily as he sat in the open window. His face seemed to naturally allow for a smile to be its neutral state. When he actively smiled it radiated like a beacon in the darkness. "Nina's right. You did something to make our parents forbid us from seeing you."

Nina nodded and looked around the room. Then she lifted the empty cardboard box off the ground. "What's this?"

Van shrugged as if that would lessen the impact of his words from a perceived lack of caring about them. "We're moving."

"What!" they both exclaimed in unison.

"When?" Lance asked.

"Why?" Nina added.

Van shook his head, willing the reason to make sense as he said it out loud. "Something about the house belonging to Dad's work and they want it back." It didn't help. It still made no sense.

The look in Nina's eyes shifted to sadness. "Where are you going?"

Van couldn't look at her so he gazed at the floor as he answered "I don't know." He didn't like how much he realized he was going to miss them.

"Van?" his mother's muffled voice called from the bottom of the stairs. "Are you talking to someone?" He could hear her mounting the stairs and climbing up to his room.

"Uh, oh," Nina said and pushed Lance through the open window. His foot slipped on the ledge as he tried to hop through it with her force pushing behind him. He ended up straddling the frame and his foot kept slipping on the roof as he tried to stand awkwardly. He was blocking the pathway so neither could exit the way they'd entered. Van's mother's footsteps hit the top of the stairs.

"Get out of the way, dork!" Nina hissed, but Lance was still halfway in and out of the window, still struggling to get his footing and maintain his balance.

"Van?" his mother called as she neared the closed door. Nina's ponytail whipped back and forth as she frantically looked around for a new place to hide.

"Van?" his mother's voice echoed just on the other side of the door.

The doorknob twisted unnervingly slow, just like in every horror movie. Van lifted the bedspread and pointed under the bed. Nina nodded and dove for the floor while Van took a giant step toward the window and shoved Lance out of it onto the flat roof of the first story of the house. He landed with a soft thud.

Nina shimmied under the bed and pulled her feet out of sight. Van slammed the window shut, and then he spun around to look at the confused expression on his mother's face as it appeared around the opening door. She paused and her forehead wrinkled in confusion as she looked back and forth from the window to Van. "What are you doing?"

"I needed some air. But it was getting too windy," he replied breathlessly, sneaking a peek at his bed, relieved he couldn't see Nina hiding under it. His mother frowned and walked over to the window and peeked out. She drew the shades closed and spun around, glancing at the empty packing box. "You're not packed yet?"

Van pinched his nose between thumb and forefinger, ready to unleash another torrent of "not fairs" when his mother wrapped an arm around him and directed him to the bed. She sat down next to him and smiled sadly. "I know it doesn't seem fair—"

"It's not."

The bed moved under him and he envisioned poor Nina being crushed under their combined weight.

"Let me finish. I know it doesn't seem fair, making us move so quickly after your father's..." Her breathing increased and she closed her eyes for a moment. "But you will see, it will be okay. My sister in Kansas offered to come out here to help. I told her we would come to her instead."

Van was more confused than before. He looked at his mother as if he didn't know who she was. "I didn't know you... I have an aunt?" What else was she hiding?

"She lives in a small town in Kansas and we are going to stay with her for a while."

"How come you never told me about your sister? Do I have any cousins?"

"No. She never married. And I never brought her up because..." His mother took a deep breath and smoothed the wrinkles out of her skirt. "We had a falling out just after high school and haven't spoken since. She found out what happened with your father and called me. She is willing to put the past behind us and move forward. And so am I. She said we were welcome to stay as long as we like."

Van knew there was more his mother wasn't explaining, but he didn't want to push too far just yet. "When are we coming back?"

She shook her head almost imperceptibly. "I don't think we can."

"But my friends are here."

"I know it sounds cliché, but you will make new ones."

Just then, Lance's head popped up outside the window and he spotted Van's mother sitting on the bed. His eyes went wide and he ducked down again out of sight.

She was tearing him away from everything. "I don't want new friends. So what if the company takes the house. We can rent an apartment. We don't have to leave San Francisco."

"The settlement from the company is not enough to afford to live in this area."

In a desperate attempt, he blurted "We can sue them!"

Her shoulders dropped. "We're not suing anyone, Van."

It was a good idea. He would make her see. He sat up straighter.

"Yeah. We'll sue them for millions. Then we won't have to move!"

She exhaled in an audible sigh. "I wish it were that easy, Van." She kissed him on the top of the head. "The moving truck will be here first thing in the morning. There is nothing more to discuss. It is settled, we are going." Van knew at that moment there was nothing more he could do. She sensed his profound sense of loss and gave him a warm hug. "It will be okay, you'll see." Then she stood and went to his bedroom door. She paused with her hand on the doorknob and looked toward the window. "You should let Lance in before he catches his death." Then she directed her attention to the bed. "Don't stay too late, Nina. I doubt your parents know where you are. And I think it will be safer if you leave through the kitchen door like a civilized human being."

After a brief moment, Nina's voice came muffled from under the bed. "Thanks Mrs. Maclean. I'll remember that."

Van's mother smiled and she closed the door after her. Van jumped up and opened his window. Lance was already on the ground and waved up at him. "We'll keep in touch with email and chat." Of course! In the modern world they would never lose touch. They might not be in the same room physically, but they could still remain close friends. Van waved back and hoped chatting with Lance electronically would maintain their friendship. Behind him, Nina wriggled out from under the bed and stood next to him.

Van watched Lance disappear into the darkness. "I didn't even get the chance to say a proper goodbye to him. He's acting like I'll see him tomorrow."

"He didn't hear what I heard. Is it true? Are you leaving in the morning?"

"I guess so." He faced her, knowing he looked miserable and realizing how she must be feeling when he saw her tear-stained cheeks. She jumped forward and wrapped her arms around him in a bear hug, burying her face into his shoulder. "I'll miss you, Van."

He hugged her tightly, never wanting to let go. "I'll miss you too. But maybe Lance is right, we won't lose touch." He felt her nod into his shoulder. They stayed that way for a long time. Holding each other without saying a word.

After a while, he heard his mother's footsteps stop outside his door. "Goodnight, sweetheart."

"Goodnight, Mom."

After a brief pause, she cleared her throat. "Goodnight, Nina."

Nina pulled away and wiped away the tears that left shiny trails down her cheeks.

"I was just leaving, Mrs. Maclean."

"I know, Nina. Be safe."

Her footsteps filtered down the hallway and her bedroom door closed softly.

Van looked at Nina and said the last thing he wanted to hear coming from his mouth. "You'd better go."

Nina sniffed in the last of her tears and smiled. "I'll keep in touch. I promise." She held her hand up and crooked her pinky finger. Van hooked his pinky in hers.

"Now you have to. You pinky swore," he said with the hint of a mischievous smile playing on the edges of his lips.

She laughed and all the tension in the room evaporated. She released the pinky hold and looked around the room. "Do you need help packing?"

"Nah. I got it."

She slowly backed toward the door. "Okay. I'll guess I'll—See you later?"

"Sure. We can Skype. I'm sure they have the Internet in Podunk Kansas."

She suddenly rushed forward and planted a clumsy kiss on his startled lips. His stomach did numerous somersaults and he froze solid, unable to even return this first kiss.

She backed away, his mischievous grin having transferred to her lips. Van was frozen in place and silently watched her open the door to his room. She paused. "Open or closed?"

Van was speechless, his mouth moving with no sound escaping from it.

She shrugged. "I guess I'll just leave the door open then." Her face grew serious. "Whatever happens, Van Maclean, I will always have your back."

She disappeared down the hallway and rumbled down the stairs noisily. She never learned how to walk gracefully, always clomping around like her feet were embedded in concrete. That's probably how his mother knew she was in his room earlier.

He stood and thought about the kiss for a moment. It was nice, but it had more of a best friend kind of feel. Not the passionate type that you see in the movies. He decided it wasn't going to help by dwelling on it. He turned toward the empty box and started haphazardly throwing belongings that no longer mattered into it. The only thing that he wanted to take with him was the warmth that he felt from Nina's hug and Lance's smiling face.

Chapter 3

In a room shrouded in darkness, a single flame flickered in the still of the night. The dancing light cast faint shadows on the face of a man who was close enough to be fully bathed in its faint light. He sat with his eyes closed and wordlessly moved his lips, reciting the incantation that would activate the unique properties of this particular candle. The flame shifted from a bright orange to a dark blue hue and grew larger until it resolved into a face looking out from the azure flame.

The man opened his eyes. He saw the eyes staring at him expectantly from the gleaming indigo flames and bowed his head. "My Lord," he said barely above a whisper.

The face glared at him. "Has the boy been located?"

The man looked up at the glimmering face. A small feeling of pride welling up within him as he answered "Yes, My Lord."

"Why has it taken so long?"

The pride fled, replaced with cautious fear. "Magic is barely functional in Techrealm."

The eyes narrowed in anger. "I do not tolerate excuses."

The man shivered from the growing fear. If he couldn't placate his master, things would be bad for him. He bowed his head again. "No, My Lord."

"Does he have knowledge of his abilities?"

This was a safe question to answer, and his fear subsided slightly. "He does not."

"I want him dead."

The man paused briefly as the fear returned in a rush followed by another shiver. His master was expecting an answer. But he didn't have the one he was looking for. "That is easier said than done, My Lord."

"Contact me again when you have done what I asked. Do I need to remind you of what happened to the last Spinner who offered me excuses instead of results?"

He visibly cringed. This time the shiver was almost uncontrollable and the candle flame wavered. He struggled to regain control. He breathed a deep calming breath and answered as strongly as he could. "No, My Lord. He will be dead by tomorrow."

"Do you stake your life on it?"

The man's heart rate increased rapidly and he tasted the iron tang of adrenaline being released. He almost lost control again. He closed his eyes, breathed a few more times, and bowed again as he said what he knew would regain his master's good graces. "My life belongs only to you."

"Never forget that," the face said with a twinge of disdain and then the flame flickered and went out, plunging the room into total darkness.

Chapter 4

Van took one last look at the room in his aunt's house that had been his home for the past five years. It seemed like only yesterday that he and his mother moved from San Francisco to Lebanon, Kansas.

It wasn't Podunk Backwater, but it was close. Van never felt so disconnected from his previous life. He spent his first thirteen years on the coast, never more than a hundred paces from the ocean.

Lebanon, Kansas was the recognized center of the United States. There was even a plaque just outside of town commemorating that it was situated at equal distance from the oceans that bordered the forty-eight contiguous states.

Van was used to the salty air from living so close to the ocean. It took some time to get used to what was unarguably the driest spot on the planet. He looked at the empty cardboard box that reminded him of the last one lettered with the same words in permanent marker. As he looked in the open box at what he considered important enough to take to his new apartment near the only college to accept him, he realized how much his life changed since his father's death.

His mind went unexpectedly to the last thing Nina ever said to him. "Whatever happens, Van Maclean, I will always have your back." Words spoken in earnest by a twelve-year-old girl after they shared their first kiss.

It was the last time he ever saw or heard from her.

She promised to keep in touch via Skype, but when he called that first time, her parents said she was not there. She wasn't there the next two times he called. And then the Skype account was deleted. The emails bounced back after the first two he sent. The same happened with Lance.

For a whole year he left his computer on twenty-four hours a day hoping she or Lance would contact him. But they never did. Sometime during the second year in Kansas he forgot to leave his computer running while he was at school. Then he forgot to leave it on during the night.

He finally admitted his quote unquote friends abandoned him the moment he was forced to leave them. It was a painful acknowledgment.

He could only assume they blamed him for moving away. He would have heard from their parents if something happened to them. So he could only surmise they were so mad they shut down all means of contact with him. Didn't they realize it was not his choice to move? He was twelve going on thirteen. If his mother said they were moving, they were moving.

Luckily, by the time he finally admitted it, he was fully settled in his new life. Adjusting to a new school wasn't easy in the beginning. It also wasn't as hard as he expected. He found being the new kid in school was replete with advantages and disadvantages alike. During the past five years in Kansas, true to his mother's word, he made new friends. Unlike his first thirteen years with Lance and Nina, most of his new friendships sparked, grew, matured, and then fizzled away. Van didn't exactly know why, but one friendship stayed constant.

At that precise moment Eddie poked his head through the open bedroom window. "Let me guess. You're thinking about me aren't you?"

Van started at the sudden intrusion into his quiet reflection. He looked at Eddie. The short, permanently disheveled hair was colored a bright neon green that only brought further attention to his ears which stuck out perpendicular to his head.

It made Van smile to look at the goofy looking but cheerful face of Eddie. Eddie was the best kind of friend anyone could ask for. He was the first to approach the new kid with an offer of true friendship and stuck by him all the way through high school graduation. That was why most of Van's friendships failed. They weren't real. Only Eddie proved time and again he truly cared about Van as much as himself and wasn't just using Van's friendship to get something. In fact, Eddie was moving with him to a new town so he wouldn't have to start over again alone. It helped that Eddie found a job in a car repair garage and was splitting the rent on their apartment situated only a quarter mile from Van's college.

Van smiled. "How do you do that?"

Eddie pointed at his ears that looked as if they doubled the width of his face. "These puppies burn anytime someone is talking about me. Or thinking about me."

Eddie clambered through the window, his lanky arms and legs

moving fluidly like a daddy longlegs spider as he stepped easily over the waist-high ledge. Once inside, he straightened to his full six-foot-seven height, his neon-green hair brushing against the ceiling before he adopted his perpetual hunch to keep from banging his head on the sky itself. He looked at the empty box and gave Van a quizzical stare.

"You're not having doubts about moving in with me, are you?"

Just then Van's mother entered the room through the open door. "Don't worry, Eddie. He did this when we moved from California. He waited until the moving truck was practically pulling away from the house to throw his belongings in the box."

Eddie bowed low before Van's mother and took her hand in his, kissing it. "Mrs. M. You are like the bright sun on a misty morning chasing away the somber fog."

Her face reddened and she pulled her hand away quickly, wiping at the spot where his lips touched. "I haven't decided if I will miss your odd greetings or not. You always come up with something new. How do you do that?"

Eddie straightened to his half-hunch as his green hair brushed the ceiling. "You inspire me, Mrs. M., like The Bard's wife inspired him to write the world's most cherished love story, Romeo and Juliet."

She reddened further and gave him a lopsided half smile. "Okay. I've decided. I won't miss it."

Eddie bowed low, one arm sweeping wide in front of him. "As you wish, M'Lady."

Her smile spread to the other side of her face. "Can you give Van and I a minute, please."

"Of course." Eddie went out the window the same way he came in. He never looked more like an overgrown spider than when he was climbing through windows. After he was gone, Van's mother shook her head and laughed, "Doesn't that boy ever use a door like a normal person?"

"Not that I recall," replied Van. And for the life of him, he rarely ever saw Eddie using a door. Even at school. Which caused no end of grief for his teachers and the principal.

She looked at Van, her face wistful but warm. "I wish your father was around to see you all grown up. You've become such a handsome and intelligent young man." A tear swelled up along her already misty eyes. "You look just like him when we first met."

Van moved forward and hugged her. She clung to him and whispered in his ear. "I wish I could tell you…"

He pulled away and looked slightly concerned as he searched her face. "You can tell me anything."

She paused, the internal struggle taking place inside reflected on her face. Suddenly, her eyes shifted and she pulled him close, squeezing the air out of him like a boa constrictor. "Your father loved you more than life itself."

"I know." He gasped.

"You couldn't possibly."

He wriggled from her grasp and searched her watery eyes for understanding. "You're scaring me, Mom. What are you talking about?"

She seemed ready to say something when she straightened up and sniffed in her tears, wiping the moisture from her eyes. "I'm just going to miss you is all."

Van felt concerned at this odd exchange but when his mom wasn't going to give him more information it was useless to push. "I'm going to miss you too, Mom."

She reached out and tugged on the edges of his sleeves, straightening his T-shirt. She brushed off imaginary dust from his shoulders and then leaned in for another tight hug.

"Your father would be so proud of you."

"I know, Mom. I miss him too."

Chapter 5

Van finally succumbed to the inevitable, packed what he deemed was important to a college student, and stuffed the box into the back of Eddie's 1988 Hyundai Excel hatchback. Eddie's skill at packing into such a limited space would impress a master Tetris player. Somehow he left just enough room for Van's box, only requiring a slight push along one edge as he wedged it into place and slammed the hatchback closed, accordioning the top rear corners of the box against the glass. He wiped his hands triumphantly. "Voilà."

Van's mother regarded the car riding low on its decades-old shocks. She turned to Van, shaking her head as if unable to comprehend anyone wishing to add their bulk to such a contraption, let alone speed down the highway at seventy miles per hour in it. "You will be safe? Right?"

Eddie stepped between them. "You have my word, Mrs. M. Van will arrive safe and sound. Old Bessie and I, we've been through a lot. This…" he waved to the overstuffed vehicle which took that very moment to let out a groan under the strain of more weight than it was designed to support. "…is nothing. She'll get us where we need to go in one piece. I guarantee it."

Van stepped around Eddie and put a hand on her shoulder. "Don't worry about us, Mom. Eddie's a good driver."

"That's true," Eddie added. "Not a single accident."

"Except for that tree last summer," Van's mother corrected him.

"Well," Eddie grinned like the Cheshire Cat. "That sucker jumped outta nowhere."

Van hugged his mother. "We'll be fine. There are no trees along the interstate."

Eddie stuck out his hand. Van's mother regarded it like a snake about to bite her, then she wrapped her arms around him in a big bear hug. Eddie gave Van a confused look over her shoulder. Van returned his confused expression layered with some of his own and a shrug to punctuate his surprise. His mother never acted like this with anyone. She always kept others at arm's length. Even her sister.

Van remembered the day they arrived and noted how the first

meeting of his mother and her sister felt like it was the first time they met. Ever. Even though they lived under the same roof over the next several years, they never acted like sisters as far as Van expected sisters to act. And now, she was acting completely out of character again with Eddie. Maybe his departure was the cause. She lost her husband to death and now maybe she felt she was losing her only son to adulthood. He decided he wouldn't let her feel like she lost him. He vowed right then and there to call her once a week at least. More if he got the chance.

She finished her unexpected hug and held Eddie at arm's length, giving him a stern look. "Eddie, you are the best thing to happen to Van since we left California. You will be in a strange town where people do things differently than they do here. You take care of each other no matter what."

Eddie's face lost its usual mirth as he returned her serious stare. "He's my best friend Mrs. M. We watch each other's back. We always have. We always will."

Van quickly spoke up to cut the suddenly serious mood. "We'll be careful mom. We have a week and a half before the semester starts. We won't push it and drive too fast or too long without taking breaks. We'll get there safe. I promise."

She let a single tear roll down her cheek as she smiled and released Eddie only to grab Van and hug him tightly again. "I know you will."

She pulled away and then wrapped her arms tightly around her chest, as if hugging herself. Van noticed she seemed to need the hugs to feel safe.

Eddie nodded at her reassuringly. "I will make sure Van calls you as soon as we get there."

She smiled. "Thank you."

One last round of hugs and laughing through tears and sniffles finally ended with Eddie and Van sitting in the Hyundai. Eddie honked twice and Van waved to his mother as they pulled out onto the road that would take them to the interstate.

Van twisted in his seat and watched as his mother's figure shrank to invisibility with the increasing distance. She remained standing right where she was, watching them until Van couldn't see her any longer. With the way she was acting she probably continued to watch the road long after she could no longer see them either. He couldn't shake the feeling she was very worried and he reminded himself to call her as soon as possible.

Chapter 6

Outside the passenger side window of the Hyundai, the power lines drooped down and then rose again, peaking briefly at the next utility pole before beginning their repetitive droop. It was lulling Van to sleep despite feeling fully rested.

Eddie's voice cut through the lull. "Look. Another sign for that Renaissance Faire. We have time to stop if you want."

Eddie spoke so abruptly, Van jerked awake. He lightly slapped his cheeks to bring himself to full consciousness. "That's more your scene. Besides, I've never been much of a fan of parading around in costumes and pretending the industrial revolution never happened."

"Don't knock it until you've tried it. There's something fun about pretending to live in a magical time."

"What was so magical about the plague? Or how about the Spanish Inquisition? The Crusades? Yeah, a real wondrous time to be alive."

"The Crusades took place two hundred years before the start of the Renaissance period."

"Whatever. I'm just glad to be alive now when we have running water, flushing toilets, and the Internet."

"Yeah. Don't tell me what you look up on the Internet."

Van struck out at Eddie, smacking him playfully on the shoulder.

"No hitting the driver," Eddie quipped.

"Wisenheimers get hit no matter what. It's in the rules. Nothing I have any control over."

It grew quiet and they drove for a few more miles before passing another sign informing them that the Renaissance Faire was at the next turnoff.

"What did your mom mean back there?" Eddie asked suddenly. Van inwardly flinched. He wondered if Eddie caught what his mother said right before they left. Eddie obviously wasn't going to let it slide and only waited for the right time to bring it back up.

"Uh. Well. None of my friends in California ever made an effort to keep in touch, even though I was just an email away. They promised to always be there for me." Van shifted in his seat, having slid down under the hypnotic trance of the undulating power lines. "The difference is they didn't mean it. But you are dropping everything to move to a new town with me, leaving everything behind." Van glanced back into the car that was crammed from floor to ceiling with boxes and loose clothes. "Well, maybe not everything."

"You never did tell me what happened. Why you left California. Other than that your dad died."

Van waited for the pit in his stomach to form. It happened every time he thought about being ripped from everything and everyone he knew and dropped smack dab in the middle of America. When the feelings of desperation didn't come, he looked at Eddie. Could he actually move on to another stage in his life? Was his subconscious finally deciding to let the past stay in the past?

"Well," he started and then paused. The heartrending emotions he so regularly observed when thinking about his sudden departure from California didn't swell up this time. Could he finally talk about it without the accompanying pain?

Eddie glanced at him briefly before returning his eyes to the road. "Well? You're keepin' me in suspense here. Not good to keep the driver in suspense."

"There isn't much to tell. My dad died at work. They said it was a heart attack. There was the funeral attended by strangers. My friends said they would keep in touch but never did. When you and I met, I decided to just put up with you to keep from being lonely." Van couldn't keep the smile from creeping across his face.

Eddie punched him on the shoulder without taking his eyes off the road. "I think you have that backwards. I put up with you, remember?

"Me?"

"Yeah. You're the one who made everyone hate us because you refused to date the most popular girl in school, even after she asked you out."

"She wasn't the one for me."

"So," Eddie glanced sideways at him. "If Cindy wasn't the whole package for you like she claimed, what are you looking for in a girl?"

Van shrugged. "I'll know it when I see it."

Eddie leaned over conspiratorially, "If you ever do, ask her if she has a sister or a best friend who likes to have fun."

He was so happy Eddie was with him on his first great foray into the real world. "What would I do without you, Eddie?"

"Besides sit around the house and never get in trouble?"

"You did know how to get us in all kinds of trouble."

"Since we didn't have girlfriends, what else was there to do on weekends? Besides, if I remember correctly, you were more than eager to join me in whatever scheme I cooked up."

Van laughed. "It was better than sitting in front of my computer waiting for an email that would never come."

Just as quickly as the conversation began, it fell deathly silent in the car. The only sound was the rumble of the pencil thin grooves in the road as the tires rolled over them at a few miles per hour above the posted speed limit. Eddie thankfully let Van ride quietly with his own thoughts. That was Eddie's best quality. As much as he could run at the mouth, and he could run at the mouth longer and louder than anyone on either side of the Mississippi, he also knew when to stay quiet.

Eddie kept the speed constant and softly whistled a soundless tune. The radio in the Hyundai stopped working somewhere during the early 2000s and Eddie just took to making his own musical entertainment rather than spending money he didn't have on a new in-dash stereo system. The tires changed pitch when they rolled onto the paved bridge that crossed the gorge formed around a wide river as it cut a path through the earth a hundred feet below.

Van glanced ahead of them at the only other vehicle on the bridge in the opposing lane and then took a sudden intake of breath, filling his lungs with air to scream.

Chapter 7

The driver of the semi-trailer truck lived and worked in the tractor that was his home away from home. He spared no expense thanks to the inheritance from an uncle he met once when he was but a wee child. As the only living heir, he received the bulk of the estate. After the lawyers took their cut, he was suddenly a millionaire.

It was enough to live off the rest of his life if he was careful. But he was a trucker through and through, and he could use that money to make more money. He knew it was a death sentence to sit around and do nothing. So he put that money to work and purchased the best tractor for long hauls across the greater contiguous states.

He maintained his personal tractor and semi-trailer in excess of all Department of Transportation regulations. Not too hard to do when the money was flowing from the business of several customers who depended on his state-of-the-art transportation to deliver their goods. He prided himself on maintaining one of the best and safest transportation rigs on the road. If you wanted your product delivered, his truck was a sure bet.

So it was quite a shock when he glanced at his side view mirror and saw one of his tires bouncing away from the side of his tractor. He slammed on his brakes and watched helplessly as the tire vaulted across the median, slammed into an older model compact car, and sent it careening over the side of the bridge.

Bluish-white clouds of smoke rose up from the burning rubber of the locked tires and engulfed the entire two lane bridge like an early morning fog. The rig finally came to a stop and he leapt from the cab, running to the edge of the bridge. The railing was torn like tissue paper where the car broke through before plummeting over the edge. He peered over at the anticipated carnage below.

The river looked wide, but not deep. The driver's forehead wrinkled as he scanned the river in both directions. Except for the bent railing, he couldn't see anything amiss. From his angle so high up, the water was clear and the river couldn't be more than a few feet deep for a quarter mile in either direction. But there was nothing out of the ordinary.

That didn't make sense.

He saw the car go over the edge with his own eyes. But now it was as if he imagined it. He didn't think the food he ate at the last diner was off. He wasn't hallucinating. But where was a car that went over the edge only moments before?

Chapter 8

Both boys screamed as their car tumbled through the air, falling toward the shallow river below. Right before they hit, the water seemed to rise up to greet the overstuffed Hyundai with a light splash, pulling it instantly down into the murky depths with minimal resistance. The weight of all their stuff packed in the car with them made the car sink like a rock. Miraculously, they survived the impact but they were sinking quickly. The view outside the windows darkened with each passing second. Then the windshield let out a loud pop and a crack appeared instantly through the center of it.

Van looked at Eddie.

Eddie looked at Van.

They both silently agreed they couldn't stay in the car.

The window buckled under the strain of thousands of gallons of water and shattered inward like someone had opened a fire hydrant and pointed it directly at the windshield. Van struggled with his seatbelt. Eddie reached over, pressed the switch with his thumb, and twisted hard. The belt snapped off and ratcheted away, but the water rushing in through the shattered window kept him pinned to his seat.

The water level rose quickly and Van took a huge breath as the last of the air pocket filled with water and the pressure equalized, releasing him from his seat. He followed Eddie out through the front windshield and they floated upward toward the faint shimmering light above.

Van slowly let out the air as he ascended, remembering something about keeping the pressure equal or your lungs would explode as you neared the surface.

Van broke through the surface and gasped for air. Eddie splashed into view near him and gulped at the air just as greedily. Van's clothes were waterlogged and threatened to pull him back under. He spun around until he saw the closest edge of dry land to their current position. "That way," he hollered over to Eddie, spitting out the water that filled his mouth when he opened it to speak.

He swam hard against the constant drag of his soaked clothing and was finally rewarded with his legs bumping into solid ground. He clawed his way up onto the shore and flopped over on his back, wheezing from the exertion. Eddie flopped down next to him and they lay panting for several minutes until the rush of adrenaline subsided and their breathing returned to semi-normal.

Van mustered up the energy to prop himself up on an elbow and looked over at Eddie. "Did you see that tire?"

Eddie was still lying on his back, but twisted his head to look at Van. "Yeah. I spotted it right before it hit us and knocked us off the bridge!"

"I thought you swerved to avoid it!"

"I didn't get the chance. It happened too fast!"

Something didn't make sense in Van's head. "We were full of stuff. A tire shouldn't have been able to move us at all. We had way too much mass to be knocked around by a single truck tire."

"Spoken like a true college-bound kid. All I know is, we went over the bridge and into the river. And it was a tire that done it."

Van looked around. But what he saw confused him even more. "Where is it?"

Eddie waved an arm in the direction of the water. "It probably sank along with my car and all our stuff."

"No. The bridge. Where is it?"

Eddie sat up with great effort and looked first one way and then the other. Van mimicked his movements and saw a lake where the river should have been. "Maybe we floated down the river and came out here?"

Van stood up slowly, his muscles screaming from the request to move again after their ordeal. Once he was standing, he scanned the lake in both directions. "I don't see a river feeding this lake."

Eddie rose cautiously and took in the entire lake, scratching his head. "Maybe we were knocked out while we floated down river?"

Van looked at him. "I wasn't knocked out."

"Yeah," Eddie scratched at his neon-green hair some more. "I don't think I was either."

Van scanned the surface of the lake. It was smooth and gave no indication as to where the car sank. He turned his back to the lake and saw a column of smoke rising up out of the middle of the forest that stretched on for miles. The smoke didn't look too far away and he could see a well-traveled dirt road leading along the lake and cutting into the woods headed in the same direction as the smoke.

Eddie spotted the smoke and broke into his easy grin. "Where there's smoke, there's fire. And where there's fire, there's someone with a cell phone."

Chapter 9

The driver remained at the scene of the accident, staring dumfounded at the bent railing until the police arrived. He flagged the police car down as it slowed. He rushed up to the police car and started yelling as the officer climbed out. "You have to call a helicopter to look for them!" he screamed.

The officer held his hands up. "Take it easy."

"Don't tell me to take it easy!" the driver bristled. "They could still be alive. We have to find them!"

"Find who?"

"A car went over the edge of the bridge!"

The police officer looked around him in confusion. Then he looked straight at the driver. "Did you see this happen?"

"I saw the whole thing. Call someone on your radio. Get help!"

"Calm down, sir. Tell me what happened."

The officer was staring cautiously at the driver as he spoke and backed away a few steps.

"I keep my truck maintained. This isn't my fault."

The officer repeated his request. "Just tell me what happened."

"I was crossing the bridge when I saw a tire bounce over the median and knock another car off the bridge. You have to find them!"

The officer eyed the driver suspiciously. Then he inspected the semi-trailer before looking back at the driver. "Which tire was it that fell off your truck?"

The driver spun around and pointed, but he was stunned to silence. "What the…"

All the tires were still on the side of his truck. "But… I saw it come off and hit the car. It crashed through the railing and went over the side!"

The policeman was looking at him with narrowing eyes. "Where did it crash through the railing?"

The driver spun around and pointed, his hand slowly dropping along with his jaw. The railing was continuous all along the bridge. There was no break in the railing where the car tore through it on its way over the edge.

The officer looked at where the driver pointed and then took a cautions step back, his hand moving slowly to rest on the grip of his service revolver. "Have you been drinking, sir?"

"What? No! What kind of pea-brained question is that?"

"There's no need for name calling, sir."

The driver sobered up and calmed down. "No. I'm a truck driver by profession. I would never drink while on a haul."

"Drugs? You know, to stay awake on those long drives?"

The driver's fist clenched but he remained calm. "No, sir."

The driver racked his brain for an explanation, but he couldn't come up with anything. He began to wonder if he was going crazy when a grunting sound made him look at the officer.

The officer slowly pulled his gun from its holster and shakily raised it to point it at the driver. The driver's face mirrored the astonishment on the officer's face. "What are you doing?" the driver demanded, his voice trembling and his hands shooting up into the air in automatic response to the gun barrel pointed at him. The officer stared at the gun in his hand. He was shaking uncontrollably and grunting noisily. His arm lowered slowly and then the officer's face registered intense pain as the gun raised again to point at the driver. "I…can't…stop," he declared through gritted teeth, visibly straining against an unseen force.

Chapter 10

The candle flickered brightly in the room, reflecting in its flame the scene of the truck driver and officer standing in the middle of the bridge. It took all his strength to replace the tire and repair the railing from across the divide between Midguard and Techrealm. But it was necessary to ensure that no one would look for the boy. Even if the fall never killed him outright, he should be dead soon enough with no one to rescue him. But there was still the matter of the witness. There was one thing left to do. And it required his full concentration.

In the flicker of the flame he could see the officer struggling against his command over the lowly human's actions. He maintained full control and there was nothing these puppets could do about it. He twisted his hands in the right configuration to release more power and felt the struggle finally give way as the officer became overwhelmed. He was back in full control. He took over the officer's hands, aimed the gun squarely at the confused driver, and pulled the trigger. Then he released one hand, guided the other hand with the gun toward the officer's head and pulled the trigger again. The light of the candle fluttered and died as the officer's lifeless body dropped to the road.

His task complete, the man collapsed; his whole body drenched with sweat. His abilities as a Spinner were advanced, but they could never have done what he just accomplished without the augmentation of the candle provided by his master. He lay there in the darkness and silently thanked Aeron for trusting him with the gift. Having that extra power was exhilarating even though it was exhausting.

The use of magic in Midguard was always limited. There were those with natural-born capabilities of elemental Spinners. But they were a tiny portion of the main Midguard population. Then there were the even rarer enchanted items used by those who wished they were granted the gift of spinning at birth. That was the extent of magic ability in Midguard. But in Magerealm, element spinning advanced far beyond the maximum potential of magic in Midguard. Most of that population was born with magical abilities, with a small population having wondrous natural skills. The people not blessed with strong magic created all manner of enchanted objects and enhancements to bring them up to their stronger peers' abilities. The candle was one of them. It enabled the user to tap into the extended magic of Magerealm and push it into Techrealm.

But, using it where magic was not in abundance caused the candle to feed off the energy of the user. This came at great cost to personal health and well-being, so the man used it sparingly in Midguard. He was reminded of the downside as sweat continued to seep from every pore in his body. If he didn't drink water soon, he might fall unconscious from dehydration and never wake again.

He stood unsteadily on his feet, reminding himself to prepare a pitcher of water for the next time he used the candle for such a strenuous task.

Chapter 11

Van stood at the point where the road split into two choices; just like it did in every children's bedtime story. One way went around the forest that stood before them. The other way narrowed as it entered the spooky woods.

Eddie let out a sigh and pointed into the forest. "The smoke is coming from straight ahead that way. I say we take the shortcut."

Van laughed nervously. "Didn't you read Grimms' Fairy Tales as a kid? Never, ever, take the shortcut through the dark forest."

Eddie pointed to the road that split off and went along the edge of the lake. "If we were driving, I'd agree with you. But the car is at the bottom of the lake and we are on foot. I'd rather not walk longer than I have to. Look, the road by the lake goes the wrong way for miles before it even begins to meander back toward the smoke. It might take us hours to go around the forest. I say we cut through it. Save some time. I mean, c'mon, we're not in a fairy tale. This is the real world. The only real monsters I've ever seen are guys with switchblade knives and a nasty drug habit. I really don't think we'll run into any of them in there."

Van looked back and forth between the wide road and the road less traveled; for obvious reasons. It looked so dark and foreboding. The path turned a corner as soon as it entered the forest and even the sun refused to shine on the trail that wandered through the densely packed trees.

Eddie headed toward the forest. He paused at the edge of the tree line and looked back. "You coming?"

Van shivered slightly and reluctantly followed Eddie into the forest. Eddie seemed to have recovered far quicker from their swim than Van. Van just wanted to sleep, he felt so drained of energy. It was a struggle just to keep putting one foot in front of the other as they trudged along. But Eddie bounced ahead, even though the forest was growing darker and the trees were closing in together above them as they moved deeper into the shadows. When the road thinned to little more than a barely used hiking trail, Van raised his head from its focus on the road and looked around. The trees looked black and sinister. Van quickly glanced behind him and noticed the path where they entered seemed to close up among the dark foreboding shadows, the bright and sunny day left far behind them.

"Wow," exclaimed Eddie. "These are some creepy trees. No leaves. The bark's all black. They look dead."

Van looked at the trees along the side of the trail. The branches grew at odd angles and seemed to be reaching across the road for them. Van thought he saw movement out of the corner of his eye. He whipped his head around, but when he looked directly at it, there were just more branches hanging low over the road. If you could still call it a road by how narrow and overgrown it became.

"Whoa! Did you see that?" Eddie asked, his voice cracking.

Van twisted quickly and looked in Eddie's direction. "What?"

Eddie was staring at a branch that was bent so low over the road, it looked like it was reaching for him. He pointed at it. "I could have sworn I saw that branch moving."

Van felt a cold knot forming in his stomach. He tried to find a logical reason that would calm his growing unease. "It was just the wind," Van offered.

Eddie, stuck a finger in his mouth to wet it and held it up. "What wind?"

Van stood perfectly still, hoping there was a breeze, but he couldn't even feel the faintest whisper. He looked around the tops of the trees, but they were as still as if he were looking at a painted picture instead of the real thing.

Out of the corner of his eye, something dark shifted and he spun around. A branch was still wobbling as if it stopped suddenly because...

Because it was moving?

It didn't make sense, but the cold knot was now threatening to freeze him in place. "We need to get out of here," he said, working hard to keep his voice from trembling.

Eddie nodded and walked faster "I second the motion and approve."

Van walked quickly to catch up to Eddie and soon fell into step next to him. Behind them, they heard the creaking of branches shifting in a slight breeze. Except there was no wind.

Van's entire spine quivered and he found himself practically running to keep up with Eddie's long stride that was increasing in pace every second. Before he knew it, they were both running full tilt, barreling through the narrowing dark forest.

They turned a sharp twist in the road and saw a ray of sunlight ahead that shone down where the forest broke for a clearing. Every instinct in Van's being told him to get to the safety of the sunlight if he wanted to live.

Eddie however, was faster than Van, his legs being longer. "Don't look back!" Eddie yelled as they bolted for the edge of the forest, Eddie quickly outdistancing Van. The creaking branches behind them grew to a hellish roar as Van's peripheral vision showed branches bending too far and breaking as they snatched for the running boys.

Eddie hit the sun first but didn't stop. Van was still a few feet from safety when he stumbled over a root that popped up out of the ground right in front of him. He hit the dirt and slid on his stomach like a baseball player going for home plate, stopping half in the sunshine and half in the shade of the forest.

Before he could get back up something bumped his foot and slid along his ankle. He dug his fingers into the dirt and pulled himself forward. His foot was suddenly released and he scuttled forward on all fours, leaving several feet between himself and the shadows. Once he decided he was safe, he rolled over and sat on the ground, daring a glance back into the forest.

His breath caught in his throat.

Everything looked normal.

Everything except for the branch on the ground that terminated right where the deep shadows shifted abruptly into sun-drenched earth. The branch was still curled at the end, sitting in the shadows, as if it started to wrap around his leg right before it hit the sunlight.

Eddie was still running full bore down the road. "Wait up!" Van yelled as he scrambled to his feet and took off at a dead run away from the nightmare forest.

He caught up with Eddie who slowed down considerably, gasping for air and settling into less of a walk and more of a plodding stumble. Eddie's normal exercise routine consisted of moving to the other side of the couch to make room for Van when they played video games in Eddie's living room. Eddie was orphaned at a young age and placed in foster care before his first birthday. He was one of the lucky ones and finally settled in with a great family when he reached junior high. The family was extremely supportive of Eddie and always treated him like he was their own child and never once made him feel unwanted. They never hid the fact he was a foster child in their care, but they reminded him that sometimes, family is who you're with, not who you're born to.

It was this teaching that enabled Eddie and Van to form such a strong friendship. Van knew Eddie viewed him as a brother, and Van felt the same. Eddie stopped plodding and bent in half with his hands on his knees, spitting on the ground as he gulped big breaths of air.

Van stopped next to him. He was breathing heavily, but being on the track team in high school conditioned him for running as opposed to Eddie the Couch Potato. Eddie coughed, spit, tried to stand up, doubled over, and spit again. When he finally stood up straight, he wiped a hand across his forehead and looked at Van. "That was weird. I swear I saw those branches reaching for us."

Van tried to shake the memory of the branches reaching across the road from his mind. "I think we're still in shock from the crash. It's causing us to hallucinate. Trees don't move their branches around like arms. And they certainly don't try to capture people."

Eddie pointed at the side of his face. "I know it doesn't make sense, but I know what I saw out of the corner of my eye. That thing was reaching for me!"

Van's breathing normalized and he stood up straight, trying to stretch out the muscles that threatened to knot up. He looked down the road that widened again. They reached the spot where the shortcut met up with the road that traveled alongside the lake. He followed the road with his eyes and saw the smoke rising thickly just over the next hill.

They were getting closer to the help they were seeking.

He tapped Eddie on the arm and pointed. "We should make it there in an hour if we keep up a good pace."

Eddie looked at the smoke. "I never was good at judging distance. I guess that's why you got the hiking badge and I didn't."

Van smiled. "No. I got it because I was willing to walk more than two feet from the couch to the fridge for soda."

Eddie smacked him on the shoulder and headed down the road. "Let's go, Eagle Scout."

Chapter 12

As they got closer, the single column of thick smoke resolved itself into numerous slimmer columns of hazy smoke billowing into the air from various stone fireplaces attached to the sides of roughly constructed wood plank buildings with thatched roofs. The buildings were situated on both sides of the road and most sported small vegetable gardens between the buildings. Low wooden fences separated the gardens of one house from another. "What is all this?" Van said aloud.

"I think it's the Renaissance Faire we saw the signs for. It said it was going on this weekend."

"But these houses look like they've been here for a while. Look at the vegetable gardens. Those didn't grow here over the weekend."

"Maybe the owners of the land let them build a more permanent town for the Faire. I must admit, it looks pretty authentic. Better than most."

As they walked past the houses, men and women, dressed in dingy cloth and tending to their gardens, watched them without saying a word. Van leaned closer to Eddie. "I thought they were supposed to be friendly to guests."

Eddie shrugged. "Maybe we came in from the back and they are surprised at seeing us here. This could be the campsite for the workers and we don't really belong here."

"Maybe we should ask if they have a cell phone."

"Let's just get to the ticket office and ask them. It's like going behind the scenes at Disneyland. It ruins the atmosphere to see Cinderella sitting at a picnic table wolfing down a plate of nachos. Maybe Faire guests aren't supposed to be back here either."

They continued down the road until they reached what looked to be a small village. The houses were spaced closer together and the road shifted from rutted mud to cobblestone. Eddie scuffed the pavement stones with his shoe. "Boy, they went all out with this place. These look hand-placed. Must have cost someone a pretty penny to get this done all the way out here."

All around them, people stopped what they were doing to stare at the visitors. Even the children stopped playing in the street and gawked at the newcomers.

Van suddenly realized why everyone was staring at them. "It's your hair," he said, matter-of-factly.

"What?"

"You dyed it bright green. You stick out like a sore thumb around here. Or more like a green thumb."

Eddie shook his head. "Even if they pretend they live in feudal Europe every weekend, you'd think they'd cut some slack for someone who dyes their hair. How do they expect to get repeat visitors with attitudes like that?"

Van looked around at all the faces casting curious glances his way. Eddie was right. It didn't make sense. He tentatively smiled at a woman. She hurriedly ducked back into her cottage and slammed the door. She appeared a moment later at the shutters and pulled them closed. Her reaction triggered a similar response from others and everyone hustled noiselessly into their cottages and sealed themselves off from the interlopers in their village.

Van smiled at a child who sat on the roof of a small cottage. The child responded by jumping off the roof and running out of sight. Something was missing but he couldn't put his finger on it.

He looked around the street. Everyone brave enough to remain outside was standing still and staring at them. It looked like they were working at their respective tasks when suddenly interrupted. They didn't look happy. Everyone he tried to silently engage with a smile acted surprised and looked suspiciously at him. The mood emanating from everyone was somber and serious.

Nobody was having any fun.

He suddenly realized what was missing.

"Hey, Eddie? Where are all the guests?"

Eddie glanced back and forth, smiling at the people who paused to watch them. He received the same reaction. "Maybe we got here before they opened?"

Van looked around the center of town. "They sure are acting strange. Do you see the main office anywhere?"

"It wouldn't be out in the open. They obviously want this place to look as realistic as possible. It's going to be inside somewhere so as not to break up the illusion of a medieval village. Which they nailed, by the way."

Eddie pointed out a large two-story building. "I'll bet it's in the tavern."

Van nodded. "Yeah. They should at least have a phone we can borrow."

They walked to the building and Eddie opened the door. He rose to his full height and strode in like he owned the place, being the normal ham Eddie always was. Everyone inside took one look at him and froze. He didn't seem to notice as he walked through the room, nodding and offering a "Hello" here and there to the people in the crowded dining area. Van stayed close behind him, feeling more uneasy as they received no welcoming responses.

Eddie sauntered up to the bar and slapped his hands down on it, startling the bartender behind the counter and making him drop the glass he was polishing. It shattered at his feet, but the bartender remained transfixed, staring at Eddie's hair.

Eddie leaned his elbows on the bar. "You got a phone behind the bar?"

The bartender, his eyes never leaving Eddie's hair, silently and slowly shook his head. Eddie grimaced and spun around, leaning back on the bar like he was Clint Eastwood in a spaghetti western. He surveyed all the faces that were transfixed on him. "Anybody here have a cell phone?"

Nobody responded. Eddie and Van exchanged a confused glance. What was wrong with these people? Were they playing at being unenlightened serfs for so long they forgot how to behave like normal people? A tiny voice coming from the floor in front of them broke the silence. "What happened to your hair?"

Van looked down to see a small boy staring transfixed at Eddie's bright green locks. Eddie knelt down, then hunched his back to meet the boy at eye level as he smiled kindly. "Is my hair really that strange?"

The boy nodded. "Did a Skrahyer do that?"

Eddie shot a questioning glance at Van and then focused back to the child. "A what?"

"Did a Skrahyer change your hair color to match that of the grasses of the plains?"

Eddie laughed. "No, I colored it myself. You like it?"

The boy's eyes grew wide. "Are you a Skrahyer?"

Eddie grimaced in confusion. "I'm not sure what a Skrahyer is. Do you know where I can find a phone?"

It was the boy's turn to grimace. "What's a phone?"

Eddie straightened up and looked at Van with a bemused smile. Van shrugged. It seemed these people were bound and determined to play the part of living hundreds of years in the past. Eddie patted the child reassuringly on the top of his head as he stood and addressed the room at large. "Somebody please, just tell me where I can find a phone?"

This got a reaction, but not one they expected. Everyone quickly jumped from their tables and ran from the tavern, streaming out the door without looking back. Within a minute, the only ones left were Van, Eddie, and the small boy.

The boy tugged at Eddie's sleeve. Eddie looked down and smiled at the boy, encouraging him to talk.

"Can you make my hair that color?"

"I will if you show me where to find a phone."

Van grabbed Eddie's arm and whispered. "Don't lie to him."

Eddie smiled and whispered back, "I'm not lying. I have some more dye in the car at the bottom of the lake. I'll be sure to get it to him when we have a tow truck drag Bessie out of her watery grave." He looked back at the boy. "Can you tell me where I can find a phone?"

"What is a phone?" the boy asked, repeating the word "phone" slowly as if unsure of what he was saying.

Eddie took a deep breath and let it out in exasperation. "Fine, we'll play it your way. I need something that lets me to talk to someone who is far away."

The boy's eyes lit up. "Oh! A Skrahyer."

Eddie shrugged. "Okay, then I guess I need a Skrahyer."

The boy nodded vigorously. "Yep. The Skrahyer can talk to people in another place."

Eddie smiled at Van. "Now we're getting somewhere." He returned his attention to the boy. "Great! Take us to this Skrahyer."

The boy grabbed his arm and pulled him through the dining area of the tavern. They burst into the sunlight and Van's pupils constricted to pinpoints as they adjusted quickly to the brightness outside.

The boy kept pulling on Eddie as he led the temporarily blind visitors through the town. "This way. This way."

Eddie laughed. "The little guy seems to be in some kind of hurry."

As he led them out of the village, Van began to feel jittery again. As they passed people working in the gardens or fixing the thatching of roofs, nobody ever greeted them or waved a friendly hello. They stopped as Van and Eddie went by, stared until they passed, and returned to their chores. It just didn't fit the feeling of any of the Renaissance Faires Van attended with Eddie in the past. He could count the number on one hand of how many he'd attended, but they all radiated with the impression of people enjoying themselves and hamming it up for the civilian guests, making them feel welcomed and entertained. This was as entertaining as watching Eddie sweep the driveway at his parent's house on a lazy Sunday afternoon. The vibe was that of slaving twenty-four-seven, with no time to relax. They didn't look like they'd enjoyed a single moment of their lives since birth.

The boy stopped in front of a small cottage that looked like it was about to fall over from disrepair. "Skrahyer!" the boy called out. "I bring patrons."

The door opened with a creak and an old woman appeared from the darkness inside. She took one look at the boy and smiled. "Rodolfo? Who have you brought for me this time?"

Her gaze glazed over Eddie, frowned as she took in the color of his hair, and then recoiled in horror as she spotted Van. She let loose a flurry of angry sounding words in a language Van never heard before. She lunged forward, yanked Rodolfo from Eddie's grasp, pushed him through the open door and slammed it, shutting Rodolfo inside. She spun around and pressed her back protectively against the door as she glared at Van. "What do you want with us?"

Van gulped loudly at the shock of her actions. "Uhh. We need to use your phone?"

She squinted her eyes at him until they were tiny slits. "Go away!"

Eddie stepped forward, but stopped when she directed her ireful glare on him and held up a finger pointed at Eddie's head. "I see that he has marked you as his servant. May the fates have mercy on your soul."

Before Eddie could toss a witty retort back at her, she returned her gaze to Van. "You must leave before you bring a plague upon this village!"

Eddie moved forward again and the woman grabbed the crystal pendant around her neck in one hand and held the other palm facing him. "Don't come any closer, I do not wish to harm you."

Eddie froze, took a long look at her, and then broke into a wide grin and laughed. "Trust me lady. If we got into it, I would be more worried about your feeble bones. Just drop the act and help us. We just want to call to our parents."

Her head whipped back and forth from Eddie to Van and back to Eddie. "Why do you need my help for that?" Her head whipped back to Van again. "Is this a trick? Did you not think I would see who you are?"

Van looked at Eddie. Neither of them entertained a clue as to what was going on. Eddie shrugged, put his hands up in front of him, and walked forward to defuse the situation like he always did. She reacted to his movement and pushed her open hand forward in a blur. Eddie exhaled sharply and flew backward, landing hard on his butt. The woman repositioned her hand and pointed it at Van, but doing so clearly made her nervous. "He gave me no choice," she apologized. "Please. Leave our village in peace."

Eddie rolled to one side and gasped for air, coughing harshly as he rubbed at his chest. "What was that? Some form of Bruce Lee kung fu strike?"

The woman kept her back pressed against her front door. "Go! Both of you. Never come back."

She kicked her door behind her open with a foot, never taking her eyes or her hand off of Van. She stepped into her small cottage and slammed the door shut in their faces. Van turned around, reached down, and helped Eddie to his feet. He was still rubbing his chest. "I didn't think she was close enough to hit me."

Van stared at the quaint little cabin. It looked peaceful and calm from the outside. A stark contrast to who, or what, lived inside. "Eddie, she didn't touch you. She was at least three feet away and never got close."

Eddie winced as he stretched out his chest. "She did that with her what? Her chi energy?"

Van shook his head in disbelief. "I don't know. But I never saw her touch you."

"Maybe she was so fast you blinked and missed it."

"She never moved anything but her hand."

Eddie coughed and cleared his lungs of the phlegm that developed. Van looked around and stiffened. He poked Eddie on the arm. Eddie turned and froze as well. The entire village formed a line in the road, blocking the path back toward town. And they all carried pitchforks, scythes, and other nasty looking gardening implements that could do nasty things to the human body.

Eddie tried to calm them and smiled, which seemed to only enrage the crowd further. Van looked behind him to see that the way was clear for them to leave. The crowd surged forward. Van was certain he heard a growl rise up from the crowd. They obviously wore out whatever welcome they could expect.

He pulled on Eddie's arm. "Let's go."

"Sounds like a great plan."

They turned around and started walking. After fifty paces, Van chanced a peek behind and was relieved to see the crowd stayed where they were. They couldn't return to the village, but at least it didn't look like the villagers were pursuing them.

"How's it looking back there?" Eddie asked.

"I think they are letting us go."

Eddie shook his head and let out a nervous laugh. "That was the most bizarre Renaissance Faire I have ever seen. What do you think their problem was?"

"I don't know."

Eddie glanced back and his head snapped forward. "They're still there and they look pissed. Maybe we should have asked about buying a ticket before we wanted to borrow their phone."

Chapter 13

In a small tavern, much like the one Van and Eddie recently visited, a man in a cloak sat at a table in the back surrounded by several drunk men, a couple of them wavering from too much nog. A small pile of gold coins rested on the table before him next to a small pile of straw. The cloaked figure regarded the gold pile and looked up at the group of men gathered around. "Two more," he said.

"Come on," one of the wavering men slurred. "That's already a king's ransom."

The cloaked figure looked at the man. "One more. That's my final offer."

"No more," another chimed in, weaving back and forth so much he spilled some of his nog onto the table. "I bet you can't even do it. You're a fraud, just like the rest who come through here all the time claiming to be a true Spinner."

The cloaked figure picked up a piece of straw about five inches long. He held up his hand and curled his fingers into a fist, leaving a small opening like a keyhole. He shoved the end of the straw into it and then reached to the other side, pulling a thin rod of gold out of his closed hand. He let it drop with a loud clatter onto the table. One of the men snatched it up and inspected it closely, his eyes crossing from drunken effort at concentrating so hard. He bit it and smiled a near-toothless grin. "It's gold!" he exclaimed.

Another man leaned over the table, spilling more nog onto the table, just missing the pile of straw. "Do another one."

"Two more, please, and I will spin the entire stack of straw into gold."

Hands fished through pockets and four more coins joined the small pile. The cloaked man scooped the coins off the edge of the table and they disappeared into a hidden pocket sewn into his cloak. He cupped his hands together and held them over the small pile of straw. As soon as he was done, he pulled his hands away and everyone gawked at the small pile of golden rods lying there. Greedy hands snatched up the rods and the fights began.

The cloaked man kept his voice low, but there was still a strong intensity to it that made everyone take notice. "I don't care how you divvy up the gold, just do it somewhere else."

The small crowd followed the man who snatched up the lion's share of the pile of golden straw and they all left the tavern. No doubt, there would be some sore heads in the morning and someone would be richer than the rest.

"How come you ask for gold coins if you can spin straw into gold? The stables are full of more straw than you could spend in a lifetime, even if you turned it into copper."

The cloaked man smiled mischievously at the woman who asked the question. She remained seated next to him when the rest stumbled off to squabble over fair distribution of the gold. "Watch this," he said with a wink and waved his hand at the candle in the middle of the table.

The flame split in two and dropped to the table. The split flames sprouted arms and legs, forming the shape of two tiny figures that approached each other, embraced, and danced in time to the music being played on the harpsichord on the other side of the tavern.

"That's cute," she said.

The man winced. "I was looking for marvelous. Stupendous. Amazing."

A man in a similar cloak sat down at the table across from the first man. He raised his hand and with a wave, a tiny waterspout formed over the glass of dirty water. He moved his wrist and the waterspout slowly moved across the table in a twisting pattern, finally landing on the dancing flames; extinguishing them.

The woman looked up at the second man. "Now that was amazing."

The second man didn't smile as he addressed the woman. "Leave us."

The woman, knowing how things worked in a tavern, left without a word and quickly sat down at another table where money was abundant and nog was flowing freely.

The men looked at each other for a long time in silence. The second man finally removed his gloves and placed them on the table. "I thought I'd find you here, Halen, hiding in the dark pulling tricks in the hope of a warm bed." He cast a sideways glance at the woman who was now fully engaged with the men at another table, sitting on one of their laps and sneaking gold coins into her skirt pocket when no one was looking.

Halen gave him a tired look, as if the conversation was already boring him to death. "I'm not interested, Calen."

Calen laughed softly. "You haven't even heard what I have to say."

"Is it coming from you, or from The Order?"

Calen took a deep breath and let it out slowly. "You were apprenticed to the strongest Spinner in all the realms. Now look at you. How could you let yourself come to this?"

Halen drew back the edge of his cloak, revealing the coal-black Wizard's Order Crest pin. "It is not by choice." He released his cloak and let it fall back into place.

Calen gave him a knowing look. "And yet you still can spin. How do you think that is possible?"

"Is there a point to all this, Calen?"

Calen smiled and pointed at the spot where Halen's crest lie hidden among the fold of his cloak. "How would you like to have that removed?"

Halen regarded him coolly. "We both know you don't have the power to even suggest that."

Calen waggled a finger and sat back, trying to get comfortable on the rough-hewn wooden chair. "My influence with The Order has grown considerably since you left."

Halen slammed a fist on the table and growled, "You of all people know I did not leave!"

Calen lifted his hands to calm Halen down. "Okay, okay. Since you were—banished—from The Order my influence has become such that I was able to convince them you were the right man for a very important undertaking. If you help me, I can help you. Besides, I've kept your secret all this time."

Halen's eyes became guarded "I have no secrets, Calen."

Calen smiled, reached across the table swiftly and tugged back Halen's cloak. "I'm sure Veren's Crest pin is in there somewhere."

Halen swatted his hand away and pulled his cloak tighter around him. "Go away, Calen. I'm busy."

Calen's face grew serious. "I'm sorry Halen, but I need you. A Spinner entered Midguard from Techrealm unexpectedly. Something like this hasn't happened in over five hundred years and we need to—"

Halen leaned forward, interrupting him. "Not everything is within The Order's control. I thank the fates for that. So another Spinner has joined the realm. What is The Order going to do about it?"

"We—" Halen's eyes turned cold and distrustful. Calen softened his own look. "—I want you to find him and bring him to The Order."

"Why? So The Order can train another monkey to blindly follow their senseless rubrics?"

Calen winced visibly, but continued. "The Order is adamant that this Spinner not be trained. He is to be returned to Techrealm with no knowledge of the power he possesses."

Halen laughed. "Isn't that just like The Order? We are facing a growing army that is amassing at the gate and it wants to prevent the training of yet another Spinner who could prevent the war? Why not just throw the gate wide open and invite Aeron in? It's what your precious Order is doing anyway. No. No way. Leave me out of it."

Halen stood up and Calen reached out a hand, grabbing his arm to stop him. "It's Van."

The memories flooded his mind. The final battle at the gate, his promise to Veren, Veren's sacrifice, and the shame he wore like a veil of darkness. The memories threatened to overload him. He settled back down in his chair to keep from collapsing to the floor. The room spun and he struggled to maintain his balance. He finally focused on Calen, who looked genuinely concerned as he continued. "You have to bring him safely to The Order. He must return to his world before Aeron knows he is here." Calen's words came to Halen as if they were filtered through rushing water. "You know what Aeron will do if he finds out Veren's son is in Midguard." Calen added, hammering the final nail in the coffin of Halen's fate.

Halen could never say no to helping a Maclean and Calen was using that tidbit of information to its fullest. But why did they need his help? Was The Order so weak they couldn't rescue one boy on their own? Or was Van in more danger than Calen would admit? He finally gathered his wits and focused on Calen. "I'm going to need some things."

Calen smiled, his shoulders visibly relaxing. "Of course. The Order has instructed me to provide you with whatever you need."

Halen gave him a hard glare.

Calen lowered his eyes briefly. "Everything but that."

"How can you expect me to protect him if I am shackled?"

"We both know you aren't exactly shackled."

"But The Order doesn't know it. How do they expect me to protect him without it?"

Calen looked at him levelly. "They trust my judgment. I said you were the best one for this. Even without your power."

Halen took a deep breath, "It's not enough," his mind focusing on the worst possible danger. "Spinning straw into gold. Dancing flames. That is the true extent of my current abilities. If Aeron finds us before we reach the Western Basilica—I need the tarnished crest removed. I have to protect Van."

Calen put a reassuring hand on Halen's shoulder, ignoring the desperate plea. "According to The Order's spies around Midguard, Aeron does not yet know he is here. The sooner you get Van to The Order, the sooner we can get him home. And the sooner we can discuss your reprieve from exile."

"I'm not doing this for me. I'm doing this for Van."

"I know. But if I can help you as well, then that is an added bonus. Remember, it is important that Van not be trained. Not even by you."

"Don't worry. As much as I disagree with the rules of The Order, I will abide by them this time. For Van's sake."

Calen smiled. "For Van's sake."

Chapter 14

Van struggled to keep pace with Eddie, whose long legs kept him several steps ahead no matter how slowly he walked. For the past couple of miles it was the same pattern. Van would jog to catch up with Eddie and then fall behind again only to have to jog to catch up again.

"Can you believe we haven't seen a car for hours?" Van asked as he jogged up next to Eddie again.

"What's even stranger," Eddie replied. "Is that I haven't seen a single telephone pole since we left that Renaissance town."

Eddie stopped and leaned his tall frame on a massive stone sitting to the side of the road. "Come to think of it. I can't recall seeing a telephone pole since we climbed out of the lake." He removed a shoe and dumped a handful of dirt and rocks out of it. "I swear I'm picking up every pebble on the road."

Van settled in next to him and removed his shoes, pouring out just as much sand and grit as fell from Eddie's shoe. "I got the ones you missed."

Van placed a hand on the stone as he kicked off his other shoe. The rock grated at his palm. "Ow!" he exclaimed as a jagged edge of rock sliced into flesh.

"What?" Eddie asked, paying more attention to the dirt pouring from his other shoe than Van.

"The rock cut me," Van exclaimed as he winced at the blood seeping from the slice on the heel of his palm.

Eddie replied with a non-committal grunt, still fixated on dumping dirt out of his shoe. Van inspected the wound on his hand and noticed a splinter wedged in the cut. He grabbed it with his fingertips and pulled, gritting his teeth against the shooting pain. His hand throbbed in relief the moment the splinter came free. He stared at it in confusion. How did he get a splinter from a rock?

He looked at the massive stone and saw it expand and contract slightly, like it was breathing. He immediately started backing away, dropping his shoe to put it on without taking his eyes off the massive rock. "Eddie?"

Eddie was in the middle of putting back on his other shoe. He glanced up. "Yeah?"

Van motioned furiously for Eddie to come to him. Eddie looked at him in confusion for a moment. Van's silent, but insistent, motions made him finally put on his shoe and walk toward Van. When he was standing next to Van, Van pointed at the massive stone that was clearly as tall as Eddie when he stood fully upright. "I don't think that's a rock."

Eddie took a long look at it. Then he turned to Van. "Of course it's a rock. What else could it be?"

Van looked around and spotted a bush growing by the side of the road. He pulled at one of the branches, snapping it off in his hands.

Eddie watched him with growing interest. "What are you doing?"

Van gripped the stick like a baseball bat in both hands. "Just watch."

Eddie observed Van approach the stone carefully and jab at it with the sharp end of the branch. The rock seemed to compress slightly where he poked it. Van pulled the stick back, ready to poke it again harder.

Just as he was about to shove the branch into the side of the stone harder, a clawed hand appeared out of nowhere and grabbed the stick, snatching it out of Van's hands.

Van and Eddie screamed in stereo as the rock rose up, its wings unfurling and spreading as wide as a small plane. It took off in the air, the dust kicking up around them as it sailed into the sky.

Eddie stopped screaming and started laughing. Van looked at him as if he'd lost his mind. Eddie wrapped an arm around Van's shoulders and gently patted his shocked face. "Did you see that? A frickin' dragon."

Van didn't find it funny. But, at least he knew he wasn't hallucinating. There was no way he was seeing things if Eddie saw it too. He was still trying to reason what his eyes witnessed when a shadow crossed over him. He searched the sky and noticed the dragon was circling above them. And then it wasn't circling anymore.

It was diving!

Straight for them!

"Run!" Van screamed and he and Eddie took off down the road. Eddie was much faster with his long legs and the distance between them grew to twenty paces in less than ten seconds. Van's brain took that moment to remind him of the joke of two hikers in the woods coming across a bear and one of them putting on running shoes. You can't outrun that bear, said the first guy. Don't have to, the other replied. I just have to outrun you.

In this case, Eddie was the one who could easily outrun Van, which became chillingly apparent as the distance between them grew. But as Van glanced at the ground, he could see by the shadow that tracked them the dragon was easily keeping pace with both of them as they ran at their top speed.

Van took in huge gulps of air, trying to force oxygen to his muscles and make them work faster. But in the back of his mind he knew there was no way either of them could outrun a dragon. He felt the wind shift as the wings beat down just above him. Van hit the dirt and skidded, the gravel tearing at his pants before biting into flesh. A claw swiped the empty air above him and soared past.

The shadow swept forward and Van watched in horror as Eddie was snatched up in an outstretched claw and lifted off the ground. There was nothing Van could do as he watched the dragon climb higher with his best friend in its clutches. The dragon wheeled through the sky and then disappeared over the edge of the nearest mountain.

And with that, Van was in the middle of the road…alone.

His heart pounded hard against his chest and his throat burned as he screamed Eddie's name at the top of his lungs. But he never received an answer. He never expected one. Eddie was gone.

He lay face down in the dirt, unsure of what to do. He'd just lost his only real friend. He was isolated, in a strange, unfamiliar world that made less sense the longer he stayed. He couldn't move. He was utterly incapacitated by the hopelessness that washed over him. He could faintly hear birds chirping from somewhere nearby, but it didn't matter. He dropped his head onto his arms wishing this was just a dream and none of it was real.

He wasn't sure how long he lay there, but it couldn't have been more than a few minutes when the cacophony of chirping birds suddenly stopped. The silence was deafening and Van's body overrode his hopelessness as he felt a shock of adrenaline hit his system, making him rush to get up and look around for the danger the birds were reacting to. The distinct shadow appeared on the grass to his right, gliding across the dry blades heading straight for him. He looked up and his heart stopped.

The dragon folded its wings back and accelerated rapidly across the sky. Its claws were empty and it looked at him with lifeless eyes as it swooped overhead before banking in a wide turn to circle back. This time, it centered on him and lowered its rear claws like the landing gear of a Boeing 747 Jumbo Jet, aiming right for him.

Eddie obviously wasn't enough to sate this monster's endless hunger and it returned for a second helping of human.

Van whipped his head around, desperately searching for somewhere to hide. He looked about him, but the road was deserted in both directions as far as the eye could see. There was a small stand of trees a hundred feet to one side. Luckily, it was not like the dank and scary forest of earlier. This one was alive with trees full of bright green leaves. It looked welcoming and cheerful and a great place to find refuge to hide from the airborne beast. If he could get there, maybe he could hide until the ravenous savage gave up and left. As he started to run, he realized the trees were farther away than he first thought.

In this new direction, the sun wouldn't be giving away the dragon's position and alert him when it was getting closer. Van was running from the sky hunter through the tall grass with no clue when it would strike. The tips of the tall weeds slashed at his face as he barreled along. He watched the grass bend away from him from a strong gust of wind, guessed what that meant, and dove for the ground. A claw caught his shirt, ripping it in half, but missing him entirely. The dragon let out a frustrated huffing sound and took off into the sky empty handed.

Van was back on his feet, running full speed for the trees. The grass was getting shorter the closer he advanced until it was only as tall as his ankle. He couldn't rely on that to warn him the next time the dragon swooped in. He wheezed breathlessly but forced himself to keep running, stumbling on the uneven ground.

He risked a glance above and behind him, but he couldn't locate the monstrosity. He stole quick glances in all directions, trying to catch a glimpse of the predator that shouldn't exist.

The glances were slowing him down as they sent a dizzying signal to his brain that made him stumble. He tripped and fell sideways just as the dragon's claw snapped loudly, missing him by mere inches. An irritated snort accompanied the whoosh of air as the dragon flew back into the sky having missed its prize for a third time.

Van jumped to his feet and realized he was close to the stand of trees. He quickly scanned the skies for the dragon and spotted the tiny dark silhouette as it angled to face him for its next strafing run.

He might make it. In a split second decision Van bolted for the trees. As he neared, he glanced back and saw the dragon was still too high to reach him before he was under their leafy protective cover. He was going to make it!

When he was ten feet from the first tree, a shape suddenly vaulted out of the forest, tackled him to the ground, wound rope around him tightly and drug him away from the safety he was so desperately trying to reach. He struggled to angle his head to see who or what was dragging him.

He was shocked to find a woman dressed in brown leather pants and a worn leather corset that looked designed more for battle than for a night out with the girls.

She pulled him out into the middle of the low grass, leaned down, without reacting to his perplexed expression, and patted him on the chest as she smiled wickedly. "You stay right there and be a good little lure."

Then she ran for the very trees he was trying to reach and disappeared from sight. He looked toward the trees in shocked outrage, then quickly started struggling against the ropes, trying desperately to free himself. But the woman thoroughly trussed him up like a calf in a rodeo and he couldn't move. At that moment a shrill cry of delight resonated in the sky. Van snapped his head toward the sound to see the dark shape of the dragon swooping down to land next to where Van lay helpless in the low, dry grass.

The ground vibrated under its massive weight as all four feet impacted with the ground. It looked around cautiously before returning its attention to Van. It reached out a tentative claw and prodded Van, seemingly confused that he was already wrapped up for takeout. The dragon pushed him harder and Van rolled around, landing hard on a sharp stone. "Ow!" he hollered. What did the woman have planned when she tied him up and left him there as bait? What kind of sick person would use another human being this way? He looked up at the dragon as it regarded him inquisitively. The dragon looked around again, then returned its attention to the waiting morsel. The giant walked over to stand next to Van, forcing him to wriggle out of the way to keep from getting crushed. The fiend took one last look around before grabbing Van quickly in its claw and taking to the sky.

"Now!" a female voice yelled from the trees.

The dragon reacted quickly, changing direction abruptly as a huge net flew out of the trees. But it was too late and the net wrapped fully around the massive creature.

Van and dragon were immediately tangled up in the ropes and they both came crashing to the ground, knocking the wind out of them. Through a haze of exhaustion and dizziness Van watched as a group of men and women, all dressed in similar brown leather outfits, surrounded the dragon and pegged down sections of the net with large wooden stakes.

Van lay there helpless in the grip of the trapped dragon. He looked at the belly of the beast and wondered, if they cut it open would Eddie pop out and say something profound, like in the movies?

This wasn't a movie, Van reminded himself. Eddie was gone.

Chapter 15

As the sun slowly dipped below the horizon, Van found himself at the impromptu camp formed around the downed dragon. They took their time before removing him from the dragon's claws and securing him to a tree. Then they built a fire against the oncoming night, but it was well away from the tree where he was currently tied. He tugged at the binds, but it was useless. He wasn't going to be loosening the ropes and escaping anytime soon.

He was at the outer periphery of the hastily erected campsite, the shadows from those closer to the fire stretched all the way to his feet. If it wasn't for the full moon shining brightly as it slowly crawled across the night sky, he would be shrouded in darkness.

Van's first day away from home was eventful, to say the least. It was the opposite of what he expected. And definitely the opposite of what he promised his mother. His heart started pounding harder as he closed his eyes and remembered Eddie being carried away by the dragon over and over again.

Right now, he and Eddie should be in some diner discussing whether to sleep in the car or find a cheap motel before they continued on their road trip to their future. Instead he was a prisoner of dragon hunters and lost his best friend to the same dragon that was now immobilized near him.

Van glared angrily at the dragon that was pinned to the ground by the same netting that was used to pull it down out of the sky. It stopped struggling against its own bindings at around the same time Van accepted that he wasn't going to escape. They were both in the same predicament and there was nothing either of them could do about it.

Only, the dragon was not innocent. It took Eddie from him. As far as Van was concerned the beast deserved whatever fate was to befall it at the hands of the hunters. Van realized he was angry. He wanted revenge for having his best friend taken from him forever. But what could he do? He was tied fast to a tree. He could see no reason as to why he was still tied up. They obviously no longer needed him for bait. They already captured the dragon. Maybe that was the reason. They could tell he wanted revenge for his friend and didn't want him to harm their precious prize.

He watched the slow rise and fall of the dragon's chest as it breathed slowly and deliberately. He caught it staring at him and, despite his anger, was unnerved when it refused to look away when they made eye contact. It was Van who always lost their game of chicken and turned away from the gaze in disgust.

Van was working through ideas on how to wriggle free of the ropes when he was startled by a sudden voice asking "Hungry?" from the semi-darkness.

Van squinted into the shadows as a dark shape approached. It soon resolved into the woman who tackled him at the forest's edge and used him as bait to capture the dragon. She cradled a bowl of something in her hands. Van didn't trust anyone willing to risk his life to capture a dragon. But they hadn't harmed him in the hours since they extracted him from the dragon's claws. What did they want with him? Van also realized he was famished and a part of him reasoned he needed to keep up his strength in case he found a way to escape this horde. If they were willing to feed him, he could use the food, but he wanted to find out why they still kept him tied up like a prisoner. Seeing she was waiting for a response, he replied "I could eat."

The woman bent down and placed a bowl with the rough handle of a wooden spoon sticking out of it in front of him. She eyed him suspiciously. "I can either untie your hands or feed you like a little baby."

Van stared at her, plastering his face with what he hoped was an innocent expression. "I'd rather feed myself."

"You won't try anything?"

He decided to lie and shook his head. "I won't try anything."

"Because if you do, I will have no choice but to make do on the bounty as is."

That was a confusing response. What was she talking about? He remembered seeing shows about bounty hunters on TV, but after his experiences today, that probably was not what she meant. Her tone made it sound like a threat. This might be a clue as to why they still kept him tied up. He resolved to find out what she meant. "Bounty?"

She smiled. "Yeah. The bounty is offering a hundred gold pieces for your head on a silver platter. I'm guessing the platter is optional."

Van's heart drummed a fast beat and he felt the adrenaline course through his veins once again. So that was why they were keeping him. They wanted to trade him for money. But to get it, he had to be dead. He couldn't tell by her expression if she was joking with him or serious.

The woman saw the confusion register in his eyes. "Don't give it too much thought. A lot of people don't even realize when they aggravate someone with a lot of money."

Van didn't know how anyone with money around here even knew about him. He'd been here less than a day and the few people he did come in contact with looked very poor; almost to the point of impoverishment. With a confused expression, Van shook his head slightly and asked "Why is there a bounty on my head?"

She chuckled softly. "It's not that hard. I must have several bounties on my head. Most of my crew are here because it is safer with me than it is on their own."

Van looked past her to the group of men and women who were enjoying themselves around the fire, drinking, and laughing. They didn't act like they were all wanted with a price on their heads.

She cocked an eyebrow at him. "You'd be surprised how many open bounties there are circulating throughout Midguard."

Midguard. He'd never heard that name before. His memory poured over the maps he studied for places to rest during their trip to college. He didn't recognize the name at all.

"I'm sorry. Where is Midguard?"

She frowned. "There is no 'where' for Midguard. Midguard is where you are no matter how far you walk. There are no boundaries. Midguard is everywhere."

"No. You misunderstand. Is Midguard a city or a county? I don't recognize the name. Is this place some unincorporated area not listed on Google Maps or GPS?"

It was her turn to look confused. She stared at him for a full minute before shaking her head and mumbling, "I don't know why anyone would pay for your head. It's filled with nonsense."

She slipped a dagger out of its sheath and held it up, letting the bluish moonlight glint off the polished steel blade. "I'm going to release your hands. Do I need to use this for something other than cutting your ropes?"

Van shook his head. He decided earlier, as he watched several muscled men and women work the nets to keep the dragon secured, that he would never win in hand to hand combat with any of them. When he made his escape, it would be while they were all asleep. He wasn't sure how he was going to avenge Eddie without waking them, but there was still plenty of time to resolve that dilemma. She reached around him and he heard the slicing of the ropes as his hands fell free. The relief in his shoulders was immediate. He couldn't help letting an "ahh" escape his lips as he crossed his arms in front of him slowly, stretching out muscles that developed knots on top of knots.

The woman took a step back and pointed at the bowl by his still bound feet. "You might want to eat that quickly. I'm not saying Hans is a master chef, but trust me when I say his stew is better warm than cold."

Before she left, he decided to see if she planned to poison him. She'd seemed forthcoming with information up to this point, so he decided just to ask and trust the answer. He didn't have much choice anyway.

"Uh, is the food safe to eat?"

She gave him an impatient look. "Yes, just eat it before it gets cold."

He hesitated, just staring at the bowl. She gave him a calculating look, then nodded. "I see. You think it is poisoned." She bent down and picked up the bowl with the spoon. "To satisfy your curiosity, I'll taste it for you."

She picked up the spoon with a bit of the stew on it, scraped the goop off of the spoon with her teeth and chewed thoughtfully before swallowing. "It's not a palace feast, but it won't kill you. Now, eat, you need your strength for the next few days."

She placed the bowl next to him with the spoon dug back into it.

He picked up the bowl and dug the spoon into the sludge the woman referred to as stew. He let go of the spoon and it stood straight up. He looked up at the woman with a slight look of disgust. She smiled and motioned for him to eat. Since she was still here, he decided to try to gain as much information as he could while he held her attention. It might prove useful. "What are we doing for the next few days?"

"Looking for someone willing to pay more for you alive than the hundred gold pieces offered for you dead."

She turned away to leave and he decided to try something he'd seen once in a movie. In it, the serial killer accidentally befriended his latest victim and she was able to stay alive, and ultimately escape, because the killer learned her name. "My name's Van. What's yours?"

She stopped and turned slowly on her heel, casting a surprised and confused look at him. She walked back over and crouched down to meet him at eye level. "Don't think that a friendly manner will keep me from killing you for the reward." She glanced at the stew. "Be assured I would never use poison. Too cowardly. But your best chance at seeing the next sunrise is to be worth more to someone alive than dead."

She was starting to rise when her head turned suddenly and she froze, staring out into the darkness. She remained perfectly still as if she were a statue. Van couldn't even see her breathing. He craned his neck to see what she was looking at, but he couldn't see anything in the darkness outside the reach of the glow from the fire. After half a minute, she visibly relaxed, stood fully, and headed back to the fire.

Despite her dark demeanor, the group she was with were the first people he saw who smiled and seemed to be enjoying themselves. She couldn't be as cold as she let on. He realized if he knew her name, he would at least have the chance at reminding her he was a person instead of a commodity. "You still haven't told me your name," he called after her with more confidence registering in his voice than he felt. She stopped dead, turned her head, and glanced at him over her shoulder. "Talia," she said and then walked away to join the rest of the group around the fire. He watched her intently and felt a small ray of hope rise up in him as she glanced his way every now and then. She would abruptly return her attention to whoever she was talking to, but he caught her stealing glances his way more and more often. She did this several times over the next hour.

He was getting to her.

She looked his way again and then motioned for him to eat. That's when he knew he'd discovered a chink in her armor. But, it also reminded him about the bowl of supposed stew in his hands. He gripped the spoon and pulled it out of the stew. The contents of the bowl seemed reluctant to let him have the spoon without a fight and when the spoon suddenly released some of the sludge splattered on his torn shirt. He dug at the middle of the brown-colored slop and lifted sloppy chunks of unrecognizable sludge with the spoon. He reluctantly brought a spoonful of the goop to his mouth and touched it tenderly to his lips. It was stone cold.

He sniffed at it, but there was no smell. He hoped the taste was as neutral as the aroma and shoveled the goopy chunks into his mouth. He was wrong. The taste hit him and he shuddered, almost involuntarily spitting the stuff out of his mouth. He sat there with the cold mush sitting in his mouth and watched as several others around the fire happily spooned the glop into their mouths until their bowls ran dry.

Talia was right. If there was any chance at surviving this ordeal, he needed to keep his strength up. And that meant eating what was given to him. His mom was never a proponent of the clean plate club, but this was his only bid for survival and he knew he should eat any chance he got if he planned to stay alive.

He tried to chew but that only made him gag. Besides, it was technically soft enough to let it slide down his throat. It felt like he was throwing up in reverse. He swallowed, gagging as the stew slowly crawled to his stomach. He took deep breaths between bites to keep it down and repeated the process until the bowl was empty. He started to think maybe it would be better if she killed him rather than torturing him with her idea of food.

He looked at the chef du jour who was happily ladling more steaming stew into eagerly outstretched bowls. Maybe Talia was right about it tasting better hot. They all seemed to be enjoying it.

He set down the bowl and realized with disbelief that his hands were still untied. He glanced at the fire and made eye contact with Talia. He smiled and then made a big show of yawning and lying back, placing his hands on his gurgling stomach as if to signal he was full, content, and ready for sleep.

He laid back on the rough ground and was about to sneak a peek to see if Talia was still watching him when a twig broke a few feet away from his head. He froze, holding his breath and straining for any sound that indicated something was coming to eat him and end his ordeal. Who knew what else there was in this place that might find human meat tasty?

He heard the scuffling of rocks close by. His breathing increased as his body prepared for the fight or flight instinct when a hand clamped over his mouth, stifling the scream that erupted from deep within.

Eddie's beaming face came into view and smiled down at him. "Come with me if you want to live," he whispered, using his best Arnold Schwarzenegger impersonation. Van stared at Eddie's face in disbelief. Was this real? Was Eddie really here? But there was no mistaking those ears, even in the shadowy light of the moon, and Van trembled with relief at seeing his friend alive.

Eddie pulled his hand away and Van sat up. "What happened? The dragon?"

Eddie winked. "I'll explain as soon as we get out of here. Just keep an eye out for anyone coming." He produced a knife from behind him. He bent forward and used it to saw at the thick rope around Van's legs.

Van watched Eddie work on the thick rope, then glanced at the fire and his heart stopped. He scanned the faces laughing and taking turns pulling a drink from the same bottle they passed around. She wasn't there. He expanded his visual search wider, but Talia was nowhere in sight. They had to get away before she came back from wherever she went. "Hurry up, Eddie."

"I'm working as fast as I can," Eddie replied right before the knife jerked upward as it sliced through the last of the rope. He let out a quiet cry of victory. "Let's go," he said and stood up. Van stood and turned to face his friend when a shadow rose up out of the darkness behind Eddie.

Chapter 16

"Eddie, look out!" Van blurted.

Eddie didn't have time to react before Talia kicked the back of his legs, sending him crumpling to his knees. Now that he was at a better height, she grabbed him from behind and held her dagger to his throat. Eddie tilted his head up, trying to keep away from the sharpened blade that bit into the tender skin of his neck.

Van's warning was loud enough to direct the attention of the entire camp at them and they were quickly surrounded by knives and daggers in swaying drunken hands.

"Looks like we have a rescue party of—one?" Talia said after everyone gathered around. Several of the men laughed and she kicked Eddie away from her. He landed on his stomach next to Van and rolled over, sitting up quickly to face Talia.

Talia looked him up and down, her eyebrows knitting in confusion. "Weren't you eaten by a dragon?"

Eddie puffed up his chest, acting brave against the reality of the situation. "He put me in his nest for later. When he didn't come back, I climbed down and followed the fire you lit here only to find my friend tied up like some criminal."

Talia stared at him stoically for a long moment before a smile spread slowly across her face. "The only criminals here are the ones with blades." That elicited several guffaws from the men and women gathered around.

Talia shook her head. "There's one problem with your story, young man. Dragons don't build nests. Everyone knows that." The crowd around them erupted in laughter and the blades lowered as they realized they weren't dealing with much of a threat.

It didn't take long for Van to be tied back up in a most uncomfortable position with Eddie restrained in ropes next to him. This time, they were brought closer to the fire so everyone could keep a better eye on them.

Van looked at Eddie. He was so happy to have his friend back and alive, he didn't care they were prisoners again. But they couldn't talk, not with so many loud drunk strangers around. After an hour Van's arms cramped up. Everyone at the camp finally turned in for the night and were drifting off to sleep. Van and Eddie were the last ones awake, still tied up side by side next to the dying fire. As a particularly painful cramp formed in Van's shoulder, he decided Eddie made a major mistake with his rescue plan. He threw an annoyed look at his best friend. Eddie noticed Van's glance and raised his eyebrows. "What?"

"Dragon nest? Really? Don't you pay attention to the movies or books? Dragons live in caves. They don't build nests."

Eddie frowned. "Of course I've seen the movies. But this isn't a movie. What if Hollywood got it all wrong?"

A man they thought was passed out nearby heard their conversation and lifted his head. "Dragons don't live in caves," he slurred. "They curl up to look like giant rocks. They sleep in the middle of wheat fields to stay warm. Everybody knows that."

Eddie smiled smugly. "Thank you. See? Hollywood got it wrong. They don't sleep in caves mister know-it-all."

"Eddie—" Van searched for the words he wanted to say and finally stopped trying and fell silent. Despite the predicament they were in, he was really just glad Eddie was alive.

Talia was still fully awake and wandered over to sit down on the log situated near the fire to silently watch Eddie. Eddie met her stare and they remained like that for a full minute. Talia finally broke the silence by embedding her dagger into the log. Eddie jumped and she leaned in close to him. "Where is he?"

Eddie looked around him in a panic. "Where is who?"

"The Spinner?"

Eddie fixed her with a new stare that was laced with bewilderment. "What's a Spinner?"

She grabbed the dagger and rushed him, knocking him onto his back. He let out a high-pitched yelp as she straddled him and held the dagger to his throat. "Tell me where he is or I kill you right now."

"I don't know," Eddie whimpered. "Please. Don't kill me."

Van wasn't about to lose his best friend twice. "Talia, please, don't hurt him, what are you talking about?"

She ignored Van and pressed the dagger against his skin. "The Spinner. Where is he?"

"I don't know what a Spinner is!"

"The man who the dragon took you to."

"Oh. Him?"

Her eyes darkened as she pressed the blade of her knife into his throat, a dribble of blood running down the shiny surface. "Yes. Where is he?"

Eddie's eyes were popping out of this head. "I don't know! He told me to wait for his signal and then rescue Van."

She sat up, the blade moving swiftly away from Eddie's neck. She looked questioningly around at her cohorts. "Signal?" She shook several of her drunk compatriots awake. "Did anyone notice anything?"

Bewildered faces answered her questions. They wiped their eyes, looked at each other, and shook their heads. Nobody heard or saw anything out of the ordinary. They were drunk, but not that drunk, they assured her.

She looked down at Eddie who would have sunk out of sight into the very ground if he could. "What was the signal!" she demanded.

"I forgot."

Her face vacillated from confusion to disbelief. "What?"

Eddie started talking faster. "I forgot what that old guy told me so I just waited until Van was alone to rescue him. I don't know where he is. I swear!"

Talia advanced on him again with the knife in her hand. "Do you swear it on your life?"

"What?" he squeaked.

In a blur of movement, the knife was back at his throat.

"Yeah! Yeah! I swear on my life! I don't know where he is!"

Talia stood up straight. She turned in a slow circle, peering out into the darkness. "Come to me Spinner. I know you are out there."

A figure emerged from the darkness and stepped closer to the flickering fire. His cloak spread out majestically behind him while the hood protected his face from the invasion of light.

The mysterious figure spoke in deep, commanding tones. "If you don't let them go, I will reduce every one of you to ash." As if in response to his threat, the fire flared brightly, sending everyone scurrying away from him and into the darkness. No one was willing to go up against a Spinner.

No one except Talia.

She stepped around the fire and stood with her feet in a wide stance, as if challenging him to a gunfight at high noon. "You don't scare me, Spinner. Or should I say, Forsworn?"

The cloaked figure pulled back his hood and glared at her. "I mean it, Talia. I don't care what you think you know. If you harm that boy nothing will stop my wrath against you and your own."

She smiled. "That's why I don't have anyone, Halen. Nobody to care about or protect. I can make a decision based on the here and now. Your powers have been stripped from you and I have a full complement of hunters at my back. I think it is I that should be setting the guidelines for out little venture."

"This is not a negotiation—"

She threw back her head and laughed. "Everything is a negotiation. Everything is up for debate as to its value at that precise moment." She glanced back at Van and then returned to staring down Halen. "And at this moment in time, what is that boy's life worth to you?"

Chapter 17

Halen ignored Talia and directed his gaze to Eddie. "I told you to wait for my signal!" he said as if they were the only two people in the campsite. Talia snapped her fingers to regain his attention. "Hey! Spinner! We were in the middle of something. Ignore the idiot sidekick," she said impatiently. "What are you going to give me for the boy?"

Halen returned his attention back to Talia. Her reputation as a superior huntress was known far and wide. Her reputation as an extortionist was legendary. He visibly widened his stance, rooting himself to the spot as if solidifying his claim. "I want both of them."

She looked at the boys and smiled, shaking her head slightly as if dealing with a fool. "I don't know why, but fine. How much for both?"

Halen barely moved as he responded, "I'll give you the dragon."

Her face frowned. "I already have the dragon."

Halen scowled at her. "That dragon is branded to The Order. You cannot take it by force or you will bring hellfire down on your head and everyone with you. You cannot escape their wrath."

Talia's face was as rigid as stone as she glared at him. And then the corners of her eyes wrinkled and she doubled over in laughter. When she finally caught her breath she let out a huge sigh. "The Order? Halen, please. They stripped you of your reason for living and still you defend them? Why do you toe the line for something that lost its way a long time ago? Wake up, Halen. The die is cast for The Order."

Halen jutted his chin out in defiance. "You don't know that!"

She laughed again. "Everyone knows it! Everyone it seems except you."

Her expression shifted and she grew serious again. "The dragon is already mine. The Order can try to take it from me if they wish, though I would advise against it. Make me another offer."

Halen glared at those dark eyes that refused to give him anything back. Then he took a deep breath and countered. "I can offer you twice the bounty being offered."

"Per captive."

Halen's eyes went wide in indignation. "There is no bounty on the other one!"

"Pretend he has the same bounty as his more desirable friend."

"Be reasonable, Talia!"

"He can stay with me."

Halen looked at Eddie and Van, both staring up at him as he bartered for their very lives. He looked back at Talia. His shoulders slumped forward and he twisted his mouth in disgust. "Fine. Double the bounty on both as if they each possessed the same bounty."

Her face broke into a wide smile. "Excellent! We leave at first light."

Halen gave her a hard stare. "We leave now!"

Talia smiled sweetly and looked at him as if she was talking to a young child "We can't. The horses will stumble in the dark."

"We can use my—your dragon to fly there in less than a day."

She indicated the dried blood along one side of her dark brown leather outfit. "Unfortunately, my dragon was injured during her capture. I was able to patch her up, but we will be traveling as a hunter troupe the old fashioned way. By caravan."

Halen looked at Van. His plan to leave with Talia and the two boys on the dragon quickly fell apart. There was little he could do to escape a band of hunters. He needed to even the odds out a little more in his favor. "We leave at first light. But we must travel alone to keep from bringing unwanted attention to ourselves."

Talia's expression changed quickly as she eyed him suspiciously. "What are you saying?"

Halen shrugged and looked at the dingy faces of the hunters who gathered behind Talia, emboldened by her courage to stand up to the Spinner. "We will be traveling to the West Kingdom. How many of you are wanted by name and image between here and there?"

Nearly every face dropped to look at the ground. Halen nodded. "That's what I thought." He looked at Talia. "We should travel as companions. Just the four of us."

Talia's face wrinkled in disgust. "I would never companion with you."

Halen let out an exasperated huff. "I'm not asking you to companion with me. Just to look like we are as we take the boys to the West Kingdom. It will arouse less suspicion. In fact, we may be completely ignored, especially if we fight as if we are husband and wife."

Talia twisted her mouth, and stared at Halen for a moment. Then she pointed a very strong finger at Halen "Fine, we act like husband and wife. But don't think for a moment I will keep up that performance when we aren't in public!" Talia spat.

Halen smiled wryly. "Perfect. Just be like that and I think we can make this work."

Hans, his apron still covered with remnants of the stew he cooked and served, stepped forward and spoke to Talia quietly. "I don't think we should separate. The Spinner might be planning something."

"I have no doubt he will try something." Talia cast a sideways glance at Halen. "I wouldn't respect him if he didn't." She gave Hans a pat on his shoulder. "Don't worry, I can handle the likes of a Forsworn. He is a toothless predator." Then she moved back a pace and unsheathed her dagger, flashing Hans a wicked smile. "While my teeth are still sharp. He has no power over me. Or anyone or anything for that matter." She raised her voice to address the entire group. "I will take the disgraced Spinner and the bounty to West Kingdom and return with enough wealth for us all to retire."

This elicited a rousing cry of huzzahs from the hunters. She smiled at Halen. "Fear not, Spinner. As long as you secure my payment, your precious boy will live."

Chapter 18

Morning came quickly and Van's muscles were cramped from attempting to sleep while tied up. The chef dropped two bowls in front of Van and Eddie, the swill splashing over the lip. "Breakfast," he muttered and returned to stirring the cauldron on the fire. Van looked into the bowl at what appeared to be grey barf. He threw a disgusted look toward the chef and watched incredulously as more steaming spoonfuls of barf were ladled out into eagerly outstretched bowls.

Eddie shuffled into a sitting position and looked down at the bowl and smiled. "Goody. I'm hungry."

Talia appeared with a stack of leather clothes in her hands. She peered down at Van and Eddie. "If I cut you two free, am I going to have any trouble?"

Van shook his head.

Eddie peered up at her. "No, ma'am. No trouble at all."

Talia dropped the stack of folded clothes. "After breakfast, get changed. If we are to pass ourselves off as a hunter family, you need to look the part."

Van looked at the pile and then looked around at the wide open campsite. "Where do we get changed?"

Talia looked at him oddly, then put her hand to her mouth and chuckled. "Don't be so prudish. For the time being you are one of us. You can change where you are." She ogled him. "Unless you have something to be ashamed of."

Eddie laughed at that. "Lady, I've had the distinct pleasure of showering in gym class with this guy. He ain't got nothing to be ashamed of. He could put a permanent smile on the face of any women here!"

Talia cocked her head to one side and regarded Van with a teasing smile. "You seem to have impressed your friend".

Van's face heated up, shifting through several shades of crimson. She laughed eyeing Van up and down. "We'll see soon enough. We're leaving as soon as breakfast is done. Be changed by then." Van's face rekindled, burning as hotly as the morning sun.

Talia laughed to herself as she slipped behind him and cut the ropes with her dagger. Van's shoulders relaxed as the ropes fell away. Eddie sighed audibly as his arms flopped forward. Talia stepped back into view, sheathing her dagger. "Eat 'till you're full. And then eat some more. We won't be stopping again until nightfall."

Eddie snatched up the bowl and started shoveling the slop into his mouth and chewing hungrily. Van gawked at how quickly Eddie finished his bowl and wandered over to the fire to ask for a second helping; which the chef gladly provided.

Van looked at the goop with the spoon sticking straight up out of the bowl. It was still warm, so maybe it was better than last night's ordeal. Eddie seemed to have enjoyed it which Van hoped meant it wasn't as bad. Van pulled the spoon out, accompanied by a sickening sucking sound, and stuck it in his mouth. It was definitely warm, but not any better than before. He remembered Talia's helpful advice. This was going to be it until dinner.

Van choked down the contents and forced himself to get a second helping while Eddie was working on the last of his thirds. How could he be eating it so easily without losing it all over his shoes?

When Van finished he set down the empty bowl, the gunk sitting heavily in his stomach and making him feel like he gained fifty pounds. He picked up the stack of clothes and was suddenly the focus of attention from the women gathered nearby. They whispered to each other, giggling excitedly, and waited for him to undress. He looked at them in disbelief. "You're not all going to stare at me while I change are you?" One of the women stepped forward and, with a wide smile, replied, "We heard you have something to see, and we don't want to miss the show." The women settled in to watch. Van could tell there was no way he was getting rid of them. The rest of the group was quickly packing to go. He needed to hurry. He glared at them as he turned away and pulled up his torn shirt, exposing his back. This resulted in catcalls and enthusiastic hoots from the clutch of women watching him in anticipation. He pulled back down on his shirt quickly, his face warming from embarrassment. This elicited some unhappy "awws" and a couple of annoyed "boos" from the small group.

Eddie smiled wide. "I guess our conversation with that hunter lady got back to the rest of them."

Van gave him a withering look. "Yeah. Thanks a lot for that."

Eddie's smile threatened to split his head in half. "Just doing my part as your wingman, buddy."

Van glanced at the group of women who were all watching him. They weren't even trying to hide the fact that they were waiting for him to strip down to his underwear. Eddie nudged him. "What are you waiting for? They want a show. Give them a show."

Van's eyes darkened. "What the... Eddie, this is—degrading."

Eddie rolled his eyes. "Come on, Van. As far as we know we're lying in a coma in some hospital somewhere. I mean c'mon. Dragons? Sorcerers? Medieval villages with superpower witches living just outside of town? None of this is real. Might as well have fun with it." He spun around and gave the women a sexy smile and winked. Well, at least as sexy as he could be with his lime-green hair and ping-pong paddle ears. He started gyrating to a beat only he could hear and pulled his shirt halfway up and then lowered it again, teasing them.

The women went wild, cheering him on. The whoops grew louder as he pulled up his shirt to his chin. He yanked it over his head, swung it around and tossed it into the air. The women dove for it, fighting each other for his discarded clothing. They were so aggressive, two of them each came away with half a shirt, but fully satisfied with their prize.

Eddie gyrated as he stripped off his pants and the women barely contained themselves. He smiled at Van, beckoning him to join in the fun. "C'mon. Like Shia LaBeouf says, 'Just do it'," he hollered as he flexed his arms in front of him, eliciting more hoots and woos from the women crowded around them.

Van looked at Eddie having fun, the women whooping and shouting with big smiles on their faces, and decided maybe he was being too much of a prude. He rolled his eyes, took a big sigh, then grabbed the bottom of his shirt and pulled it off. The women responded with catcalls and whistles. He quickly decided this just wasn't for him. He wasn't a natural performer like Eddie. He needed to get down to business, get changed, and go. Van dropped his pants and quickly dressed in stiff leather pants, cotton shirt, and dark leather tunic before Eddie's pants were completely off. Eddie took his time as he redressed, to the amusement of several women who formed a circle around him and clapped in time to his gyrations. He was thoroughly enjoying himself. When he was done, Eddie bowed, only to be rewarded with a slap on his behind. He jerked straight up and waggled a finger at the offender. She winked at him and then bit a lone fingernail between her teeth, tilting her head and doing her best to be his favorite.

Van sat back down to work on the seemingly hundreds of laces needed to close his tunic. As he worked, he caught the eye of one of the women in the group. She shook her head at him and then returned her attention to Eddie and draped her arms over his shoulders, edging out the butt-slapper for dominance. Multiple hands worked on all the loose strings of Eddie's clothing, helping him finish dressing in record time.

Talia came over and sat down next to Van. She saw him struggling to keep the laces tight while tying them. She let out a sigh and turned to face him. "Let me help you," she said as she swatted his hands away and roughly took over tying his tunic properly. She finished and turned to watch Eddie enjoying his attention. She finally lifted Van's old T-shirt and studied it. "Where was this made?"

Van looked at it and shrugged. "I don't know, China?"

"Ahh," she said. "It came from the nations beyond the waters. Figures. It is so thin. Provides no protection from the elements."

Van gave her a curious look. "Yeah, well. Where I come from, the elements can be kept at bay by a simple nylon Windbreaker in the summer and a goose down parka in the winter. We don't have to worry about dragons. Or roving bands of killers chasing us down."

She narrowed her eyes at him. "I'll try not to take that personally."

Van laughed sarcastically. "Take it any way you want. I'm beginning to think that Eddie is right. None of this is real anyway, so—"

She moved so quickly and fluidly, Van didn't realize her dagger was unsheathed until she slashed it across his arm in a blur.

"Ahh!" he yelled and gripped his arm where the blood welled up. She wiped the blood off the blade onto his pant leg. "Did you feel that?"

"What do you think?!" Van blurted. He pulled his hand away and saw blood slowly dripping from the paper-thin cut just below his shoulder. He gripped it again tighter. "What did you do that for?"

She sheathed her dagger. "The scar will give you character."

"I have enough character, thank you very much!"

She motioned with her head to Eddie. "Not as much as he does."

Van watched as Eddie did the robot dance, much to the delight of the women still gathered around him. "Maybe not as much, but you didn't have to cut me."

"Yes I did."

"Why?"

Talia turned to face him. "Did you see it coming?"

"No."

"Were you expecting it?"

"Of course not!"

"Then that should prove to you this is not a dream. If it were, you wouldn't have felt it because you didn't see it. It wouldn't have happened."

Van checked his wound, his arm feeling hotter around the area where she sliced through his skin. It started to scab over and the bleeding finally stopped. "How do you know?"

She fixed him with a serious stare. "Because I am real. And if I didn't exist apart from the fantasies in your mind, I would be unable to do anything to you that you weren't expecting. I can tell by the look on your face—it is the same look from when I first saw you—you are astonished by everything you see around you. Accept that this is all real. That is a much more interesting concept than living in a dream."

Van looked away and studied his shoes. How could he tell her he thought he was living five hundred years in the past? He didn't even understand it himself. He looked up at her, unable to find the words to express his confusion as to what happened to them since the car crash. She patted his knee. "Don't worry, little one. We have a week to get to know each other better."

"A week!"

"It will take that long to reach the far end of the West Kingdom and turn you over to The Order."

Before Van could manufacture a response, Talia stood up. "Okay," she shouted above the doting women, each clamoring for Eddie's undivided attention. "Time's up, ladies." She strode into the throng of women and grabbed Eddie's wrist, pulling him free of the pack. The women protested noisily, but none made a move to challenge Talia.

Talia pulled Eddie along and glared at Van. Her look made him stand up right away. She pointed toward a wagon on the edge of the campsite where Halen stood silently waiting. "Time to go," Talia said and walked briskly to the wagon.

Van and Eddie exchanged a glance and then they both ran to catch up with her. She climbed up onto the driver's seat and grabbed the reigns. Halen climbed up to sit next to her, staring straight ahead. He didn't speak a word to anyone after he finished his negotiations with Talia and seemed lost in quiet reflection. She looked down at them, acting surprised that they were still standing by the wagon. "In the back! Both of you."

Van grabbed Eddie, stopping him from climbing onto the wagon. He looked up at Talia. "Where are you taking us?"

She frowned. "Haven't you been listening? Halen promises to double the ransom for your safe delivery to The Order."

Van matched her frown. "What does that mean?"

She titled her head to one side and gave him a penetrating stare as she nodded slightly with every other word. "You get to keep your heads."

Eddie's eyebrows shot up. "Sounds good to me," he said as he scrambled into the back. Van stood his ground. "What does this Order want with me?"

Talia twisted in her seat and addressed Halen. "Are you going to tell him something that will get him in the wagon or do I force him into it?"

Halen let out a long breath and looked at Van. "They are going to send you home."

Home? How did they know where he lived? "If that's all they want to do, why go through all this? I mean, taking a week to get to someplace called the West Kingdom only to send me back here?"

Halen shook his head. "You won't be coming back here. You will be going home."

"But I must live a couple hours' drive from here." He pointed at Talia. "She's saying we're going to take a week to get to someplace called West Kingdom. School starts next week. I don't have time to go all the way there just to be sent back here!"

"Get in, Van. I will do my best to explain what I can. But we need to get moving to keep you safe."

"Safe from what? Everything I've run into so far has been out to kill me."

Halen's eyes sparkled with an anger that proved he wasn't as dead and motionless as he portrayed. "I would never hurt you, Van. I made a promise to your—" Halen turned away and looked straight ahead. "I made a promise to someone." He faced Van again. "I will do everything in my power to keep you safe. That promise I will not break. Now get in the wagon."

Van's body moved of its own accord as he realized he was climbing into the back of the wagon without thinking about it. Before he was settled, Talia urged the horse to move and Van nearly fell back out of the wagon as he fought inertia to sit next to Eddie.

Wherever they were headed, Van wasn't convinced it would be an improvement over what he and Eddie already experienced. He looked over at Eddie who nestled between the burlap sacks of vegetables and watched the scenery roll by, as if they were on a leisurely hay ride at the county fair.

"How can you be so relaxed?" Van said to Eddie.

"Why not?" Eddie replied. "This is better than any dream I've ever been in. Did you see the ladies back there? They acted like I was a Greek god or something. That has never happened to me before. Not with these flappers," he said and pointed to his ears. He settled back against the side of the wagon and took in a deep breath of the crisp clean air. "I don't think I'll mind if I never wake up from this coma. I could stay here the rest of my life."

Chapter 19

Without the benefits of air-filled rubber tires and gas-piston shocks, the wagon jarred Van's teeth so much, he thought they were going to crack and crumble under the constant juddering. Eddie, as usual, was soaking up this new experience as if it was the best thing to happen to him.

They passed through several small towns, and one medium sized village, without stopping as the sun crawled across the sky to mark that they were also progressing through the day. Eddie smiled at various people along the road who walked beside their cows and sheep, but nobody ever smiled back. Despite the constant state of melancholy all around him from those they met on the road, and while crossing through the towns, Eddie retained his jovial attitude and started whistling a tune.

He suddenly stopped and looked at Van, then at the back of the man who still wore his cloak, even in the heat of the middle of the day.

"Hey," Eddie called out. "Isn't your name Halen?"

The man turned around in his seat, looking at Eddie questioningly. "Yes."

Eddie broke into a huge grin. "Oh, Em, Gee!" He looked at Van. "Okay, this is too weird to be happening for real. Now I know I'm in a fevered coma dream in some hospital bed somewhere."

Van squinted against the bright sunlight and realized his friend was finally succumbing to the relentless rays of the sun. "What are you going on about Eddie?"

Eddie grinned even wider. "Did you notice that together," he said while pointing to each of them in turn. "We are Eddie Van Halen?" Eddie shook his head and returned his attention to the road ahead of them "Wild."

Halen looked at him for another moment, realized the question didn't deserve an answer, shook his head, and turned back to watch the road ahead. Van shook his head as well at Eddie's obtuse thought pattern, then checked his arm where Talia slashed him the night before. The cut was still there. This wasn't a dream. He wasn't sure what it was but it sure wasn't a dream.

They sat in silence for another few miles before Van got the courage to inch over to Eddie, letting the vibrations of the wagon on the rutted dusty road do most of the work for him. "Eddie?"

Eddie turned toward him and smiled. "Yeah?"

"Why do you think this is all a dream?"

Eddie took in another big breath of air, his thin chest swelling up and then deflating as he let it out. "You smell that air, Van? That's the fragrance of a sky that has never tasted the burn of diesel fuel. From everything I've seen, this is so far beyond pre-industrial that I doubt they invented the steam engine yet. I sure hope it ain't a dream 'cause I kinda like it here."

"What about the dragons? And the people in that town who kicked us out? It isn't all good."

"Are you forgetting what it was like back home? Sure, our parents loved us and we were blessed with thousands of choices of movies on Netflix to satisfy our whimsical desires. But I don't care how many times I watched DragonHeart. It pales in comparison to actually being snatched by one and carried up into the air in its talons."

"I thought it ate you!"

Eddie's eyes sparkled. "I thought it was going to also. But it dropped me at the top of a mountain and this crazy old guy in a robe came running over to make sure I was okay. I tell you, when he realized that I wasn't you, he practically slapped that dragon back into the sky to go get you. I know I'm not much to look at, but I've never seen someone so disappointed to get me instead of you. I was always the popular one in school while you kept your distance."

"Do you have any idea why they all want me?"

Eddie shrugged. "I don't know. Maybe you should ask him?"

Van watched the back of the man in the cloak jostle around in his seat as the wagon rumbled along the road. They passed through the previous town a couple hours before and it would be getting dark long before they reached another one.

Then his eyes fell on Talia jostling about in the seat next to him. He couldn't talk to Halen with her sitting so close. He might not be willing to discuss what was really going on in front of her, or worse yet, he might lie and then Van would be acting on false information.

Van settled back against the sideboard and let the wagon rattle his teeth until they ached. He would have to find a way to get Halen alone if he expected to learn where he was and why he was wanted; dead or alive. And if Talia was telling the truth, the preference was dead.

Chapter 20

Halen kept his eyes forward, refusing to look back at the son of the man he made a promise to on his honor. The futile fight with his brethren over that man's final decision, which ultimately destroyed his life and kept him from fulfilling that promise, brought up overwhelmingly painful memories. Van's presence kept reminding him how The Order decreed that Halen was to become a Forsworn. His powers were stripped from him and his intended protégé prohibited from participating in The Order's noble mission to protect Midguard. When all seemed lost, he lost his resolve. He stopped fighting.

Absentmindedly, he reached under his cloak and touched the Wizard's Order Crest pinned secretly on the underside. This was not the pin that The Order blackened as a badge of his dishonor. This was the one given to him by Veren right before he used his life to close the gate between worlds. A gate he knew could be opened again in seven years. That should have left Halen plenty of time to train Veren's son to be ready for Aeron and his growing army. But The Order judged his final deed as a disgraceful act. It still angered him to the core that they never waited until the blood congealed on the dead and dying before making their declaration. Instead, right there in the middle of the battlefield, The Order shut down the entire Maclean line and stripped Halen's reason for living.

No matter what anyone said, no one deserved what happened to him. Even if he had lied to the highest Spinner in the land about receiving Veren's pin from him before he plunged headfirst into oblivion.

He still wasn't quite sure why he'd done that. It was not how a Spinner or Apprentice should behave. Nor was it how Veren trained him. Honesty and virtue were staples of The Order. Halen willingly violated his training when he withheld Veren's crest from Falen. But, deep down, Halen determinedly clung to the belief that Falen, nor anyone else in The Order, was worthy enough to hold Veren's crest. That was for his son alone. The crest was a physical totem to enable him to focus his power and fully accept his place in the universe as protector of Midguard. A call that the son of Veren was forbidden to answer.

Halen closed his eyes. The biting words of Talia echoed in his head. She was right. He wallowed for so long in self-pity he refused to let himself see it. The Order was becoming weaker with each passing year, encumbered by the increasing number of rules placed on the activities of a Spinner. The new rules and added restrictions were now a burden to preparation instead of the advantage they were supposed to be for the next wave of Spinners. When Aeron next came knocking at the gate, they would not be ready.

He should have admitted it before this. The limitations placed on Spinners during his training almost lost them the war five years before. If it were not for Veren's sacrifice, all of Midguard would still be fighting and dying as they resisted the armies of Aeron. At least those that didn't go along with his bloodthirsty lust for total dominance.

Halen's finger traced the crest pin, his skin sliding easily along its polished surface. Behind him, he heard the voice that was a near match for the tone and tenor of his father. Halen's heart pounded heavily as he realized what he should be doing. But was it really the right decision now? Given the circumstances? He promised to train Van. But he also promised to protect him? Which was the more imperative obligation?

His heart sank as he realized training Van would put him in more danger than Veren could have imagined. He could never give Van his father's crest pin. Besides, The Order would probably find them and take it long before Van ever put it to good use. Then where would Halen be? Despite The Order's insistence on following the ever expanding, and emasculating rules, Halen doubted they would bend any when meting out the punishment for his deliberate defiance of a mandate given to him directly by the High Spinner himself. That would leave Van to their mercy. Halen tasted bile deep in his throat as he admitted to himself he couldn't trust The Order to do what was right.

He listened to the speech pattern and voice modulation that made the years fade as if time never progressed beyond Veren's death. Halen was unable to shake the feeling that his master's spirit was resurrected in the son, despite Van already being on the cusp of apprenticeship age when Veren sacrificed himself.

Halen truly wanted to tell Van how his father saved three realms with his unselfish act. Tell him of the promise he made to a man with only seconds to live. It would have been his honor to teach him the ways of The Order. No. That was not what Veren wanted. For the first time in a long time he remembered Veren's exact words. They echoed in his head as if Veren uttered them at that very moment. "Train my son as I trained you. Protect him as I protected you."

Halen resisted the urge to look at the boy. He clenched his jaw, his teeth aching from the constant pressure. He stayed that way until the urge to commence Van's training subsided. It deeply saddened him that he chose to agree with The Order's edict. But, as much as he wanted to pass on the Maclean line of the Spinner arts, following through on his promise only ensured Van's fate would come to a tragic end. If they began his training as a Spinner, The Order would never let him return to Techrealm. And because of the decree, he would never be allowed to be fully trained and become a Master Spinner. Even if they allowed some training, he would be surrounded by brethren who could never defend his back; they were so inadequately trained themselves. Van's life would be over, sent to guaranteed slaughter in only two years' time.

Halen couldn't let that happen to the son of the hero who saved The Order and half of Midguard from certain death. Even if it meant going against a promise made to that same man.

Halen dipped his head and let it rest in his hand as he bounced along in the seat next to Talia. Life was never supposed to be this difficult. Especially the life of a Spinner. A Spinner performed but a single function. To protect the gate every seven years, during a year of the tri-moon, when the barrier between realms was the weakest.

Talia was right. The Order was adrift. It was so encumbered under the weight of its own rules that it ceased to be effective for its original purpose. Halen's thoughts turned to the growing contingent of Forsworn. Like him they broke the rules and were removed from The Order; their crests blackened. They could no longer spin the elements and were forbidden from training others. If the rumors spreading across the land were to be believed, the ranks of the Forsworn now numbered greater than the ranks of the Wizard's Order in Midguard. It was a hard metric to determine since most Forsworn kept to themselves and rarely showed their face in public.

But if it were true, with fewer Spinners learning the art of magic, and now learning it half-heartedly, they were in no position to defend the gate. They were much worse off than they were five years ago. What didn't make sense was that Veren saw this coming. He knew this was happening, which explains why some of Halen's more battle-worthy training was done in secret, beyond the prying eyes of The Order. But why couldn't the High Master not see what was obvious to Veren, even back then, and loosen the rules so they could be stronger? They would have lost the gate to Aeron's army five years ago if Veren wasn't forced to perform his final act alone because his brethren weren't strong enough to stop Aeron.

The other Master Spinners in the Circle Tribunal were too afraid to go against the High Master and remained silent when another of their own was Forsworn and sent away to hide among the shadows in disgrace. This seemed to be happening more and more often. Halen didn't like the way this train of thought was pulling him.

But training Van was out of the question. Halen would have to figure out something else to help Midguard, but Van was not the answer. Van spent the last five years living as a normal human in Techrealm instead of training as a Spinner under Halen's tutelage. With only two years left before Aeron made his next attempt to breach the gate, even a Master Spinner would be hard pressed to train an inexperienced Spinner to be ready to repel the invading forces.

Besides, if Halen tried to train anyone The Order would stop him. There simply was no way to hide from the Watchers who could sense the use of magic, especially spinning magic, from hundreds of miles away. The Order may have become powerless to defend the realm from invaders, but it still retained the authority, and the desire it seemed, to quell any unsanctioned spinning within Midguard.

Halen heard from those still willing to talk with him in The Order about how Van was relocated to the middle of his world; away from any significant source of water. Early testing showed his predilection was for water spinning. In fact, the testing showed he could become one of the strongest Spinners in the history of Midguard. It was the decision of The Order that he be sent from his home by the ocean and moved to where the only seas were made of sand and dust. The less Van was given access to large bodies of water, the less chance his substantial powers of spinning would present themselves unexpectedly. It was in Van's best interest to never know where he came from and be sent back to his desert home.

But if that were true, how was he in Midguard? Calen never provided any information other than The Order noticed Van shifted realms and they were to return him before he made the mistake of discovering his powers and drawing attention. Halen knew there were supporters of Aeron here. If Van fell into the hands of Aeron's supporters, and they convinced him to join them and they trained him, they might gain the advantage. It was why there was a price for Van to be delivered dead.

While gathering his resources to rescue Van, Halen tapped his contacts in the underground and was shocked to discover that someone put out a contract on Van's life. It lit a fire, so to speak, under Halen to find Van as quickly as possible. But Halen luckily possessed the edge in finding Van over everyone else in Midguard. His hand reached under his cloak and felt the cool metal of the untarnished crest pin. That was all the magic Halen needed to keep track of Veren's son. It could detect anyone carrying the bloodline of a Maclean across continents. Using it like a compass, Halen found Van in less than a day after learning he was in Midguard. It should have been long before any hunter was able to locate him. But, as fate would have it, Talia chanced upon him. It made Halen wonder, once they got away from Talia, how many more bounty hunters he would have to fight off to keep Van alive? He shook his head as he realized more than likely, half of Midguard's less than questionable population was now actively looking for Van.

He stole a quick glance at Talia. She stayed focused on the road ahead and kept the horse in the center of the lane. How she found Van as quickly as she did was still a mystery. She swore up and down that it was the dragon she was after. But, while her huntress reputation was known far and wide, how did she locate a dragon that he'd only just secured twelve hours before? It all happened far too quickly. That kind of pinpoint accuracy didn't come without a price. The price of magic.

Her ruthlessness in carrying out a contract was legendary. It still bothered Halen that he somehow convinced her to risk venturing into the West Kingdom. She was taking a big risk in accompanying them to The Order. The risk far outweighed her negotiated reward, even if Halen was able to make good on his promise to pay what amounted to quadruple the original bounty for Van's head.

Why was she taking this risk? It was frustrating he couldn't just come out and ask her. But, he knew her reputation well enough to know she would never tell him the truth. She retained a secret agenda that would eventually reveal itself. Hopefully they could get away from it before it was too late. Halen was already successful in separating her from the rest of her hunter troupe. The sooner he got Van and his friend away from her, the better.

Chapter 21

Talia stared straight ahead, worrying what kind of trouble she was bringing down on herself. The bounty bond was specific. Because of her connections in the underworld, she was promised a twenty-four hour head start to fulfill the contract before an official bounty bond was issued.

She was alone with the disgraced Spinner and the two boys. She knew the bounty identified Van as a man, and his body designated him as young man, but his behavior clearly delineated him as a mere boy and she couldn't think of him in any other way.

She kept a careful eye on the Spinner with her peripheral vision. He seemed lost in his own troubled thoughts but she detected him sneaking a glance at her every now and then. The bond instructions were very clear. Kill the boy, and the Spinner with him, on sight.

She'd easily killed wanted men and women before, as long as they truly deserved their fate. It was how she made her living for years. She gathered a group of trusted hunters, who happened to be people she hunted over the years who proved to her they didn't deserve the price on their head, and promised them each a portion of the reward. The whole group was ready to make the capture when she saw the dragon. Or more accurately, Hans, who for reasons unknown considered himself the resident chef, saw the dragon and demanded they catch it alive for an even bigger reward. Everyone was overwhelmed with the idea of how much a kidnapped dragon would bring on the black market and she couldn't dissuade the group. Once she agreed she was unable to make good on the bond conditions until after the dragon was captured. A dragon would never be drawn in with dead prey. It needed to be very much alive and squirming if the dragon was to be enticed to come close enough for them to capture it. She knew it was risking finding out if the boy didn't deserve his fate and losing yet another bounty, but the dragon was too great a prize.

And it worked beautifully. They ended up capturing both the boy and the dragon. But Talia was too good a huntress. She recovered the boy too early. The bond details were for the heads of both the boy and the Spinner. Now she needed to keep the boy alive to draw the Spinner in just like the dragon. Which meant she was most likely going to interact with her target. And that always made her job harder. She had a reputation to uphold, despite the fact she reneged on more bond orders than she fulfilled.

As soon as the boy's friend showed up to rescue him, she cursed her noble heart. She realized at how inept and confused they both were. They didn't deserve the bounty and she only killed those who deserved it. Once the Spinner joined the party, she decided to make an omelet of the broken eggs and parlay what she already planned to do, keep them both alive, into a greater reward. That way, she could blame her refusal of the contract obligations on greed. It was a flimsy excuse, but one she would cling to for as long as she could.

She needed to find a Skrahyer to inform her source that she met the contract conditions and would bring the corpses to him by the end of the week. She didn't like taking the risk of lying to a paying customer, but if she didn't secure the fulfillment of the contract to keep it from release, the bounty bond would go public and it would become impossible to keep them alive with every known hunter out for their heads. Not to mention anyone protecting them would likely die somewhere in the fighting, reward or not.

Behind her she heard the whispering of frightened and confused boys. She shook her head trying to understand the puzzle. They didn't behave like anyone she ever met before. Living the life of a huntress along the boundary of the badlands caused her to come in contact with just about every type of individual imaginable. Some good; most bad.

But these boys were different. While she never felt like she belonged, these boys truly were fish out of water. It was more than the strange clothing they wore that tore so easily, provided almost no protection against the elements, and seemed to be more decorative than functional. Their reaction to the dragon is what really threw her for a loop. They purposely put themselves in danger! Every child, no matter their station in life, was drilled with the knowledge of what to look out for in Snapdragon territory. Snapdragons curled into a ball, looking just like a massive stone, then when you ventured too close, they would snap you up unawares. Hence the name. But knowledge was power and Snapdragons failed to claim a new human victim since long before Talia was born. Their actions back along the road flabbergasted her. From her vantage point in the forest, she watched in utter confusion as they deliberately leaned on the waiting Snapdragon. It was as if they didn't know what it was. Why didn't they see there were no other massive stones for miles in either direction? Animals were simple enough creatures to fall for the deception, but humans were supposed to be smarter than that. What happened to these boy's basic life education?

It was as if they didn't belong here. If that was true, where did they belong? And why did someone from here want them dead? While most bounty bonds didn't go into details, such as specifying the crime committed by those named on the bond, this specific bounty failed to even identify the boy by name. Nor did it mention the fact there was a friend of the same age traveling with him. It was as if the bond was created without this knowledge.

And the amount was quadruple the normal going rate. Someone was very anxious to acquire their lifeless corpses. It was almost too good to be true, and her greed got the better of her so she didn't ask the appropriate questions. She accepted the bounty with the hope of squirreling away a large portion of it for retirement and because the task didn't seem too daunting. While she never shied away from killing someone who deserved it, she didn't like killing innocents. And these boys were as innocent as fresh newborns.

As the sun struck the mountains in the distance, she saw the smoke rising above fireplaces long before she saw the roofs of the town ahead of them. The roofline was unmistakable. They were about to enter Brandhaven. Its claim to fame was its close proximity to the trail that cut through Ridge Mountains straight to the badlands.

She'd come this way before and knew the town was big enough to easily find a place to rest and feed the horse. But the memory of her last visit was a hard one to shake. She would rather sleep in the mud than pay money for a room in that flea-ridden god-forsaken place. But she wasn't alone this time, and the rooms were a good place to hide the three fugitives for a night. Besides, maybe the place improved a bit since the last time she'd visited. It sure couldn't have gotten worse.

She guided the wagon down the road that passed through the middle of Brandhaven. It was an ugly town to say the least.

As soon as she passed through the main gate, Halen hopped out of his seat. She pulled the reigns and glared at him for assuming they were stopping for the night without discussing it with her first. He looked up at her without a hint of malice or regret for his actions. "I'm going to find proper accommodations for the night. Maybe even something to eat. Meet me at the local inn as soon as the wagon is secure."

He spun around, not waiting for her answer and headed for the two-story building on the other side of the town square. She silently agreed with him, they should stay the night. But Halen made certain assumptions without discussing it with her first. There was little she could do about it now. Once they were on their way in the morning, she would have words with him. In the meantime, she was forced to deal with Hicksville for the night. She nicknamed the town to be more illustrative of its occupants, which the Brandhaven name refused to color properly. Halen said he was going to try to find proper accommodations and food. If history was any indication, she was sure he would fail on both counts.

The taller of the two boys poked his head over the back of the seat and regarded Halen walking away from the wagon. He twisted his head until he was looking straight at her. "Where's he going?"

She narrowed her eyes at the boy. "What was your name again?"

His face broke into an easy smile. "Eddie."

"Well, Eddie, he's going to see about getting us food and lodging for the night."

Eddie tucked his hands into the small of his back and stretched. "Good. After sleeping on the ground last night, and the lack of shocks on the wagon, my body is nothing but one big bruise. It will be good to have a real bed just like at home."

She stifled a sour smile. She knew he would be disappointed as soon as he saw what passed for a "bed" around here. Then she knit her eyebrows together realizing he gave her a great opening to learn more about them. She opened her eyes a bit to look interested and smiled slightly to calm him. "Where is home?"

He looked around and then frowned. "I don't really know. Well, I mean I know where my home is. It's just that I don't know where it is from here."

That was a puzzling response. She couldn't help drawing her eyebrows together in confusion. "Then how did you get here?"

His frown deepened. "That's even stranger. We fell into a river and came out here."

The river. She knew the north contained most of the water around these parts. "Ahh, so you came from the north?"

"I don't think so. Tell me something…" he paused and raised his eyebrows, asking the obvious question with his silence.

"Talia," she replied with a slight bow of her head.

"Tell me something, Talia. Have you ever heard of an airplane?"

What was he talking about? He was watching her closely, waiting for her answer. She didn't know what to say in response to the gibberish, so she shook her head.

"A computer? A car?" he continued.

She shook her head in response to every strange word coming from his mouth.

He shrugged. "And you look like you've been around."

That she understood. She nodded. "I've been to the four corners of Midguard. To the ocean that surrounds this continent on all sides." That thought drew up her memories of what drove her to become a huntress in the first place. When her heart started racing at the usual emotional response accompanied by the painful memory she shoved the thoughts away quickly and concentrated on learning what she could from Eddie. "I also spent some time in the Southern Colony." She prompted.

"And you've never heard of a television?" Eddie asked, using another bizarre word that sounded to Talia like he made it up on the spot.

She shook her head again.

Eddie shifted uncomfortably as he hung over the back of the seat. "Where are you taking us, if you don't mind me asking?"

She'd lost him. The gibberish he was speaking distracted her enough, she didn't put the proper questions in place in time and he shut off the conversation of home. Now he was probing her for information. She knew better than to continue now, she would try again later. She pulled up to the public stables and hopped down. He watched her, waiting for an answer to his last question. She decided it best to stick with a truth that was safe and neutral. "For now, you and your friend are coming with me to find Halen."

Eddie sighed. "His name's Van," he said and hopped down to join her. She glanced back, half expecting Van to jump from the wagon and run away. Instead, he climbed out of the back and twisted his torso to force the cramps out of his muscles. She gave him a half smile of sympathy. It was why she always kept control of the reins. The bench seat in the front, while not a great improvement, was constructed better for sitting on long drives. The back of every wagon was designed for the storage of hay bales that required no acceptable levels of human comfort. Van and Eddie were suffering from that lack in engineering now.

She slipped out a few copper coins from her purse and quickly paid the groom enough to cover the storage of the wagon, food for the horse, and a little extra for the stable boy to ensure a good brushing to get the day's dust out of the horse's coarse fur. She liked to take care of those in her service. It engendered loyalty for the times when she would need it most.

She was glad to see that Eddie and Van were hanging around close to her and not making as if they planned to run. She hoped the reason for their compliance was they were afraid enough of her and decided attempting to escape was futile. That would make the night go much smoother.

They gawked at the bustling town that was shutting down for the night as the sun dipped below the edge of the mountain ridge in the distance. She realized, as they looked at everything with newborn eyes, their insistence on staying close was more caused by having no idea where to go. They looked completely lost in this environment.

She walked past them without stopping. "Come with me," she barked over her shoulder, then strained her ears to listen behind her, ready to change direction if they proved not to be as obvious as they seemed. A smile crept across her face as she heard them scrabbling around to follow her, finally jogging to catch up, and then falling in line behind her. They followed her like little lost puppy dogs. She hoped she could train them like puppies, and by giving them enough positive rewards, they would develop loyalty towards her. That would make her job much easier.

More than ever she was anxious about her immediate future. Bad things happened the last time she visited Brandhaven. If anyone recognized her, she might be forced to leave quickly and have to drag the trio with her. She kept her head low as she made her way to the pub and prayed that enough time passed for her features to change and for memories to fade. As she strode through the middle of the town square, the same question kept repeating in her mind like a mantra. What was she getting herself into?

Chapter 22

Van stayed close to Eddie as they both stayed right behind Talia. The townspeople here seemed to be ignoring them, which was a welcome change from the last town they visited. Then he noticed a few people were casting wary glances in their direction. Van looked at Eddie. He didn't seem as out of place this time, now that he was wearing the clothing Talia provided, but his bright green hair still made him stand out.

Van willed his nervous heart to slow to a more regular beat as he kept telling himself that they might not be shunned as abruptly from this town like they were the last one. He was with guides who knew this area and didn't look so out of place. Looking for a safe place to direct his gaze, so he didn't accidentally upset any townsfolk by non-verbally challenging them with a stare, he decided to watch the back of Talia's head as they followed her. But before he realized it, he found his eyes wandering lower until they breached the expanding curves just below her thin, but still sexy, hourglass waist. Suddenly he heard "Eyes forward!" Talia was looking at him over her shoulder, her eyes dark and threatening. Van's head snapped up, nearly giving him whiplash. He glanced over at Eddie who was smiling wide and silently asking him the same question on his mind. How did she know?

Van closed his roving eyes each time they threatened to look at her backside and adjusted to look past her at the brightly lit two-story building with a wooden placard on the side that dubbed the establishment, Mocking Bard Inn and Pub. They followed her through the open front door into what looked like the Renaissance era version of a comedy club.

All around the open floor people were seated around tables brimming with food and drink. They were all turned and staring raptly toward a stage where a single man stood with an odd looking guitar in his hands, clearly in the middle of a song. He continued strumming the musical instrument and a melodic tone spilled from the strings. "The real magic is happening up here, fellas," the guy on stage said. It sent the crowd into fits of laughter, a couple of them choking and letting food fly from their mouths.

Van looked at Eddie who shrugged. He failed to understand the reference either, but it must be extremely funny if it sent the crowd into hysterics.

Talia glanced to where a crowd gathered around a table in the corner of the room, ignoring the man on the stage. The man on stage kept glowering in the direction of the corner table and sang louder.

Talia nodded toward the table. "Stay with Halen. I'll be right back."

Van looked closer and saw Halen seated at the table. A small stack of gold coins sat next to a small pile of dried grass in front of him. Van moved closer, with Eddie following him, and saw Halen smile at one man in particular from among the small crowd. "Surely you can do better than that?" Halen prodded.

"Of course I can," the man replied, puffing up his chest. "But I want to see you do it first. I think I have paid for that much."

Halen studied him for a long time and then swept the gold coins across the table with an arm, letting them disappear into his cloak. "Fine. You have secured one rod of pure gold."

He picked up a piece of dried grass. When Van looked closely, he noticed it was actually a piece of straw about five or six inches long. Halen balled one hand into a fist and then thrust the piece of straw into it. He reached around and pulled a thin rod of glittering gold from his now empty hand. It was the same size and shape of the straw that entered his hand.

Halen held it up and then let it drop to the table surface. It rang with the resounding clink of metal on wood. The man who challenged him reached for it. Halen grabbed his wrist and glared at him. "You only paid to see it. You must pay the agreed amount if you wish to touch it."

The man glared back for a moment before his face softened. "Of course," he replied. He pulled a small bag from the pocket of his coat and dropped it on the table next to the small rod of gold. Van couldn't tell who was faster to remove their item from the table. Halen with his bag of coins or the man who snatched up the golden rod and hurried out the door.

Suddenly, more bags of coins dropped on the table as others demanded to triple their money like the first man. Halen stood abruptly. "Sorry, everyone. I told you, I will make the first one to ante up my asking price richer than when he walked into the pub. The rest of you are out of luck," he said as he stood to leave.

A man larger than the rest pushed his way to block Halen's exit. "You will make me as rich as you did the baker."

Halen grimaced up at him, having to tilt his head back to make eye contact with someone so large. "My offer was for the first person to meet my price. If you were so interested, you should have spoken up sooner."

The man glowered at him. "Name your price."

Halen smiled and appeared calm despite the muscled man, who stood a whole head and a half taller and was easily twice as wide, blocking his path. "Sorry. Only one transaction per evening. It's one of my rules."

The man cracked the knuckles of one hand with the other. Because of the size, it looked more like he was pressing two cooked hams together rather than his fists. "Break your rule. Or I break you."

Halen rolled his eyes and smirked. "You really don't want to make me disregard a rule. That would prove disastrous for both of us."

"Big words from such a little man," Meathead responded and flexed his chest, letting the muscles on his biceps stretch at his already tattered shirt sleeves.

"Then let me use a word you might be familiar with but, judging by your size, I doubt you hear very often." Halen rose up on his toes to close the distance between their faces. "No."

The crowd suddenly surged back, knowing what was coming. "Oh, crap," Eddie said suddenly. "Halen's gonna get his butt handed to him."

Van was forced back by the crowd as they made room for the upcoming fight. He didn't notice that Eddie became separated from him as all his attention was on the standoff happening in the corner of the pub. Halen stood his ground and watched as Meathead took a couple steps back, twisted his torso back and forth, and flexed his arms for the benefit of the growing crowd. The musician on stage quickly joined in the excitement and started to play a hard-driving fight soundtrack on his guitar.

Halen was still smiling at the large man without a care in the world. The crowd around them was clearly rooting for Meathead and eagerly watched Halen to see how the fight would start.

The innkeeper was suddenly between them. He glowered at Halen and then turned to Meathead, holding up his hands trying to calm the massive man down. "I just got all new furniture." He pleaded.

The large man responded by snapping his fingers. Two smaller men appeared and handed the innkeeper two large sacks of coins. The innkeeper's hands drooped under their weight and he smiled. "I didn't like the new design anyway." And just like that, Halen and Meathead were facing each other down in the middle of the pub with no one to stop them.

Chapter 23

In a small room on the opposite end of the town square from the pub, Talia was just settling down in her chair. She regarded the Skrahyer with what she hoped looked like respect and admiration. No sense tipping her hand and showing the chills and distrust Talia truly felt for all Skrahyers.

The Skrahyer gave her a curious look. "Have we met before?"

Talia refused the request of her body to squirm uncomfortably in the chair. Instead, she forced the muscles of her face to smile. "I don't think so."

The Skrahyer leaned in closer. "Your face is familiar."

Talia met her steady gaze, not about to let this old woman trip her up. "Have you ever worked beyond the East River? That is where I was born." A lie, but one carefully constructed over the years with plenty of corroborating evidence; should anyone start poking into the history of a huntress who went by the name of Talia.

The Skrahyer seemed on the verge of true recognition. If she remembered Talia for who she really was they would have to flee Brandhaven earlier than Talia wanted. Just as the Skrahyer was about to ask another question, the door to the private room burst open. The Skrahyer whipped around and verbally assaulted her attendant with a flurry of curses that would have curdled milk still inside the cow. The attendant's eyes sparkled with terror. She gave her apologies and quickly explained she knew she would be in more trouble if she didn't tell the Skrahyer immediately. "A Spinner is about to fight a mortal," she said breathlessly. Talia couldn't tell whether the attendant gasped for air because she'd run to deliver the unusual news or was having trouble breathing because of the excitement of the news. Either way, Talia stopped breathing entirely when she heard it.

Half a second later, Talia was alone in the room. Both the Skrahyer and her attendant left all the doors open in their haste to witness such a monumental event before it ended.

A Spinner about to go at it with a mere mortal? They couldn't be talking about Halen, could they? What were the odds there happened to be another Spinner in town?

Talia cursed under her breath.

Why was it so hard for outsiders to maintain a low profile in this town?

She followed the crowd to the bottleneck at the entrance of the pub. Talia was thinner, and more aggressive than most, and successfully elbowed her way into the pub, ignoring the curses and return shoves. A few bruises were nothing if it meant she could find out if the Spinner was Halen and, if so, get enough of a head start to extricate him and the boys before anything horrible happened.

Ignoring the sour stench of villagers crammed into such a confined space she stood on her tiptoes and peered across the dingy, matted heads at the combatants.

Her heart sank.

It was Halen.

"Crap!" she muttered.

The man next to her smiled a toothless grin. "My money's on the big guy," he said, his rancid breath searing the hairs of her nose. "You can still place a bet with the innkeeper if you hurry," he added and then returned his attention to the impromptu clash that looked to be very one sided. She couldn't afford to lose Halen this early in their journey.

She needed to do something, and do it quickly; before it was too late. She elbowed her way back out of the pub and headed for the stables. What she needed to end this fight swiftly and decisively was safely locked up in the trunk behind the seat of the wagon. But using it would remind everyone in Brandhaven who she was and why they chased her out the last time she dared set foot in their town. If they caught her, it would be much worse for her this time; and anyone who claimed to be with her. If she didn't do something, Halen might not survive. And he was needed to gain access to The Order. She wasn't ready to end the journey now, but still she hesitated; her hand on the chest. Was it really worth the risk?

"Okay," she whispered to herself as she unlocked the chest and pulled out a very specific tool. "I just won't get caught this time." How hard could it be to avoid a vengeful angry mob anyway?

She was suddenly aware of the tightness of the deep scar that ran down the length of her back, reminding her of the last time she said those same words.

Chapter 24

Halen glanced around at the faces that were eager to see the blood of a Spinner spilled in their small town. Having such a thing happen would place their little corner of the world on every map. The fact that the Spinner was obviously a Forsworn and stripped of his powers was even better. There would be no consequences for killing him.

Halen cursed the routine of always showing his tarnished Wizard's Order Crest before he offered to spin straw into gold. Normally it was a great idea. It enticed the crowd's pity for his devalued status in society, like a homeless beggar, and it announced non-verbally that he held the capability to do as he promised.

This time, his plan backfired and now he was forced to either get beat up or reveal that he wasn't as magically neutered as they all believed. But he wasn't ready to reveal that he could do more than a Spinner with a tarnished crest.

Halen stood as tall as he could and watched as Meathead paced to and fro, waving his arms back and forth and getting them prepared to enjoy a good beating. Meathead's jaw was set at an awkward angle and informed Halen that this was not the big guy's first fight. Despite the mismatched contestants, the giant was unaware he was about to lose. But Halen didn't want it to be too obvious. The last thing he needed was any level of scrutiny from The Order. He knew his power was still not as strong as a full Spinner, but doing anything other than parlor tricks would be perceived as something unique. Word of a Forsworn with the powers of a Spinner would spread far and wide very quickly. Too quickly. He didn't want to do anything that would make people in the room think he could still access high-powered magic despite the tarnished crest. But he also didn't want to let Meathead beat him senseless. He still needed to get Van home. He very well couldn't do that if he was recovering slowly in a convalescence room.

That left only one good option. Get out of this fight without using his powers. That meant outthinking the brute.

"You really don't want to do this," Halen said and took a step backward, keeping his arms at his sides and trying to look as non-confrontational as possible.

This only made Meathead move in closer, matching Halen step for step as he tried to back away. Halen bumped against the far wall and quickly scanned left and right. He was trapped in a corner of the pub with crowds of onlookers pressing in on all sides and no way around the approaching mountain of a man. He didn't have time to reason with the man. Besides, he wasn't going to listen anyway. It was at that moment Halen worried he would have to employ magic to stay alive. Doing so, though, would solve one problem while creating a slew of new ones.

Meathead cracked his knuckles one more time and the murderous look in his eyes increased. He gave the impression he was going to enjoy this. Halen gave in, closed his eyes, and turned all his energy on using Veren's crest pin to compensate for the tarnished one he could never shed on his own. He needed to be careful about what he did. He needed to make it look as natural as possible without losing the fight.

Meathead suddenly slapped a hand against his own neck. He pulled something out and glared at the thin needle pinched between meaty fingers. Then his eyes glazed over and he pitched forward, landing on a table and smashing it to kindling under his massive frame.

The crowd fell silent, all eyes staring at the town hero who collapsed without a warning.

A hand reached out of the crowd and pulled Halen roughly into the mass of stunned bodies. As soon as they broke free of the overcrowded pub, Talia started running without letting go of his hand. Van and Eddie were already standing around outside, having been pushed out by the overcrowded and stinking tavern. They watched Halen and Talia rush by in confusion. Van and Eddie broke into a run and quickly fell in step beside them. "Hey," Eddie said breathlessly. "What's the hurry?"

Talia pointed back toward the pub. Halen glanced back in time to see the large crowd turning their attention to the fleeing group and giving chase.

Chapter 25

Van looked back to see the angry mob surging after them. He felt his adrenaline spike, keeping him running at full speed alongside Talia and Halen. Eddie, with his long legs, was actively slowing down to keep from outrunning all of them. He didn't want to be ahead of them in case they turned down another route than he took.

"What happened in there?" Eddie asked through panting breaths. Despite his long-legged advantage, he was not in the best shape.

Talia glanced back as they ran. "I helped Halen win his fight. Some might consider it cheating."

Eddie glanced behind them at the growing crowd chasing them and then he pulled ahead of the small group. "From the looks of it they all consider it cheating," he said between gasps for air.

They turned a corner and dashed into the darkness of an alleyway, pressing themselves against the wall as the crowd poured past. Van gasped for air as quietly as he could. When the last of the angry mob disappeared from sight, Talia pointed into the darkness outside of town. "We have to leave. Now!"

Halen gave her a startled look. "What about the wagon?"

Talia shook her head. "The wagon isn't suitable for where we're headed."

Halen shook his head. "I can get it back!" he insisted.

He started to walk away when Talia grabbed his arm and yanked him back, glaring into his eyes. "It's not worth the risk! I have—history with this town. If they catch us," she started and then pointed at Van. "He will be dead by morning light."

Van's heart skipped a beat. "Me?"

She nodded.

"What did I do?" he squeaked.

Talia looked at Halen, sadness, and regret, written on her face. "I received a twenty-four hour advance notice on the bounty order with a specific condition that both you and Van be killed on sight."

The world started spinning and Van leaned on the wall for support. Eddie took over for him. "What! We only just got here. Who could possibly want him dead already?"

Talia shook her head. "I don't know. The order is coming through a clearing house to hide the identity of the client."

Van's heart finally started beating, sending vital oxygen to his brain allowing him to think again. He stepped forward and scrutinized Talia's eyes. "You were going to kill me?"

"That was what the bounty order stipulated, yes." Her eyes refused to give up any emotion she may be experiencing. If she was experiencing any at all.

Van moved in closer, ignoring the fact she could easily kill him before he saw her make a move. "You were going to kill me?"

She met his gaze and he could see the irritation welling up inside her and spilling out through her carefully constructed defenses. "I didn't!"

"But you were going to!"

"But I didn't! Look, I brought us here so I could tell the client the contract was complete. That would have bought us a week to get you home where they could never get to you."

Van felt hope coming back. "So you told them you fulfilled the contract? They think I'm dead?"

Talia's face turned to Halen in disgust. "I was about to when Mr. Showoff here got into a fight and ruined my communication channel. Now it's too late. We have to run."

Van was about to ask Talia how he could possibly be expected to trust her when Eddie stepped between them and held his hands up in a paltry attempt to defuse the situation. He looked at Van and smiled easily. "Why don't we focus on the fact you are still alive and try not to force her to change her mind?"

Van caught Eddie's eyes and the tightness that gripped his heart loosened. Eddie was always able to calm him down. Eddie always took life at face value rather than making demands on how it should be. It was one of the things Van admired in Eddie, and he was glad to have him here.

Talia glanced around and started talking quickly. Van watched her speaking animatedly, but didn't really hear her. He wondered if Eddie was right. Was he trying to goad Talia into killing him to prove a point? And what would that point be? He was still clueless as to where he and Eddie ended up; and why everyone was after him.

Maybe Eddie was right and they were in a coma and this was all a dream. Then he remembered the knife and Talia's lesson. But if it wasn't a dream, where were they? A chilling thought ran down his spine. Maybe they weren't in a coma, like Eddie proposed, but they were dead. Maybe they died when the car went over the bridge.

"Hey," Eddie said and shook Van out of his trance. "Were did you go buddy? We have a situation here and we need your undivided attention."

Van's eyes focused on Eddie. "What?"

Eddie sighed in relief. "You worried me for a second there. Talia says she knows a way out of town where we won't be discovered. If we can make it to the next town, she can get a message back to her hunter camp and get a fresh horse and wagon. We'll be on our way with only a single day delay and hopefully ahead of the throngs of hunters coming after us. Weren't you listening?"

Van nodded his head despite not hearing a word she'd said. He was still in a fog, wondering what he did to deserve ending up here. He let Eddie grab his sleeve and lead him slowly out of the town. Every now and then, Eddie pressed him back against a building in the darkness while they waited for a smaller subset of the angry mob to pass by; searching for them.

Chapter 26

They were deep in the woods before Talia agreed to ease up and let them walk at a more manageable pace. They walked for half the night when Van sensed the ground start to incline. He looked up between the closely spaced trees and glimpsed the tall mountains that drew a jagged line across the dark sky rising up before him. When they could no longer see the faint twinkle of lamplights from the extended outskirts of Brandhaven, Talia sat down on a fallen tree. "We can spend the night here and be in the next town by late morning."

Halen fixed her with an accusing stare. "How is your reputation in the next town?"

She shrugged and stared back at him. "They haven't come after me with torches and pitchforks yet. Are you planning on changing that for me?"

"As if this was my fault." Halen said sardonically and then took a deep breath before letting out an uncharacteristic sigh. "I'll look for a good place to bed down for the night," he added and crashed off through the bushes.

Eddie sat down next to Talia and took several deep breaths before he could speak again. He turned to her and asked his question as if she only just stopped talking. "What if they are still mad?"

She smiled, chuckling softly. "It is my experience that angry villagers have the attention span of a gadfly. They flit about from one reason to another. I guess it helps them get through the drudgery of their meaningless lives. I wouldn't worry too much about it. It should blow over along with the early morning fog, especially since no one was killed and everyone still has their money."

She fixed him with a steely stare. "I, however, am a huntress. I never forget those who wrong me."

Eddie gulped loudly and turned away.

Halen crashed back through the bushes and hooked a thumb over his shoulder. "I found a small clearing that should shield the light of a fire. We'll want to extinguish it before the first light to keep anyone from seeing the smoke, but it will keep us warm through the night."

He pushed back through the bushes and disappeared into the

forest. Talia looked at Eddie. "Follow him. I know of a stream near here where I can catch some fish." She disappeared through bushes in the opposite direction, leaving Van and Eddie staring at each other. Van looked around and then back at Eddie. He was shocked Talia left them alone. "This is our chance to escape!" he said suddenly.

Eddie looked at him like he had antlers growing out the side of his head instead of ears. "And go where? Halen said this Order is planning to send you home. And Talia said that by tomorrow, everyone will be gunning for you. If we can get away from Talia, that might be beneficial. But we should stick with Halen if we want to get home in one piece."

Eddie crashed through the bushes in the direction Halen disappeared. Eddie was right. Between the two of them he was the one with the level head. Van pushed his way through the bushes, the branches and spike-edged leaves grabbing at his shirt sleeves. He caught up with Eddie and saw Halen setting up camp. He joined in clearing away branches and rocks, making a comfortable place for them to rest for the night.

When they were done, there was a nice smooth area to sit with a small stone-encircled spot ready for a crackling fire. Halen stood over the dark circle of stones and swirled his hands in front of him slowly.

Eddie nudged Van in the ribs. "What's he doing?" he whispered.

"I don't know," Van whispered back.

Eddie watched him transfixed, forming his hands in the same shapes he saw Halen executing. Van glanced at Eddie and was surprised Eddie was mimicking the movements to near perfection. At least, to the untrained eye they looked perfect.

A glow emanated from within Halen's cupped hands. He bent down and placed his hands over the branches stacked like a teepee in the center of the campfire. He opened his hands and a ball of fire dropped onto the dry cone of branches, igniting them with a whoosh. Halen stood up and dusted his hands off. He sat down on one of the small stones he placed around the campfire and prodded at the burning branches with a stick, coaxing the fire to life.

Eddie's mouth hung open and he looked down at his hands as if he expected to see fire there as well. He shook his hands out and went over to sit down on the stone next to Halen. "How did you do that?"

Halen glanced over at him. "It's called spinning. Those of us who can spin the elements are called Spinners. We are natural-born magic users who can manipulate the world around us to a certain degree."

"Can you teach me how to do that?"

Halen glanced at him without taking his attention away from the growing flames. "It is not something you can learn to do. You either have the ability to control the elements or you don't."

Eddie wasn't going to give up that easily. "So you've been able to do that ever since you were born?"

"I definitely had the inclination. But I couldn't control it. It was something I needed to learn to regulate so I didn't hurt myself or others."

"How did you learn to control fire?"

"I was apprenticed to one of the best Spinners in Midguard. He taught me everything I know. I hoped someday to pass on my training to another. But it never came to be."

Halen stared into the fire, lost in a memory that made his face grow somber. The quiet crackle was the only sound for a few minutes until Eddie broke the silence. "You can train me!"

Halen set his stick down and turned fully to Eddie. "I can't train you if you don't have the ability for it already."

"How do I know if I have this ability or not?"

Halen faced the fire again. "Don't worry, kid. You don't."

"Fine, then tell me how you know?"

Halen faced him again. "Magic users can see the magic that flows and ebbs around the aura of other magic users."

Eddie suddenly looked at Van. "Hey. That crazy lady in that first town. She looked at you like she'd seen a ghost. Maybe she was seeing this aura around you." Eddie looked back at Halen, his eyes sparkling with excitement. "Does Van have the magic aura?"

Halen stared into the fire and never once glanced in Van's direction. "No!"

Eddie frowned, the lines deepened by the dancing flames of the campfire. "You didn't even look at him. How do you know?"

Halen shrugged, never taking his eyes off the growing flames. "If he had the gift, I would have seen it."

Eddie was like a dog with a bone. He wasn't going to let go so easily. "Look closer. Just in case you missed something."

Halen's face started to frown, his voice giving a warning tone. "I told you, he doesn't have it."

"But that old lady—"

Halen stood abruptly. "Let it go!" He took a deep breath and calmed himself, lowering his voice again. "I'm sorry to disappoint you but neither you nor your friend have the ability to spin the elements. Now, if you'll excuse me, I need to be alone."

Halen spun around and stomped into the forest. Eddie watched him go and then turned to Van. The strange look on Eddie's face morphed into a sly smile. "He doth protest too much."

Van looked after Halen, but there was no sound in the forest anywhere around them. It was like Halen magically disappeared into thin air. The key word being magic.

Eddie hopped over and sat next to Van. "Do you think you have this spinning thing Halen and Talia keep talking about?"

Van stared at his hands. He laughed out loud for even considering the possibility.

Eddie frowned. "Don't laugh. That old lady in town. She wigged out the moment she saw you."

Van shook his head. "I think it was your hair that scared her. You look like a troll doll with that bright green mop. Or maybe you look like an actual troll, considering where we ended up."

Eddie stroked his thin chin in thought and then snapped his fingers. "I know how we can test it!"

Van gave him a quizzical expression that matched how he felt inside. Eddie positioned himself in front of Van, making him look sinister with the light of the fire to his back. He grabbed both of Van's hands and held them up. "Cup your hands like this," he said.

Van pulled his hands away. "What are you doing?"

Eddie grabbed his hands again and lifted them. "Humor me. Cup your hands like this," Eddie added and showed Van what he wanted.

Van cupped his hands and Eddie painstakingly repositioned them until he was satisfied. "Okay. Now let me move them around until you feel the rhythm."

Eddie started moving Van's hands around. "Loosen your arms," he commanded and Van released his muscles, letting Eddie control him like a marionette. Eddie stopped and let go of Van's hands. His face fell into a disappointed pout. "It's not working."

Van laughed. "Of course it's not working. I'm not a magician—"

"Spinner," Eddie corrected him.

"Whatever. Just accept that it was your killer good looks that freaked out that old lady."

Eddie's eye developed a calculating look. He thought for a moment, looked at Van, then back at his hands before positioning them in front of him. He looked up at Van, his eyes filled with anticipation. "Do what I do."

Van started to get up. The fire was getting hotter and he was getting uncomfortable being so close. Eddie pushed him back down. "C'mon. Just do what I do."

Van sighed. "Fine." He shaped his hands to look like Eddie's. Together they swirled their hands around in front of them.

Nothing happened.

Big surprise.

Van stopped but Eddie urged him on again. "C'mon, you were almost there."

"Nothing is happening Eddie."

"That's because you haven't quite matched the angle. But you're almost there. Try again."

Van sighed, then circled his hands again, taking less care than before.

"Van. You're not even trying. Here." Eddie adjusted Vans hands again. "Hold that pose. Don't move until I tell you to."

Van sat there feeling like a department store mannequin, letting Eddie manipulate him and freeze him in place. Of course, without a television for hundreds of miles, at least this was entertaining in an oddly absurd way. Van smiled to himself. With Eddie around, life really was a hoot and a half. It never took long for him to pull everyone near him into his child-like wonder of the world. Eddie held his hands close to Van's and started moving them slowly. "Match my movements."

Van studied Eddie's hands and moved his the same way. After a few revolutions they fell into sync and Eddie nodded his head vigorously. "Good. Now I'm going to start going faster. Just stay with me and do what I do."

Van kept pace with Eddie until both their hands were swirling around like they'd seen Halen doing when he lit the fire.

Eddie looked at him expectantly. "Anything?"

Van frowned. "Like what? Flames shooting from my hands?"

Eddie shrugged which threw off his concentration. "Sure. Anything like that."

"Of course not!" Van retorted. He should just stop, but Eddie was so into it, he couldn't be the one to let him down. Besides, there wasn't anything else to do and it passed the time.

Eddie stopped rotating his hands but prodded Van to keep at it. "Keep going, Van. You almost have it!"

"How do you know?"

"I have a hi-def camera built into my brain. It records everything I see when it comes to mechanical stuff. I learned how to fix Bessie by watching guys do repair jobs on YouTube. I can tell if you are doing the same things as…"

Eddie stopped talking about the same time that Van's hands started getting uncomfortably hot. "I'm too close to the fire," Van said. "My hands are getting warmer."

"Don't stop," Eddie said. "I think I see a glow. You almost have it."

Van kept spinning his hands around each other. Nothing was happening except that his hands were definitely getting warmer. Maybe it was his imagination making him feel what Eddie wanted him to feel. There was no way he possessed some deep hidden power, the knowledge of which was kept from him since birth. The idea was ridiculous.

He spun his hands around and thought he saw something happening within his hands when someone grabbed his wrist tightly and pulled him off balance. He looked up into the pitch-black eyes of Halen, the reflection of the fire demonizing them. "What are you doing?!" Halen demanded as he clung to Van, his eyes wild with rage.

Van's heart raced in panic. "I—"

"Shh," Halen said to silence him and cocked his head to one side as if listening for something. A whistling sound carried through the air and Halen suddenly let go of Van as multiple objects thudded into the ground around them. Van and Eddie screamed in terror as a dozen arrows embedded in the dirt all around them. Fortunately, none of them were hit. And then Van saw the feathered end of an arrow sticking up out of Halen's shoulder.

Halen ignored it and spun his hands around quickly. The fire from the campfire responded by rising up in the air and spreading over them like a canopy. Halen dropped his arms and the flames followed. Van screamed and ducked down as the fire enveloped the three of them. But it didn't engulf them and roast them like a thanksgiving turkey. Instead the flames formed a giant dome made out of burning fire.

Arrows pelted the dome from above, some snapping in half. Halen suddenly collapsed and the fiery dome collapsed along with him. Van looked at Halen and then at Eddie.

"What the...?"

"Wait!" Eddie said, holding up a finger to silence him. Van strained to listen in the quiet darkness. All the animal sounds were gone; which he didn't notice until he started listening. A low whistling sound grew louder followed by several muted impacts around them as arrows embedded in the soft dirt around the camp again. Eddie grabbed Halen's feet. "Grab his arms. We have to get out of here!"

Van didn't wait for the next volley of arrows and grabbed Halen under the arms and hefted his bulk up. He wasn't expecting Halen to be so heavy. He lost his grip and dropped him right away. A small silvery object dropped from Halen's cloak unnoticed and was immediately covered with dirt as Van's foot moved around while he struggled to lift the unconscious Spinner. When he finally stabilized, he looked at Eddie. "Which way?"

Eddie glanced around and then nodded to his right. "We need to get up over that mountain."

Van exhaled sharply. "The mountain? Wouldn't it be easier to carry him on flat ground?"

"Sure. But it will also be easier for whoever is shooting those arrows to follow us."

Van nodded. "The mountain it is."

They headed into the darkened forest with an unconscious Halen in their hands. Van wondered how long Halen would be out cold. They couldn't carry him for too long. He was just too heavy and awkward.

It was at that moment he heard the excited barking of dogs picking up a scent. Eddie pulled faster on Halen and Van struggled to stay on his feet as they ran as best they could heavily burdened through the forest with no way of knowing where they were headed or what dangers they might run into.

Chapter 27

Talia used a sharpened stick to spear a few fish from the shallow stream and, pegging them on the end, headed back to the campsite. She was still a good quarter mile away when she heard something she shouldn't. Howling dogs.

No. Not just howling dogs. Something far worse.

Hunting dogs.

She dropped the stick filled with fish and ran full speed through the forest toward the campsite; the same direction she heard a deep male voice call out urging someone to release the hounds and begin the hunt.

She heard the dogs barking fade away as they took off after their prey. She sucked in air to provide oxygen for her weary muscles and sprinted for the campsite, ignoring the screaming agony of her legs.

She hit the clearing and, without stopping, spotted the owner of the deep voice and tackled the bigger man at the back of his knees. It was always best to eliminate the biggest threat first. He went out cold as soon as his face slapped squarely on the ground. She rolled to one side and kicked up between the legs of the second man still facing away from her.

The disabling move proved ineffective at driving the second man to his knees. Instead, he grunted with a high-pitched voice and then dropped the empty leashes and a long barreled device. He spun around to face Talia.

But it wasn't a man!

It was a woman!

Talia's intended incapacitating attack only filled her attacker with a growing rage. Talia rolled to her feet with her dagger out just in time to deflect the woman's blade as it cut through the air. Their daggers collided with a ringing sound accompanied by the sparks of finely shaved off steel. The woman's blade was obviously kept incredibly sharp. It whistled through the air as she slashed right in front of Talia's face. Talia saw the move telegraphed by the woman's shoulder angle and ducked away fast, but not fast enough to keep the blade from slicing off a stray tendril of hair.

Talia backpedaled quickly but the woman kept charging forward, intent on keeping Talia on the defensive. Talia tripped on a rock and landed on her back. She used the momentum to keep rolling. The woman lunged after her but, as Talia somersaulted, she kicked out a foot at the blade trying for an angle that wouldn't send the finely crafted blade through the sole of her shoe and into her foot. The woman cried out as the fingers on her hand cracked and bent backward at odd angles. She stumbled to the side, dropped the blade, and gripped her injured hand with the other.

Talia was on her feet, her own blade ready for anything. When it was clear the woman was disarmed, Talia stood straighter. "What do you want?"

The woman scowled. "What do you mean, what do I want? You attacked us!"

Moaning came muffled from the man lying face down in the dirt. Talia noticed the woman glance toward the sound and took the opportunity provided by her distraction. Talia moved swiftly and cracked the hilt of her dagger across the woman's head. She collapsed like a marionette with its strings suddenly severed. Talia stepped quickly over her body and did the same to the man, sending him back into a deep sleep.

Talia crouched next to the fire and glanced around hurriedly, her eyes taking in everything at once. All around her were arrows embedded in the ground; some of them snapped in half. She stood and peered into the darkness, but the couple was alone. She looked down at them lying on the ground. Brother and sister? Husband and wife? Either way, it spelled trouble.

She scanned the ground and spotted a smoldering ring of fire that was the only place missing feathered arrows sticking out of the ground. A few arrows lay just outside the ring, snapped in half.

A multi-bolt crossbow leaned against a tree near the fallen man. It could hold and shoot thirteen bolts simultaneously on a spread that could be as narrow or as wide as the operator wanted. It was an unlucky weapon for the target. She checked and found it empty. Since they were generally stored fully loaded, an empty multi-bolt crossbow meant it was recently fired. As she finished her sweep, she spotted a splotch of darkness near the ring of fire. As she bent down to inspect it, her heart skipped a beat when she realized it was blood soaking into earth.

The arrows struck someone when they rained down on the campsite. Excited barking drew her attention momentarily. When she returned her attention to the ground, she noticed Van and Eddie's footprints leading into the woods. She followed the path they took with her eyes. The barking was definitely coming from the same direction. As she continued to follow the trail her tracker ability told her something was missing. There wasn't a third set of prints. Where was Halen? She focused to make better sense of the tracks. She bent down and ran a finger along the shapes in the dirt. They showed two sets of tracks carrying something large and heavy. Did they carry Halen out of the camp? If he was the one hit with an arrow, it might force them to grab him and run. She scanned the dirt again. Several small drops of crimson fluid were splattered all around the ground.

More excited barking drew her attention back toward the night. She used dogs in the past to hunt down many a creature and she immediately recognized the message they were sending back to their owners. They had trapped whatever it was they were after.

Chapter 28

Van waved the tree branch in front of him, keeping the snarling dogs at bay. Or at least trying to. Eddie crossed the river, pulling a still unconscious Halen after him and looking like a lifeguard rescuing a drowning victim. Van swung the branch back and forth; the dogs snapping at the leaves with sharp teeth. Van cringed every time one of them grabbed the branch and tugged on it. That gave him an idea. They seemed very intent on following the branch. Maybe throwing a stick would distract them.

Van scanned around his feet and found what he was looking for. He let go of the large branch and lifted the small stick, wiggling it enthusiastically. "You wanna chase the stick?"

He waved it back and forth slowly in front of him, making sure the dogs eyes were fully engaged with the movement of the stick. Then he hauled back and threw the stick as far as possible to his left. The two dogs watched the stick fly into the forest and then both heads snapped back to see what Van would do next.

Van was shocked. He'd never met dogs that didn't run after something thrown. He made a big motion with his arms toward the direction of the stick. "Fetch!" he hollered. The dogs sat down and just watched him. He decided to try one more time. He picked up another stick and threw it behind the patiently watching dogs. They ignored it and kept their watchful eyes trained on him.

He glanced back to see Eddie pulling Halen out the other side of the river. It was his turn to swim across. He hoped the dogs didn't know how to swim. Or at the very least wouldn't follow him. He took a step back and the dogs stood quickly. One of them barked at him, giving him an obvious direct order. Which he immediately followed and froze in place.

"C'mon, Van! Quit stalling," Eddie called from across the river.

"Working on it!" Van replied. He lifted his foot to take another step back. He saw the muscles of the dogs tense up and he stopped moving, one foot hovering in the air. He lowered his foot behind him and both dogs started to growl. He lifted the same foot again and brought it forward, back in line with his other foot. The dogs calmed down and sat again, watching him.

He quickly took a small step backward and they stood abruptly, barking viciously at him until he returned to his original spot. Only when he was back in place did they calm down and sit again, watching him carefully. They weren't going to let him move a single step, let alone let him get to the river and cross it.

"C'mon," Eddie pleaded from across the slow moving water.

"Shut up, Eddie!" Van called out. He decided he didn't have a choice. If he was going with Eddie, he would just have to make a run for it. After the experience with the dragon he was never going to lose Eddie again. He would try to outrun the dogs. If they got him, they got him.

His heart was hammering heavily in his chest and his adrenaline was spiking in preparation for the chase. Just then, the dogs whined and looked behind them into the forest. They looked back at Van, as if asking him if it was okay to investigate this new interest.

They whined and looked behind them again. The dogs looked at each other and then suddenly took off into the woods, leaving Van with a shocked expression as he stood alone by the side of the river.

He wasn't going to naïvely wait to see if they were coming back. He bolted for the water's edge, tightly focused on running as fast as he could. He hit the water and kept running, raising his legs higher with each step as the increasing depth pulled on his clothes and slowed him down. He waded in until he was chest deep before looking back to see if the dogs were after him. To his relief, they were nowhere in sight. He didn't know what was more fascinating than eating him, but he silently thanked it for the distraction and hoped whatever it was got away too.

Chapter 29

Talia blew on the dog whistle again and waited. She'd spotted the small silver flute tied to a leather necklace hiding down the woman's blouse while they were fighting. When the woman was unconscious, Talia snatched it from the leather strap, realizing it obviously called the dogs and would be a faster way to save the boys than trying to catch up with them.

She blew the whistle again. While she waited for the dogs to return she went over to inspect the odd looking device the woman dropped earlier. She bent down and picked up the largish cylindrical object. Upon closer inspection, Talia was pleased to see it was a net gun. Its name was very fitting since it shot a net with weights evenly spaced out along the edges. It was a superb weapon to take down even the most nimble of creatures. If a net gun was fired in your direction, and you were within range, you were caught. She was just about to inspect the trigger mechanism when she heard something crashing through the forest, headed her way. It must be the dogs. Even though she held the whistle, it never hurt to be cautious when dealing with hunting animals for the first time. You never could tell when a creature would decide to not follow its training and turn on you. And she was a complete stranger. She held her finger pressed against the cold lever. As the sound grew closer, she pointed the net gun in the same direction. As soon as the dogs ran into the light of the campfire, she squeezed the trigger. The release mechanism responded to her slightest movement and the net catapulted from the gun, spreading wide and enveloping the dogs. They stumbled to the ground with surprised yelps. They writhed around until she blew the whistle again. They immediately cringed and gave her a sorrowful look. Luckily for her, hunting dogs were all trained the same. Whoever operated the whistle was the master. "That's better," she said. "It's best you recognize who your new master is."

She worked for the next few minutes to untangle the dogs from the net and gave them each a celebratory rubbing of their bellies once freed. They rolled around, their tongues hanging loosely from their mouths, and thoroughly enjoyed the affection she was lavishing on them. It wasn't necessary since she owned the whistle, but she knew from her past experiences, giving a little kindnesses to the dogs made them work harder for you when you were in trouble.

Back on their feet, they took position on the same side of her and leaned heavily against her legs, trying to knock her over with their combined weight. They were letting her know they would happily be her hunting dogs. Talia kept the couple tied to the tree with their legs secured together to keep them from standing. No sense giving them any wiggle room. Even an idiot could escape from ropes if there was even a little slack. She made sure they were securely bound to the tree before they woke up. Currently, they were both alert and glaring silently at her. She ignored them and tossed another handful of branches on the fire that long ago had reduced itself to a small pile of glowing embers. It flared brightly and hungrily consumed the dry vegetation; returning to its former glory as a roaring campfire.

She approached the couple. The woman's scar ran down the left side of her face and forced her left eye into a perpetual squint. There was obviously a great story behind a wound like that. The man was missing all his hair. Even his eyebrows. It was hard to look at him and Talia focused her attention on the one with the character building scar. "Where are your tools? Your horse and carriage? Maybe a wagon?"

Scar smiled up at Talia. "You're bleeding."

Talia touched the side of her own face, her finger coming away covered with a thin sheen of blood. She touched her face again and realized the woman's blade sliced off more than just a piece of her hair during their fight and had, in fact, connected with skin. It was a tiny cut and would heal without leaving so much as a hairline blemish. But it didn't make Talia happy that someone got close enough to break her skin. She was getting soft in her old age. She chuckled silently to herself at the absurdity of that notion. She wiped away the blood and glared at Scar. "Where is your transport?"

Scar laughed defiantly. "We came in on foot."

Talia raised her hand, ready to backhand Scar. But she noticed the muscles on the woman's neck tense up in preparation. This woman was used to a rough life. Talia could beat her for hours and never get her to talk. What she needed was to find Scar's weakness. Everyone was cursed with a weakness. Something to be used against them. Talia reminded herself she had one too, once. It was why she was helping the boy rather than fulfilling the original bond order and killing him outright. She suppressed her feelings and brought herself back to the here and now.

Talia looked at Baldy again. His features did not resemble those of Scar. If they weren't related, they must be married. Talia looked back at Scar. "I give you one more chance to tell me the truth."

Scar jutted her chin out boldly. "I told you, we don't have one. We were hunting deer in the forest on foot. We didn't know someone was camping here."

Talia sighed audibly. "Suit yourself." She reared back and kicked Baldy hard in the stomach. All the air in his lungs expelled sharply and he gasped and coughed, visibly straining to breathe again.

The look on Scar's face changed from defiance to horror. Talia went to kick Baldy again when she cried out. "Wait! Please! I'll tell you!"

Talia raised her eyebrow to punctuate her previously stated question. There was no need to verbalize it again. She could see Scar's resolve evaporate like butter on a hot skillet. She nodded to her left with her head. "A hundred yards to the east," she said through upwardly curled lips.

Talia looked at the dogs and pointed to the couple tied against the tree. "Guard," she commanded and the two dogs took position, growling deep and low to let the couple know that they obeyed a new master now. Talia walked the short distance until she located the horse and wagon right where the woman said it would be. Her eyebrow raised in surprise at what she found inside. Most of the items were enchanted.

She held up a compass that spun in place, occasionally stopping in a certain direction before spinning again. She glanced back in the general direction of the campsite with a renewed interest in the couple. How did they get their hands on a Watcher's compass? This special type of compass did not detect the magnetic pull of north, but instead detected the faint emanations left behind from magic use. She inspected the device and found it calibrated specifically to track Spinner magic.

It was the reason they found Halen in the middle of the dense forest at night. He used his magic to start the fire.

She found a few more useful items, along with some food, which she packed into the saddlebags of the horse. Unfortunately, she was forced to leave the bulk of the items behind. They would be worth a fortune on the illegal black market, but she couldn't take the cart and save the boys. If she wanted to keep her reputation and a modicum of trust with what was left of The Order, she needed to bring the boys and Halen back with the greed excuse. Arriving in the west empty handed would brand her as unreliable so she packed what she considered the most valuable items and walked the horse back to camp.

As soon as her eyes fell on the glowing embers of the fire her stomach growled. She selected a jar of beans from the saddlebag. It was best to eat something before heading out, she decided. Since the dogs weren't on the hunt anymore, the boys were relatively safe. Besides, with her new dogs she could follow their trail a week cold.

She also needed to conduct a little local hunting expedition of her own. She needed information. Based on how many enchanted items they had in their wagon, she determined they were working for The Order. If she could get a name from them she would be that much closer to discovering who put out the contract on the boy. She stomped back to her captives and squatted to put herself at eye level with them.

She tilted her head to one side and looked from Scar to Baldy and back to Scar. "Who do you work for?"

Scar glared at her while Baldy looked away.

Crap! Baldy was the weaker one. Which meant he would get the bulk of her attention if she wanted to find out anything.

She grabbed Baldy's jaw in her hand and twisted him to face her. "Why are you hunting the Spinner?"

Baldy swallowed loudly. His eyes suddenly grew watery, glazed over, and his mouth slacked opened to spill out the saliva he no longer cared to swallow. He looked right through her as if she wasn't there. She recognized that look and her heart sank. He hadn't swallowed from fear but instead took a hallucinogenic substance that was embedded in a false tooth. This immediately identified him as a former inmate of the Southern Colony. Now that he was flying higher than a dragon he wouldn't be useful while his body dealt with the effects of the drug coursing through his bloodstream. Then there would be the subsequent crash and the violent withdrawals that lasted several days. That left Scar. Talia would have to handle this delicately.

It was time for a new tactic. "Are you going to check out like Baldy here?"

The woman glared at her. "We only had enough for one. But I'm not afraid of you. Do your worst," she said with a sneer.

Before Talia could do or say more, screeching sounds from the sky made her freeze as her blood curdled. She knew that sound intimately.

Dragons!

A responding screech echoed from a different direction.

And there was more than one!

She scanned the dark sky. It was hard to see anything through the thick canopy of trees.

There!

She spotted the jagged outline of a dragon's leathery wings as it whizzed by overhead. And then another. And another!

Talia couldn't stay here. Not with dragons so close. There was still blood on her clothes from the dragon they injured while trying to capture it. The scent of dragon's blood was almost impossible to wash out. It was so strong, another dragon could detect it from miles away. She wasn't as worried about it initially. There were so few dragons in the wild, and she was so far from any major city that she shouldn't have seen another dragon until she reached the edge of the West Kingdom. But now there were three of them inexplicably wheeling overhead in the sky in the middle of a forest. And they most certainly smelled the blood on her, judging by their excited shrieks that tore through the night.

She looked at Scar. She was about the same size as Talia. She smiled apologetically at the woman. "Sorry about this," she said and used her hand to wipe some of Baldy's spittle from his chin and then smeared it on Scar's lips. Scar tried to struggle, but she could barely move and Talia got enough of the drug into her mouth that her eyes glazed over fairly quickly.

Talia used her dagger to sever the ropes and arranged the two drugged hunters in front of the fire. She worked quickly, positioning them to sit against each other, as if they became enraptured with the flickering flames because of the drug coursing through their bodies. It would be days before they could speak coherently. By then, Talia would have delivered the boy to the West Kingdom and made her request.

She wasn't completely honest with the Spinner when she said all she wanted was the money. She knew The Order would be in her debt if she delivered the boy alive. And she expected to collect her reward. But it wasn't just the monetary compensation she was seeking. She cleared her mind. She didn't have time to be distracted by what she would lose if she didn't escape the dragons.

She ran for the wagon and dug out a new set of leather clothing. Thank the fates she came across a pair of hunters, one of which was female. She would have hated changing into a dress or even men's clothing that was less combat worthy. She changed hurriedly into a new outfit, one free of dragon's blood, and mounted the horse.

With a sharp whistle across her lips, her dogs quickly fell alongside her horse as they sprinted through the forest away from where the dragons landed nearby.

Chapter 30

Calen waited impatiently in the sitting room of the private chambers reserved for the High Master Spinner of the Order. He only just arrived at the Western Basilica an hour before and was drawing a bath to remove hundreds of miles of road from his skin and hair when he was unexpectedly summoned by the High Master. He stared absentmindedly at the carefully arranged cut stones that made up the thick walls of the stronghold and thought about the place he called home since the day he was inducted into The Order.

The Western Basilica was built on the same extensive grounds as the Citadel of the West that in turn was built around the gate at Devil's Claw. It was the final defensive position should Aeron burst into Midguard from Magerealm. While the gate at Devil's Claw was not the only way to cross from one realm to the other, it was the only gate Aeron controlled on the other side. If he ever got through, he could use magic to slowly conquer all of Midguard, killing thousands upon thousands along the way. Once he controlled all the gates in Midguard he could easily conquer all of Magerealm. And then he would set his sights on Techrealm. Aeron's goal was simple. Bring magic to all the realms and connect them under a single unified monarchy with him on the throne.

Every child born into the ruling family was purposely named Aeron. And since there was always an Aeron on the throne, few dared question their sovereign right to be there.

In Magerealm, Aeron only maintained control over his tiny kingdom. The other kingdoms in Magerealm were tolerant of the tiny volatile nation-state and let it continue as an independent monarchy since it never bothered the rest of them. But that little kingdom held one of the gates. The Wizard's Order was formed after the first Aeron tried to cross over to Midguard and use it as a staging area to take over the rest of Magerealm. He destroyed several areas of Midguard, killing thousands of innocents in the ensuing fighting, before some other kingdoms in Magerealm learned of his plans. Seeing how this small tyrant could actually gain enough power to threaten the rest of Magerealm, they formed an opposing army to stop Aeron. But fighting in Midguard was not what they expected. They sustained heavy casualties and many more thousands of the natives of Midguard were killed during the Mage Wars. When they finally pushed Aeron back to his little kingdom in Magerealm, everyone agreed to establish a guard post at the gate to prevent the tiny annoying kingdom from bothering anyone else ever again. For a thousand years, the Wizard's Order did its job, stopping one Aeron after another. But the Aerons never gave up on their thousand-year-old dream to conquer all three realms.

As long as he was confined to Magerealm, Aeron wasn't a threat. The other kingdoms were powerful enough to crush Aeron like a bug if they wanted, but they were more interested in keeping the peace and left his kingdom untouched. And as long as the Wizard's Order successfully defended the gate at Devil's Claw, the kingdom of Aeron could be summarily ignored in the grand scheme of things.

Calen carefully manipulated events around him until he was a highly respected Spinner in The Order, one who could wield great influence with the Council of Elders of the West Kingdom who, in turn, oversaw the principles of The Order.

Only one person commanded greater influence with the Council of Elders. And right now, Calen was sitting in his private chamber waiting for an audience with him in the middle of the night. Such a late request unnerved Calen and, despite looking straight at the door to the High Master's private study, he was not really seeing it. His mind was running through scenarios about the questions the High Master might ask.

The door opened and Falen stepped out, smiling warmly at Calen. That was not a good sign. In his experience, Falen never once cracked a smile. It was as if his face was incapable of holding anything but a perpetual frown.

"Spinner Calen," Falen said as Calen stood abruptly to his feet to show respect for the status of the High Master Spinner.

Calen bowed his head. "High Master."

Falen touched Calen's elbow. "Please. We are alone. There is no need for formality. We have known each other for far too long. You may call me Falen." He turned and led Calen into his private study, a place few but the High Master and his closest advisors ever entered.

Calen's heart beat faster as he stammered his reply while following Falen into a room reserved for the elite of the elite. "Of course High—

Falen." It felt unnatural to roll the High Master's informal name across his tongue.

Falen chuckled at Calen's obvious discomfort. "Don't worry, Calen. You'll get used to it." Falen motioned to one of the chairs sitting at canted angles to the small table between them. Calen sat in the indicated chair and Falen slowly set his thin frame in the other one.

Between them, a tea set was arranged on an impeccably polished silver tray. The small clear pot was adorned along the sides with intertwined brightly colored red and orange dragons. A small leather box, with copper rivets that looked like they witnessed better days, sat on the table behind the tray in stark contrast to the bright tea setting.

Falen carefully poured steaming liquid into the matching gold rimmed crystal cups, stopping well before they were even half full. He lifted the cup closest to him and peered over the rim of the cup at Calen. "Dragon's Breath Tea. Have you ever had the pleasure?"

Calen shook his head.

Falen smiled. "Watch this."

He flicked the side of the cup. It rang with a single solid tone. The vapor rising from the cup immediately turned a bright orange before shifting to a dark red and then fading back to white steam. His smile widened and then he closed his eyes, breathed the vapors in deeply, and slowly sipped from the cup.

Calen couldn't stop his anxious mind from wondering what Falen was up to. Why did he call Calen in to this unprecedented private meeting and then serve him exotic tea as if they were old friends?

Falen kept his eyes closed as he continued. "The leaves grow only in the highest mountain ranges of Magerealm."

He opened his eyes and regarded Calen as casually as if they were two bond-farmers discussing the weather. "Sadly, I must pay ten times the going rate to import it through one of the other gates since we have to keep ours under constant lock and key."

Falen motioned to Calen to pick up the other cup.

"Try it. You'll like it, I promise. But be sure to flick the rim first. They have been exactly fashioned to deliver a precise resonant tone when struck. The tea is deadly unless you release the vapors first."

Calen fought the urge to bolt from the room. He felt his hand trembling on his lap, so he kept it in place. He didn't want his host to see that he thought the High Master might just poison him. Despite wanting to show he fully trusted the leader of The Order, he found himself unable to reach for the offered cup.

Falen regarded him warily, his smile fading. "Are you not going to try the experience of a lifetime?"

Calen swallowed dryly and tried his best to smile, despite feeling like running and never looking back. He willed himself to hold out just a little longer. "My apologies, Falen. I just arrived home from a long journey and have not yet taken the time to be properly cleansed. I do not wish to defile your tea set with traveler's hands."

Falen set his teacup down, his face shifting to one of concern. "Please forgive me for my lack of patience. I heard you were back and asked for you. I had no idea you only just arrived."

Calen felt his hands shake harder. Why was Falen apologizing to him? A terrifying thought compelled his heart to pound heavily. Did Falen know? How could he know? Calen's breathing increased in short, brief bursts. If he didn't calm down, he would pass out from too much oxygen in his brain. There was no way Falen could have found out, he reminded himself. He was careful.

Falen gave him a curious look. "Are you okay, Calen?"

Calen gathered his wits and smiled weakly, pressing his hands into his lap to suppress their quivering. "I just realized I missed both lunch and dinner today, I was so eager to complete my journey home."

Falen nodded. "Of course. You left the dragon with Halen. He should have found Veren's son and arrived long before you. Have you heard from him?"

Calen lowered his head. "No, High Master."

Falen set his tea cup down. "Then I might have some news for you. I received word from the dragon master that the dragon I provided you was injured earlier in the day. Dragons can telepathically communicate with other dragons when in danger, were you aware of that?"

"Of course."

Falen nodded. "Well, I ordered a contingent of Riders to investigate. They arrived within hours and found the dragon had been captured by a group of hunters. Unfortunately, the hunters were not willing to return our property without a struggle. Suffice it to say that none of them survived first contact with our Riders." Falen shook his head. "Our troops are not used to dealing with non-magics. I will have to look into better training for the Riders if we find we are using them for more civilian-contact operations."

Calen was riveted to his chair. As much as he wanted to jump up and run from the room, he found he wanted to stay and hear the rest of Falen's report.

"Did they find Halen? Or the boy?" Calen asked, his voice wavering slightly from the anticipation of what he wanted to hear.

Falen reached for the box behind the tea set. He set it in Calen's lap.

"This was recovered at the hunter's encampment."

Calen looked at the object on his lap and then at Falen. "A box?"

Falen raised his eyebrows impatiently. "Look inside."

Calen lifted off the leather-bound lid and peered into the dark interior. He pulled out strange fabric that was torn and bloody. He looked quizzically at Falen. "What is this?"

"It is material from Techrealm. It is Van's clothing along with the clothing of another who must have crossed over with him."

Calen's heart skipped a beat. "You found him?"

Falen's eyes bored into his. "These clothes were found in the hunters' camp along with the dragon. It appears the hunters captured the dragon and killed the boys. Must have left them in the desert for vultures to pick their bones clean because we were unable to find their bodies in the camp."

Calen stared at the clothing that could only have been worn by Veren's son. He looked up at Falen. "What about Halen?"

Falen's expression darkened. "Apparently the hunters split up after capturing the dragon and killing the boys. A couple of them took Halen."

Calen frowned. "Why do you think that?"

"Our dragons caught the scent of someone covered with the blood of the injured dragon. They followed the scent and found two more hunters. Among their belongings was an outfit belonging to the woman. It was covered in the blood of the injured dragon."

"Enough about the dragon! What about Halen?"

Falen ignored Calen's intensifying demand to his voice and responded as if the lower Spinner had not made a considerable breach of protocol. "He wasn't anywhere to be found. The Riders did however find fresh blood around the small campsite. A Skrahyer was brought in. She verified the blood at the second campsite matches that of a Spinner. A closer inspection showed it was from Halen's bloodline. Since he is the only surviving member of his line, it could be no one else but him."

"What did the hunters say?"

Falen shrugged. "The hunters had taken Boars Blood and were staring blindly into the campfire. An odd way to celebrate the killing of a Spinner."

Calen's head spun as the implications of what occurred tumbled through his mind. "So they found some blood. That doesn't mean Halen's dead. He could be injured. We have to find him."

Falen held up a small object squeezed carefully between his index finger and thumb. "They also found this at the second campsite."

Calen took it and inspected it. Realization of what he held in his hand hit him like a ton of bricks and his chest constricted as if a dragon stood on it. His head snapped up. "This is Veren's Crest pin!"

Falen nodded. "I knew Halen kept it from us when Veren sacrificed himself, but I couldn't prove it. It explains how he was able to still spin, even if only a little, after his crest pin was tarnished by my own hand. Now we know the truth. He was using Veren's pin to counteract the censorship of his magic. I can think of only one reason he would ever let go of this."

The room spun around Calen and he nearly fell out of his chair. Falen took the crest pin from him and tucked it into a pocket. He looked at Calen with sadness in his eyes. "Do not blame yourself for what happened."

Calen stared at him in wide-eyed silence.

Falen responded to his unspoken question. "It was you who recommended Halen look for Veren's son and bring him here, was it not?"

Calen finally found his voice. "I recommended him because he would have given his life to protect the boy."

Falen's eyebrows raised. "It appears he did. As much as our way does not condone death, it seems the problem of Veren's son appearing unexpectedly in Midguard has been resolved. Maybe not in the best way, but resolved nonetheless."

Calen nodded. "What of the hunters who killed Halen?"

"We brought them back here for questioning. It will take a few days for the effects of the Boars Blood to wear off. Once that happens, we can verify who they are and find out who hired them to kill the boy and a Spinner."

Calen's heart jumped into his throat. He swallowed it down quickly. "You think someone hired them to kill Veren's son and Halen? Who would do that?"

Falen lifted his tea cup and peered at Calen over the top of it. "It is too coincidental that these hunters would come across them only hours after they entered the realm, and somehow end up killing both the boy and the Spinner before the day ended. Only someone who possessed knowledge of who the boy really was could have sent them."

Calen pressed his hands into his lap to keep them still as he restated his first question, his brain unable to formulate any new words as it swirled out of control. "You think they were hired to kill them?"

"The woman appears to have taken a smaller dose of the Boars Blood. She should be speaking coherently in a matter of hours. I will personally ask her and let you know."

Calen felt the coolness of sweat evaporating from the perspiration that formed along his hairline. "Hunters have their own code they adhere to as much as we adhere to the code of the Wizard's Order. She will never tell you who hired them."

Falen narrowed his eyes into thin slits. "She killed a Spinner, Calen. This is not something The Order can take lightly. This is not something I can allow. She will tell me."

Chapter 31

It required all of Calen's strength and concentration to walk out the door of Falen's private chamber and into the hallway without collapsing. He heard the door close behind him. He struggled to force himself to keep walking until he turned a corner and was completely out of sight of the Master Spinner's chambers. Then, his body froze. Despite gritting his teeth until his jaw ached and silently ordering his leg muscles to move, he couldn't take another step. The world spun around him in circles and he placed an outstretched hand on the wall for support. He focused on his breathing until it steadied and then worked on getting his heart rate down from its accelerated drumroll. He'd never seen Falen like that in all the years he lived with The Order. Calen held no doubt about the resolve of Falen to convince the huntress to surrender the identity of who hired her. And he wouldn't have to threaten her life to do it. All it would take would be the promise of double the original payment. She would flip instantly like a click beetle on its back.

Calen pushed off from the wall. He must find a way to stop her from revealing what she knew. He focused all his energy on putting one foot in front of the other, taking the floor one step at a time until he made it all the way across the basilica to his room. He closed and latched his door, relaxing his jaw muscles for the first time since leaving Falen's private chambers. For good measure, he grabbed the chair from his reading table and wedged it under the door handle. He knew he hadn't been discovered yet, but it was only a matter of time. The chair wedge was a small comfort that it would take several large men just as many minutes to break through that door. That would give him just enough warning and he could be out the window before they broke through. It didn't matter that he was several stories above the ground. Once they were coming for him, he was a dead man anyway.

Calen needed help. His hands still shook like he was an elderly man with the tremors. It made lighting his candle nearly impossible, but finally the flame took and he set it down in the middle of the room. He sat cross-legged in front of it and closed his eyes, focusing his energies on making contact with his true master through the channeling fire.

He wordlessly moved his lips in the specific incantation that would activate the unique properties of the candle. The flame shifted from a bright orange to a dark blue hue and grew larger until it resolved into a face looking out from the azure flame.

Calen opened his eyes. He saw the face of Aeron among the gleaming indigo flames and bowed his head. "My Lord," he said barely above a whisper.

Aeron glared at Calen, his image not solid enough to obscure the rest of the room behind him as his facial features danced along with the flickering blue flame. "You'd better have good news," Aeron said.

Calen sat up straight. Feelings of well-deserved pride welled up inside him. "It is done. They are dead."

The face nodded but didn't shift from its sour expression. "That is not good news."

Calen caught his breath and clenched his fists in a panic. What could Aeron mean? The impossible task given to him was fulfilled. How could it have disappointed Aeron? Was he being betrayed? He could be in the badlands by nightfall of the following day. Nobody could get to him there. He was about to blow out the flame and ready his escape when Aeron's face broke into a wide smile. It looked so unnatural. More sinister than the bizarre smile that was on Falen's sour face earlier.

"That is excellent news!" Aeron exclaimed.

Calen let out his breath in a heavy sigh of relief. The alleviated pressure extended to every muscle in his body and he sagged a few inches as he relaxed for the first time in years. He'd done it. He'd accomplished what no other follower of Aeron could do. Thanks to him, the way was finally clear for Aeron to gain entry to Midguard. The Maclean line, undoubtedly the strongest line of Spinners, was gone. It was Calen, and Calen alone, who singlehandedly defeated the Macleans. Veren's son sired no offspring before his life ended, so there was no future threat that could unseat Aeron from his self-professed claim as the one true ruler of the three realms.

Aeron's head bobbed up and down with the flame. "As for the huntress you hired, I suggest bringing in another hunter to cut that thread loose."

Calen stiffened again and swallowed coarsely, his throat rough and dry from the combination of fear and the dehydrating effect of the channeling candle. He still needed to stop the huntress from betraying him. Maybe Aeron would help. But he must ask carefully. Aeron destroyed anyone who demonstrated weakness.

"That is not possible at this time." Calen stammered.

Aeron frowned, the anger in his eyes growing steadily. He hated to be challenged. The consequences on those who defied him were legendary. And the names of his victims were never forgotten. But Calen didn't want to be remembered like that. He wanted to be remembered for his part in unifying the three realms. And for that to happen, he needed to appeal to a side of Aeron that quite possibly didn't exist. "She has been captured and brought here to the basilica to answer for her crimes against The Order."

Aeron studied him. "Does she know your face?"

"No, My Lord."

"Does she know you are with The Order?"

"The chances are remote, but it is possible she could determine the source of my Skrahyer; for a price. I had no choice but to use a local Skrahyer to avoid raising suspicions among my peers."

"Unfortunate."

"I know," Calen said and clenched and unclenched his hands repeatedly. "That is why I need to be brought to Magerealm as soon as possible."

Aeron raised a single eyebrow and his face returned to the normal frown Calen was more familiar with. "I need you to remain at The Order and be my eyes and ears."

"It has become too dangerous for me here."

"Then handle it."

"I don't know that I can. The huntress will become lucid soon and she will identify a Spinner as the one who hired her to kill Halen and the boy. Once he starts looking it won't take long for the High Master to determine it was me. The magic is too recent. My usefulness at The Order will be at an end. I can no longer function as your spy here. Bring me to Magerealm where I can continue to serve you."

"I need you to remain with The Order until my triumphant return to Midguard."

Calen clenched his fists tightly, but nothing inhibited their shaking.

"Once the Huntress informs the inquisitor about me, that won't be possible."

"Then make sure she doesn't."

It was Calen's turn to frown. "You cannot ask me to do this."

"I'm not asking you to do anything. But if you want to remain useful to me, it is important that the huntress never speaks of your involvement in another Spinner's death."

The flame flickered out when Aeron severed the connection from his end. He was refusing to assist Calen. The task Aeron asked of him was more than unsurmountable. It couldn't be done. Yet Aeron was right. If Calen wanted to remain useful he would have to find a way to get to the huntress before she was given the chance to expose his crimes against The Order. He worked too hard to gain the influence and power he enjoyed to let it all be unraveled by a single hunter who prized wealth over everything else.

Calen let out a long slow breath that calmed his shaking hands and reset his heart rate back to normal. He reminded himself that it was the huntress' personal choices that landed her in the position she found herself. Calen was just the vessel that conveyed her fate to her. He was not to blame for any of it.

Now that his head was clearer he began to formulate a plan that would do more than just protect his influence with The Order, it would secure him a better position in the hierarchy itself. His frown shifted to a smile as he realized how he could move up the ranks of The Order by eliminating a loose thread that threatened to bring him crashing to the ground, all with one fell swoop.

"Two birds with one stone," he said quietly to himself as a plan developed in his mind. He sat in the darkness of his room until the sky outside his window started to lighten. Once the sun peeked over the ridge of the distant mountains he knew exactly what he needed to do.

Chapter 32

As the sun rose from beyond the edge of the world, Van was barely able to keep his eyes open. Eddie wasn't faring much better as they crested the top of the mountain they spent the better part of the night climbing. Halen's dead weight slowed them down further with every step. Van's arms went numb an hour before and it felt like the blisters on his feet were forming blisters of their own. Before he started working on his third layer of blisters, Van stopped, forcing Eddie to halt in his tracks. Eddie wavered in place as he clung to Halen's feet. "Why'd you stop?"

Van lowered Halen to the ground carefully. "I can't…"

Eddie jerked up on Halen's feet to keep from dropping them as he struggled for a better hold. "Can't what?"

Van felt his muscles tremble from the release of carrying Halen up the mountain. Now that he was relieved of his burden, all he wanted to do was curl up on the ground and fall asleep. "I can't take another step."

Eddie's mouth fell open and he looked around in a panic before fixing his eyes on Van. "We have to keep going."

Van sat down and the cramp in his leg immediately knotted up until any weight applied to it was agony. He used his useless fingers to knead the screaming muscles. "I'm tired. I'm hungry. I'm thirsty." He looked at Eddie who hugged Halen's legs tightly to his waist. "I'm done. You want to keep going, be my guest."

Eddie dropped Halen's feet. They landed with a soft thud on the dry grass. Eddie rolled his shoulders. "We can't stop here."

Van looked up at him. He was sure his face reflected the defeat he felt. "Why not? This is as good a place as any."

Eddie glanced around and then looked imploringly at Van. "You're just thirsty. I know I am. If we can find some water we will have enough strength to get somewhere safer than here."

Van squeezed his shoulders with swollen fingers. "We're at the top of a mountain. There's no water up here. We should have stayed down by the river."

Eddie's face contorted in frustration. "Have you forgotten that loud screeching? I know you heard it. Whatever it was would have eaten us if we stayed there!"

Van winced as he massaged his tired muscles and stretched his foot out, unfurling the multitude of knots along his leg. "It was circling the camp. It wasn't coming after us."

"You don't know that!"

Van shot him a hard look. "And you do!"

Eddie jerked back reflexively. The hurt look on Eddie's face told Van there was more he wanted to say, but held back for some reason.

Van didn't want to hurt Eddie. He was exhausted. He was done. He held up his hands in surrender and looked at Eddie apologetically "Look, we've been walking all night and now the sun's coming up," Van said, gesturing in the direction of the warm morning light. "If something wants to eat me now–" he said with a yawn as he lie down on his back. "Then just consider me breakfast."

Eddie nodded, accepting the silent apology and sat down next to him, looking at Van's prone form while hugging his long legs close to his chest. His silence spoke volumes and the space between them thickened with tension. After a short while Van turned his head and finally cut through the anxiety with his words like a sharpened knife. "There's obviously something you want to say."

Eddie looked sideways at him, as if gauging if this was a good time. Finally he said. "Yes. We should talk about this."

"Okay. Talk about what?"

Eddie motioned to the air around them with his arms. "All of this. I've been keeping track of everything up here," Eddie tapped the side of his head. "If this was a dream, or we were in a coma from the accident, we would be jumping from one event to another with no coherent passage of time."

Eddie was babbling and making very little sense. Van propped himself up on an elbow to try to listen closer "What are saying, Eddie?"

"I'm saying we need to discuss what is happening to us."

Van laughed, surprising even himself that he could find their situation remotely amusing.

Eddie's face acquired a serious look that Van rarely saw. The last appearance was during finals week before graduation. "I'm serious. I don't believe this is a dream."

"What clued you in, Sherlock?"

Eddie gave Van a sideways glance "The passage of time. It's happening as it should."

Eddie wasn't making sense again. "What are you talking about?" Van asked.

Eddie looked at Van as if he was slow. Then holding out his arm, Eddie pulling back his sleeve to show his massive diver's watch. "What time does it say?"

Van squinted at it and then frowned. It was slow, or fast, depending on whether it was hours early or hours late. "It says two fifteen." He looked quizzically at Eddie. "In the afternoon?"

"Or two fifteen in the morning," Eddie offered. "Either way, it's obviously wrong."

Van looked around at the early morning sun poking into the sky. Neither time fit. They didn't travel far enough to change time zones. There was only one explanation he could think of. "It must've broke when we hit the water," he offered.

Eddie vigorously shook his head. "Nope. If that were the case it would say ten in the morning. This is a Navy Seal diver's watch and it kept working for a short while after we climbed from the river. It can handle far worse than what happened to us. It stopped later."

"Okay, so it stopped. How does that prove we aren't dreaming?"

"Before you looked at my watch, what time would you have thought it was?"

Van looked around. "I don't know. Seven or eight in the morning?"

"Precisely!" Eddie said sharply. "If you were dreaming, you should have seen my watch tell you what time you thought it was, not what my watch actually shows. Or, at the very least, the numbers would have been all jumbled up. Supposedly, the part of the brain that tells time doesn't work so well while you're asleep. No. I've been glancing at it all night, and it never jumped or changed. It stayed at a quarter after two this whole time."

The wind picked up and rustled the tall grass. Eddie jerked to one side nervously as if expecting another dragon to rise up and devour him. He looked back at Van, his face white as a sheet. "That's what is freaking me out Van. We're not dreaming. This is all real!"

Van gave Eddie a half smile and shook his head. "Welcome back to reality, Eddie."

Eddie clasped his hands together and stood up, walking around in a big circle nervously, muttering to himself. "Where are we? What happened to us?"

Van sat up and looked down at Halen. He could tell by the soft rise and fall of his chest that he was still alive. But he remained comatose for the long tortuous climb to the top of the mountain and showed no signs of waking up any time soon. His last act, before falling into a death-like sleep, was to save Van and Eddie's life. But not without getting an arrow lodged into his shoulder first. Van owed him one and was paying it back by carrying his sorry, unconscious butt over the mountain.

Van studied the arrow and decided it was best to keep it in place for the time being. The bleeding slowed and stopped soon after they reached the river. The crossing of the river wasn't any worse for the wound and, during their trek to the top, it never reopened. Since it wasn't bleeding at this very moment, it was better to leave the arrow in place until they could get him to a—did hospitals even exist where they were?

Van closed his eyes to let the morning sun wash over his face. He came to the realization long before Eddie that all of this was real and not some coma induced dream state. Everything around them was actually happening, despite very little of it making any sense. He needed to accept it and roll with it. There wasn't much choice in the matter.

Now that he was at the top of the highest peak, he could get a good look at the world around him. He sat up straight and studied the mists that shrouded the valley behind them. The tops of trees poked out of the white haze adding green splashes of color in an otherwise full basin of fog. It looked like a tranquil scene from a painting. But, he realized, it was anything but peaceful. The rain of arrows, and subsequent dog chase down there, is what caused them to take refuge up here.

He turned his attention to where they were headed. Limitless desert filled his view. Dull orange sands stretched on to the point of infinity. In the distance they met up with the tops of another mountain range hundreds of miles away. It looked barren and hostile. He glanced back at the serene fog enshrouded forest with its large lake at the opposite end of the basin. It beckoned him to return to its sparkling clear waters and use it to find his way home. Maybe they never traveled to some imaginary land after all and it was like he first thought, they simply floated down the river away from the bridge. Maybe if they went the other way they would have come across the road in a matter of hours instead of venturing deeper into the abyss of this nightmare. But, this rationalization couldn't explain the town they passed through, the dragons, or the use of magic by Halen. Wherever he and Eddie were, it didn't function like the world they knew.

Eddie waved a hand past his eyes as he gazed into the desert, interrupting his thoughts. Eddie's child-like enthusiasm returned as he pointed down the side of the mountain. "I see a road down there. And look! Someone's coming."

Van squinted into the distance and saw dust rising up along the horizon's edge.

Eddie stood quickly, grabbed Halen's legs, and gave Van a longing look set in place by a half smile. "If we hurry, maybe we can reach the road before they pass by."

Van took one last look at the dissipating fog behind them and noticed it revealed a harsher looking reality than his imagination conjured up when it was concealed by the soft mist. That way was uncertain. At least, toward the desert, someone was coming who might offer help. He stood, dusting the grass off his pants and leaned down to grab Halen's arms. He lifted, every muscle screaming in agony. He plastered on as decent a smile as he could muster, despite the growing pain, and looked at Eddie. "What are we waiting for?"

Chapter 33

Calen didn't sleep a wink the entire night, but he never felt more alive and awake as he waited for the woman from the cleaning service to arrive. He was purposely clothed in a robe, giving the illusion of someone who awoke before the sunrise and hadn't bothered to get dressed when he called for the pageboy.

After ensuring the pageboy noted his robe and disheveled appearance, he requested his room be revitalized with fresh aromatic flowers and his bedsheets improved. The boy immediately ran down to the lower levels of the basilica to fulfill his master's desire. It was one of the benefits afforded to the Spinners in The Order. The Western Basilica was officially part of the West Kingdom's extended castle grounds. As such, the Spinners in the Western Basilica were provided with the same embellishments in life that kings, queens, and lords and ladies of the court were accustomed.

The servants in the West Kingdom were also aware of the additional privileges seized by members of the court and The Order. The special attendants pushing the decorated carts around the castle were always infinitely more beautiful than most of the regular servants.

Calen was aware of these less than admirable customs. Though he shunned them in the past, they were perfect for his plan. He purposely used the code words that informed others of his desire to have someone, who was beautiful and willing, come to his room and help him toss his bedsheets vigorously. For most, this perk was a definite improvement over being alone in bed. For Calen, it was the ideal cover for his true motive.

The selective attendants' pushcarts were always adorned with roses from the royal garden, fresh cut that same morning prior to sunrise. Calen first noticed them upon his appointment to the Western Basilica when he was but a young apprentice. Shortly after learning of the "services" these women, and a few men, provided to those living in the castle grounds of the West Kingdom, he purposely ignored them. They became all but invisible to him and anyone else who knew of them. To notice them would be to admit you knew what was about to happen in the room they entered and that was more information than most wanted to know about their fellow Spinners and the surrounding nobility.

Over the years, he pondered how they were ignored by everyone of importance, from the king all the way down to the lowest pageboy, and how that knowledge might come in handy someday. Calen never fully settled on whether the invisibility of this specific sect of "servants" was beneficial or demeaning to who they were and what they did.

But, for his current plan, it was of great benefit. As he waited for his specially ordered service to arrive, he was anxious to obtain the "benefit" of moving freely around the castle grounds without being noticed. There was no magic powerful enough, not even in Magerealm, to render a human fully invisible. But the obscurity possessed by these attendants, as they traveled unhindered and unnoticed through the most secured halls of the West Kingdom, came pretty close.

A faint knock at his door made him jump slightly. "Come!" he said and the door opened quietly. A young woman stepped into the room, pulling the cart in with her. She closed the door and shed the scarf that hid her appearance from scrutiny while she ventured through the halls on the way to perform the shameful chore of her special brand of services.

As Calen looked upon her unmasked visage, he noted she was a classic beauty. Her features were perfectly proportioned and, if she were born at a higher station in life, she would be the porcelain hand the princes across Midguard would battle each other for.

"My Lord," she whispered, her head still bowed and her hands crossed demurely in front of her at waist height; gripping her scarf tightly. While he silently appraised her entire body, her hands twisted at the scarf, wrinkling the brightly decorated fabric.

The stage was set. With him still clothed in the morning robe he established the expectation of what he wanted before he took the time to get properly dressed. No one would expect anyone to emerge from this room for a while.

Calen suddenly found himself trembling. Not from excitement but from fear. He'd never ordered a room servant before except for actual room cleaning and to deliver meals when he studied late into the night before the many tests he took while still an apprentice.

Now, a woman was in his room in the early hours of the morning expecting things to happen that were better left undeclared. He found himself as nervous as when he was a young apprentice who attended his first state dinner with the king and queen. He refused to eat then for fear it would come right back up from the nerves. He felt the same way now.

She stood perfectly still, obviously waiting for him to set the tone of their interaction. He knew he should do something quickly before she suspected anything out of the ordinary. He hoped he could act correctly. Not having done this before left several areas for missteps. He cleared his throat and then remembered the tea he especially prepared for this spontaneous rendezvous. "Would you like something to drink? I brewed some tea," he said, his voice wavering from sheer terror that she might see through his ill-conceived plan and alert the court guards.

She looked up at him, shaking her head almost imperceptibly. "No thank you," she replied softly and smiled timidly.

That wouldn't do. She must drink the tea. He must convince her. He took a very slow and deep breath to steady his nerves. Then he reached down deep and found his courage. He took a step forward and smiled as warmly as was possible to convince her to trust him. "It is a special recipe handed down by my grandmother. And from her grandmother before that. The aroma is enough to knock you off your feet. You have to at least try it. I insist."

She looked at him uncertainly, and then warmed a bit as he kept his eyes on hers and his smile as charming as he could muster. She finally glanced around to see that they were alone, dropped her shoulders a bit, and nodded hesitantly. "Okay," she said barely above a whisper. He crossed the room to where the tea service sat on a table. He poured the tea into a single cup. He looked back at her and saw the glimmer of confusion in her eyes as she noticed he only served her. He never anticipated her second guessing his actions. His mind raced for a reason why he'd done something as unexpected as not joining his guest in a cup of tea. He needed to make it look more normal. He was forced to improvise, not having enough foreknowledge of how these transactions were normally conducted.

He took down another cup and poured one for himself. Luckily, she never moved from the spot where she removed her scarf, as if waiting for his invitation to sit. That gave him the excuse he needed to hand her the cup first without having one for himself. She took it from him delicately and watched him, waiting. He knew she expected him to go back and get his own cup to join her. He needed to get her to start without him. Then a flash of brilliance. "I'll go and get my cup, but please, first I just want you to smell my grandmother's recipe. It will make me happy to see that I prepared it with the same pleasurable scent she always made. It reminds me of home and the smile in your eyes at the aroma will let me know we shared a common experience that I love."

She looked at him with sad eyes. How many times had she been called to a room to please someone's carnal desires and then summarily discarded as if she were but a sitting chair around the royal dining table? Used but for a singular purpose and then ignored the rest of the time.

He saw the edges of her eyes moisten with tears. He was treating her as a person and it affected her deeply. Ever since he'd sent for her, he thought of her as a mere object to be used. Something necessary for his plan. But now that she stood in front of him, he saw her as a person with feelings. Someone with memories and desires of her own. Aspects of humanity that could never be stripped away no matter how much she was treated like nothing more than a possession.

He knew what was about to happen must happen, or he wouldn't have a future. He needed to shed the feelings he suddenly felt for this young woman and do what needed to be done. He kept the warm smile and pushed the cup in her hands toward her face. "Just smell the aroma. If I did it right, there is no equal in all the realms."

She smiled at him, at ease finally, and willing to do as asked. She breathed in the vapors rising from the cup and the lines on her forehead softened, all her cares seemingly erased as she made soft, happy sounds, closed her eyes, and lowered the cup a bit. Calen knew the scent was heavenly, until the effects took. He waited for her to start to fall. Then unexpectedly, she raised the cup to her nose to take another deep breath. Calen started to panic and reached to stop her arm, but it was too late. She inhaled deeply. This was too much of a dose. Her eyes suddenly popped open in shock as the effects came on too quickly.

She opened her mouth to speak but nothing came out. Calen

snatched the cup from her hands and set it down on the table merely seconds before she collapsed to the ground. In a swift, single motion, he caught her before carrying her carefully to the bed.

He looked down at his sleeping beauty and marveled at how trusting she was, despite the treatment she received at the hands of the animals that claimed to live as civilized human beings around the castle. He watched, mesmerized, as her chest rose and fell with each breath she took. She'd taken an unexpected second deep breath of the vapors and would sleep far longer than he originally intended. She would most likely awake with a horrendous headache. This transformed his carefully constructed timeline since someone would miss her long before she left his room. He would need to come up with an excuse that would curb the questioning as to why she stayed much longer than usual with him. But there was time to worry about that later. Right now, more urgent matters needed attending to.

He leaned over the bed and carefully extracted the scarf from her slack hands. He stared at it for a short moment and then directed his attention to the rest of her clothing. He removed her blouse and skirt, stripping her down to her undergarments, and then straightened her out on the bed, taking the time to cover her gently with the comforter, ensuring she would be comfortable and warm while she slept. He might be aiding Aeron in his conquest of the middle realm, but he wasn't a monster.

He took the teacup to the rest of the service and poured all the tea down the floor grate in the corner of his room. Then he carefully rinsed it with his daily wash water and put the tea service away so nothing would jog her memory should she awake before he returned.

He removed his robe and dressed in her clothes. The last article he donned was her scarf. He checked his reflection in the mirror and cringed. If word got out that this was his big plan to help Aeron defeat Midguard, he would be the laughing stock for generations to come.

But, Calen knew, covered in the servant's dress, and wearing her head scarf to hide his manly features, he was now able to go anywhere in the castle as if he were invisible.

Chapter 34

Van and Eddie shuffled down the side of the mountain, every rock threatening to twist Van's ankle as he struggled with the deadweight of Halen. They hurriedly descended to ensure they were at the road before whoever was coming reached the spot where they would intersect.

Van focused on the ground to keep from slipping too much and sending all three of them tumbling end over end down the incline. But Eddie was obviously tiring. No matter how much Van prodded Eddie to go faster, he was slowing down. If they kept their current pace, the caravan would pass by before they got close enough to flag them.

Van realized, if they hurried now, they would meet up with the caravan right at the base of the mountain. In an impatient move, Van picked up speed and pushed Halen forward to try to force Eddie to pick up the pace. Eddie wasn't prepared for the sudden surge of speed and he stumbled sideways. He let out a sharp cry as he went down. Halen suddenly became heavy, forcing Van to hunch over as he tried to compensate for the sudden increase in weight and the just as rapid decrease in speed. Halen's feet hit the ground and dug in like a stake, stopping his forward progression completely. Van toppled over Halen's body head first and landed on top of him. Eddie rolled a few feet away and grabbed at his ankle, hissing loudly between clenched teeth.

Van scrambled off of Halen and checked him over quickly. Except for some torn clothing and light scratches, Halen survived the pedestrian crash intact. Time to check on Eddie.

He crouched next to Eddie who sat on the ground, massaging his ankle with both hands. Eddie looked at him, anxiety filling his eyes. "I think I broke it."

Van looked at the swelling ankle and then glanced at Eddie. "May I?"

Eddie's forehead wrinkled with confusion. "Can you tell if it's broken or not?"

Van smirked. "No. But I did stay at a Holiday Inn last night."

Eddie laughed through the tears.

Van laughed with him.

That joke never got old. "If you're laughing, it can't possibly be broken. Can you stand?"

Eddie grabbed Van's outstretched arm and stood on his good foot. He slowly lowered the other one and winced as he applied the weight of his body. "It hurts a lot."

He lifted the weight off his foot, leaning heavily on Van. Van struggled to remain standing. They were still on a sloped part of the mountain and it wasn't easy to stay vertical with Eddie pushing him to one side. He looked at Van. "Should we take off the shoe?"

Van shook his head. "No. Even if you only twisted it, it would swell so fast we'd never get your shoe back on."

Van glanced down the mountain and looked along the road. He could now see the individual wagons pulled by horses as the caravan made its way down the road in their direction. He judged the speed and distance of the wagons. It didn't look good. With Eddie's twisted ankle, and Halen still out cold, there was little chance they could all make it to the road in time. But they could still try.

He helped Eddie stand and pointed to where the road turned at the base of the mountain and followed it for several miles. "Get down there as fast as you can. I'll drag Halen down. Hopefully, even with your ankle, you can get to the road before they pass by." He indicated the slow moving caravan with a wave of his hand and then turned to pick up Halen. Eddie placed a hand on his arm. He turned back and Eddie's eyes searched his. "I'm sorry. I don't know what happened, but I suddenly went off balance and fell."

Van looked at him sheepishly. "It was my fault, I tried to go faster and didn't warn you. Do you think you can make it down there quickly?" Eddie hobbled around a bit, but was still able to move around pretty quickly. Eddie nodded and hobbled away down the hill. Van reached down and hefted Halen up. He laced his arms under Halen's armpits and pulled him, angling to drag him down the mountain while walking backwards.

As he hit the tree line, he took one last glance down at the road before it was lost in the thick forest. He looked over to the caravan once more and judged the speed at which it was moving. His heart sunk. The caravan would be long gone before he came out the other side of the forest. It was up to Eddie to get there in time to stop them.

A quick glance down the road revealed that it turned to follow the snaking path of the mountain along the desert floor.

Not only would the caravan pass by before he reached the road, the caravan would have followed the road out of sight and there would be no one to help them. The world around Van started spinning as he concentrated on keeping Halen in his grip. The last thing he needed was to collapse from exhaustion and lose his only chance to save Halen, no matter how remote.

He entered the dense forest and the temperature dropped slightly, providing a little relief from the rising heat as the morning progressed. The bad news was that he could no longer see the road. All he could do was race down the side of the mountain as quickly as possible, dragging the slack body behind him, and hope the caravan was moving slowly enough that Eddie could chase it down before it got too far.

Unfortunately, the trees were so closely spaced, Van spent more time twisting and turning Halen to get him around and between massive trunks than progressing forward. It didn't look like they would make it to the road in time. With each step Van moved slower and his hope faded. The longer it took him to pull Halen around another tree, the harder it became to remind himself that help was just on the other side. If he kept slowing down, help would be miles away by the time he reached the road.

Chapter 35

Calen loaded the cart with the supplies he needed and then checked the sleeping maiden in his bed. She would definitely be out for several hours. He cursed himself for not reacting fast enough and letting her take that second breath. No matter. He would deal with this new wrinkle in his plan when he returned. For now, there was a far more important issue to resolve.

He checked his outfit, complete with head scarf, in the full length mirror one last time. He turned his head back and forth, scrutinizing himself from every angle. As long as he kept his head low, which was not uncommon for servants walking through the corridors of the palace, he would not be recognized.

He glanced at the girl on the bed and then worried she might not stay asleep as long as he was anticipating. If she possessed a fast metabolism, or if he was detained longer than expected, she might wake up here alone. With her dress gone along with him, she would wonder what happened. He reached down and pulled on the strings to her undergarments, loosening them to create the illusion of physical play. To complete the illusion, he ruffled his side of the bed and pulled away the top edge of the blankets, as if he left the bed only moments before. Should she wake, and decide to leave before he returned, he wanted her to have a plausible conviction that something actually happened. If it looked odd, she might say something to arouse suspicion among the servants. And nobody was better at spreading rumors than those in the lowest stations. It was better she thought something did happen, thereby compelling her to typical silence.

He removed several bottles of port wine from his wall cabinet and poured their contents down the grate in the corner of the room. He then laid them all around the room, leaving one on its side among the rumpled bedspread.

He took a step back and surveyed his handiwork with a sly smile. If she woke up she would think they drank too much while they were fooling around. That would explain to her naïve mind why she couldn't remember anything that happened after she arrived. One of the benefits of the tea he used on her was that it also erased the victim's memory of the tea's existence. He could use it as many times on someone as he wished, as long as they never found out about the existence of the tea right before falling under its influence.

He placed his hands on the handle of the push cart and noted how much they trembled. He took several deep breaths to calm his nerves, but it didn't help. He was about to do something he never thought he could do. He'd killed before, but it was always through the candle. It was always so surreal, controlling the actions of another through the candle's power. The humans in Techrealm were weak-willed and retained no natural defense against the dark arts practiced by followers of Aeron.

He never dared use the candle's influence to direct any deaths in Midguard. The trace of magic could have been followed back to him if used improperly. While his innate Spinner skills were honed with experience, he was still only slightly more than an apprentice level in the use of enchanted magic. Enchanted magic was normally used by those who did not have inborn magical ability themselves. For a Spinner to practice magic with enchanted objects increased the power and strength of the enchantment magic nearly to the level of magical potency only achievable in Magerealm. It was why Spinners were barred from using their natural-born abilities in conjunction with enchanted magic. If too many Spinners started enhancing their abilities through enchantments it would tip the precarious balance between magic and technology in Midguard too far in the direction of magic, thereby eradicating the potential of technology to exist at all. Midguard was the one safe place where both magic and technology existed in equilibrium to each other; neither gaining a foothold in the realm. To tip that balance could cause catastrophic events all across the realm as technology such as wagons, carts, bridges, anything mechanical really, suddenly failed. But, he was only one Spinner, and only used the enchanted candle occasionally. Not enough to cause much of a ripple as long as he kept its use to a minimum. Calen could use the candle to eliminate the hunters before they were questioned by Falen. But that came at a price. Such powerful magic could easily be detected by the Watchers; which would expose him and his unauthorized use of enchanted magic.

It was why he didn't use the candle to deal with Talia. If she died, the king would order a full investigation. Any use of magic to end her life would be detected by the Watchers and lead right back to whoever performed the magic. He must do this the old fashioned way. Besides, he reminded himself, there's a first time for everything. If he planned on becoming a viscount for Aeron then he needed to prepare himself mentally for sending innocent people to their deaths. He needed to learn firsthand how to be judge, jury, and executioner; with no remorse. It was Aeron's way, and he was fully aware of it. But the downside of becoming a cold-blooded murderer was far outweighed by the wealth and riches he would attain once Aeron was in control of Midguard.

Reminding himself of why he was doing this soothed his trembling hands. He had the resolve to finish what he started. He was only fooling himself if he thought for a minute that the huntress could be allowed to live after she completed her task. He originally hoped to hire some other hunter to complete the bloody job, but since it fell on him to handle it personally, he needed to show Aeron he could be trusted to get the job done; no matter what.

He took one last look around his room and then pulled some clothes from his dresser and strew them about the room, leaving his robe lying over the edge of the bed. If anyone came in, or she woke before he returned, all they would see was the collateral damage of a morning of zealous passion. It was her profession within the castle walls. It was why he asked the pageboy to send for her. The level of people she serviced prided discretion above everything. No matter what she believed might, or might not, have happened in this room, there was little worry she would talk to anyone about it.

He took a few more breaths and tugged the scarf over his head and pushed the cart into the hallway. At the first corner, he almost bumped into a guard on morning patrol. Calen lowered his head and rolled quietly past the guard who didn't even cast a glance in his direction. He was being completely ignored now that he donned the outfit of someone worth less than the dirt kicked from farmers' boots each night.

He moved past the guard without so much as a "good morning" and into the next hall that led toward the dungeons. Whatever happened from this moment forward, Calen was fully committed now.

Chapter 36

Van found it harder to pull Halen across the ground after him as the terrain leveled out. Gravity was no longer helping him and he used all the strength that remained in his overtired muscles to keep putting one foot in front of another. If he stopped, he wouldn't have the energy to pick Halen back up and keep going. It was keep moving or stop permanently. There were no other options.

The sun crawled higher into the sky, signaling the passage of time. Enough that the caravan must be long gone and he was convinced he was rushing to an empty road. He lost Eddie to the forest some time ago and wondered if he was sitting by the empty road at the bottom waiting for him.

Van's sweating and aching hands made it hard to keep hold of Halen. Even more painful was the twinge that developed in his back after pulling a grown man down the side of a tall mountain. "Come on, Halen. Wake up! I can't keep lugging your sorry butt all through the countryside," he said, grunting through the effort of pulling the motionless body around another fallen tree.

He pulled harder, Halen's feet catching on something. He unexpectedly lost his grip and fell backward into the shallow pit generated by the roots that tore up the ground back when the tree fell. Whether or not the tree made a sound when it fell in the forest, Van made plenty of noise as he let loose a flurry of expletives when his spine compressed with an eruption of nasty sounding crunching noises upon impacting with the dirt. Halen broke free from whatever held his foot and he landed directly on Van. Van lay flat under the immovable weight, cursing himself for the predicament he found himself in. He pushed his hands under Halen's unconscious ribcage and shoved Halen off, rolling away until he was clear. Then he stood up, brushing the clumping dirt off his clothes. It couldn't get any worse than this.

He bent down to brush dirt off his leg when an oddly shaped shadow fell across his line of sight. He looked up at a massive barrel of a chest. He looked higher and came across a very large, very square face. It belonged to the chest that filled his entire view a moment before. The man looked as tall as the trees around him and was looking down at him with a frown. Van's heart went into overdrive, an immediate fear response to the imposing figure of the unexpected frowning giant. This forced oxygen through Van's whole body in preparation for the standard fight or flight response.

The man twisted his entire torso to face away from Van. It was an awkward looking maneuver, but it didn't look like his massive neck could turn on its own so it was all the man could do to look behind him. He hollered into the forest. "I found them. And it looks like one of them is already dead."

Before Van could register that the giant wasn't about to kill him, more men streamed into the forest and surrounded Van. A woman pushed her way through the crowd and looked Van up and down. She grunted in displeasure and then bent down to inspect Halen lying peacefully on the ground. She tugged at the bolt stuck in his shoulder. Van winced as if the arrow were stuck in his body as she manipulated it around, not caring about the blood that seeped from the reopened wound. "That's going to have to come out," she said and then looked up at Van. "That looks like a hunter's bolt. Any idea why they were shooting at your friend here?"

Van was stunned to silence. She understood the look of confusion on his face and pointed at the barrel-chested man. "Buff here drives the lead wagon. He saw you climbing down the mountain. I decided to have the caravan wait for you to come down and see if you needed assistance." She glanced back down at Halen. "It's a good thing I did. His wound is starting to get infected. The fever would have set in after another day or so. He would have lost that arm entirely if he lived."

The pounding of Van's heart softened. These people didn't seem to pose a threat to him or Halen. They were actually offering help. It was a nice change from just about everyone else he met since he and Eddie crawled out of the water into Neverland. Van found his voice along with a little courage. "You can help him?"

She smiled warmly. "Of course. I have food for you back at the caravan. Your friend visibly drooled when he saw it. He told us where to find you and how you got here."

Van was confused. What did Eddie tell her about how they got there? She glanced up at the peak of the mountain that towered over everything and then back at Van. "You must be hungry after that climb?"

Van's stomach gurgled loudly in answer to her question. He was more than hungry. He was famished.

She bent down and tugged out a crystal pendant that was tied around her neck with a plain leather strap from just inside the collar of her shirt and gripped it in one hand. She placed her other hand over Halen's forehead and began mumbling incoherently.

She took her hand away and Halen's eyes popped open. Van's heart fluttered with excitement. Halen was awake!

Halen blinked at the brightness of the morning sky that filtered in through the trees and then his eyes focused on the woman bent over him. His face went sullen and a wave of panic flooded his eyes. "Oh no!" he croaked. "Travelers!" He started to flail his arms and legs in a panicked flurry as if he were trying to run. But instead, it only looked comical as he lay prone on the ground. He realized his error and did something unexpected as he dug his heels into the dirt and pushed up, bending his back and resting on his head like he was attempting the Upward Bow Pose Van's mother performed repeatedly during her yoga phase.

The woman produced a small wooden bat from within the folds of her clothing and cracked it across Halen's forehead. His feet shot straight out and he collapsed to the forest floor; motionless. This time it really did look like he was dead.

The woman stood and spoke to Buff while pointing her stubby bat at Halen. "Get him to the caravan and secure him for travel."

Buff lifted Halen as if he weighed nothing and tossed him over a shoulder like a sack of potatoes. Van watched in dismay as the giant headed through the forest. Van never felt the urge to run more than now. He took a reflexive step back, but strong hands clamped down on his arms from behind and held him in place. The woman turned to him with a smile spread wide across her face. "Lucky for you we came along."

Chapter 37

Calen pushed the cart to the end of the hallway and breathed a sigh of relief. He made it all the way to the guards' quarters unhindered. It helped that it was still early in the morning and the sun was well below the horizon despite its light shifting the hues of the sky to lighter shades of azure. There were very few people moving about the castle at this hour. Even less in the lower section where the dungeon housed criminals and dissidents.

Calen glanced around and snatched the key ring off the cart. It was another reason this disguise was perfect. These particular servants kept a set of keys to every door in the Citadel of the West. That included every door in the basilica, the main castle, and the government houses. There was no place this class of servant could not gain entry to in the most secure place in the kingdom of the west. It was the one weakness everyone willingly overlooked. Nobody wanted to hinder a servant's ability to attend to them anytime and anywhere. Convenience always won out over privacy and security.

Calen wondered how much the world would change in an instant if the servants decided they were unhappy with their station in life and stopped protecting the secrets they discovered. So far, nobody had upset the apple cart, so to speak. It was this complacency that allowed Calen to wage the battle against Aeron's enemies from within.

It took only four attempts to locate the correct key and open the doors that led down to the prison cells. Calen pushed the cart in ahead and then turned and locked the doors behind him.

He turned around and jumped out of his skin when he came face-to-face with a guard. The man glowered down at him and addressed him gruffly. "What are you doing here?"

Calen kept his head low and was thankful that the lack of available light in the dungeon further hid his masculine features to someone so close to him.

"Hey! I'm talking to you," the guard said again.

There was no time to pretend to be a lowly servant, it wouldn't work with the guard so close. Before the guard became suspicious, Calen jerked his arm up swiftly and smashed the heel of his hand into the guard's chin. The guard's head snapped back and he went down with a clatter of armor, his helmet spinning away across the floor.

Calen held his breath and listened intently in the silence, waiting for someone, anyone, to come running to see what all the commotion was. When nothing happened, he let out a sigh of relief and spun around, peering into the dank interior of the jailer's domain.

The first two cells were empty and Calen felt the nervous sweat start to seep from along the hairline above his forehead. He was certain this would be where Falen requested the hunters be detained until they could be questioned. Where could they be? He lit a portable torch from the one mounted to the wall and headed down the center walkway, checking each cell with the light from the flame.

He walked past cell after empty cell, his nerves increasing with each vacant space until his hands were jittery again. He reached the end of the short hallway and spun around. He fought to get his anxiety under control and to think clearly. The hunters should have been in one of the prison cells waiting for interrogation once they were fit.

But the cells were all empty!

If they weren't here, where were they? He headed for the door and stopped right before grabbing the handle of the push cart. He heard the unmistakable sound of keys rattling on the other side of the door.

Someone was coming!

He extinguished his hand torch, grabbed the unconscious guard by his feet, and pulled him along to sink into the shadows of the last cell, well away from the main torchlight. If he were discovered he would be unable to explain what he was doing here. That would lead to a series of questions he wasn't ready to answer. And breaking The Order's policy of honesty was the least of his worries.

Keys clanked noisily in the iron lock. Calen breathed as quietly as possible, hoping beyond hope he wasn't discovered in the dungeons dressed as a woman; with an unconscious guard at his feet.

Chapter 38

Rough hands pushed Van alongside a caravan of wagons. Each one was built from wood, fully enclosed with a door. Most included side windows and small chimneys, but every one of them was brightly colored. Buff took charge of Van from one of the other burly men and directed him up the short stairs into a wagon in the middle of the caravan. Inside, it was ornately decorated with an open design that accommodated a table in the middle with loose wooden chairs around it. There were cabinets built alongside one wall and shelves of books on the opposite wall. In the corner, hanging from a hook mounted in the ceiling, a canary softly twittered a song-less tune while sitting on its perch in the small wooden cage.

Eddie and the woman who woke Halen before knocking him back out again were seated at the table. Buff shoved Van down into the chair next to Eddie. They looked at each other. Eddie gave him a sheepish look of apology and shook his head. "I'm so sorry, Van. They were waiting for me when I came out of the forest. I told them where to find you and Halen. I thought they stayed to help. I didn't know they were going to take us prisoner until they left me here alone and I couldn't get out the door."

Van pasted on the most reassuring smile he could conjure. "It's okay, Eddie." He wasn't about to blame Eddie for any of this. They were both eager to get help and catch up with the caravan. There was no way to know who they'd run into.

Eddie's shoulders dropped. "You know what the worst thing about all this is?" He adjusted the angle of his head to look at the woman who sat in the chair opposite them. "I was promised breakfast."

The woman laughed. "And I will make good on that promise. I only have a few questions for you and then we can discuss your breakfast options."

"Thank you," Eddie replied and settled back in his chair, crossing his arms. Van mimicked Eddie's body language and scowled at the woman. The longer he spent in this odd place, the weirder it became. The last time horse-drawn gypsy wagons were in practical use was over a hundred years ago. It was like he stepped back in time to a world before the industrial revolution and magic was still believed to exist by the masses.

He worked over every angle in his mind, puzzling out where they were ever since the crash. He ruled out method actors at a Renaissance Faire pretty quickly. He ruled out death and a bizarre version of the afterlife. He ruled out coma induced dream state. Maybe they were somehow transported back in time by several hundred years. That would explain a lot of things, but it still didn't answer how.

The woman scrutinized him for a long time before she relaxed. "My name is Madam Ryes. I am the matriarch over The Rootless."

Eddie sat up straight in his chair. The look in his eyes was one of sheer terror. "The ruthless?"

She smiled warmly. "No, Eddie. The Rootless. We have no history or roots to any one place. So we travel in our own moveable town. Our houses are on wheels for a reason. We don't stay in any one place long enough to form roots."

Eddie leaned over and whispered to Van while she spoke. "Maybe they should call themselves The Restless."

Madam Ryes raised an eyebrow. "That is also an apt description of my people. We haven't found what we seek, so we keep moving and keep searching."

Van couldn't keep his curiosity in check, so he asked the obvious question. "What are you searching for?"

"It's not a what. It's a who."

Van took the bait. "Okay. Who?"

She smiled, a sparkle in her eyes. "Why, we have been searching for you."

That caught Van off guard. His pulse quickened and he felt a sheen of sweat form along his brow. She was looking at him like she'd won a prize. He didn't know why but it reminded him of a cat watching a juicy mouse. "Me?" he squeaked.

She laughed. "Well, not you specifically, but you nonetheless."

Eddie took over since Van's throat constricted and he couldn't find his voice. "What is so special about us?"

She tilted her head and looked at Eddie. "For starters, you have brought me a Spinner."

Eddie was always a fast thinker and an even faster talker. He could have easily attained the nickname Fast Eddie if he ever let anyone get a word in edgewise. "Can you save him?"

She nodded. "The arrow has been removed and he is recovering in our healing wagon."

Van finally found the courage to speak. "Can we see him?"

He saw the answer in her eyes long before she spoke. "We gave him something so he can—sleep peacefully—to let his body heal. I'm afraid he won't be awake or alert for several hours."

Eddie took a big breath and asked the question that was on both their minds. "Are we prisoners here?"

She laughed again. She laughed so easily, it was hard to think of her as the ruthless leader that conked Halen on the head and dragged Van down the mountain. "Of course not. But I can guarantee that you will not survive long in the badlands. I'd be surprised if you lasted a single day on your own."

"What is the badlands?" Eddie asked.

She regarded him coolly, not responding to his question. "I've told you about me. Now it's time to find out who you are."

Good old Fast Eddie was ready and rattled off a small speech as if he had practiced it for days. "We are pages hired by the Spinner to help him travel through the badlands. Unfortunately, we were attacked by bandits. They shot Halen and took our stuff. We were lucky to get away at all."

Her expression changed the moment Eddie mentioned Halen by name. Van could tell she stopped listening as soon as he said it. She sat forward in her chair and looked at Eddie. "Did you say the Spinner in my healing wagon goes by the name of Halen?"

Eddie nodded. "Sure."

Her head snapped to look at Van. He didn't like how she evaluated him, her eyes moving up and down and studying his face intently. It was worse than the cat regarding a tasty mouse look from before. Her dissecting eyes made him squirm around uncomfortably in his seat. She suddenly sat back, held up a finger, and a smile broke out on her face. She stood up from her chair and went through the cabinets built into the inside walls of the wagon. She produced a small round stone with a hole worn through it. She held it up to her face, peering through the hole, and gazed at Van.

Her mouth opened slightly as her eyes widened at him in wonder. Then she opened another cabinet and shuffled various items around as she rooted through it for a short while. She produced a sliver of worn cotton fabric that looked as if it was torn from a larger piece. She inspected it through the hole in the stone and then brought her attention back to Van, examining him through the same hole in the smooth stone once more.

She glanced from the fabric to Van and back again at the fabric. She walked over, no longer concerned about keeping a safe distance, and held the fabric up next to Van while she inspected both of them through the stone.

She lowered the stone and then walked to the small cage. She opened it and the tiny bird inside hopped onto her finger. She slowly turned and held up her hand, showing off her brightly colored yellow canary. "This is Walter. He lied to me once." She glared at Eddie. "Once."

Eddie gulped loudly.

Van's stomach cramped up in knots.

She sat down and Walter hopped up her arm to sit on her shoulder. "Since you are obviously strangers to this land, I'm going to be lenient this time. But my tolerance for lies does have its limits. Which you have already reached. Now. Who wants to tell me the truth?"

It was Fast Eddie to the rescue again. He told her about the tire bouncing across the road and their subsequent crash into the river. She interrupted him and asked lots of questions about the car as if it was the first time she ever heard of such a contraption. Then she let Eddie continue his tale. He told her about appearing in the lake, the reaction of the old woman in that first town, the dragon, Talia, everything up to when they carried Halen over the mountain and hurried to the road despite his twisted ankle. "Speaking of which," he said. "Whatever you put on it is working great. I haven't felt any pain for a while now."

She smiled. "Keep it rested. It still needs to heal properly so you won't be encumbered with a limp the rest of your life." She looked expectantly from Eddie to Van. "Is that all?"

Van and Eddie looked at each other. Eddie was very thorough with his retelling of their unusual adventures. Eddie looked at her. "I think so?"

"You're not leaving anything out?"

Eddie frowned. "Not that I can think of."

She stroked the belly of Walter with her fingertip. He warbled in appreciation. It was a clear message. She was letting Van and Eddie know that if they held anything back, they would be punished just like poor old Walter.

"He told you everything that led to us sitting here at the table. I swear. That's all there is," Van offered.

"Yeah," Eddie added. "We swear on–" Eddie looked around the small room. "Whatever you want me to swear on, I'll swear on it. I've told you the truth, the whole truth, and nothing but the truth."

She narrowed her eyes at Eddie. "What's your family name?"

Eddie's face looked stricken. "My what?"

Van knew what she meant and nudged Eddie with an elbow. "She wants to know your last name."

Eddie's head snapped back to look at Madam Ryes. "Hardaway. My dad always joked that I always did everything the hard way, so my last name was very fitting. I'm adopted by the way. My dad wasn't my real dad."

She was taken aback. "Why did you tell me that?"

Eddie shrugged. "I didn't want you to think I was keeping anything from you." He pointed at the tiny bird on her shoulder. "Like Walter did."

She laughed. "Thank you Eddie. It is good to know I can trust you to be completely honest with me. Which is why I will ask you one more time. Are you sure there isn't something you're leaving out of your story, as exciting as it was, that I should know?"

"Uhh, I don't think so," Eddie stammered. He looked at Van who shrugged. Eddie transcribed the events flawlessly up to the point where they were forced into the pre-industrial version of a mobile home. There was nothing after that. There was nothing more to tell her. What could she possibly be expecting?

Her eyes shifted back and forth as she scrutinized them. Van could tell she didn't completely believe them. But Eddie didn't hold back and had told her everything. He felt the pit in his stomach grow larger and heavier. What was it she was looking for? Eddie told her the truth. If she wasn't willing to believe that, then there was nothing more they could do. They were doomed to be turned into birds. She twisted in her seat and Walter got the message. He flew back to his cage and landed on the perch inside.

Madam Ryes turned back to the boys. Eddie was visibly shaking and Van felt like his whole body was about to flip inside out. Was she casting some magical spell on them already? Van wrapped his arms around his stomach to keep his guts from exploding outward in case she turned him into a canary. But she didn't. Instead, she drew a deep breath and let it out slowly. "I was hoping you boys would be honest with me."

"We have been!" Eddie countered. "I told you everything!"

She clucked her tongue. "But you left out one crucial bit of information. Something more important than everything else."

Van felt the walls closing in on him. Eddie was rambling at the mouth. "I didn't leave anything out!"

"Why are you making me draw it out of you? I thought we trusted each other?"

Eddie was thinking faster. "We do trust—I trust you not to turn me into a bird for a stupid reason. Why don't you tell me what I forgot?"

"I'd rather you told me," she replied calmly as the room started turning ice cold.

"I don't know what you want to hear!" Eddie screamed as he jumped from the chair.

Madam Ryes didn't move a muscle but Eddie suddenly froze solid. Van's heart raced as Eddie whimpered through his immobile mouth. "What's happening to me?"

Madam Ryes stayed seated. "It's the enchantment of the negotiation table. If any party makes a move against someone seated on another side, the table freezes them."

"How long does it last?" Eddie said, unable to enunciate any of the words as saliva dripped from his open mouth.

"Until you calm down."

Eddie slowly wiggled a finger and then flexed his hands. In a few seconds he was able to move again and sat down, casting a wary sideways glance at Van.

Madam Ryes smiled. "Now, where were we?"

Van glared at her, but was cautious to not let it grow into anger or animosity. The table might take it the wrong way. "We told you the truth. But for some reason you don't believe us."

"I didn't say whether I believed you or not. I said you left something out. Something important."

"We didn't leave anything out. Everything happened exactly like Eddie said."

"Then when were you going to tell me?"

Eddie massaged and flexed his jaw as he answered her question with a question. "Tell you what?"

"Tell me something about your friend?"

Eddie looked at Van. "Like what?"

Her eyes narrowed again. "Something personal."

Eddie sighed. "Okay. Van enjoys quiet walks on the beach, sipping wine in front of a roaring fire, jazz punk fusion. What more do you want to know?"

She turned her steely gaze on Van. "Why won't you tell me?"

Van's face contorted as he struggled to understand her circular questioning. "Tell you what?"

"That you are a Spinner?"

Chapter 39

The door to the dungeons creaked open and two guards strode in. Calen kept to the shadows as he peeked around the edge of the cell door. The first one through the main door looked at the servant's cart and playfully hit the second guard, pointing at the cart with the telltale flower on it. He peered deeper into the dungeon and called out softly, as if unsure about disturbing his fellow guard. "Isaiah. Grunt once if we are interrupting anything?"

Calen relaxed a little. His chosen disguise was again working its magic. Calen did his best to lower his voice a couple of octaves, hoping to match the tonal quality he heard before he knocked Isaiah out cold. "Go away!" he said, adding a little heavy breathing to secure the illusion Isaiah was with a servant woman.

The man stood up taller and peered deeper into the dungeon. "Isaiah? That doesn't sound like you."

Uh oh, thought Calen. This was how everyone would remember him. Dressed like a servant woman sneaking into the dungeons to rendezvous with a male guard. It didn't help that he knocked Isaiah out cold. They would think he did it to have his way with a man who preferred the company of women.

The first guard started walking down the line of cells, slowly drawing out his sword as he headed for the last one Calen was in with an unconscious Isaiah; Calen's mind racing on how to save himself. "Isaiah? Are you sure you're okay?"

Calen ducked back into the cell and looked at Isaiah lying on his back on the ground. He sighed heavily and then struggled to pull Isaiah's pants down and bunched them up around his ankles. Thankfully, Isaiah wore underclothes, so he wasn't rudely exposed and Calen didn't have to touch anything untoward as he straddle him and began gyrating his hips with his back to the open cell door. He sensed more than saw the other guard at the cell door. Calen grunted as he spoke, masking the fact that he didn't sound at all like Isaiah. "I told you I'm, ah, ah, ah. I'm fine. Go away!"

Calen didn't dare look back, but smiled to himself when he heard the guard sheath his sword and back up quickly. Loud whispering continued until the door closed and the dungeon was silent except for the rustling of cloth against cloth as Calen kept moving around on top of Isaiah. As soon as he heard the key relock the door, Calen hoped off Isaiah, patting the man's chest with a hand. "Thanks. You were great."

Calen dashed to the cart and spun it around. He listened at the door until he could no longer hear the guards' voices laughing about what they thought they witnessed. Calen unlocked the door and pushed the cart out of the dungeon. He locked the door and headed back to his room, fuming. There was still the sleeping woman in his bed to deal with. And he never accomplished what he set out to do. He was back to square one. He still needed to find out where the huntress was being kept and make sure she never talked.

Ever.

Chapter 40

Van ears filled with the rushing of blood. All he could hear was his heart pounding heavily. It sounded like he was underwater as Eddie stared at him in shock. Then a smile broke out across Eddie's face and he laughed. Hard. So hard, he could barely catch his breath. He looked back at Madam Ryes and hooked a thumb in Van's direction. "You— you think he's a Spinner? A magician? A wizard?" Eddie waggled his head and waved his hands in front of him while he joked, laying on a thick British accent. "Guess what, I'm friends with Harry Potter." That sent Eddie into another laughing fit until his face turned a bright red and he gasped unsuccessfully for air.

Van wasn't laughing. And when he looked across the table, he noted that Madam Ryes wasn't laughing either. Eddie was finally calming down and placed his forehead on the table's surface. "Whew!" he exclaimed as he raised his head to look at Madam Ryes. "Thanks. After all we've been through, I really needed that." He started up again and couldn't shake the giggles. Then he exploded again into fits of laughter.

Madam Ryes looked at him and shook her head, then she looked directly at Van. "I think it's time you and I spoke alone."

A harsh whistle from Madam Ryes brought Buff quickly into the wagon. He must have been standing just outside the door the whole time. She tilted her head in Eddie's direction and Buff half-lifted the still giggling Eddie out of the chair and carried him from the room. Despite closing the door after they left, Van could hear Eddie start up again until his laughter faded away as he was taken away. Van watched the door, wishing he'd been removed from the wagon along with Eddie. Once the interior of the cabin was finally silent Van swallowed dryly and turned to Madam Ryes. "What are you going to do to him?"

Madam Ryes regarded him amiably. There was no malice in her eyes and no edge to her voice as she spoke. "He will be fine. Let's talk about you."

Van gripped the edge of the table with white knuckles. There was no getting out of this conversation, as crazy as it sounded, so it was best to get it over with. "Okay. Why do you think I'm a Spinner?"

"Because of your father. He was one of the best; before he died."

Van frowned. How did she know his father was dead? None of this was making any sense. "My father was an insurance adjuster. He wasn't a Spinner. There's no such thing as Spinners where I come from."

It was her turn to laugh. "And just where do you think you come from?"

"Earth?" It sounded just as weird saying it out loud as thinking it in his head.

She laughed again. "What you call Earth is really Techrealm. The Spinner spawn are taken there after being born."

Van frowned. "Spinner spawn?"

Madam Ryes rolled her eyes. "Fine. All Spinner children are taken to Techrealm until they are of age. Then they are brought back to Midguard for training."

"Why would they do that?"

"It's the safest place for them while they are still too young to control their powers."

"Are you saying Earth—Techrealm is full of Spinners who don't know they are Spinners?"

Madam Reyes shook her head. "Let me try to make this simple to understand. Magic and technology are locked in a cosmic battle with each other. For some reason they cancel each other out. Magic was allowed to die out in Techrealm so that your industrial revolution could take place. Your world is able to plunge the depths of technology without interference. But in Magerealm, all technology was removed to test how far the human body could manipulate magic. Here, in Midguard, technology and magic live side by side, but they each suffer at the hands of the other. Magic can only become so strong and technology can only advance so far. As long as both are here, we are trapped between two worlds of perfection, with neither gaining a foothold over the other. We are the focal point of that balance. The Spinner children are taken to Techrealm to suppress their powers until they are ready." She canted her head and looked at him curiously. "But you weren't brought back, were you?"

Van understood only half of what she said. He recognized the words individually, but strung together they didn't make any sense. He shook his head in response to her question. He hoped he was giving her the right answer.

"Of course not," she continued. "The Maclean line is to be stripped of their status and all future generations forbidden from training. So the High Master of the Wizard's Order decreed after your father broke a cardinal rule and sacrificed himself to save Midguard."

The room spun again. She knew his last name. How did she know that? And what was she talking about? His father died at work from an unexpected heart attack. He wasn't an all-powerful wizard. There were no such things as wizards. There were also no such things as dragons, his brain reminded him, but he was almost eaten by one.

He looked up at Madam Ryes. The look in her eyes told him she believed everything she was saying was the gospel truth. But how could that be? He was a normal kid. He wasn't a wizard—a Spinner. That type of reveal was reserved for characters in a movie. This was real life, with real-life responsibilities. Trying to reassure himself of those real-world responsibilities he blurted out, "I'm supposed to be registering for college classes right now. I don't belong here."

She smiled. "That is true. But someone went to great lengths to get you here. They also made sure you met up with the one man who was the apprentice to your father."

Van's heart skipped a couple beats that time. "Halen?" he asked.

She nodded. "He was banished from The Order; his training invalidated when your father sacrificed himself. Someone wanted you two to meet. The question is who. And why?"

Van clung to the table to keep from falling over as the room continued to whirl. Why wouldn't the room just settle for a moment and let him think? "Halen knew my father?" he said quietly.

"Yes. He was Veren's apprentice." She suddenly locked her eyes onto his. "If he had never been banished, you would have been his apprentice."

Van's mind reeled and focused on something she said that didn't fit. "What did you call him?"

"Who?"

"What was the name you used for my father?"

"Veren."

That was it. That wasn't his father's name. She must think he is someone else. He pointed at her. "Hah! You do have me confused with someone else. My father's name wasn't Veren!"

She snapped her fingers. "Oh right. That was his taken name when he joined The Order. What was his normal name? His Techrealm name? Ah, yes. Paul. He went by the name Paul before he joined The Order. You see, trivia knowledge about The Order is something of a hobby of mine."

Van's triumphant smile faded. This was too much for him to take in all at once. "This is crazy. None of it is true. I'm a normal kid who lost his father when he was young and moved across the country to stay with his aunt. I got okay grades in school. I never really dated. I mean, I like the idea of girls, but actually talking to one is just plain terrifying. They're so judgy, and they pounce on the smallest detail you say and twist it. I was hoping that college might prove me wrong there. Maybe find a girl who wasn't trying to find every little fault with what I said. I'm just a normal guy. I'm not some boy wizard. Maybe Maclean is a common name like Smith or Jones?"

She laughed softly. "The Maclean family name is anything but common, Van. You come from a long line of Spinners. Great Spinners of legend I might add. I know what I am talking about."

"How do you know?"

She held up the piece of torn cloth and the circular stone with the hole. "I saw it with my own eyes." She held out both objects to Van. "Maybe it's time you saw it as well."

Van took the stone and cloth. This was all too surreal. She must be wrong. There was no way he possessed the ability to perform magic. Magic didn't exist except for the elaborately constructed illusions of professional "magicians" with television specials or those who worked the strip at Las Vegas. Then his mind swirled around everything that happened the past couple of days. Was magic real? Was it possible that there was some big family secret kept from him? Was his father's death caused by something more than natural causes? Did his father really break some magician's code? That would explain why they were forced to move the day after the funeral. That made a lot more sense than the company owned the house and they were forced to move once his father no longer "worked" for the company. No company would ever do something like that. But what about his mother? Why did his mother accept this and keep it from him? He would ask her about it when he got back home. If he got back home, he corrected himself with a shiver along his spine. It would make things simpler if he did have magical abilities. He might even figure out how to use them to get back home. There was only one way to find out. His hands trembled as he examined the innocuous items. He glanced up. "What do I do?"

"The stone has been enchanted to identify the family colors of magic. Look through it at the cloth."

He placed the cloth on the table and held up the stone to his eye and looked through it. A dark swirling haze that went from a bright electric violet to a dark, almost black, eggplant color surrounded the cloth.

Madam Ryes explained. "Every Spinner family line has a specific color of magic that courses through their body. That magic becomes imbued on the clothing they wear most often, like a cloak. That little remnant is definitely from your father's cloak. The seller explained it was the one he was wearing the day he died, or so I was told when I paid a king's ransom for it."

Van lowered the stone and looked at her as she stood up and crossed to the book shelves, selected an ancient looking tome, and returned to the table. "This journal has been passed down through our family from generation to generation. I have spent the better part of my life looking for the one mentioned in it."

She opened the cracked-leather-bound book and removed a piece of square cloth from the inside cover. It looked old and worn, but still more carefully preserved than the torn fragment on the table. "This belonged to my great-great-great-great-great-great—well, you get the picture. A very distant relative. She wrote, and I quote, the wearer of this cloak is the most powerful of all Spinners. Seek them out for every generation to protect the family from what is to come."

She closed the book and her forehead wrinkled as she looked at him. "Unfortunately, we never did locate anyone that matched the line of Spinners who wore this when it was part of a full cloak. That is until I bought that little piece there. But I was too late. The owner of that cloth was already dead. I obtained that small piece along with the story of the banishment of his entire family line."

She set the square cloth down next to the ripped fragment on the table. "Look at these two pieces side by side."

Van held up the stone and saw the identical swirling of purplish mists around both strips of cloth.

She let out a sigh. "It seemed my family would never find another Spinner cut from the same cloth, to turn an apt phrase. Now look at yourself in the mirror over there," she said as she pointed to the wide mirror mounted on the back wall.

Van looked up at his reflection through the stone and almost dropped it. The same purplish haze swirled like a living creature all around him. He took away the stone and gazed at his normal reflection in the mirror. He looked over at Madam Ryes. "What does this mean?"

She regarded him with a broad smile. "It means my search is over. I have found the one who matches the family magic of the cloth passed down to me from my foremothers. You, Van Maclean, are my ticket out of the badlands."

He brought the stone to his eye and peered through it at the miasma of magic swirling around him. Everything he knew about his father, about himself—about everything—was a lie.

Van lowered the circular rock. According to what he saw with his own eyes, he was coursing with magic. He looked at his reflection without the stone. He looked normal. It must be some kind of trick. The mirror was doing something to make it look like the purple haze swirled around him when he peered through the stone. He held his hand out and looked at it through the stone, not using the mirror.

The living smoke of undulating shades of purple rolled and swirled around his hand. He angled his head, looking at as much of himself as he could. Everywhere he looked, his body was surging with magic. The purple smoke was more prominent where his skin was exposed, so it wasn't a trick of the mirror. He pointed the stone at Madam Ryes and looked at her through the hole in the stone. There was no colored smoke surrounding her, but there was a white hot glow, almost painful to look at directly, radiating through her blouse. No idea what that meant. He lowered his hand with the stone and looked at her. "What does this mean?"

Madam Ryes held her hand out. He placed the stone in her hand and then she gathered up the fragments of cloth. "Most parents lie to their children in one way or another. I wouldn't dwell too much on it. The important thing is that you are here. Now. Just like the journal predicted. You have come to rescue my family from our rotten existence. Best of all, you brought someone along who can train you."

He looked at her in alarm. "Train me?"

She frowned through her smile. "Of course. You won't last two minutes in The Gauntlet if you can't spin the elements."

Chapter 41

Calen made it to his room and pushed the cart in just as the sun rose. It took him longer to get back than he anticipated. He completely forgot about the repairs being made to the south wing of the castle. The first time he passed through, it was too early for people to be awake so he was able to navigate the cart around the piles of stacked bricks and pre-cut wooden beams. On his journey back, however, it was teeming with workers preparing to continue their tasks. He didn't want to risk any too-close glances at his face and eventually found another way through the castle. It took longer, but he finally made it back to relative safety.

He closed his door quietly and leaned his back against it, breathing a huge sigh of relief. He glanced up at a faint sound of surprise and his heart stopped as he looked right into the eyes of the woman sitting up in bed staring back at him. Her eyebrows were stitched together in confusion. "Are those my clothes?" she said as she gawked at him in disbelief.

He pushed off the door, pulled off the scarf, and slipped out of her clothes. As he headed toward her he pasted on his most disarming smile. "Good, you're awake. I thought you might have drunk a little too much."

She looked at him bleary-eyed. "Why were you wearing my skirt?"

He tossed the clothes on the floor at the foot of the bed and sat down on the edge. "I wasn't wearing them."

Her eyebrows knitted further. "But I just saw you—"

He patted her shoulder. "You're seeing things, child. Why would I wear women's clothing? It's a ridiculous notion and not one worthy of my station in life." He picked up the empty wine bottle, regarded it with a chuckle, and then leaned in toward her while smiling warmly. "Isn't it entirely possible you are disoriented from drinking this much alcohol?"

She looked at the bottle, and then at the others strewn about the room. She looked at the bed, saw that it was thoroughly disheveled and then placed a hand on her forehead. His smile widened. The headache was setting in.

"Maybe you're right," she replied.

He placed his hands on her shoulders, slowly lowering her back into bed. "Of course I'm right. You go ahead and sleep it off. I have matters of The Order to attend to. You can let yourself out?"

She nodded, still confused about what happened.

He smiled again. "Good. Be sure to lock the door when you leave." He tucked her in and kissed her tenderly on the forehead. "Thanks. You were great."

He stood up and dressed quickly in his normal, and expected, Spinner attire. As he was crossing the room to go, he walked over to the cart and removed a small item he stored there earlier. He looked back to ensure the girl was laying down and not watching him. Once he was certain, he also removed the other few things he stocked in the cart for his trip to the dungeon and hid them in a drawer nearby for later. He then strode out of his room without looking back. He closed the door behind him and leaned on it, breathing a second sigh of relief.

He mentally patted himself on the back. He handled that beautifully. One crisis averted. One still left to deal with. He looked down at the tiny needle housed inside a small glass vial still in his hand. All it would take was one tiny prick and he would never need fear the huntress again.

Before he could do that he needed to determine where she was being held. And there was only one person who knew for certain where that was. But was he willing to give that information to Calen? There was only one way to find out.

Chapter 42

Van stared bug-eyed at Madam Ryes. "The what?"

"The Gauntlet," she repeated. "You, my boy, are going to make me rich beyond my wildest dreams."

"What is The Gauntlet? Some kind of contest?"

"The Gauntlet is a competition between two Spinners. The element you can spin will be your weapon. The two Spinners battle until one of them is victorious."

Van's heart caught in his throat. He swallowed it down so he could talk. "And the other one is dead?" he squeaked.

She laughed. "Of course not. It's a technical competition. Nobody fights to the death anymore. I don't care what you've heard about the inhabitants of the badlands. We're not barbarians. But we do enjoy a good fight. We love it so much, we're willing to pay to see a great one." She looked at him with a twinkle in her eye. "But better than that, people are willing to pay more to be entertained. With your pedigree, and a real Spinner of The Order to train you, we're going to give them a show they will never forget."

He was still trying to come to grips with learning that he might have the ability to perform magic. If that's what the swirling purple cloud around his body really meant. But he'd never done anything magical before. He still didn't know if he was capable now and here she was already talking about entering him into Spinner tournaments? Things were moving way too fast.

He needed time to think. He needed time to figure out what all this meant. He didn't want to be rushed into a tournament he would definitely lose without having any idea how to perform magic. Maybe he could bluff her out of her plan? He took in a deep breath to gather his courage. She seemed to respond to power. Maybe he could demand his release. "You can't enter me in a tournament without my permission. I don't belong to you! I demand you let Eddie and Halen go."

She adopted a bemused expression. "And if I don't meet your demands, you'll do what, exactly?"

Van glanced back and forth, his mouth opening and closing without uttering a sound.

Madam Ryes chuckled. "That's what I thought." She held her hands up in front of her. "Look. I'm not interested in keeping more mouths around to feed than are necessary. But let me warn you, the badlands is not a place to be without friends. You have landed yourself in a dangerous place, my boy. However, you and Eddie are free to go."

Van knew she was right. They wouldn't survive without friends.

"What about Halen?"

She shook her head. "He stays with me."

She was determined to only let Eddie and himself go. Maybe if he pushed the right button she would let Halen go as well. He decided to try the tough act one more time. "I'm not leaving without him," he said, trying to sound strong without being overtly threatening.

She laughed in response, a brief snort emanating from deep within her throat. "Then I guess you are staying. He's in no condition to travel. We have stitched up his wound, but he is under my care for a few days. That is final."

Van realized he was trapped, but he didn't want to look like a loser in front of Madam Ryes. He jutted his chin out. "Fine. Eddie and I will stay until Halen is fit to leave with us."

She smiled. "Since you made the choice to stay, you may do so under two conditions."

Van closed his eyes and lowered his head. He knew he was stuck and he knew what she wanted. "That I participate in this Gauntlet thing?"

She laughed again. "Good boy. I knew you would do the right thing."

"And what is the second condition?"

"Stay away from the green wagon, the one without any windows."

"Okay," Van said hesitantly. "What's in the green wagon?"

She narrowed her eyes. "Promise me you will stay away from that wagon."

"Okay. We will not go near the green wagon."

She smiled again and her face brightened. "Then I accept your proposal. There is the small matter of payment for lodging and meals, though."

Van frowned. "I don't have any money."

"I would never accept money from you. I know the tricks Spinners use to secure real gold coins. No, you will pitch in where needed to pay for a space in my caravan. If you learn nothing else from your time in Midguard, remember this. There are no free rides in the badlands."

Chapter 43

After she sent Van away to find Eddie and tell him the good news that there were two more hands to help with the duties of running a successful caravan, Madam Ryes took a slip of paper and wrote a note on it in code. It was a short letter to her sister in the Outskirts, the last bastion of civilization before the badlands claimed the territory between the West Kingdom and the more fertile lands on the other side of the Grand East River.

She rolled the tiny paper into a miniature cylinder and whistled. Walter flew from his cage and landed on her outstretched finger. She tucked the message into the tiny holder permanently mounted to his foot.

"Take this to Kaylie."

Walter tweeted his acknowledgment and shot out the open window and took to the skies. She watched him until he became a tiny yellow speck and then disappeared entirely in the distance.

The letter he carried would ensure the future of the caravan for generations to come. The moment she realized Van was the missing Maclean heir, she hastily formed a plan that would make her wealthier beyond her wildest dreams. And her dreams could get pretty wild, she mused.

She was as honest with Van as she dared. The certainty of his lineage was all true. And when she first looked through the stone at him, she nearly wept from excitement at the possibilities. But she maintained her composure and kept her emotions in check. Her generation would be the first in several hundred years to have a Spinner at their disposal.

This stroke of luck was beyond her craziest imaginings. After hearing of Veren's death, she resigned herself to never finding anyone of the Maclean line in her lifetime, or any lifetime after. Not after securing the strip of cloth at great personal cost and hearing about the family banishment decree. She looked at the square of cloth that still held the magical stain of the Maclean who previously occupied the cloak it was cut from.

She held it close to her heart, the only part of her that still held a trace of Maclean blood in her body. Her family became diluted throughout the generations, but the man who formed this caravan was a full blood Maclean. The people and the wagons were replaced many times over throughout the years, but deep down at its roots it was still the Maclean Caravan that set out from Devil's Claw, a jutting finger of land referred to by that unfortunate name on the authoritative maps of Midguard, a hundred years before. The Maclean name used to mean something to some people. It certainly meant something to Madam Ryes.

She held the round stone to her eye and gazed at herself in the mirror. There was not even a hint of the power that coursed so strongly through Van's blood. Her blood was so far removed from his that she was literally a relative stranger. That one simple fact made her decision easy. She wanted to tell Van that they were distant, distant cousins. But then he would expect more from her than she was willing to give. A weak leader was a dead leader. And no leader meant the caravan would disband and the true Maclean line would end with it. Madam Ryes was not about to let that happen, even if they were known now only as the Ryes family by everyone they came in contact with. They survived this long by hiding their true family name.

He was wrong when he claimed he was not her property. He belonged to everyone who carried the Maclean bloodline, no matter how faint. His obligation far exceeded his personal wants and desires.

In her mind, Van returned home—to his true home—to fulfill his destiny. To get the Maclean's out of the badlands forever. It would be his greatest accomplishment. Even if he never lived to see it realized.

She looked around the empty room and stood, closing the shutters on the windows and plunging the interior of the wagon into complete darkness. She turned to face the center of the room by instinct since she couldn't see into the gloom. She spoke softly. "Get me what I want and I will consider your debt paid in full."

After a moment, the darkness responded. "It will be done."

Chapter 44

Talia stopped by the side of the road to give her horse a drink of water from her leather water canteen. Her two hunting dogs, Brutus and Davon, sat down and waited for their turn at the leather bag. She rode slowly most of the morning to keep from kicking up the fine dust along the road through the badlands. The last thing she needed, traveling all by herself, was to alert bandits that she was coming with enough time for them to form an ambush.

She set out early from the Outskirts after spending the night in one of the many rooms for let. It was a shorter night than most, but it was better than falling asleep in the saddle or sleeping on the ground where rattlesnakes and scorpions rummaged about for hapless victims.

She watered the dogs and then helped herself to enough to stave off the sensation of dehydration. Under the blazing sun of the badlands, it was hotter here than anywhere else in the world. Maybe not the most entirely accurate statement, but she was here and not anywhere else.

She patted the side of the horse's neck. "You about ready to keep going, fella?"

He tossed his head with a whinny. She laughed and hopped up onto the saddle, grabbing the reins in one hand and shifting her weight to be more comfortable on the seat that was designed for someone twice her size. She was about to kick the horse back into a slow trot when the dogs started acting odd.

Their ears perked up and they whined, hopping back and forth impatiently from one front foot to the other. "What is it?" Talia asked.

She squinted against the blinding sun to look in the direction they were watching intently. She slipped her spyglass from the pack on the saddle and pulled it to its full length. Peering through it, she couldn't see anything but bright blue sky.

She looked down at the dogs. "I don't see anything."

The dogs were adamant that something was out there as they whined louder and became more agitated with each passing second. Whatever it was, it must be getting closer.

She gauged the angle the dogs were focusing their attention and squinted one eye while gazing through the spyglass. She finally spotted something yellow against the clear sky. And it was coming this way.

She watched, keeping the scope centered on the pinpoint object until it resolved into a small bird. She lowered the spyglass and shook her head at the dogs. "It's just a bird," she said and packed away the spyglass.

But before she could get them moving again, the dogs grew far more excited than they should over a stupid little bird. Then she remembered this breed was specially attuned to perceiving magic at great distances. It made sense. Just about every piece of equipment the hunters filled their wagon with was designed for hunting magical and enchanted creatures.

She looked at the dogs again. They were still focused on the bird flying toward them high in the sky. But instead of the agitated dance they exhibited moments earlier, they were both stock still as they tracked the bird through the open sky.

Then something tickled the back of Talia's memory. A recollection of a time long past and a pain deeply buried. Talia's head snapped back up to the oncoming creature. Could it be? She suppressed the urge to let hope swell in her over what could be nothing. She gave up actively searching for him long ago. After years of looking in vain, she knew her only hope would be to stumble upon him one day in the distant future. The years went by and it cost a lot of money to keep the grim reaper at bay. She eventually turned to hunting as a profession to pay for more time to randomly stumble upon him.

She admonished herself with a well-placed curse. What were the odds that he would appear the moment she controlled the means to snare him? It was ridiculous. She looked for him everywhere. But she searched for so long, it was entirely possible he was already dead of old age and she was simply going through the motions out of a futility.

She knew it was unrealistic and delusional, but she never allowed Father Time to take her and couldn't willingly give up the promise she would one day obtain her deepest desire. She simply wasn't a quitter. She glanced at the arsenal of enchanted weapons strapped around her horse. If she planned to see if this enchanted bird might be her long lost one true love, she'd better get ready.

She hopped off the horse and looked seriously at the equipment. The bird was coming in fast and she needed something with range. She spotted the net gun. It was the only thing she owned that could remotely capture a bird in flight. But, at the speed it was going, it was a little risky. Hopefully, if she somehow managed to catch it, the bird's small size and the net's soft weaving would cushion the little bird's fall. Then she would just have to keep the bird until she could figure out how to determine if this bird was indeed who she was looking for. She slid the net gun from its holster beside the saddle. She checked that it was fully charged and the safety was disengaged. Then she glanced at her dogs. Their heads were dropping slowly. She knew that meant this bird was performing the normal flight-pattern maneuver for a long-distance flight. Most birds would expend a lot of energy to climb quickly high into the sky and then cover greater distance while they glided slowly back down to the ground. She sighted down the barrel at the same area her dogs watched vigilantly.

It took a few seconds for the yellow speck to resolve in her vision. She tracked the bird as it flew closer and closer, now only ten feet off the ground. She kept the net gun trained on it as it flew overhead and, once it passed her, she held her breath to steady her aim and squeezed the trigger.

The net flew from the gun, spreading out in a multi-pointed star to engulf the bird from behind. She didn't shoot the bird on approach or else it would see the net flying toward it and swoop to one side, successfully avoiding capture. This way, the net enclosed around the bird before it even noticed something was surrounding it.

The net wrapped around the bird. Talia smiled triumphantly, then her smile turned into a look of utter shock as the trapped falling bird instantly expanded in size, changing color from a bright yellow to a dull pink, and plummeted to the ground with a baritone scream that sounded all too human. Whatever the bird turned into hit hard and skipped along the ground as it bounced and rolled for a dozen feet before coming to a sickeningly crunching stop in a cloud of dust.

Talia was frozen in place. What just happened? The bird suddenly change into something else. Something big. Something that was probably dead from the sound of that last bounce. She focused on her racing heart, reminding herself through conscious logical arguments that this wasn't her fault. She didn't know the combination of the net and bird would somehow make the bird change. She dropped the spent net gun and ran forward to the spot where her quarry hit the dirt. The dogs gathered around it and settled down, sitting idly nearby. They no longer focused on what was under the net and took to grooming themselves while they waited for their master.

She got closer and slowed down. She looked at the dust-covered figure under the net and her hands shot up to cover her mouth and nose in horror. It was a man. A naked man at that. He was lying on his side with his back to her. His arms and legs were bent at awkward, unnatural angles. And he wasn't moving.

She'd made a real mess of this, even unwittingly. She felt terrible looking at his battered and broken body. Her body shuddered at the thought of the amount of pain he would be in if he was still alive. She didn't want to leave him broken and bleeding in pain in the middle of the desert if he somehow lived after falling several feet through the air and tumbling end over end across the desert floor. Was he still alive? How could he be?

She walked slowly around to the other side to get a look at his face. She crouched down, but was still unable to get a proper look. He was lying in a fetal position and a rubbery arm flopped over his face, blocking her view. She raised a trembling foot and pushed very gently on his shoulder with her toe. The man flopped onto his back, pulling the head along with it on a rubbery, broken neck. She let out an audible gasp, feeling as though she was sucker punched in the stomach while she gazed at a face she hadn't seen in over a hundred years.

All thought process froze. It was too much for her brain to comprehend. Her mouth worked but emitted no sound as she stared through blurry tears at her hearts deepest desire, the love of her life, broken and bleeding in the settling dust. The tears came faster and she found it difficult to see his face clearly. She scanned his whole body. It was bruised and broken from head to toe and covered with dirt and drying blood. He hit the ground naked and unprotected and still wasn't moving. It didn't look like he was even breathing. There was no way he could be alive with his neck bent at that angle. She finally found her one true love, after more than a lifetime of searching, and then unwittingly killed him.

Magic could do many things, but there was a line drawn in the sand with death clearly on one side of it. Anyone who crossed over was never coming back.

She dropped to her knees and looked at his battered body. She finally found her voice. "Walter," she whispered, tears filling in what was left of her obscured vision.

Talia looked up at the heavens, directing her attention to the gods who gazed down on her pathetic little existence with indifference. "What!" Her screams echoed across the surrounding desert. "What have I ever done to you? Why! Why!"

Then she hunched over, covering her lover's still form with her own and let a hundred years of pent up guilt flood out and over his mangled and lifeless body.

Chapter 45

Calen knocked on the door to the High Master's room. "Come," came the muffled reply. He pushed open the door and stepped for a second time into the room that, until two days ago, he never thought he would ever see in his lifetime.

Falen sat at a wide desk filled with scrolls and leather-bound books. He held a quill hovering over a piece of parchment, having paused mid-sentence. He smiled, but couldn't mask the quizzical look in his eyes. "Calen? What are you doing here?"

Calen closed the door, keeping his back to Falen long enough to calm the nerves that sent his hands trembling again. He turned around and Falen was still paused, his eyebrows furrowed to meet just over the bridge of his nose. "Have you changed your mind about sampling Dragon's Breath?"

Calen pasted on his sincerest smile and took a step forward. "I was hoping to question the hunters."

Falen set down the quill, clearly taken aback by Calen's request. "You?"

Calen took another hesitant step forward. "I was the one who requested Halen bring the boy here. I know you said I shouldn't feel—guilty."

"And you shouldn't," Falen confirmed.

Calen lowered his head and took a deep breath to regain his confidence. He raised his head and fixed Falen with a hard stare. "I want a few minutes with the hunters. Alone."

Falen held his gaze. "I'm afraid that's not possible."

Calen took another step forward and was now at the front edge of the massive desk. "I deserve to know why they did it. Why they—killed him."

"And we will get that information as soon as they are capable of speaking coherently. They took Boar's Blood and are still quite unreachable."

"I want to see them."

Falen frowned, his eyes growing darker. "Why?"

Calen took a momentary pause. Falen was getting suspicious. He needed a compelling reason that sounded absolutely sincere. And then it came to him. "Halen and I—what we had was—a special friendship. I was the only one in The Order willing to speak with him. He may have imprinted on one of the hunters a final message to me because of our—history. Since I was the one who recommended him for what would be his—final mission. I have to check if there is residue of such a message on the hunter who killed him."

Falen regarded him warily. "We are not even sure which one killed him."

Calen leaned on the table, placing his palms face down and took the chance that it would be interpreted as not thinking straight due to his grief over Halen's death. "Let me see them. I will know instantly if one of them carries such a message for me."

Falen tapped a finger against his pursed lips and regarded him silently.

Calen shifted his stance to seem insistent yet vulnerable, needing closure. "Please, High Master. Give me the peace I deserve. The peace Halen deserves if he left such a message for me."

Falen sat back. "I inspected the hunters personally upon their arrival. Even a Skrahyer examined them. We saw no residue of a message from Halen."

"If it was left specifically for me I would be the only one capable of seeing it." Calen carefully bowed his head and masterfully lowered his voice to an almost whisper as he said "Let me try. I owe him that much."

Calen remained for a short while with his head bowed, then he slowly raised his eyes to meet Falen's. They stared at each other for a long time before Falen finally let out a soft sigh. "I understand you feel somewhat responsible for the death of Halen."

Calen nearly smiled at his triumph but checked himself as he grabbed the thread being offered. "Yes. I need to know if a part of Halen survived his body's demise. I could never forgive myself if I didn't at least look for it."

Falen nodded. "Very well. I guess it can't hurt for you to look upon them. They won't even know you are there. The chemists say they will be like that for another day. And then we have to deal with the withdrawals. But at least they can answer by then, even if it is difficult to get them to focus on the question."

Calen wasn't listening to what Falen said. All he focused on was getting the chance to be near enough to the hunters to use the poisoned needle hiding in his pocket. "Can I see them now? Before the magic fades any further?"

Falen glanced at the first morning light spilling in through the window. "Now?"

"I haven't slept a wink, but I didn't want to disturb you too early for my request."

Falen waved to the open books and unspooled scrolls around him. "The life of a High Master is one of constant study. I dare say, I may be awake before you most mornings."

Calen lowered his head, unsure if he misspoke. He didn't want to lose his chance to see the hunters. "Of course, High Master. I meant no disrespect."

He kept his eyes cast down, his mind racing as he worried he may have insulted the High Master and ruined his opportunity. He heard rustling and looked up to see Falen scribbling on a blank sheet of parchment with the quill. Falen finished and blew on the paper, drying the ink fully, before he held it out to Calen. "They are being kept in the lower section of the tower. Show this to the captain of the guard. It should give you the few minutes you require."

Calen took the paper and bowed again. "Thank you, High Master." He spun on his heels and already had a grip the door handle when Falen called out to him, stopping him in his tracks.

"Do you really think Halen would have imprinted a message to you on his killer?"

Calen turned back toward Falen. "That's what I intend to find out."

Chapter 46

Talia lay on Walter's body and ignored the burning sun. She'd cried for what seemed like hours until she no longer retained enough liquid left in her body to produce tears. Her dogs shuffled back and forth in the burning sand, fighting each other for the tiny oasis created by the shadow of the horse that stood patiently nearby.

The heat of the lengthening day took most of the fight out of them, and their battle reduced to half-hearted shoving of each other into the blistering sun until the heat became unbearable and the one most out of the horse's shadow pushed back with greater force.

Talia wanted to lay there until she expired from dehydration now that her reason for living lay dead under her.

Davon, decidedly the less aggressive of the two dogs, lost access to the shade more often and came over to lick her face. His tongue was dry and scraped across her cheek like a patch of rough tree bark. She raised a weak hand and stroked the back of his neck. "I'm sorry to keep you out here like this. Maybe you were better off with the hunters."

"I'd stay with you no matter what," Davon replied, barely above a whisper.

That was too strange to be ignored, even in her current state. Talia raised her head and looked at Davon, her forehead wrinkled in confusion. "Did you say something?" Davon panted, happy to be getting attention from his master.

Despite the sorrow that filled her heart at what she lost after all this time, Talia chuckled softly at the absurdity of her initial thought. "Of course you didn't. I've been out in the sun too long and now I'm hearing things. I'm also talking to a dog as if he were a person."

Then she heard the voice again.

"Your knee is digging into my back."

This time, she was certain Davon wasn't talking to her.

The voice originated from under her.

Walter!

She quickly scrambled up and looked down at the dust-caked man lying in a crumpled heap. Despite his neck bent at an odd angle, he was looking up at her with sparking clear eyes. "Talia?"

She laughed and cried at the same time. "Walter!"

"I thought I recognized your voice," he said and smiled weakly for the briefest of moments before his face scrunched up in pain. "Why can't I move my arms?"

She gazed into his face, his wonderful face. She needed to touch him with her fingers. To know if he was really there. She reached between the cords of the net to stroke his face. Her face shifted to a look of horror as her hand aged instantly, at once turning into the gnarled fingers of an old woman. But it didn't stop there. It continued progressing to the dried skin of the dead before it flaked and blew away in the dry breeze, leaving only a desiccated skeleton hand with which to touch Walter.

She yanked it out in terror and confusion and looked at her hand which was instantly restored to normal. Well, as normal as the magic that kept her body in its youthful state would allow.

He'd changed from canary to man as soon as the net surrounded him. Her fingers aged as soon as they were past the boundary of the netting.

Of course! It was obvious now that she thought of it. The net gun was enchanted to negate magic and he was in human form while inside the net and she in her youthful form outside of it.

She sat back and looked at how broken his body became when he plunged unexpectedly to the ground. He was like this because of her.

"You look older," he said. Walter was always one to tell it like it was. That was what she loved most about him. He never sugar coated anything. She gazed at him and marveled how the magic that turned him into a canary also stopped the clock on his aging. She begrudgingly thanked whoever cast the spell.

"And you look exactly the same," she said, her eyes burning because they couldn't produce any more tears.

"Are you okay, my love?" he asked. She laughed again. He always showed more concern for her than himself. Even now when the slightest movement of his head could permanently end is life. Walter gritted his teeth in pain. "I can't move my head."

She wanted to touch him, but the net negated the magic that kept her alive just like it negated the magic that kept him a canary. Then she flashed on an idea and it started her heart racing with hope. If magic kept him alive, and also kept him young, could it save his life? There was only one way to find out.

She quickly lay flat on the ground, tilting her head to be in line with his, and peered deeply into his eyes. "I'm going to try something to help you," she said softly. "Do you trust me?"

He looked at her with his shining eyes and smiled. "Always".

Her face scrunched up as she fought back the emotions that urged her eyes to produce more tears than humanly possible. She forced a smile to give him courage. Then she stood up and carefully pulled at the net. She worked the loops off, careful not to let her hands slip inside, and slowly removed it from his broken body.

As soon as the last loop was off, Walter let out a blood curdling scream. His body jerked violently, accompanied by gut-wrenching, joint-snapping, bone-breaking sounds.

Talia watched in frozen horror wondering what she'd done. Did she just make things worse? Had she squandered the last remaining moments with him on a foolish bid for more time? She reacted and reached for him. He suddenly shrunk down to a tiny yellow bird and hopped upright onto his feet. He stretched his wings and flapped them. Then he twisted his head back and forth.

He looked up at Talia and tweeted excitedly, hopping back and forth on his tiny feet. He looked around and saw the net sitting on the ground. He hopped over to it and looked up at her expectantly.

She finally got her mind to register that he wasn't dead and her gamble might have paid off. She blinked twice at him in confusion and then the slow realization of what he wanted washed over her. They could always communicate without a word and this came in handy now that he was a bird. But just to make sure she received the right message she asked, "You want me to cover you with the net?"

He tweeted again and hopped back and forth. She lifted the net and tossed it over him. He hunched down as the net flew over him. Within moments, he was human again. He stood up tall and in full health.

Talia once again grudgingly thanked the magic that kept him a bird but also kept his human body in full health and with the youthful vigor she remembered.

They were finally together.

After all this time.

She longed for his touch but knew going under the net would destroy her, so she decided to reconnect with him on a deeper level until they could find a solution to their inability to connect physically.

He smiled, ignoring the fact that he wore no clothes to speak of. "Hello, my love."

"I've missed you—" she started, the tears returning as if her body kept some in reserve for this very moment.

He struggled over to her, the net making it difficult to walk. "And now we are back together."

He held his arms wide and she decided not to worry about the danger as she rushed in to be enveloped by their comforting embrace. The net made it challenging for them to properly embrace, but they did the best they could, being sure not to cross through the net. After a short while, she felt him shift his weight. "How long has it been?"

"A hundred and twelve years," she replied.

After another long pause, he released her and she took a step back. He looked her up and down. "Magic?"

She nodded. "I would have died fifty years ago as an old woman…" She couldn't finish because she felt her heart breaking further apart with each word.

He lifted up the net in his hands. "I saw what happened when you reached into the net. Out there, you are young, but I am a bird. In here I am a man. But you are dead. The same magic that has kept us alive all these years now keeps us apart." He smiled at her. "At least we're not as far apart as we were yesterday."

That brought a smile to her face despite the frustration at yet another thing keeping her from truly being with him. She took a step forward and her face returned to one of strength and resolve, the weakness and sadness all but gone. "I'll figure out how to fix this."

"No, you won't," he replied.

Her frown made him smile unexpectedly and laugh lightly as he gazed lovingly into her eyes. "We will fix this together. I am never leaving your side again!" He glanced down at his naked body. "Well, more like your shoulder until we can fix this magic problem and actually stay alive without it."

"Whatever," she retorted, "I just want to have sex again!"

They both laughed and, just like that, the years apart faded away.

Chapter 47

Calen held the access order from Falen gripped tightly in his hand and strode to the lower chambers of the tower in the southern section of the castle. The southern tower was the first section of the castle built. It was the tallest of all the spires as it was designed to keep watch in all directions while the castle was being constructed.

The Central Valley to the East, while technically under the West Kingdom's rule, was a hotbed of illegal activity and roving bandits, many of whom were wanted on multiple continents and cared nothing for the laws decreed by the leaders of the Western Kingdom. It wasn't that the West Kingdom couldn't keep control over its borders, but the every-seven-year battles that raged when the gate to Magerealm opened was an incredible strain on every available resource just to prepare for the next fight. Thus, the Central Valley was not watched as closely as it should be.

The southern tower was the first structure built to keep watch for any potential invaders from the wild Central Valley during construction of the castle. Thankfully, nothing ever happened, but it was always wise to be careful with anarchy living so close to the seat of government for the West Kingdom.

Calen walked up to the sleeping guard perched on a chair, tilted up on two legs, its back resting against the wall. Without a word, Calen kicked one of the chair legs, sending the guard and the chair both crashing to the floor. The guard scrambled to his feet and held his tongue when he saw who disturbed his nap. He snapped to attention and saluted, a mixture of confusion and grog-induced sleep in his eyes.

Calen held out the signed order that gave him unrestricted access to the prisoners the supposed "guard" was keeping watch over. The guard studied the paper and then pulled a ring of keys from around his belt. He unlocked the door and stepped to the side to let Calen in before him. Calen took a step into the room and glanced around. The room was empty except for a spiral iron staircase that led up through the middle of the room. He spun around and glared at the guard. "Where are the prisoners?"

The guard pointed up at the ceiling. "Follow the staircase. They are at the top."

"I thought the cells were underground?"

The guard shook his head, still so groggy he nearly lost his balance with the simple act. "After someone escaped by digging a tunnel, those were filled in. The cells were moved higher to prevent any further attempts."

Calen looked at the wrought iron staircase and smiled to himself. This new development was perfect. These prisoners were about to escape, but he needed to get rid of the guard to make it look convincing. He glanced back at the guard. "When does the next shift come in?"

The guard glanced at a candle on a shelf. The flame burned slowly closer to the scratch gouged into the side of the wax. "My relief should be here at the next mark."

Calen glanced at the candle. Someone would be relieving the guard soon. But it was more than enough of a span to the next candle mark to execute his plan. He turned away from the guard and quietly slid out a dagger from among the folds of his cloak. The dagger was one he procured from a trader who purchased it in the badlands, where most of the hunters took refuge from the authorities. When the investigation into the guard's death took place, they would have a hunter's dagger to give them a false clue to pursue, taking the authorities hundreds of miles away from the person who actually committed the murder.

Calen spun around and stabbed the guard in the heart, leaving the knife embedded in his chest. The guard looked into his eyes with confusion and clutched at the dagger hilt. Calen watched with a thrill as the life faded from the guard's eyes and he stumbled forward to collapse with a thud at Calen's feet.

Calen spun around and checked his clothing. He accomplished his brutal task without getting any blood on him. Very good, there would be nothing to lead this killing to him. He rolled the guard over and checked him for signs of life. When he found none, he pulled the signed order from the man's balled fist and stuck it back in his pocket. Then he grabbed the guard's set of keys and stood, heading for the stairs while purposely trailing bloody footprints in his wake.

As he pounded quickly up the stairs, the story of what happened formulated in his mind, his lips silently mimicking what he would say.

"I came to the chambers and found the guard dead. I heard a scream from above and ran up the stairs. But I was too late. Someone killed the hunters and then jumped from the window into the moat. I got to the window just as someone was swimming away. If we send the dogs now, maybe we can find the killer before the trail grows cold."

He hit the top stair, the wrought iron still thrumming from his drumbeat footsteps, and headed for the only door on the other side of the small antechamber. He inspected the ring of keys and found the one most worn. This would be the front door. He then found the next one that looked most used and tried it in the lock. The lock clicked and he swung the door open.

He stepped through the threshold and a blur of something that looked like a striking snake flew into view from the side and slammed into his face. Pain radiated from his nose all the way to the nape of his neck. He stumbled back out the doorway, his vision seriously impaired. A dark shape stumbled into view, and as his vision returned, the shape resolved into a woman with murderous intent in her eyes. She raised a rope with a giant knot in the end in her hands. That was the "snake" that struck his face. She whirled it over her head like a flail, ready to finish what she started.

Calen's eyes focused on the huntress. He possessed just enough sense to spin his hands in the practiced motions taught to him by his master. At his expert level, they were second nature. He was a Wind Spinner, and when he spun the elements, he commanded the very air around him.

A great tempest rose up out of nowhere and circled around him and the huntress. He shoved his hands at her and the cyclone did the rest. A gale force pushed her back into the room, toppling her end over end, and sending the rope flying from her grasp.

Calen stopped spinning his hands and the indoor hurricane instantly died out. He mistakenly pressed his fingers against his injured nose and pain temporarily blinded him once again. He took his hand away and blinked several times. When his vision cleared he looked at his fingers. They were covered in blood. His blood.

Her skills as a hunter and warrior were legendary. She recovered from the effects of the Boars Blood sooner than her partner, who still looked comatose, and now she was getting ready for a counterattack after being tossed across the room.

Calen spun his hands again, forming a miniature tornado around her before she could get back up and lifted her off the floor. He held her in place and walked up to the edge of the swirling storm. "You are resourceful. I will grant you that."

Her arms and legs flailed as she tried to maintain her balance while being held aloft. "Where are we? Why are you keeping us here?"

"I wanted to thank you personally for the service you provided. It is time to collect your payment."

"What are you talking about? I've never worked for you."

He laughed. "Of course you have, Talia. I'm the one who hired you."

"Talia? Who's Talia? My name's Bailee. I haven't taken a job in over a fortnight. You have me confused with someone else. You have the wrong people. Let us go!"

He held one hand palm side up to maintain the magic as he produced the needle from a pocket with the other. "I'm sorry I have to do this, Talia, but this is bigger than the both of us."

"Stop calling me Talia! My name is Bailee!"

He walked over to the hunter lying on the mattress that was on the floor instead of inside the timber frame of the bed. That's where she got her weapon. She'd fashioned the support latticework of rope from under the mattress into an improvised flail.

He bent down and held the needle above the sleeping giant of a man.

"What are you doing? Stop! Don't hurt him!" the huntress screamed.

He wasn't going to be deceived by Talia pretending to be someone else. It was the oldest trick in the book. He pricked the man in the shoulder and then stood up. The man started convulsing violently for a few seconds and then his eyes opened wide and the light extinguished from them an instant before the pupils clouded over.

"Nooo!" the huntress screamed.

Calen faced the swirling tornado with his captive floating within it.

His face throbbed and his nose still stung. She took the items at hand and fashioned a devastating weapon in short order. That was how she was able to kill Halen. If Calen hadn't practiced constantly, he would already have been dead and she could have escaped. With the guard already taken care of, the way out was clear.

He flipped his hand so his palm was facing the floor. The tornado vanished and the huntress fell from her hovering position in space. She hit the floor and sprawled out. Calen was on her in a split second. He pressed his knee into her back and held her down with all his weight.

She struggled against him. "What did you do?! Why did you kill him?!"

He bent forward so his lips were mere inches from her ears. "Don't worry. It is painful. But it will be over very quickly."

She struggled but couldn't escape before he stabbed the needle into the flesh of her shoulder. She screamed and then convulsed, blood spewing from her mouth as she bit down hard on her tongue.

And then she fell silent and still.

It was over.

The loose ends were all tied up neatly in a bow.

"Hello!" a voice called up from below.

Calen glanced around the room and then grabbed the rope. "Help!" he screamed and then swung the rope, shattering the window and sending the rope reeling out through the new opening. He dropped to the floor, balled his fist, and punched himself in the face. Not too hard, but not gently either. Stars filled his vision, but the desired affect worked. Blood gushed from his already broken nose and he was still struggling to stand when a guard rushed into the room, sword drawn.

Calen pointed to the shattered window with the strand of thick rope hanging over the windowsill.

"He went that way!"

The guard rushed over and peered out the window. He grabbed the rope and pulled it back up until he retrieved the blood-covered knot at the end. He inspected it and rushed back, reaching a hand down to help Calen stand. Calen slapped it away as he tried to get up on his own, thought better of it when the room started spinning, and settled into a seated position against the wall. "Don't worry about me. Check the prisoners!"

The guard was good at taking orders and felt for a pulse on both bodies. Calen already knew he would find none but looked at him expectantly. The guard shook his head sadly.

Calen slapped his hand on the floor, leaving a bloodstained hand print on the grey stone. "Dammit! Contact the outer guards! Don't let the killer escape! Look for someone with blood on their clothing." He held up his hands covered in a rosy sheen of liquid. "My blood."

The guard rushed for the stairwell. Calen called after him. "And get me a healer!"

"Yes, sir!" the guard shot back and disappeared down the stairs.

He looked at the carnage around him and then gingerly touched his nose. It was not the ideal outcome for his plan, but the damage the huntress did to his face was enough to eliminate all doubt his story wasn't the absolute truth.

Despite the pain, he laughed. Talia's final act gave him the perfect alibi for what happened here. He glanced at the body of the huntress lying face down on the polished stone floor. She wouldn't be causing him any more problems.

Chapter 48

Talia located the tiny message tube among the dirt under a bush. She held it up. "Found it."

Walter stood up, stretching his back after being hunched over for so long looking among the bushes and rocks. "I forgot how much of the human body can get aches and pains. Being a bird does have its advantages." He lifted at the edges of the net, like a lady in a long gown about to cross a muddy road, and walked over to meet her.

She slid the message out of the holder and unspooled it. She held it up, but the words didn't make any sense. Her shoulders dropped. "Who wrote this again?"

Walter gave her a calculating look, "Madam Ryes. Why?"

Talia frowned and looked back at the note. "She wrote it in some kind of code. I can't read it."

Walter held out his hand, careful not to let any of it slip past the webbing of the net. "I've been watching her write these for quite some time. I might have picked up a word or two."

She handed the note through the net. The tips of her fingers withered and the skin flaked away to leave bony tips holding the paper. Walter snatched it quickly from her grasp and she pulled her hand out. She marveled at how quickly the skin returned and her hand looked young again.

Walter squinted at the note and then looked up at her. "From what I can tell, she is asking her sister to bet all the money they have that the boy Spinner loses in the third bout of The Gauntlet."

Talia's mouth fell open. "Did you say Spinner?"

Walter nodded. "He is the son of Veren Maclean."

"A Maclean? And she's entering him into The Gauntlet?"

Walter nodded. "Right. She made him promise he would do it in exchange for his freedom."

Talia held up the note. "But if she is betting on him to lose, then he won't be getting his freedom."

Walter shook his head. "It's not like that. The Gauntlet is a technical battle. The outcome is based on points scored. Losing won't necessarily harm him physically."

Talia gave him a hard stare. "But if he wasn't losing she would kill him to guarantee he lost wouldn't she?"

Walter nodded.

"Then we need to stop her."

"Why?"

"Walter. You know the Macleans are the most powerful Spinners to ever imprint Midguard with their footsteps. If anybody has the power to bring us together again, it is that boy."

Walter looked at her skeptically. "But he has never been trained. He has no idea how to use his power."

Talia looked at him intently, "Halen's with him right? He learned the Maclean style. But if that boy truly is the last of the Macleans, we convince Halen to train him no matter what. We have to save that boy because he is the only one who can save us!"

Walter looked at her, understanding finally dawning in his eyes. "Right. But if we wait until the boy is trained, it might take years to get to the point where he can help us."

Talia smiled at him "At least we know that help is on the way and it's just a matter of time. Let's go and make sure that hope isn't snatched from us."

Walter smiled and tossed aside the net. He shrunk down to a canary and landed on her shoulder. She stroked his breast with a finger and then mounted her horse.

Talia no longer needed to track the caravan. She knew exactly where they were headed. If she cut through the middle of the badlands, rather than follow the road, she would be in front of the wagon train and get to The Grease a day ahead of Van. It was not a place she ever wanted to set foot in again. And it wasn't because the name was more descriptive of the environment than most city names.

She made enemies all across Midguard, mostly by trying to do the right thing and coming up against racketeers who were more interested in preying on the weak to turn a quick buck than in helping their fellow man. She made lifelong enemies of these types of people over the years. And a very powerful one lived in The Grease.

Chapter 49

Van walked behind the caravan, his face covered by a scarf tied over his nose and mouth to keep out the choking dust lifted by the hooves and wheels of the moving caravan. Tinted goggles protected his eyes from both the sun and the swirling dust. His task, part of his payment for staying with the caravan, was to sweep away the horse prints and wagon wheel tracks. A caravan was protected from raiders if there was no evidence they passed recently along the road. Sweeping the tracks made them look older and thus presented the assumption the caravan was farther away along the road. Raiders were lazy, if nothing else, and rarely ventured too far from their main encampment to find victims. So, as long as they were in raider country, it was Van's job to sweep the caravan's tracks. At least they provided him with some protection from the mindless but dirty task. Van paused to adjust the goggles and pulled the scarf tightly around his mouth to keep from breathing in too much dust. He wasn't able to keep all of the dirt from being sucked into his mouth, but the scarf kept his airways relatively clear. Almost.

Eddie sat in a chair at the back of the final wagon of the caravan, watching Van sweeping away at the tracks. He pointed to a set that Van hastily brushed away. "Those look too fresh. Sweep them again."

Van held up the wide straw broom. "If you think you can do better, by all means."

Eddie smiled and lifted his bandaged ankle. "I would if I could, but you know I'm supposed to rest."

"Too bad you didn't land on your mouth," Van muttered.

"What was that?" Eddie asked.

"I said too bad you didn't land on your mouth. Then you would need to rest that too."

Eddie's face fell, showing Van how much his comment hurt. He sat back in the chair and waved a small hand fan to fight off the heat and the flies. "Fine. If you don't want me to talk to you, I won't."

Van stopped sweeping and looked at Eddie sulking in his chair. Van felt tired, uncomfortable, and sore and knew he was unnecessarily taking it out on Eddie. "I'm sorry, Eddie. It's hot out and I'm tired of sweeping the road. It's not like I'm making any difference."

Eddie sat back up. "That's because you're sweeping side to side. If you..." He stopped when he saw the look on Van's face. "Sorry," he said and suddenly became enthralled with a loose thread on his shirt.

Van glanced back at the road. All that was clearly visible was the single trail of his own footsteps. It really did look like he was walking through the badlands alone. The tracks embedded in the road from previous caravans looked to be days or weeks old, the wind having whipped around loose dust to fill in the prints. Van wondered if they were only hours behind another caravan, but because of this little broom trick, it gave the appearance of being isolated from everyone else by several days' travel.

Van swept half-heartedly as he looked at Eddie who still ignored him in favor of the thread that was unraveling and loosening the sleeve of his shirt.

"Eddie?" Van tentatively said.

"Yeah," Eddie responded while pulling the thread even more, dislodging half his sleeve.

Van took a deep breath. "Do you think anyone has noticed us missing yet?"

Eddie stopped his destructive pastime and gave Van a serious look. "Well, it has been a few days and we obviously didn't make it to the apartment as planned. Since you haven't called your mother in all that time, I'm pretty sure she has every state trooper, along with the FBI, the NSA, the CIA, and quite possibly the United States Army out looking for you right now."

"That's not funny, Eddie."

"I didn't say it to be funny. If I know your mom, and I think I do, that's what's happening. And not because they are concerned about a missing college student on a road trip with his best friend. Nope. They are calling in everyone just to appease her. I know I would. She can get kinda scary when she wants to be."

Despite trying to remain serious, Van laughed and a snort escaped his nose at the last comment and he smiled wide. "Yeah. You're probably right."

The rocking motion of the wagon vibrated Eddie's chair toward the edge of the platform until he was close to falling off. He shifted to reset the chair more securely on the back of the wagon. "You never told me what that old lady said to you after she kicked me out."

Van shrugged, focusing his attention on sweeping away the hoof prints and wheel ruts left in the dust. "It wasn't anything important."

"Not important?" Eddie exclaimed. "She told us both you were a magician and have the ability to do what Halen did. Only without passing out."

Van shrugged. "I don't know if I believe her."

"I don't care if you believe her or not. You have to make her think you believe her."

Van stopped sweeping, but kept pace with the caravan. "I don't follow."

Eddie leaned forward, despite the threat of toppling out of the wobbling wagon. "If she believes you can do what Halen can, then maybe we can negotiate from a better position. Maybe even get some perks."

Van shook his head. Eddie was always thinking of ways to manipulate the system. "I already negotiated our release on one condition."

Eddie's eyebrows lifted. "Yeah. What was that?"

"I participate in a contest."

Eddie's face was full of curiosity. "What kind of contest?"

"As far as I can tell, it's a magic contest."

Eddie's eyebrows rose even higher. "Then you better hope the old lady's right and you are one of these Spinners or whatever they're called."

Van looked at him, "Yea? Why's that?"

Eddie smiled wide "So we can win. Then we can get out of here and back home."

Spinner was the right term, Van recalled. But what he didn't remember was whether Madam Ryes requested he win the contest or not as part of their deal. At the time he thought he'd found a loophole in their agreement. Now he was not so sure. She said he came from a long line of Spinners. The best, actually. But he didn't know about it and lacked training on how to use magic. He didn't know if he could learn how to use his supposed powers in time for The Gauntlet. And self-doubt was the first indicator of failure, no matter the undertaking.

Chapter 50

Calen sat in the room with the dead hunters and waited for the circus of castle guards that would be joining him soon. To his surprise, the first one through the door, after the thrumming of the metal staircase announced his impending arrival, was Falen.

Falen swooped into the room, taking in everything at once. He scrutinized Calen. "What happened here?"

Calen was ready. He rehearsed what he was going to say, only modifying a few points to match what he and the room looked like.

"I got here and found the guard dead downstairs. I ran up the staircase and was ambushed. I tried to fight back, but I couldn't concentrate enough to bring up even a light breeze."

Falen wasn't fazed. "We train for precisely these times. Instinct should have taken over."

Calen motioned a bloody hand in the direction of his face. Even that small movement sent shooting pains down his neck and along his spine. "Look at my nose. I can barely breathe."

Falen looked at the other two bodies in the room. "The hunters?"

"I was too late. He would have killed me too, but a guard showed up and he escaped out the window."

Falen looked around the room, taking it in again. He circled back to Calen, "I hold you responsible for their deaths."

Calen's heart was suddenly in his throat and he tried to swallow it back down so he could respond. He put up the best defensive glare he could muster. "They were dead before I got here. The guy was still bent over the woman with something in his hand when I came in." He looked around and spotted the needle he left by the huntress' body. "There. I think he poisoned them with that."

Falen crossed over and inspected the needle without touching it. He turned over the huntress and inspected her foggy dead eyes. He rolled the body back into position. "It appears they were indeed poisoned."

Calen struggled to stand. He fought off waves of vertigo in the attempt. "You cannot blame me for their deaths."

"I do not blame you. But I make you responsible for finding out who did this."

Calen leaned on the wall, his hand leaving dark red smears on the rough-hewn stone. "You wish me to find out who did this?"

Falen held his gaze solidly on Calen. "I also want you to find out how Van Maclean came to be in Midguard. Whoever hired the hunters to kill Halen and Veren's son didn't want them talking to us. Did you get a good look at the assailant before he escaped?"

Calen stood up straighter, releasing the wall and finally standing on his own two feet. "It happened very quickly."

"Would you recognize him if you saw him again?"

Calen worked quickly through the faces of those who slighted him throughout his life. Any one of them would do. "I might."

Falen nodded slightly and strode from the room, his words fading as he left. "Then it's settled. You will not rest until their killer has been brought to justice."

Chapter 51

Van couldn't remember a day taking so long. He and Eddie tried to pass the time by amusing themselves with jokes and reminiscing on growing up in Lebanon, Kansas. But that world seemed a lifetime away and talking about their adventures growing up made them a little homesick for a world without dragons, magic, or wizard contests.

As the sun dipped low in the sky the caravan circled for the night. The driver of the last wagon pulled into position before hopping down and glaring at Van. "Go around the camp and clear away any wheel tracks and horse hooves before you call it a day."

Van nodded. He looked at Eddie. "Feeling strong enough to walk a little?"

Eddie nodded "Sure. Ankle feels fine. I think I can do one lap or so around the camp." Eddie followed behind him along the road as he brushed away the tracks. Van suddenly paused sweeping.

He was staring directly at a green colored wagon with no windows.

Eddie stopped next to him. "What is it?" he asked.

Van pointed at the wagon. "That's the wagon Madam Ryes told us to stay away from."

Eddie titled his head and looked around. "What do you think is in there?"

"I don't know. But I think we should keep moving."

Eddie grinned. Van knew that smile. It always preceded trouble. Van shook his head. "No, Eddie. She was pretty specific that we stay away from that wagon."

"I wonder why?" Eddie said and started walking toward it.

Van looked around anxiously. "C'mon Eddie. Let's just keep going."

Eddie flashed his eyebrows up and down. "I love a good secret, don't you?" He walked up to the wagon and glanced around before placing his ear against the side. After a moment he frowned in concentration. "I think I hear something."

Something slammed into the wall from the inside, rocking the wagon and lifting it up onto two wheels. Eddie jumped back as the wagon settled back to the ground. A chilling scream emanated from inside the wagon and they both ran without looking back.

Van collided with Buff, Madam Ryes' right hand man, as they rounded the corner of the final wagon in the half circle. It was like hitting a brick wall. Eddie slammed into Van from behind, squashing him between them. They stumbled back and Van looked up at Buff, trying to keep his face from telegraphing the knowledge that they ventured too close to the windowless green wagon. Buff looked down and held out his hand. "I'll take the broom."

Van gratefully handed him the dusty broom. "Did I do a good job?"

Buff scowled at him. "If we aren't attacked by bandits during the night I would say you did an acceptable job. Go ahead and make yourself comfortable around the fire. You earned your keep for the day." He turned to Eddie. "How's the foot?"

Eddie hopped up and down on his feet. "That goop your doctor put on it really does the trick. I can barely feel it."

Buff tossed the broom to Eddie. "Good. You'll take over for him tomorrow."

Van and Eddie glanced at each other before Eddie looked at Buff. "So I'm working with Van tomorrow?"

Buff made Eddie shrink back with his look. "You will be sweeping alone."

"What will I be doing?" Van asked.

Buff snorted as he laughed. "You will be busy."

Eddie held up the broom. "Is this the only way to sweep the road behind the caravan? Surely, after all this time, you must've come up with something that automatically erases the tracks behind the last wagon as you move."

Buff frowned. "We have no use for machinery that's just going to break down in a short time anyway. Besides, we have you." He spun on his heel and stomped off.

Van and Eddie looked at each other and Eddie shrugged. "Oh well. I guess it beats getting attacked by bandits."

The sun dipped below the horizon, the light in the sky shifting quickly from a pale powder blue to a deep dark purple. The smell of food drew them to where others gathered for the dishing out of supper. They stood in line and received their tin plate of beans and a chunk of something that looked like meat. Or possibly bread. Van looked at the greasy man who ladled equally greasy food onto his plate. "Are there any vegetables?"

The man smiled, his toothless grin making his smile dark. "Sorry. Fresh out."

Eddie pulled him away before the cook decided to take offense and start trouble.

"Where do we sit?" Van asked.

Eddie's eyes moved past Van and he smiled. "Looks like someone wants us to join them around the fire."

Van turned as Eddie walked toward two attractive young women sitting near the fire, his limp barely perceptible. They were smiling and one of them beckoned with a curled index finger for Van to join her.

Eddie turned around. "Are you coming?"

Van suddenly felt like sweeping the road again for another fourteen hours despite the desire to join them welling up in him. It was an odd internal war going on in his head, but the longer he watched them, the more he couldn't resolve the conflicting desire to run or go to them.

Eddie walked back to Van and grabbed a handful of his shirt sleeve, spilling some of the congealed beans from his plate. "Come on, Romeo. They're not gonna bite. Unless you're lucky."

Eddie dragged Van past the campfire and stopped in front of the two young women sitting on the log. "Have you met my friend Van?" He said as he shoved Van down on one side of them while taking his position on the other side.

Eddie immediately went into overdrive, causing the young woman next to him to giggle as he turned on the Eddie charm. It always worked. He was a natural-born schmoozer and was instantly everyone's longtime companion. Meeting Eddie for the first time was like reconnecting with an old friend.

Van didn't have the natural skills Eddie possessed and instead sat silently as he choked down the tasteless meal. They took turns smiling at each other and then looking at their plates in embarrassment.

When their plates were empty she finally gathered enough courage to turn to him. "My name's Maura."

Van smiled uneasily. He rarely talked to the female gender outside his family. Sure, he made friends at school, but they were definitely just that, friends. As for dating, he was waiting for the right one, and no one he met ever quite met that definition. Being unsure into which camp this young woman fell made him very nervous.

"Van," he replied, swallowing down the excess saliva that developed suddenly in his mouth.

Great opening line, he thought. Me Tarzan. He shook his head, admonishing himself. Real smooth Van.

Her smiled sent his heart fluttering and his stomach flipped repeatedly, which was not easy with the thick bean stew sitting heavily in it. She looked at him expectantly, but all he could do was stare back at her, smiling like a mute fool.

"Uhh," she said hesitantly. "I hear you are a Spinner?"

Eddie caught the word and leaned over and intruded on their "conversation" without so much as skipping a beat. "And not just any Spinner. He's from the Maclean clan."

The young women giggled at Eddie's silliness. That only spurned Eddie further and he adopted a thick Irish brogue as he continued. "The Maclean clan is the most powerful Spinner clan of all. They have directed history for thousands of years."

Van closed his eyes as his heart hammered in his chest. He curled his fists, turning his knuckles stark white as he listened to Eddie make a farce of his life and what happened to his father. He tried to shoot Eddie a look to make him stop. Eddie, unfortunately, was lost in the moment and his new audience.

"The Macleans have made kings out of peasants and peasants out of kings. Van Maclean is the last, and thus the most powerful, of all Macleans. There can be only one!"

Van stood up abruptly. "That's enough, Eddie!"

Eddie looked up at him, the campfire throwing menacing shadows across his confused face. "Dude! Relax. That's Highlander."

"I know what it is. But that's not me!"

Eddie raised his hands, palm side out. "Okay. I'll back off."

Maura gently touched Van's hand. He reflexively jerked away and she cringed, raising her arms defensively, as if he was about to hit her. He quickly looked down at the sudden movement and noticed her frightened face. He knew he was overreacting and needed to calm down. He walked to the other side of the fire and sat down to be alone.

He watched Eddie enjoy every minute of this hell they found

themselves in. Playing for a new audience who ate up his every word.

Van spun around, putting his back to the fire and stared out into the darkness. The sun's light had faded enough to allow the faint twinkle of the brightest stars to appear. Not long after, the sky was completely dark and every star in the sky made its presence known to all. He craned his neck upward and marveled at how many there were. He could even see the dense ribbon of the Milky Way. The last time he'd seen the sky like that was during an overnight backpacking trip with his father when he was ten.

He closed his eyes and let the memory play in his mind's eye, showing him the small campsite his father made with the two-man pup tent, which was nothing more than camouflage-printed fabric thrown over a rope stretched between two trees and staked to the ground to keep it in place.

His father poked at the small fire with a can of open beans heating up on one edge of the grill. The label was already burned away to reveal the ribbed aluminum metal that blackened along one side. Pleased with the progress of the campfire, his father sat down next to him, placed an arm around him, and pointed up into the night sky. "What do you see up there, Van?"

Van looked into the sky and shrugged. "Stars?"

His father laughed. "Yes. To the scientific mind, those are stars. But to the imagination they are whatever you want them to be. Souls of our forefathers. Gods. The eyes of heaven." His father turned to him. "All your young life, people are going to push science, math, and history on you. What I don't want you to forget is the wonder you first felt when you looked at the world around you. Until you learned about the surface tension of water, and how water striders developed special legs to stand on the surface, you thought it was magic that kept them from sinking into the lake like you and I. Do you remember that?"

Van shrugged as he blushed. "I was a stupid kid back then."

His father smiled. "No, Van. You believed in magic. I don't want you to ever stop believing in magic."

Van smirked. "What about Santa Claus?"

His dad laughed. "He's just a guy in a suit at the mall."

"The Easter Bunny?"

"Your mother gets up extra early to hide the basket."

Van smiled. "I know. I watched her last year."

His dad gave him a curious look. "Is that how you found it so quickly?"

Van nodded. "I pretended to look as long as I could. But I had to eat the ears off the chocolate bunny before breakfast."

His dad punched him playfully on the shoulder. "For shame, Van. Your mom was so proud of herself when it took you half an hour to locate the basket. Well," he said as he hugged Van closer to him. "It will be our little secret. Whaddya say?"

Van snuggled into his father's embrace. "Sounds good. But promise me that we won't keep secrets from each other."

"I promise," his father said. But now that Van was remembering that conversation, he knew his father broke that promise the moment he made it. And this was bigger than not telling his mother he peeked while she hid the Easter basket. Why did his father keep such a big secret from him? What was the benefit of lying to his family about who he really was?

Van felt his chest constrict and take away his breath when he realized how his mom reacted when the "company" his father worked for kicked them out of their home. She knew the truth. That's why she didn't put up a fight. Who knew what people with magic abilities could have done to them if they resisted. But if she knew all along, why didn't she tell him? Why keep his father's secret so long after his death? But Van knew the answer. She kept the secret because it was too crazy to be believed.

A hand on his knee yanked him abruptly from his waking dream and back to reality. If this could be considered reality. He never even noticed Maura approach and sit down next to him.

She smiled sweetly. "Your friend was only having fun," she offered.

"Yeah. I know," he replied. "But sometimes he goes a little too far."

She lowered her head. "I'm sorry I reacted like that."

Van felt a sudden need to reassure her. He carefully placed a hand on her shoulder. "No. I'm sorry I made you think I was going to… I would never hit—hit anyone unless I was fighting back."

She smiled demurely. "That's good to know."

They fell silent as they continued to smile at each other.

"Hey," Eddie said. Van looked up to see Eddie with his arm around the other young woman. "Me and Harmony are going to her wagon to check out her clock. Don't give me that look. She says it stopped working last week. I think I can get it ticking again."

Van grimaced. "How do you know if you can fix it?"

"It's worth a look." Eddie winked. "Don't wait up."

He spun around with Harmony under his wing and they giggled into the darkness as they made their way to her wagon in the outer circle.

"Don't worry," Maura said. "Harmony is—experienced."

Van laughed. "Then she's gonna be disappointed."

Maura's face went serious. "Is he...?"

Van reacted quickly. "Oh, no. There was this one year at summer camp..." Van waved his hand in front of his face, dismissing the rest of his explanation. "He knows his way around the garden, if you know what I mean. But once he starts working on that clock, he won't stop until it's fixed. They might never get around to—that."

Maura smiled slyly. "What about you?" Her cloak took that moment to slip from her shoulder, exposing her porcelain-white skin. "Are you—experienced?"

Van wasn't sure how much he should tell her. He looked around the caravan's circle of wagons for something convenient with which to change the subject easily. But all he saw were couples pairing off and heading for wagons or further into the dark beyond the revealing light of the fire. Though he went on a few dates, and experienced a couple steamy encounters, he never went too far. He believed in his heart it was important to wait for the one who was waiting for him. He never could explain the feeling. He just knew that one day a special woman would steal his heart and they would love each other forever. He was waiting for her and wanted that big moment to be a truly wonderful experience. Not a hookup because they were the only ones around.

Maura shuffled closer on the log and placed a hand on Van's thigh. Van's body reacted and, to his surprise, so did his heart. It started to flutter in a way he never experienced before. But he didn't even know her. He wasn't about to allow anything to progress, but he was quickly realizing his body might betray him if he let her touch him for much longer.

Van jumped to his feet. "Maura. I think you are sweet and very pretty. But I have a lot on my plate right now and—"

She stood and placed her hands on his face, holding him in place. She looked at him a little questioningly as she moved her face closer to his. "Don't worry, Van. I won't pressure you. I know what that's like."

That spiked Van's curiosity, he removed her hand and looked at her gently questioning "What do you mean?"

She looked at him with a sad expression in her eyes, then stared at the ground. "I just meant… People force me to do things all the time I don't want to do and I just meant I would never do that to someone else given the choice."

Van's eyes started to look at her protectively "You don't mean you were forced to…."

She quickly raised her head and looked at him with a sad smile, "No, no, not like that, just other things for….family. Do you understand?"

Van thought he did. He didn't know why but he felt he could trust Maura. He was comfortable talking to her about things he normally kept to himself. "When I was twelve my father died and I was forced to move away from everything I knew and everyone I cared about, so my mother could keep a roof over our heads. Do you mean things like that?"

She smiled. "Kind of."

He looked at her and, despite being very worried about his body's reactions, that brief sadness brought out a protective instinct he wasn't expecting. He wanted to know more about her. He guided her back to sit on the log and face him. "Like what?"

She looked into his eyes again, as if a little confused, "Why don't you tell me what you look for in a woman?"

Van was caught a little off guard. Was she flirting? His brain tried to tell him this was dangerous territory but that protective instinct wanted to continue. To get to know her better.

"If I answer your question, will you answer mine?"

Maura gave him a slightly surprised look, but quietly nodded. "If I can."

Van decided to roll with it. Hopefully he'd be rewarded with more information about her. He'd known what he wanted in a woman since he was fifteen. Unlike Eddie, who was very happy going with the flow,

Van would only settle for the right one. "Well, I'm looking for a partner. Someone who will be by my side through thick and thin. An equal, someone who is strong and capable and will be a true companion in life." Van looked down at the ground as he was explaining, but when he looked up, Maura held the oddest expression on her face, almost as if she was calculating and hopeful all at the same time.

She looked into his eyes and said "Van, do you really want a woman who is an equal to you? Even if someone was as strong as you?"

Van smiled and dipped his head a bit as he looked at her "I guess around here that seems a little odd, but yes, I want a girl that is an equal. I also wouldn't mind if she was stronger than me."

Maura sat back for a moment with an almost shocked expression on her face as she searched his eyes for a long moment. Then she suddenly smiled. "You truly mean that don't you?"

Van took her hand and pulled it toward his chest. "Cross my heart and hope to die."

He was shocked when she snatched her hand away from him and shook her head, a look of horror crossing her face. "No! Don't even joke about that."

Van looked at her confused, "Maura, it's just a saying where I come from. It doesn't mean anything."

Maura's breathing slowed down as she calmed down. "I've been looking for a strong partner too. Someone who would like me for me. My strengths as well as my weaknesses."

Van didn't understand why but he felt more of a connection with Maura than with any girl he'd met before. She was undoubtedly beautiful, but it was something about her, something both painful and strong, steel against silk, with a little bit of melancholy thrown in. It was very attractive. It made him want to protect her while at the same time stand by her side to take on the world. "You know Maura, I would really like to get to know you better."

Maura looked at him a little cautious, "Oh? In what way?"

Van saw the meaning and quickly corrected her, "No, not like that, just know you. Who you are, what you want in life, that kind of thing."

Maura gazed into his eyes as if he'd just thrown her a life preserver while she was drowning in the middle of a tumultuous ocean. "Really?"

Just then she looked beyond him and her eyes became dark and round. She quickly looked back at Van and with a sadness he didn't comprehend. "Van? Will you kiss me?"

Van was surprised, he was about to say they should talk a little longer first, but she quickly moved in and brushed her lips to his. His eyes grew wide as hers closed. Then the armor he spent half his life building around his heart to wait for the one melted and he closed his eyes as his body stopped listening to his mind and he returned her kiss. She responded hungrily and wrapped her arms around his neck, pulling herself to him.

The world around him, the world he grew up in, and the one he now found himself in, faded away. Nothing mattered except the warmth of her lips on his. He felt himself merge with her as if they were always meant to be. Was this what true love felt like? If it was, it was definitely worth waiting for.

Not too far away, but far enough from the light of the fire to be barely visible, a striking figure of a woman observed them from a distance. She watched as Van succumbed to the siren call of the young woman who took his defenses down one by one. The woman smiled and then silently faded away, as if the very darkness of the night took her.

Chapter 52

Madam Ryes, her private carriage set apart from the rest of the caravan, sat on the rear porch of her wagon and watched as the young woman led Van away from the fire to one of the wagons in the outer circle. She closed her eyes. Everything she did in her life led directly to this moment. She was about to get everything her heart desired and more.

A shout of panic pulled her from her reverie. She watched in horror as the fire at the center of the encampment grew, standing up on legs born of fire and stretching out tentacles of flame for arms. The eyes formed like dark pits and gazed around at the panicked men and women running away. It stepped out of the stone fire pit and started attacking everyone in sight. Wagons caught on fire as people ran in circles, trying to extinguish the monster with buckets of water. Madam Ryes shook her head. She knew such efforts were ineffective against this particular creature.

She hopped down from the back of her wagon and headed straight for the medical wagon. She sprang up the stairs, flung open the door, stepped inside, and glared at Halen. He was awake, sitting up in bed, and moving his hands around in a circle. In his lap, a small crystal glowed brightly. She snatched the crystal from the bed and the glow died down along with the screams outside. She crossed her arms. "You have my undivided attention. What do you want?"

At that moment Buff poked his head through the open door. "Was that the Spinner's doing?"

Without taking her eyes off Halen, Madam Ryes barked her commands at Buff. "The Watchers will have seen that. Get everyone ready. We break camp in half an hour."

"Yes, ma'am."

"And close the door."

Buff disappeared, slamming the door in his haste. Madam Ryes glowered at Halen. They stayed that way for several minutes before Madam Ryes broke the silence. "I'm not asking for much."

Halen sighed heavily. "I cannot train him. The Order has decreed."

"I don't care one whit about what The Order wants. And I'm

guessing neither do you."

"I was taking him to The Order before you intervened."

She couldn't hold in the spurt of laughter. "That's not how I remember it. As I recall they were carrying your lifeless carcass over a mountain. Or was that your way of getting out of having to walk all the way to the West Kingdom?"

"Hunters ambushed us. I did what was required to protect them."

"You mean protect the son of Veren."

Halen's shoulders drooped and he closed his eyes briefly. "How did you find out?"

"I've been looking for him my entire life."

"He's just a young boy."

"You know what I mean. My family has been searching for a Maclean since before I was born. And I found one."

Halen gave her a dark stare. "I won't train him."

She raised an eyebrow and smirked. "You don't want to see him die in The Gauntlet, do you?"

Halen sat up straighter. "You can't be serious? He doesn't know who he is. What he is capable of."

"He does now. And he swore to me he would participate in exchange for your release."

She could see Halen biting back the words that hovered just below the surface of his tongue. "He's not ready," he said through gritted teeth.

"Then make him ready. You have two days."

Halen let out a surprised gasp. "It takes years to learn the ways of a Spinner. Even more to become proficient."

"Give him the basics."

"Even the basics take a year's time, I can't do it in two days!"

Madam Ryes winked and tossed the crystal back onto the bed. "That's all you have. Make it work. I'm glad to see you already know how to use that. It should help speed things along. Just be careful with it. I don't want The Order coming down on us for illegal magic activity."

Chapter 53

By the light of a candle, Calen sat at his reading desk and tried to focus on the scroll unspooled in front of him. But it was a useless endeavor. His mind kept reminding him of his success.

He accomplished the task of trying to kill Van in Techrealm by sending his motorized vehicle plummeting into the icy waters of a river. When Van's powers triggered and brought him to Midguard, Calen was ready and implemented Plan B. Send Halen to find him while simultaneously sending the huntress after both of them. She eliminated them most expeditiously and he in turn eliminated her to tie up all the loose ends. The Maclean line was finally sealed, and with Halen's death, there was nobody left to teach the Spinner ways of a Maclean, a unique form of instruction that created some of the most powerful Spinners in Midguard. The most dominant Spinner line to ever spring forth from creation was finally gone forever.

He singlehandedly ensured the success of Aeron at the next triple moon when he could traverse the gate again. That was still two years away but there was nobody left in all the realms to challenge him. At least nobody capable of challenging him on their own. It was an amazing stroke of luck that The Order became so encumbered by rules and regulations that all the Spinners, masters and apprentices alike, would not be strong enough to stop Aeron's impending triumphant arrival to Midguard. He would break through the meager defenses The Order provided and start his conquest of the realm. There would be no Maclean charging to the rescue to stop him the next time. And it was all thanks to Calen.

He smiled to himself, his eyes not seeing the words written on the scroll in front of him. Aeron would be so grateful he would have no choice but to make Calen important in his new kingdom. Calen would ascend from his low station in life and finally everyone would see him as he saw himself.

Worthy of the power he deserved.

The title of High Master should have always been his, but the Council of Elders never saw it that way. Someday soon, they would all see the true power Calen commanded when he was reinforced by the mighty army of Aeron.

A knock on his door snapped him out of his fantasy and his damaged nose throbbed from the sudden movement as he turned instinctively toward the sound. He cleared his throat and returned his attention to the scroll in an attempt to look busy.

"Yes?" he called out.

The door opened and two figures darkened the doorway. It was Lance, a young apprentice who showed great promise. But not nearly enough for what was coming Calen mused while struggling to keep a wry smile from spreading across his face.

Standing next to him was Calen's own apprentice, Nina. She represented all the qualities of a great Spinner, save for one. Her training was less than adequate thanks to Calen's withholding of certain crucial lessons. Another way he was helping the already weak Order by undermining the potency of those under his control. The Order's fight against Aeron would soon be over.

He pasted as sincere a smile as he could muster. "What is it, Lance?" By addressing the man who entered instead of his own female apprentice, he hoped to jab yet another stake into the heart of his apprentice, keeping her feeling less than worthy and destabilizing her confidence.

Though it never seemed to work as she pushed her way past Lance and spoke first anyway. "Master. We have been hearing certain— rumors filtering through the halls of the basilica."

He tilted his head to convey his curiosity, despite already knowing what she would say. "What rumors would that be?"

Nina fidgeted as she looked at Lance beside her and then took a calming breath. "A Spinner was killed in Midguard."

He closed his eyes, letting a pained expression cover his face before looking at her. He did his best to not smile while he spoke. "It is not a rumor."

"But we've been hearing–"

He raised a hand. She was always interrupting him. It showed an inner strength but also reflected an immaturity that Lance lacked. At least, that was what he always told her to keep her spirits down. "Let me finish."

Her mouth snapped shut, but he could tell she wasn't happy about remaining silent.

"It is true that hunters, acting alone and without provocation, killed a Spinner."

"It was Halen!" she said a little too loudly for the small study, her voice echoing off the spines of leather-bound books.

"Calm down!" Calen demanded.

Instead of following his instructions, she approached quickly and leaned forward over the edge of his desk, invading his personal space. "They are saying the son of Veren was also killed. Are they talking about Van?"

He fixed her with a sorrowful gaze. It was the opposite of how he felt inside but there was no way he was going to give away how exhilarated he felt at his success. "Yes."

Lance was still letting her do all the talking. Come on, Lance, Calen silently urged. Put her in her place for god's sake.

"But the decree? He was banished! He was never to know his heritage. How was he in Midguard?"

"We are still looking into how he crossed over from Techrealm." It was a "mystery" Calen knew would never be properly solved now that he was in charge of handling the investigation. He could tell by the look on her face she would be like a dog with a bone trying to find answers. He needed to placate her and keep her from causing trouble. "I know you were childhood friends but there are more pressing matters that deserve our attention. We can't do anything to bring him back."

"We can't let his death go unanswered!" She emphasized her statement with a fist pounded on the top of the table that made the candle stick jump, the flame flickering wildly.

Calen stood abruptly, his chair tipping over with a loud clatter. "Enough! Know your place, apprentice!"

She shrank away from the table immediately and Lance placed his hands on her shoulders. Calen chose that moment to address Lance directly since he was unwilling to take matters into his own hands and appeared to only be here for moral support. "Take her out of here. Remind her of her duty to The Order."

"Yes, sir," Lance replied. He turned Nina around and placed an arm around her shoulders. He whispered to her as he led her from the study. He glanced back at Calen and nodded that he would take care of her and then closed the door.

Calen stood there, his fists clenched from having to raise his voice at an apprentice. She possessed no Maclean blood in her veins. But she did possess the same willingness to ignore the rules that made the Maclean line a blight on The Order.

If he didn't break her soon she would become a problem that he would have to deal with severely. But once news of the huntress' death spread across Midguard it would be impossible to find someone willing to kill a Spinner. Even an apprentice Spinner.

He took a deep breath and relaxed his hands. When the time came he would do what needed to be done. Even if he had to do it himself.

He worked the rest of the night, compiling a list of suspects he could frame for the murder of the hunters.

Chapter 54

Van woke with a start and looked around him in a panic. He felt queasy, as if he were in motion. But his eyes told him he was lying in bed in a small room, nestled comfortably among silky soft animal pelts. But his inner ears told him otherwise. The lamps hanging from hooks on the ceiling swayed back and forth, confirming to his eyes they were indeed moving.

His head pounded and he squinted against the small light coming from the lamps. He looked around and noted that this wagon was missing windows. His heart skipped a beat as he wondered if he was inside the green wagon.

The last thing he remembered was kissing Maura by the fire. Where was she? He sat up slowly, easing himself to his elbows as a wave of nausea overcame him. He tried to keep the contents of his stomach down, but the bile rose in his throat.

He jumped from the bed and shoved his way through the door that was thankfully unlocked. He jumped from the slowly rolling wagon, ignoring the stairs. He nearly collided with a horse when he hit the dirt. "Whoa!" the driver said and stopped his wagon.

Van ignored the whinnying animal as he ran for the bushes. He barely made it when he fell to his hands and knees, retching heavily and losing part of what remained from dinner. When he finished, he sat back on his heels and wiped his mouth with an arm.

"You too?" a familiar voice said to his right. Eddie was sitting half in and half out of a bush several feet away. His face scrunched up and he doubled over, spewing brown chunks across the desert floor. That was enough to send Van back into convulsions and he emptied his stomach of everything.

They were still dry heaving when a shadow fell across them and a straw broom hit the ground between them, accompanied by a deep voice. "Madam Ryes wants you sweeping." Buff said.

Eddie squinted up at him. "Both of us?"

"No. Just you." He turned to Van. "You are to follow me."

Van stood and took one look at Eddie. He wanted to ask him what he remembered from last night, or if he knew where Maura or

Harmony went, but Eddie just smiled and picked up the broom. "Go. Train to be the next David Blaine. I'll keep the bandits at bay."

Van tried to extend the conversation. "What about your foot?"

Eddie stood and hopped back and forth on both feet to show Van that he was no longer in pain. "Whatever they gave me really worked. If I bring that back with us, and get it into pill form, I'll be a multi-billionaire inside of a year."

"Enough talking!" Buff demanded.

Eddie waved Van away. "Go. You showed me how to do a lousy job sweeping yesterday. I'm sure I can't do much worse. It's only fair."

Van snickered. "Fair would be me sitting in a chair sipping lemonade and cracking jokes while you swept the road."

"Touché, pussycat," Eddie replied with a grin. "Now get out of here before I change my mind."

Van spun around and inspected the wagon he had exited. He was relieved to see it painted a bright blue with red highlights. It was not the green wagon. Buff hollered to him and he jogged to catch up with him at the back of one of the wagons.

"Inside," Buff said as he pointed up the short staircase. Van climbed the stairs into the brightly colored yellow and turquoise wagon, not sure what to expect.

Chapter 55

Halen sat at the table inside an empty wagon. Anything he could use to escape was removed. It didn't matter. He wasn't going anywhere without Van. He made a solemn promise to Van's father to protect him. He also promised to train him. It looked like he was going to get that chance. Although not in the manner he would have preferred.

He studied his wrinkled hands folded on the table in front of him. They looked like the tired hands of a man decades older than he was. It didn't help that he stayed awake thinking about everything and nothing at the same time since Madam Ryes left him alone. He was still awake when they moved him from the medicine wagon to the wagon used for long-term guests of the caravan.

He knew they were in trouble the moment he first woke up and recognized the face of a Traveler. And not just any Traveler, but the worst of the lot. Madam Ryes of the infamous Ryes Caravan.

Halen was well aware that she possessed a journal, scribbled by a senile old woman hundreds of years earlier, which referenced a lost land rights certificate claiming heritage to the Maclean family line. It was a ludicrous concept. Hard to believe by anyone except the delusional Madam Ryes who clung to it as if she finally belonged to something more important than a collection of nomads adrift in the badlands.

Truth be told, no family proved more important to Midguard than the Macleans. Down through the ages, whenever Midguard was in danger, the Macleans were there to save it. Veren sacrificed himself to keep with that tradition, and asked Halen to break the cycle, knowing his son would probably follow in his footsteps to protect Midguard. What he never anticipated was The Order's decree that the Maclean line never be allowed to practice magic again.

Halen already resolved himself to the fact that Van Maclean would not be encumbered with his family legacy. Midguard's greatest danger was the danger it put itself in through its misguided policies.

There was nothing Halen could do about it so he decided to live the rest of his days alone with the hope that he wouldn't be affected when Aeron's army overran Midguard. When that day came, Halen planned to ensure they left him alone by proving too unimportant to notice or bother with.

His fingers searched his pockets again but still came up empty. He'd lost Veren's crest pin. It was the only thing that enabled him to counteract the tarnishing of his own crest. Spinning the elements took a lot out of him since he was fighting the banishment decree. Sending up the shield against the barrage of arrows to protect the boys took all his strength, even with Veren's pin helping him focus his energies.

It must have fallen off somewhere on the mountain while the boys carried him up one side, over the peak, and down the other into the badlands. If they had any idea where they were headed they would have turned the other way around and run as fast as their feet could carry them.

But there was no way they could know.

They were strangers to this strange land.

The door opened and Halen looked up.

Van stepped in and looked around before his eyes settled on Halen's.

Halen took a deep breath and nodded at the empty chair across the table from him. "Have a seat, Van."

Van stood there unmoving. Halen didn't need to be a magician to read the message engraved on Van's face. The look in his eyes told Halen everything. Betrayal and lack of understanding overtook Van and he seemed mistrustful and hurt.

Halen stood and crossed the room, closing the door himself as he glared at Buff outside to silently remind him they were not to be disturbed. He took Van's arm and led him back to the table and helped him settle into a chair. Halen sat down across from him and smiled. "I have the answers you seek. All you need to do is ask the questions."

Van's eyes shifted to his. Halen could see the pain and confusion reflected there. He wished he could wave his hand and make all the anguish and fear fade away, but that wasn't how magic worked.

Van's eyes shifted away from his. "Why?" Van asked. He spoke so quietly Halen thought for a moment he'd only heard the wind pick up outside.

"Why what?" Halen replied.

Van's eyes shifted back. Gone was the confusion. It was replaced with a building rage. "Why didn't my father or, for that matter, my mother tell me!"

"Every child born of Spinner lineage is sent to Techrealm to be raised as a normal human. On their thirteenth birthday their abilities and where they came from are revealed and they are brought to Midguard to begin training."

"Are they brought here to attend some big school for wizards?"

Halen gave a derisive laugh. "Magic is not something that can be taught en masse, like math or history. It is personal and requires the bond of master and apprentice to ensure the student flourishes to the best of their ability."

"So I was supposed to have been brought here?"

"Yes."

"What happened? Why wasn't I brought here?"

Halen swallowed dryly. He never anticipated talking to Van would prove so difficult. He'd faced ogres and wild dragons, coming out unscathed each time. But those encounters paled in comparison to the difficulty he felt having a simple conversation with the son of his former master.

"Your father—died."

"I know that. Was he supposed to train me?"

"That is usually the practice. The father trains the son in the ways of their family line."

Van's forehead wrinkled. "Family line?"

"Every Spinner family developed their own training methods thousands of years ago. Methods passed from father to son, mother to daughter. There are no gender roles for Spinners. This resulted in creating Spinners of varying degrees of ability. Some families became sloppy with their training and only produced Spinners with limited magical ability. Most families follow a common style and share among each other. A few families kept their training methods a trade secret to ensure their influence as Master Spinners over the other families. You can imagine the strife this caused as families who wanted to increase their status attempted to steal the carefully guarded training methods of the more prominent magic users."

"Where did the Maclean family fall within that range?"

Halen smiled. "At the top. It created an unhealthy jealousy among the other families when your father was always the first called to deal with troubles throughout Midguard."

"Why was the Maclean training so much better than the others? What's the secret?"

Halen leaned in letting a twinkle sparkle in his eye. "The secret? The secret is, there is no secret. The Maclean family practiced far more than anyone else and trained longer before presenting themselves to the Wizard's Order to be commissioned as Spinners. Everyone else was in a big hurry to become a Spinner. They took shortcuts and progressed through their training faster than they should have so they could graduate with just enough skills to be accepted by The Order. The Macleans never took shortcuts. They practiced until it was second nature. They were able to control the power within better than anyone."

Halen sat back, his eyes showing a sadness as his eyebrows knitted together. "Some families became too lazy yet still insisted their children be accepted as Spinners. They put up such a fuss The Order reduced its requirements to accommodate them. They made people who should only be considered mere apprentices as Master Spinners in The Order."

Halen lifted the edge of his cloak and revealed the Wizard's Order Crest pin. "That was unheard of as recently as your dad's childhood. The Order was for fully trained Master Spinners to stop the enemy at the gate. An apprentice isn't prepared to go into battle because of their lack of control over the power. But after several generations of lazily trained spinners, and more and more losses every seven years, The Order's numbers were dwindling. It was seen as a way to bolster enrollment and make The Order look good on paper. With so many undertrained spinners the few good ones, like the Macleans, were almost required to make huge sacrifices to win the battles. Your dad didn't want that for you. He didn't want you to have to sacrifice needlessly for The Order."

Most of the rage dissipated in Van's eyes. He leaned forward, soaking in the information. Halen sighed heavily as he continued. "There is a Spinner in Magerealm who wishes to conquer Midguard so that he can build an army big enough to conquer Magerealm. His country is small in Magerealm and is not seen as a threat, so no one there bothers to stop him. Instead, they put The Order in place to protect the gate between the realms so he wouldn't be a problem here either. As long as he is small in Magerealm, and The Order is strong here to protect the gate, he is no threat to anyone."

"Is he the one who killed my father?"

"Your father sacrificed himself to close the gate during the last battle."

Van sat back, his eyes wide and sad. "He killed himself?"

"He did what was necessary to close the gate. The rest of The Order's Spinners weren't strong enough to hold Aeron back much longer. He was about to come through with his army. Midguard would be defenseless against Spinners from Magerealm and, in the resulting war as Aeron's forces swept across Midguard, millions would die in this world."

The lines increased on Van's forehead. "So with the death of my father there is no one left to train me in the Maclean ways?"

Halen closed his eyes, breathing deeply before opening them again. "Your father made me promise to train you as he trained me but to also find a way to keep you from having to make his sacrifice."

"Are you related to me?"

"No. I am from another family."

"I thought you said the families never shared their training secrets. How come you were trained by my father?"

Halen was afraid Van would ask that question. Regardless, he wasn't prepared to answer it at this time. Maybe someday he would tell Van everything, if he had the chance. But that day was not today. "Because of the manner of your father's death I was unable to honor your father's final wishes."

Van stared hard at him. "You didn't answer my question."

Halen met his gaze. "Because of the current situation it looks as if I will be training you after all."

"Why did my father train you?"

Halen paused for a moment, suppressing the feelings welling up within him before continuing. "It is a good thing he did or the ways of the Macleans would have been lost with him."

"How many of the families bring in apprentices from other families?"

Halen realized Van wasn't going to let it go and gave a partial answer. "It is rarely done."

"How rare?"

Halen clenched his teeth as he suppressed the memories being brought to the surface by Van's incessant questioning. "Just rare."

"Then why do it for you?"

Halen concentrated all his energy to suppress the memory that needed to remain locked away. He couldn't allow it to overcome him. He silently recited the mantras that kept his emotions in check until he felt his heart rate slow down. He was then able to look at Van, his face devoid of all emotion. "We will begin your training after breakfast."

Van pushed harder for an answer. "Why won't you tell me?"

"When the time is right you will not have to be told. You will know."

"That's rather cryptic."

"And that is how it shall remain until the time is right. It has no bearing on your training so I suggest you let it go."

"Is this my first lesson? Learn how to let go of the past?"

"If you wish it to be."

Van slouched in the chair. "This isn't gonna be some kind of Mr. Miyagi Karate Kid spiritual cliché thing, is it?"

Halen frowned. "I have not heard of the Miyagi family."

Van laughed. "It was a movie. Don't worry about it. So how long do I sit and focus on my chi before we start doing some real magic?"

Halen tilted his head in confusion. "Chi?"

"Yeah. You know, my inner child. Who am I, really? Stuff like that."

Halen smiled internally while keeping his face stolid. Van exhibited just enough attitude to make the unexpected choices that were the hallmark of the Maclean way of spinning. "There will be no need to sit and contemplate your place in the universe, Van. As soon as you have finished your breakfast we will begin. No sense learning who you really are on an empty stomach."

Chapter 56

Van carefully stepped down the short staircase and joined Madam Ryes and Buff next to the wagon. Madam Ryes was whispering something to Buff but stopped as soon as Van opened the door. She looked expectantly at him. "Is he going to train you?"

"I think so," Van replied.

She smiled. "Excellent. Buff will take you to breakfast." She swept past Van and entered the wagon, closing the door after her.

Van looked up at Buff's glowering face. Despite it still being early in the day, the oppressive heat of the sun was already causing Buff to perspire. Sweat ran down the side of his cheeks. "This way."

Van shook his head. His stomach was still sore from his rude awakening and roadside evacuation. "I just need some water."

Buff shrugged and took him to the water wagon and poured a cup of crystal-clear water into a wooden mug from the tap. Van drank it, the smell of the mug making the water taste funky. But it was wet and calmed his stomach instantly. He was feeling much better and then his nose detected something familiar. He glanced around and noted that the caravan set up camp right where they stopped when he and Eddie jumped from their wagons. The cook was sliding stacks of golden silver-dollar sized pancakes onto stained tin plates.

Pancakes?

Van's stomach grumbled, indicating that the unrest earlier was long forgotten and was ready for something delicious. And the stacks of fluffy griddle cakes looked appetizing. Van looked at Buff. "On second thought. I could go for some pancakes."

Buff frowned. "Pan what?"

Van pointed to the food the cook was sliding onto someone's plate. "What do you call those?"

Buff squinted and raised his eyebrows. "Dropped scones," he replied gruffly.

Van joined the line and received his short stack of dropped scones that looked exactly like pancakes. He followed the line to the next table where various jams were laid out. What he didn't see was syrup. He watched as others scooped jam onto their scones and moved to find a place to eat.

He selected what closely resembled strawberry jam and scanned the crowd for the girl from last night. She wasn't anywhere to be seen, but Eddie smiled and waved him over.

He sat next to Eddie on the ground and set the plate in his lap. Eddie chomped into his scone and looked around them. "So. Are you an evil wizard yet?"

Van laughed. "Not yet. My training begins after breakfast."

Eddie laughed. "Okay. I'll ask you again at lunch."

Van scanned the people milling around the temporary campsite. "Have you seen Maura?"

Eddie took another bite of scone, crumbs flying from his mouth as he replied. "Nope. Have you seen Harmony?"

Van swiped the scone through the jam and bit into it. It melted in his mouth with a burst of berry flavors mixed with the perfect pancake recipe. He closed his eyes as he chewed slowly and swallowed heaven.

When he opened them again, Eddie was smiling. "Good, huh? It's a far cry from that meaty bean dish last night. It's like night and day with that cook. Unfortunately, I don't know what the norm is for him. Is he a great cook that can't do beans, or a terrible cook with one good recipe?"

Van smeared his scone through the berry jam and took another bite. "It's kinda hard to ruin pancakes."

"That's what I was afraid of," Eddie said. "He's a terrible cook with really good pancakes. Let's hope these are a daily occurrence or I might starve."

They ate in silence. Eddie finished first and licked his plate clean before looking at Van as if he wanted to ask a question.

"What?" Van finally said.

"I just didn't want to upset you again by running at the mouth."

"I said I was sorry about that. I was exhausted from sweeping the road all day. Forget I ever said anything. You are Fast Eddie, and we all know what that means."

Eddie smiled. "Okay. After Harmony and I left, did you go back to Maura's wagon?"

Van blushed. "A gentleman never kisses and tells."

Eddie grinned like a fool. "But a man always boinks and tells."

Van looked around uneasily but was saved from having to answer when Eddie started talking. "The last thing I remember is stopping in front of her wagon to kiss. The next thing I knew I woke up in a windowless wagon and she was gone. Then my stomach started flipping around and I felt the urge to throw up something awful."

Van thought about the kiss he and Maura shared by the fire. The next thing he remembered was waking up in what he assumed was her bed in another windowless wagon. "Me too," he said.

"The funny thing," Eddie added, "is that I don't remember seeing the clock she said was broken. I don't remember anything about last night."

Van looked stricken. "Do you think we…?"

Eddie shrugged. "We did wake up in strange beds. But I was still fully dressed."

"Me too," Van said.

Eddie frowned. "I think they slipped us a mickey and put us to bed alone. That sucks. I finally meet a girl interested in me and she drugs me. And not the fun kind."

Van was puzzling through the blur of his memory. "But why?"

"Why what?"

"Why drug us? It couldn't have been to rob us. We don't have anything."

Eddie chuckled. "And Harmony didn't need to do that to get me to sleep with her. I would have done it in a heartbeat."

"We were fully dressed when we woke up. I don't think they did it to sleep with us."

"Then what did they do it for?"

Realization dawned on Van like the rays of the morning sun breaking through the fog when he was a young boy in San Francisco. "Maybe to keep us here. If we were passed out, we wouldn't escape during the night."

"And go where?"

"I don't know. But better safe than sorry I guess?"

"I hope they don't do that again tonight. I don't like waking up in pukesville."

Van looked around again. "I guess that's why we don't see them. They were following orders to keep us here and must feel ashamed about their part in it."

A bell clanged and everyone rose at once. Van and Eddie sprang to their feet. "What's going on?" Eddie asked, looking around him in a panic. "Bandits?"

Van turned and collided with Buff. "Breakfast is over," Buff said. He turned his scowling face toward Eddie and pointed a thick finger at him. "You. Be ready to sweep in ten minutes."

"Why?" Eddie asked. "What happens in ten minutes?"

"We are continuing our journey to The Grease."

Eddie frowned. "What's The Grease?"

Buff smiled for the first time since they met him. "You'll see. Now get to the rear and start clearing our tracks."

Van looked up at the beast of a man. "What about me?"

A voice responded from behind him. "You're with me."

Van spun around to see Halen sitting on a horse holding the reins of a second horse next to him. The horse's dark eyes examined Van with aloofness. He'd never seen a horse this close up. Its feet were enormous. More than big enough to crush a man flat with two swift stomps. "You don't expect me to—whoa—whoa—whoa," Van howled as he was lifted up from behind by strong hands that put him on the saddle like a young child being placed on a brightly painted wooden horse at the county fair carrousel.

He stared at the back of the horse's neck for a moment dumbfounded and then grabbed frantically at the horse's mane. Halen frowned at him. "You have ridden a horse before haven't you?"

Van swallowed his fear down but it kept coming back up, threatening to bring the pancakes up along with it. "Do merry-go-rounds count?" he whined.

"I don't know what that is. So I will assume your answer is no."

Van nodded but kept a firm grip on the horse's mane.

Halen sighed loudly. "Take the reins." He shook them at Van. When Van failed to move, he rolled his eyes. "Take them!"

Van reached out a hand and snatched the reins, grabbing the horse's mane again as he tilted in the saddle.

"Hold the reins tight, but not too tight, and simply let your horse follow me," Halen stated as he turned his horse to face Buff. "We will catch up with the caravan at the night camp."

Buff glowered at him without saying a word.

Halen chuckled bitterly. "And let Madam Ryes know I understand what she will do to us if we don't return."

Buff smiled briefly and turned away.

Halen clicked his tongue twice and pulled his reins to the side. His horse shot off at a fast trot.

Van stared at the quickly moving back of Halen in slack jawed shock when Eddie came up beside his horse. "Well don't just stand there, follow him." Eddie smacked the horse's backside, accompanied by a cringe-worthy loud clap, and it exploded into action.

Van clung to the reins and was distressed to find himself sliding precariously down one side of the saddle as they galloped away from the main road and deeper into the untamed badlands.

Chapter 57

Halen kept the pace quick to cross a large distance in a short amount of time. He didn't want to be anywhere near where people could witness him training Van in how to spin the elements. Even though it was the middle of the badlands, it was not unusual to stumble on a small enclave of Travelers who refused to use the established roads for one reason or another.

Halen rode hard for nearly half an hour until, when he looked back, several low hills separated them from the road they left behind. Halen noticed Van struggled to remain in his saddle as his horse kept pace with Halen's.

Halen yanked the reins to one side and his horse skidded in the loose dirt. He quickly glanced around and took note they were completely alone. This was as good a place as any.

Chapter 58

Van clung to his horse for dear life. He lost the reins almost immediately and ended up wrapping his arms around the horse's neck. He hugged it tightly as they bounced over one hill after another, wondering if it was possible to choke a horse out accidentally.

He tried several times to call out to Halen to get him to stop. But his voice caught in his throat and he could do nothing but hold tight and let the wind whip the horse's mane across his eyes.

Thankfully his horse finally started to slow down and Van felt confident enough to lift his head to look around. For the past half hour all he could see was the horse's legs galloping across the dry desert. His own neck grew stiff as he held himself in one position fearing any movement might loosen his grip and send him flying off the horse.

He spotted Halen circling around ahead and let out a sigh of relief. They were stopping. The muscles of his arms and legs took that moment to cramp up now that it was no longer a life or death struggle to hang onto the horse.

"Ahh," Van cried out as his body contorted from the pain and promptly fell out of the saddle. He hit the dirt flat on his back and all the air ejected from his lungs. Stars filled his vision and he gasped for oxygen, gulping in dust instead which sent him into a coughing fit.

A shadow fell across him and he looked up. Halen stood over him, shaking his head. The sun created a halo around Halen's head as he smiled down at him, held out his hand, and helped Van to his feet.

Van coughed and spit dust-filled mucus onto the ground. The grit crunched between his teeth, threatening to activate his gag reflex. He concentrated on clearing his mouth out before he cleared his stomach out.

Halen waited patiently while Van coughed and spat. Van finally stood up straight. "Whoo!" he exclaimed and coughed once more before finally taking a long deep breath that filled his lungs with clear air.

Halen looked him up and down. "Not bad for your first pony ride."

Van dusted off his clothing, causing a translucent beige cloud to form around his legs that took a long time to settle on the ground.

Halen grabbed the reins of both horses and led them to a gnarled tree that was little more than a glorified bush. He loosely draped the reins over the branches. If the horses wanted they could easily pull free and take off toward the horizon in any direction. It was more to let them know where they were expected to stay put until needed again.

Halen opened the saddlebag on his horse and removed a large unlit torch and a cylindrical tube made from a thick bamboo stalk. He turned and faced Van. "You crashed into the river with your wagon before ending up in Midguard, correct?"

It took a moment for Van to realize Halen meant car. "Yeah. That's right."

Halen nodded and started walking sideways, dragging his toe in the dirt.

Van walked over to him, still dusting off the last of the desert floor that hid in the creases of his leather jerkin. He originally called it a vest and was corrected by Talia's hunters who provided one each to him and Eddie.

Talia!

He forgot that she left to get food right before the arrows rained down from the sky into their campsite. Between dragging Halen over the mountain and then finding out he was descended from a long line of Spinners his brain disregarded any extraneous information, like, where was Talia?

He wondered if she escaped or was captured by their attackers. Or, worse, ended up killed by whoever shot Halen with an arrow.

He looked at Halen, who was determinedly drawing a large circle in the dirt. Van watched him with his eyes slightly squinted against the bright sun. While it had only been a few days, it felt like a lifetime since he set off on the road trip with Eddie to get on with the next stage of their lives. He expected it would include studying, late night beer bash parties, and maybe hooking up with a pretty co-ed. How was he expected to know the next stage of his life included surviving a real-life Medieval Times nightmare of dragons, sorcery, and pretty young maidens who drugged men to sleep at night for some unknown purpose?

Halen finished his circle in the sand and faced Van. He popped a cork off one end of the bamboo tube and set it on the ground. Then he lit the torch and stuck it in the ground next to the bamboo.

He stood and looked at Van with a strange smile, as if he was going to enjoy what he was about to do. "Your training begins, now."

Chapter 59

Walter spotted the horses along the horizon long before Talia could have seen them. Even if she were looking through her spyglass she couldn't beat Walter's keen bird sight. Having a canary for a husband did have its advantages. But there were still a lot of disadvantages.

She stopped and lifted the spyglass to her eye. She recognized Halen immediately and knew the thinner one with him was Van. Halen stuck a lit torch in the ground and walked away from it. Years of secretly witnessing Spinner training gave Talia the experience to know what Halen was planning, and that he shouldn't be disturbed.

Talia scanned wider across the desert. Eddie was nowhere to be seen. He must still be with the caravan, which meant there was little she could do here. Van wouldn't go anywhere without his friend. That much she surmised. Based on what little she knew of him, his sense of loyalty was not lacking.

She folded the hand-held telescope and kicked the horse back into a trot. Her dogs fell in step on either side of her, keeping whatever pace she set, and never once complaining. She didn't have any other choice. She would still have to beat the caravan to The Grease and figure out a way to save the Spinner and his new apprentice there. It wouldn't be easy, but then again, Talia always seemed to prefer tasks that were considered impossible by any measure.

Chapter 60

Van watched intently as Halen walked to the opposite edge of the circle he had drawn in the dirt. Van looked down and noticed that he was standing just outside the same circle. He glanced up and Halen motioned for him to join him inside.

Van took a step forward and then Halen tossed a small metal globe into the center of the circle. A rush of strong wind blew dirt into the air and enclosed them in a dome of dust. Van looked all around, but he couldn't see through the dome to the wasteland around them. He guessed it was to hide the secretive training of a Spinner.

The space inside the dome looked to be about fifty feet in diameter. It seemed bigger now that it was the only space visible and not offset by the expansive desert. Halen pointed to the bamboo cylinder standing up on one end in the middle of the enclosed space. Next to it was the flaming torch, the fire burning but not consuming the cloth wrapped around one end. "I'm going to guess you are a Water Spinner based on how you arrived. There is water inside the bamboo for you to use against me. I am a Fire Spinner. I will be using the torch."

Van frowned in confusion. "Using the torch? Wait a minute. Did you say against you?" Van jabbed a solitary index finger at Halen to punctuate his next question. "Am I supposed to fight you?"

"There are no shortcuts to becoming a Master Spinner. But we don't have time for you to connect with your powers the normal way. I will have to draw them out by any means necessary."

Van held his hands up in surrender. "Any means necessary? What are you...?" Van didn't have time to finish his question when Halen spun his hands in a blur and a glow emanated from under the collar of his shirt. A ball of fire suddenly shot out from the torch heading straight for Van's head.

Van brought his arms together to protect his face. The fireball slammed into him and knocked him off his feet. He hit the ground and slid backward a couple of feet. There was no time to recover before another fireball exploded on the ground next to his chest, throwing him into the air.

He hit the dome's wall of dust and fell back to the ground. He scrambled to his feet and pounded on the wall of shifting sands. It was solid and didn't budge no matter how hard he banged against it. The dome was obviously not only created to keep anyone from seeing what was going on in the arena. It was also designed to keep him trapped inside.

He spun around when he heard flames rippling through the air in his direction. He ducked and the fire exploded against the dirt dome. The dome was obviously very strong. The flames didn't do anything other than barely shift the sands slightly. There was no hope of escaping through the hole created by goading Halen into shooting fire at him and into the undulating dirt wall.

The only option Van could think of to keep Halen from killing him was to beg. "Stop," Van pleaded. "Enough!"

"Stop me!" Halen shouted and sent another fireball screaming across the open space straight toward Van.

Van ducked and rolled to the side as the fireball exploded, leaving a small crater in the ground. "How do I stop you!" he screamed back.

"Use the water!" Halen commanded.

Of course thought Van in a flash of enlightenment. He dashed forward, ducking under another fireball launched at him from the torch, and grabbed the bamboo cylinder. He doused the torch with the water in the bamboo container and stood triumphantly over the extinguished flame with his legs splayed apart, breathing heavily.

Halen shook his head and spun his hands even faster than before. The torch ignited again and burned Van right in the crotch. He jumped back with a yelp of pain. "What the...! I used the water! Just like you said."

Halen was still spinning his hands, a ball of flame hovering in the air above the relit torch. "That was a mistake. Now it will be harder for you to use the water as it soaks into the dry ground."

"What are you talking about?"

"Think of the water as a weapon to use against your opponent. The arrow is not your enemy. Neither is the bow. It is the archer. Don't fight the flame with the water. Fight me!"

Van looked at the short bamboo tube in his hand and darted straight for Halen. A fireball exploded at Van's side, sending him pinwheeling to the ground. He landed hard, the bamboo cylinder somersaulting away.

"Don't fight me with your physical body. Fight me with magic!" Halen shouted as another fireball expanded above the torch.

Van glared at Halen. What was he doing? Van didn't know how to use magic! Halen never bothered to shown him how before deciding to burn him to death.

Several smaller fireballs split from the larger one and shot through the air, headed straight for Van. He scrambled to his feet and ran along the edge of the dust dome. Explosions rippled along the dome's edge behind him, peppering him with pebbles and sand like buckshot from a double-barreled shotgun.

Van watched Halen out of the corner of his eye as he ran. The smile spreading wide across Halen's mouth showed he was enjoying this. As Van ran, and explosions peppered scorching grit all over his skin, he knew he must think of something. He couldn't keep this up for long. Halen was grinning like an old fool and spinning his hands in tight circles.

Van looked down at his hands and decided it couldn't hurt to try to mimic Halen. He cupped his hands and moved them around. He glanced at Halen who was laughing and shooting more fireballs at him.

Van spun his hands faster in similar motions to Halen's, glancing at the puddle of water in the middle of the arena soaking into the dry earth. But nothing happened.

A fireball rocketed straight for his head and Van raised his spinning hands to protect his face from being burned while he continued the motion.

The puddle of water suddenly shimmered, gathered together, and shot up into the air, creating a defensive wall between Van and the approaching fireball. The fireball hit the water and went out like a light. The wall of water splashed to the ground as soon as Van stopped spinning his hands.

"That's it, Van!" Halen hollered. "Keep it up!"

Halen increased his barrage of fireballs exploding around Van. A massive fireball started to form over the torch that filled the ceiling of the dome. Van could feel the heat from the expanding reverse pool of fire and watched in horror as Halen didn't stop, but kept filling the interior of the dome with sizzling flame.

Then Van's eye spotted something dangling around Halen's neck. It was a large crystal that glowed brighter each time the flames increased and then faded again. Was that the source of Halen's power? There was only one way to find out. He didn't have time to make a wrong decision. The heat was almost unbearable as the entire top half of the dome was brimmed with liquid fire.

Van spun his hands again and concentrated on the puddle—but it was gone! Halen increased the heat inside the dome to evaporate the water on the ground. Van didn't have any water to fight with. Halen was going to defeat him if he didn't think of something quickly.

An explosion blew him off his feet and he skidded on his side across the ground. He sat up and felt wetness running down his upper lip. He touched a hand to his face and brought it into view. There was blood on it. He was bleeding from his nose!

Wait!

Blood was a liquid!

Van stood and sprang to the side to avoid another exploding ball of fire. He spun his hands and concentrated on the blood spilling from his nose. He saw a drop of crimson red spinning in the air in front of his face. The drop expanded into a larger sphere as he pulled more blood from his streaming nose until he formed a golf ball sized glob of bright red thick fluid.

He whipped his hands in Halen's direction, ignoring the fireball flying at him. He closed his eyes as the fireball slammed into his side, lifting him off his feet and slamming him into the dome wall. But not before his ball of blood splattered against Halen's face. It impacted with Halen's left cheek and expanded to splash into his eyes.

Van hit the ground and bounced back to his feet, running for Halen as fast as he could. Halen was still wiping the blood out of his eyes when Van reached him. Van grabbed the leather strap visible around Halen's neck and yanked hard. The strip of hide snapped, suddenly ending Halen's connection with the focusing power of the crystal as Van pulled it away from him. But now that power was coursing through Van.

The pain suddenly consuming Van's body was like nothing he ever felt before.

Halen scrubbed furiously at his eyes to clear them of Van's blood.

When he finally could see, he looked at Van, his eyes growing wide as he held out his hand and rushed toward Van screaming. "Van! Stop!"

He reached for the crystal necklace and Van pulled away, trying to run. But he suddenly didn't have the strength to move. He collapsed to his knees and looked down at the hand that held the crystal. It glowed as bright as the sun and was quickly being eclipsed by a large glob of red. Van's eyes grew wide as he witnessed his blood evacuating his body out of every pore on the skin of his hand. His vision tunneled as his mind reacted to the sudden loss of blood. Just before everything went black he realized the same thing was happening along his arm. His blood was being drawn out of every pore and coalescing in the air above his skin.

The world tilted and his head spun out of control. He faintly heard Halen screaming at him but then the sound of his own blood rushing out of him overtook everything.

The world narrowed to a pinpoint of light in front of him. And then it went out, shutting him off from the world around him.

Chapter 61

Halen grabbed the necklace and pulled it from Van's unconscious grasp. As soon as he did, the crystal's glow died and the blood seeping from every pore in Van's body soaked back in, leaving only a faint red stain over his skin.

Halen breathed a sigh of relief when he felt for a pulse and found one. It was faint, but Van was still alive. He stopped him before he pulled too much precious lifeblood from his own body.

Halen glared at the crystal in his hand and then threw it. It bounced off the dome interior and landed in the dirt, its color shifting to a dark black. All the light that previously glowed from within was gone.

Halen sat on the ground and cradled Van in his arms. What was he being forced to do? He'd ignored his own training and took it too far. He glanced at the crystal. It was now the color of obsidian. Madam Ryes provided it to him to counteract the suppression of his magic by The Order. It was the first time he'd obtained enough power to fully counteract the tarnishing of his crest pin. He felt what it was like to be a Master Spinner again. And it felt good.

But when Van took the crystal, it fell into the hands of a Spinner who wasn't being suppressed. It was too much power for anyone to handle. Especially for someone using magic for the first time.

Halen rocked Van in his lap and wiped away the blood-soaked hair from Van's eyes. He smiled down on the unconscious form.

Van did it. Despite almost dying, he figured out how to use his magic to distract Halen and take away the source of his enhanced power. But he used more than magic to defeat Halen. He combined a magical attack along with a physical one. That level of cunning would save his life one day. Halen chuckled softly to himself. There was hope for the boy yet. If Van could do what he did on his first attempt at spinning the elements, there was no telling what he could do after years of training.

Then Halen quickly scolded himself for even thinking such a thing. The Order made their proclamation. The Maclean line was closed. They were no longer the heroes Midguard called upon to save the realm. But then why was Van here? Van couldn't have come to Midguard by accident. He may have unknowingly activated his powers to move across the realms, but somebody must have been behind the accident that drove him into the river.

A sudden thought chilled Halen to his bones.

Somebody wanted Van in Midguard. Somebody went to great lengths to get him here from Techrealm and then hired hunters to kill him.

But why?

What threat was Van to anyone?

Someone must wanted Van dead and caused all of this to happen.

Whoever it was, they had miscalculated. They should have left well enough alone. Van was in Techrealm with no possibility of discovering his true identity. And Halen was hiding out on the fringes of society with no desire to buck the status quo.

But due to the attempt on Van's life, he was in Midguard and being trained as a Spinner, by none other than Halen himself. And he was being trained far away from the oppressive rules of The Order. This was exactly what Veren wanted. What he had asked him to do moments before death.

Halen didn't bother fighting back the tears that flowed. He was, by a cruel twist of fate, following Veren's final wish. A request he never thought he would ever fulfill.

But if he hoped to continue, and make sure The Order didn't mess everything up, he needed to figure out who wanted Van dead. And find out before it was too late.

Chapter 62

Calen pushed away the scroll and stared blindly at the open book in front of him. It was impossible to concentrate on anything. He was still running high on endorphins. Van was dead. Halen was dead. All ties to him were severed. It didn't matter who he found to be his scapegoat. He would wrap up this investigation and it would fade to time as just another tragic series of events that meant little to the overall record of history.

Nobody but Calen understood the significance of these events. Aeron was coming and there was nobody left to stop him.

A knock on his door broke him from his trance. "Yes!" he called out.

The door opened slowly and Nina poked her head in cautiously. "Master?" she said hesitantly.

He frowned at her. "What is it, apprentice?"

"Uh, my lessons?"

He glanced at the sun casting its rays onto the sundial outside the window. He was an hour late. Unusual, but he hadn't slept a wink the night before and was kind of busy all morning.

He smiled warmly at his apprentice. "Of course. I'm sorry, Nina. There will be no formal instruction today. Work on your mantras."

She fidgeted but stayed by the open door. Her passive-aggressive ways were never more infuriating than they were now. Calen wanted her to leave, but he knew she wouldn't until she said what was on her mind. "What?"

"I was wondering when I can start spinning elements. I've been in training for five years and have yet to use my powers to their fullest. I think it's time."

He gave her a withering look. "When you are ready…"

She expelled a puff of air from her mouth in irritation. "I am ready!"

Calen stood and slammed his book shut loudly. "Nina!"

She immediately shrunk into herself and lowered her head in supplication. Calen stomped around the desk and approached her quickly. "Look at me."

She was slow to raise her head so he grabbed her chin and forced her to look him in the eyes. Anyone with fewer secrets than he retained would never have detected the defiance concealed just below the surface of her gaze. He knew that look in her eyes. It was a hallmark of their family line, being able to keep deep secrets just beneath the surface. It was the same look he saw in himself every time he passed by the mirror.

He wished he could introduce her to Aeron. He would see her potential and then there would be two champions within The Order working toward victory. But Aeron insisted it was better if Calen's involvement with him remained a secret. She would have made a good addition to his team. Instead he kept her down. And if her current behavior was any indicator he would have to keep pushing her down. She just wouldn't stay down on her own.

He held her chin firmly in his grip and leaned in. "You will not be ready until I say you are ready."

"But my father let me—"

He tightened his grip and she went silent. "Your father is not your master. I am. And you should be thankful for that. After his banishment, your training was invalidated. You are lucky I was the only master in our family with no children of my own, or there would have been no one to take you in as their apprentice. And a young Spinner without a master is no Spinner at all. That is the rule of Spinner Law."

"Thank you, Calen, for taking me in."

His eyes burned into hers. "And?"

He could see her struggling to keep her defiance in check. He hoped that by taking her under his wing after her father was expelled from The Order, he could reshape her. Mold her into what was needed for Aeron's triumphant arrival. A Spinner who knew her place.

But there was too much of her father in her. Truth be told, she carried the family defiance within her like it was hereditary. Her father questioned a decision of the High Master and paid the price for his insolence. While she bit her tongue, he could see the uncertainties in her mind forming as she examined her training, his instruction, her place in The Order, and her place in the grand scheme of the universe. "And I am grateful for your generosity," she said through gritted teeth.

He released her chin with a flick of his wrist. Her head whipped to the side and she massaged her jawline while looking at him.

He turned his back to her. "Double studies today."

He could feel her heated gaze on his back and smiled. As he returned to his desk, he heard the door close quietly. It satisfied him to no end to see her having a hard time controlling the rage building inside her. There just might be hope for her yet. It only required a little redirection of her rage. Then maybe she could be shaped into a follower like the rest of the apprentices.

Every generation a natural leader always emerged among the apprentices. Everyone always assumed the current crop of apprentices would be led by Van Maclean, since his family was the strongest.

When that possibility was eliminated with the banning of the entire Maclean line, Calen prayed that this generation would be different, and there would be no leader. That would make his life simple. But Nina Heise stepped up to the plate and every apprentice quickly fell in line behind her.

Banishing her father was supposed to crush her informal leadership position among the apprentices. It did the opposite, everyone rallying behind her with their support. Calen needed to find another way to undermine her influence so he agreed to train her in the ways of the family. He managed to effectively delay her training. There was no way she would be seen as a powerful Spinner and her status as leader would diminish when others could spin the elements better than her. His resolve to keep her spirits down and her skills untrained as long as possible was unwavering.

Calen tread carefully to make it look like he was training her while at the same time stunting her knowledge of how to harness magic. He was successful in getting her to believe that it was her failings, and not his teachings, that always kept her at the bottom of the measured range of Spinner ability. What confused him most was how easy it was to get away with subpar training and still have everyone think it was Nina's inability to learn. But then again, the Council of Elders were split among other matters that demanded their attention. And Falen was too wrapped up in presenting The Order as anything but perfect. Calen watched Falen actively suppress the acknowledgment of failing apprentices and didn't waste time looking into why they might be failing.

Life couldn't be more perfect for Calen.

The Order was being weakened from the inside out. Any Spinners who might have posed a threat to his plan conveniently violated the growing list of rules of The Order and were banished. One by one the Spinners' crests were tarnished and they were exiled to the far corners of Midguard, far away from the Citadel of the West. By the time of the next third moon, there would be no one left to oppose Aeron on this side of the gate.

Chapter 63

Talia rode into The Grease. Her horse's head drooped and the dogs plodded slowly along her flank. The sun beat mercilessly down on all of them and her canteen ran dry a couple hours before. Her entourage was too large for her to carry enough water without using a wagon. But a wagon would only slow her down. She needed to lighten her load. It wasn't fair to the animals. If not much had changed in this town since her last stopover she could find someone who would give them a good home.

Despite the reputation of, well, just about everyone who passed through The Grease, nobody would harm two perfectly good hunting dogs. Only fighting dogs were in any danger here. But these two were hunters through and through and would be invaluable to anyone in the badlands. She could rest easy they would be well cared for.

As she rode through the middle of town people who looked more natural with a scowl on their face grinned broadly and pointed at her as they murmured to those around them. More faces turned her way as people gawked, laughed, and prodded others to look at her too.

She drew her eyebrows down at the reaction. This was not the level of attention she expected. Or wanted. Was it possible that the biggest warlord in The Grease circulated her picture all around town and gave an embarrassing story along with it on the slim chance she would ever return? It didn't seem likely. Then again, Koby Dameron rarely did what was expected of him.

Laughter erupted to her right and she jabbed her heels into her horse to prod him to a faster trot.

"Hey huntress," a man suddenly called from her left. She stared straight ahead and ignored him, urging her mount to trot even faster. Maybe coming to this town was a bad idea.

"Nice falcon," he added as she rode away quickly. His statement was met with waves of laughter from both sides of the street.

She glanced to her shoulder suddenly remembering Walter sitting there looking majestic as he rode on her shoulder as skillfully as she rode her horse. She stifled a smile realizing the reason for all the attention. Walter spun around and tweeted insults at the man who called after them. She felt a great weight lifted from her shoulders. She wouldn't have to worry about Koby if she kept her head down.

She shook her head and suppressed a smile. She must have looked the odd sight. Riding into town on her horse, two hunting dogs loping in her shadow, and a bright yellow half-ounce canary perched heroically on her shoulder.

She couldn't stifle it any longer and laughed out loud, causing Walter to turn on her and twitter angrily. She couldn't keep from laughing. This only enraged Walter more and he took off into the air, spewing chirped insults in his wake.

She called out after him. "Don't be like that, Walter. Who cares what these knuckleheads think?"

"What did you call me?" a man who was almost as tall as her horse strode up angrily toward her.

She glanced down at the irritated face. "Davon," she said and her dog moved closer at her command, growling at the man. The man took a step back, wide eyes suddenly in rapt attention on the angry looking dog. Davon approached slowly, still growling. The man kept taking steps backward. He was so focused on the dog encroaching on him he failed to notice the vegetable cart until he tripped into it.

The sidewalls cracked under his weight and split open. Apples rolled out from the broken cart across the cobblestone road. Everyone's attention suddenly shifted to the broken cart and bystanders started laughing at him instead of her. He stood up, glaring around him at the laughter he was receiving.

He pointed up at Talia. "Watch your back." He turned, stumbling over rolling apples, and ran into a back alley to get away from the embarrassment he sustained.

"Davon," she said again and he fell into place behind her. "Good boy."

She scanned the sky, looking for her husband. Where could he have gone? She continued on until she found The Dark Mole Tavern. The sign was a lot more faded than the last time she passed through town but, surprisingly, the place was still there.

She commanded the dogs to wait with the horse tied to the hitching post in reach of a water trough. All together the horse and the dogs thirstily dove their noses into the waiting water.

She took one last glance into the sky. Walter was nowhere to be seen. There was no doubt he was watching her, though. She smiled up, did a small wave and a wink, and then passed through the door into the tavern.

She paused just inside the door to let her eyes adjust to the dim light cast by the lamps sitting at the center of every other table. On the other side of the room the bartender was hanging glasses behind the bar.

She walked past tables half filled with men who sat sullenly by themselves and drank quietly. It was not the usual tavern scene with drunk men standing arm in arm singing drinking songs. In The Grease, if you so much as looked at someone for more than a few seconds, it started a fight.

Talia walked up to the bar and propped one dusty boot on the foot rail. To her surprise the man who turned around must have been no more than twelve years old. He stepped down from the crate he was standing on that made him look adult height while hanging the glasses and grunted at her, which she interpreted as "Drink?" right before he grabbed a half-full glass of lager and sipped from it.

Talia frowned. His face was clear of the blemishes that would signify his entry into puberty. He was definitely too young to be serving lager let alone drinking it.

"I'm looking for Markus," she said.

The young boy put down his lager and frowned. "Why?"

Was he capable of saying anything more than monosyllable words?

Her eyes widened with insistence "He's the owner."

The boy puffed up his chest. "I'm the owner," he mumbled almost imperceptibly.

Talia was taken aback and about to respond with some choice words that would surely get her in more trouble than she wanted when an elderly man at the end of the bar spoke. "Not 'til I'm dead, Eugene."

"Stop calling me that! My name's Galen," the boy mumbled back.

Talia glanced at the man. The first thing she noticed was the large hairy black mole on his left cheek. The next thing she noted was that, while he was looking in her direction, he wasn't looking directly at her. The pupils of his eyes were a milky white and he was only looking in her general direction as he spoke loudly. "The boy thinks he's going to be some kind of wizard and has already taken a Spinner sounding name," he grunted.

"I turn thirteen in a fortnight," Eugene spat back. "They will come for me. They will see that I have the gift. And then, old man, I will be rid of you."

"No, Eugene. Technically, I will be rid of you. Unfortunately, I fear I am stuck with you until I draw my final breath. Now go check on the few customers you haven't scared off yet with your sparkling personality."

Eugene stomped off, mumbling profanities under his breath.

"Kids," Markus countered as he scrutinized her with cloudy eyes for several moments. "My old eyes don't see so well any more. Mostly shapeless dark splotches in a formless light. No big loss. I never developed a memory for faces. Or anything really. But I could never forget your voice. Dameron won't be pleased to learn you are here."

Talia slid across the bar until she was next to the old man. "I'm kind of hoping he won't find out."

"It's a small world, Talia. You can't hide forever. Don't worry about me, though. If anyone asks, I didn't see you."

"Is the special suite available?" she asked.

"Well, I guess you could hide out forever in there. Yes. I haven't been down there in a while, it might need some tidying up."

"Thank you, Markus."

"I could never refuse a request from you."

Talia looked around, noticing the corner booth was empty. "Where is Yareli?"

His face drooped and he lowered his head. "She passed on to a better place."

Talia placed a hand on his arm. "I'm so sorry. I really liked her."

Markus laughed sadly and placed a hand over hers as it rested on his arm. "So did I. She was a lovely woman who saw past this to the man inside." He motioned to the large mole on his face. His forehead wrinkled and he frowned at her as his hand stroked hers. He suddenly looked at her differently, despite not seeing her clearly. He raised a hand to feel her face. Talia didn't move away and let him feel her cheeks, her neck, and around the edges of her eyes. He pulled his hand away quickly. "You haven't changed."

"I needed more time."

He lowered his head and shook it. "I warned you about selling your soul—"

"I found him, Markus," she said quickly, interrupting his impending lecture.

The old man looked at her in alarm and then smiled, revealing that all his teeth were missing. Time had not been as good to him as it had been to her. "Was it worth it?"

"Of course. But we have a little problem that I'm working on. I just need a place to stay for a few days."

"Of course. Whatever you need." Markus' nose crinkled and he turned to the bar. "What is that smell? Boy! Boy! Where is that kid! Never around when—"

"Let me help. What do you need, Markus?"

"Nothing. I can't repay you for everything you've already done. I must be decades in arrears with you. Boy!"

She smiled knowing he would hear it in her voice even though he couldn't see it with his eyes. "I can help a little more. And just for you, free of charge."

Markus smiled. "Okay fine. At least it's a price I can afford."

Talia went around the end of the bar to investigate the smell. A drunk ambled up and slapped down coins while ordering a lager. Talia slid the coins off the bar and dispensed his order from the tap. He dropped an additional coin on the counter and added a wink for her tip. She smiled sweetly back, playing the part of sultry beer maiden, and slid the extra coin into a pocket. The man smiled and carried his lager back to his table, spilling it as he swayed across the floor. Talia slipped the coin back out of her pocket and placed it in the owner's tip box under the counter.

Word spread quickly that there was a new bartender at The Dark Mole Tavern. And she was a looker. The bar was standing room only before the midnight bell tolled. Gone was the somber mood of the few patrons sitting alone at their tables. Now the place was filled with dozens of burly men singing at the top of their lungs. Every one of them off key but enjoying themselves immensely. The impression from the street as to how much fun people were having inside The Dark Mole enticed even more patrons to squeeze themselves through the crowded entrance to join the festivities. This was no longer about a sexy barmaid but about people having a good time and spending a ton of money to keep their spirits high.

When the activity of pouring and carrying became too much for her, someone magically arrived with pretty maidens from the companion house across the street. In exchange for a hundred percent of the tips they earned they were willing to take orders and carry drinks. Talia readily agreed and, even if just for one night, the glory days of The Dark Mole Tavern were back.

Talia was pulling lagers and depositing tips in the box all night. She estimated, based on how empty the tip box was on her arrival, they matched several months' worth of business in but a few hours.

But, looking over at Markus, the satisfied look on his face as he talked with patrons who came by to say how they thought he closed down or needled him for keeping his thriving business such a secret was worth more than the money they were earning.

When the orders backed up, Markus slipped behind the bar, and despite his visual handicap, was pouring drinks nearly as fast as Talia. They worked flawlessly together and never once got in each other's way as they crossed back and forth fulfilling a steady stream of orders.

As Talia set two mugs down and slid them out to the waiting server she glanced over at Markus who was chatting up the patrons at the bar without missing a step on the drinks he was pouring. She smiled to herself. Some things never changed no matter how much time passed and it felt good to be working side by side with her younger brother again.

Chapter 64

Van woke abruptly and sat up, looking around in a panic. This was becoming a bad habit. He was in bed in a small room. All he could see through the window was darkness. He must have passed out and slept the entire day away. The swaying lamps hanging from the ceiling indicated motion. He recognized the brightly colored and decorated ceiling. His heart rate slowed and he settled back into the bed.

He was back with the caravan.

A faint snoring drew his attention to a dark shape at the foot of the bed. Halen was asleep in a chair with his feet propped up on the edge of the bed.

Van settled his head on the pillow and closed his eyes for what he felt was only a second. When he opened them again, the sun was already shining and Halen was watching him. "Good, you're awake," Halen said abruptly. "Time to continue your training."

Van sat up and his stomach growled. "What about breakfast?"

Halen scowled at him. "Breakfast ended hours ago."

"I'm hungry."

"I'll find you something while you get dressed."

Van tossed aside the blankets and then realized he was naked. He grabbed the sheets and wadded them over his privates. "What happened to my clothes?"

"They were soaked with blood. There's a fresh set on the chair."

Van suddenly remembered seeing his blood oozing from every pore on his arms and hands. He looked at Halen with worry and confusion written across his face. "What happened?"

Halen swooped in closely and startled Van as he whispered, "Not here. We will discuss it under the dome."

Halen dashed to the door and glanced back. "Get dressed. You have slept away most of the morning and we don't have nearly enough time to get you ready for tomorrow."

Van turned confused eyes to Halen. "What's tomorrow?"

Halen kept his face serious as he replied, "The Gauntlet."

Halen shut the door leaving Van alone in the wagon. Van dressed quickly and went outside. His stomach growled again to remind him that Halen promised to be searching for something to eat.

"Hey, sleepyhead."

Van spun around to see Eddie's smiling face. He was leaning on a wide straw broom and shook his head while still smiling. "So? The mortals are stuck getting up at the crack of dawn and sweeping away the trail of the caravan while the pretty boys get to sleep in as long as they want?"

Van punched Eddie in the shoulder. "It's not like that."

Eddie's face grew serious. "The washer woman told me your clothes were so soaked with blood she recommended burning them instead of wasting half the caravan's resources to clean them. What happened?"

Van tried to remember, but everything came in disjointed flashes. Nothing comprehensible or complete enough to give him a mental picture of the day before came to mind. He finally just shook his head. "I don't know."

Eddie held his hands up. "I get it. Trade secrets and all." He moved in close and half whispered. "Just tell me one thing. Were you able to perform any—you know—feats of mystery and magic?"

Van's memory came in snippets and fractured events. His eyebrows knitted in confusion. "I think so?"

Eddie smiled and slapped Van on the back. "That's my boy! I always knew you would amount to something."

Buff cast a shadow over both of them. Eddie jumped and looked at him. "Geez, man. For someone so big, you move like a house cat. I'm surprised the ground doesn't vibrate with each footfall like the T-Rex in those Jurassic Park movies."

Buff frowned and looked at Eddie, but Van could tell he was giving him a sideways glance, never letting him go beyond his peripheral vision. Buff pretended to ignore Van as he spoke to Eddie. "I have never met someone who says so many strange words. I have no idea what you're talking about."

Eddie half lidded his eyes and his mouth became a thin line. "How soon before I have to start sweeping again?"

Buff held his hand out slowly, keeping one eye on Van but clearly directing his attention to Eddie. "Your duties as sweeper are on hold. Word has gotten around that you are good with mechanicals."

Eddie's smile was back as he nodded. "I've re-built not one, but two, working mini-bikes before graduating high school. One of them was even a GP RS-R with a 40cc, four-stroke, air cooled engine that could hit 10,000 RPMs. On a good day I could get that baby up to forty-two miles per hour on the open road. Just ask Van, here. He clocked me using Old Bessie."

Buff looked like his head was going to explode as he puzzled out the words Eddie fired at him. "Old Bessie?"

"Yeah. My 1988 Hyundai Excel hatchback. She's sitting at the bottom of a lake somewhere. I must say, a burial at sea was unexpected but no less than she deserved."

Buff's face scrunched up as he struggled to understand Eddie. He finally shook his head. "The cook is having trouble with one of his stoves. Do you think you can fix it?"

"As long as it's not a microwave or one of those computer controlled ovens. I hate silicon chips invading everything sacred. Those eggheads," he looked at Van. "No offense. But those eggheads should leave our stuff alone. Build mainframes. Build your whole cloud-computing civilization-ending Skynet for all I care. But stop putting a computer in my toaster."

Buff frowned. "Was that a yes?"

Eddie laughed. "Yes. Geez." He said and then turned to Van, placing a hand conspiratorially against the side of his mouth. "These people really need some television to get them caught up. And I don't mean those new curved high-def sets with five hundred digital channels and built-in Netflix. I'm talking an old black and white set with rabbit ears and the pliers so you can change the channel 'cause the plastic knob broke off." Eddie's eyes glazed over and he was no longer looking at Van despite looking straight at him. "My grandfather left me that TV. I got it working, but there wasn't much being transmitted over the air it could receive. A shame. But those were still the good old days."

Buff shook his head. He finally gave up on trying to understand Eddie and spun on his heels. "Come with me," he shot over his shoulder as he walked away.

Eddie snapped out of his private fantasy and headed after Buff. He spun around to walk backwards and held his fists up in front of him.

"Keep up the good fight, Van. See you tonight."

Eddie spun around and jogged to catch up with Buff, only to start pummeling him with more phrases and idioms that meant nothing to the citizens of Midguard.

Van heard the clomping of horse hooves behind him and groaned. Halen decided to get going immediately rather than wait until they ate. He turned and his mouth hung open in surprise. Instead of Halen's sour mug, he found himself staring at the smiling face of Maura. In one gloved hand, she held a jet-black parasol that shaded her from the sun. In the other she held the reins of a horse. "This is Shadow," she said. "She's a more—understanding horse for novice riders than Lightening is."

He smiled at her still unable to remember the time he spent with her beyond the initial kiss. "Was that the horse's name yesterday? Lightening?"

She nodded.

"Fitting," Van quipped. "I felt like I was hanging onto a bolt."

She held out the reins. "You shouldn't have any trouble with Shadow. She's my horse. She will take good care of you."

Van took the reins and his hand lingered with hers, their fingers slowly intertwining, before she blushed, pulled away, and looked around as if afraid someone was watching.

She took a step backward. "Maybe I will see you tonight if you are up for it?"

Van couldn't keep the smile off his face, his lips threatening to split his cheeks in half. "I'd like that. I'm sorry I missed dinner last night."

She blushed and quickly interrupted him. "That's okay. I wasn't feeling well and stayed in my wagon. Maybe it was something we ate?"

Van nodded. "I knew those beans tasted a little off."

She took another step back. "Take care of yourself, Van Maclean." She spun and disappeared between two wagons before Van could ask her about that night. Van thought about going after her when a sharp voice made him jump.

"Mount up, Van. There is much to be done and we have very little time," Halen barked as he steadied his horse. Van never heard him ride up, he was so focused on watching Maura leave.

He looked up at Halen, holding up a hand to deflect the sunlight streaming in from behind him. The sun's position directly behind Halen gave him an impressive glow that made him look heroic sitting up on his steed.

"What about breakfast?" Van asked, his stomach growling again as if adding its voice to the question.

Halen held up a small cloth sack and tossed it at Van. "Scones. Courtesy of the cook. You may eat them on the way."

Van frowned. "On the way?"

Halen sighed. "I don't want a repeat of yesterday. It took a long time to get you back while you were—asleep. This time we will be where the caravan plans to spend the night. They will come to us if we have any trouble."

Van winced. "How about if we just try not to kill me this time?"

Halen's horse tossed its head and he pulled on the reins to turn it around. He twisted his head to keep Van in view as the horse fidgeted in a tight circle. "That I cannot promise. But we will start off with some instruction before you attempt to spin again."

Van bunched up his shoulders and glared at Halen. "Why didn't you start off with instruction yesterday?"

"Because you weren't ready."

"Wouldn't not being ready automatically count for needing instruction?"

Halen impatiently shook his head "You have now controlled the power inside you intentionally. That was not the case yesterday."

Halen kicked the sides of his horse and galloped off down the road before Van could say another word.

Van tightened his grip on the reins and went to climb into the saddle. Shadow sensed his trepidation and stepped sideways away from him as soon as he put one foot in the stirrup. Van found himself hopping along on one foot, with the other firmly locked in the stirrup, as he chased Shadow around in a circle.

"Come on, Shadow. Maura said you would be nice."

To his surprise Shadow stopped immediately and stood still, as if she understood his words. He crawled up into the saddle. Then, wanting to be nice back, he patted the side of her neck. "Good girl."

He looked up to see Halen long gone, already a small figure against the horizon. "Maybe I do need Lightening if I plan to catch up with

Halen," he said to himself out loud.

Shadow suddenly shot forward, nearly sending Van tumbling backward out of the saddle. He regained his balance, leaned forward, and held onto the reins tightly this time. Luckily, Maura was correct, Shadow was much smoother and it was easier for Van to stay in his saddle. It didn't take long for Shadow to catch up with Halen and then fall into an easy trot beside him.

Halen looked over with a faint smile. "We are going to have some fun today."

Van laughed nervously. "More fun than yesterday I hope."

"Oh yes," Halen responded. "A lot more fun than yesterday."

Halen kicked his horse back into a fast gallop and Shadow followed suit. Van clung to the reins and let Shadow's steady gait take him wherever Halen was leading them.

Chapter 65

Maura stepped between the wagons of the caravan quickly and nearly collided with Madam Ryes. "Oh!" she cried out in surprise and then bowed her head in supplication. "Madam Ryes. I didn't see you there."

Madam Ryes narrowed her eyes suspiciously at Maura. "But I saw you."

"Of course, Madam Ryes. I should be more careful." Maura tried to step around her but Madam Ryes stepped to the same side quickly, blocking Maura's path.

"Interesting," Madam Ryes said.

"What is?" Maura said quietly, keeping her head down.

"That you would risk coming into the sun to provide the young Spinner with a horse."

Madam Ryes swatted at the parasol and knocked it away temporarily. The sun burned brightly and Maura stifled her reaction as she tilted it back to block out the damaging rays. Madam Ryes bent at the waist to peer at her under the edge of the parasol. "Why are you favoring him?"

Maura's head shot up along with her parasol but she was careful to not let any sun reach her skin again. She met Madam Ryes' confident gaze with one of her own. "Mother told me how much he means to you. To the entire caravan. I was only doing my part to clear our debt."

"Did you do what I asked the night before?"

Maura lowered her gaze. She spoke so quietly it almost sounded like the faint hiss of air seeping from a steam engine. "Yes."

Madam Ryes smiled. "Then, as I told your mother, your debt is clear. You and your sister are free to leave any time."

Maura should have been ecstatic at hearing that statement from Madam Ryes but now, more than ever, she had a reason to stay. She finally found someone who could, and would, love her for her. Someone who she could be a true partner with and build a real life. But her mother would never approve of her giving her heart to a human boy. Her mother always told her and her sister, ever since they were very young and learning their vocation, "Never, ever, give your heart to a human. It is our intent to take his from him."

Madam Ryes took a deep breath and let it out. "You are, of course, welcome to stay. But remember, there are no free rides in the badlands."

"I understand," Maura replied and this time was able to get around Madam Ryes. She hurried between the stationary wagons of the caravan to her own windowless one. She climbed the steps and secured herself inside before taking her next breath.

Her sister, Harmony, gave her a startled look. "What were you doing outside? In the daytime?"

"Why aren't you asleep? In your own wagon?" Maura shot back.

Harmony's face suddenly shifted instantly to alarm. "Oh my god! Your face! You let the sunlight touch you?"

Maura brushed past her, slid into the lower bunk mounted on the wall, and pulled the curtain closed.

Harmony opened the curtain again and looked at her sister with concern. "Maura? Why were you outside?"

Maura gave her a look that immediately silenced any further questions. "Leave me alone!" she said a little too harshly and pulled the curtain closed, cutting her off from the outside world in concept only.

She hoped she could convince Harmony to never tell mother that she ventured outside in the daytime. It wouldn't take long for Harmony to figure out why. And it would take her mother even less time.

She lay in the bunk and caressed a finger across her face. The skin was tender to her touch. It would heal when the moonlight cast its reflective rays across it. But she couldn't be that careless again. If her mother discovered how Maura felt for a—human—she would make things difficult for a lot of people. Especially for Maura.

Chapter 66

Talia woke slowly to a different world. A world where she knew she was safe, wanted, and loved. She sat up slowly, easing herself vertical to keep the pounding in her head from overtaking her. Being a bartender in any tavern in The Grease meant you were required to match shots with a successive queue of heavy drinkers. And Markus' unique concoction, The Wart, went down easily. But like its namesake, it formed roots that attached to your memory and refused to let you forget how much you drank the night before well into the following day.

And that day was today.

She blinked in the dimness of the hidden room buried fifty feet under the main road that went past the front of The Dark Mole Tavern's front door. She helped build this room long before a town grew up around the small one-shack watering hole. It was originally built to shelter outlaws crossing through the badlands in a time when thugs were lone wolfs and crime wasn't an industry.

Back then, it was called The Dark Hole Tavern. But as solitary criminals banded together and started carving out territory it was not deemed a clever idea to advertise the defining secret of the place. After a short deliberation the tavern was renamed after the mole on one of the partner's face. As the town grew, the watering hole expanded into a tavern, growing in size as the population it served increased. Over the decades The Grease changed from a single watering hole for horses to one of the largest towns in the badlands.

Talia placed a hand on the cool dirt wall and closed her eyes. It was good to be home, even if just for a little while.

The door opened and Markus stood with a tray of biscuits and fresh fruit sliced on a plate. "Room service," he said softly and smiled.

Ignoring her pounding head, Talia crossed over and took the tray from him. She helped him locate the chair and then lit the candle.

The room brightened slightly and he squinted around. His forehead wrinkled in confusion. "You're alone?"

She went back and sat on the bed and placed the tray in her lap, digging into the fruit first. "You didn't think I'd bring some boozer down here after we closed the doors, did you?"

"No. I thought Walter would be with you."

She stopped chewing. "Walter and I—we sorta had a fight I guess. He took off as soon as we entered town and I haven't seen him since."

"This is not a safe place for someone to be wandering around alone."

"I'm pretty sure Walter will be fine. But I don't think you came down here to talk about him."

Markus looked up at the ceiling briefly before facing her. "You always go straight to the heart of the matter. Just like mom."

"And you always pussy foot around the issue. Just like dad. Out with it Markus."

"Well, unlike you, I'm not getting any younger…"

"I've found Walter. I don't think I'll be taking any more—treatments," she added quickly.

Markus laughed. "And you've seen what my protégé is like. The tavern will shutter its doors to bankruptcy five minutes after I am laid to rest."

This was the one conversation she hoped to avoid. "I turned over the tavern to you, Markus. We both agreed I'd have nothing to do with it thereafter."

He laughed. "Right. When I was nearly two decades younger than you and with big dreams. Our fates have reversed, Talia. You must be what? Three or four decades younger than me now?"

She looked at the wrinkled and weathered face of her younger brother. "Why'd you stop, Markus?"

His gaze moved around the room, seeking out the direct spot where her voice came from. "We both stopped forty years ago. We wanted to grow old together and see what life brought us. But she was murdered, Talia. My beautiful Yareli. My reason to keep on living died right along with her."

Talia's eyes misted. Her plate was already full and now Markus was adding to it. If he asked she would gladly avenge the death of Yareli. But there was much to do first. If he asked for her help, it would have to wait.

He chuckled softly. "I know what you're thinking. I took one more treatment after she was gone. Those responsible have already paid for what they did. You are not the only one capable of imparting absolute retribution. No. I need you to take the deed for the tavern. As my only living relative, it is yours when I die. Which I fear will be soon."

"What about Eugene? Why aren't you giving it to him?"

Markus laughed harshly, sending him into a choking fit. It took him a while to calm down before he could answer. "He's not my son. He was the son of one of my regulars. I promised to watch him for a couple months while she looked for a new place to live outside the badlands. To get him away from the harsh life, she said. That was five years ago."

"Sorry. I thought he was yours."

"I was lonely after Yareli died. So very lonely." Despite his eyes not seeing much to begin with he seemed to be lost in his memories for a moment before snapping back out of it. "No. There could be no one after her. And when I go the tavern is yours."

Talia shook her head. "I have spent a long time cultivating a new life and a new persona. Last night was fun for nostalgia's sake. But I'm afraid you would have a hard time convincing anyone I was your sister. The Talia who started the tavern with you so very long ago has been killed many times over."

"I can name whoever you are today in a new will."

She smiled, knowing he would hear it in her voice. "You would have to be of sound mind and body for a new will to stick."

He smiled back getting the joke. "You have me there."

"No, Markus. Let the tavern go. It was something we started in a different time. It is no longer relevant to my life."

"And that's why you came here to hide out? Too many options to choose from?"

"An important part of my new life will be passing through The Grease in the next day or so. I needed a safe place to rest my head until it arrived."

Markus looked hurt. "You didn't come here to see me?"

She leaned forward and placed her hands on his face, looking into his cloudy eyes. She still recognized the sparkle of her brother behind those milky pupils. "You were the only reason I was happy they would be passing this way. You were my first stop in town."

He smiled, his toothless grin making him look even older. "And your last, I'm afraid. I don't think I'll be around the next time you pass through the badlands."

She shook her head. "Don't talk like that, Markus. You're going to live forever."

His smiled shifted to sadness as his eyes adopted a faraway look. "I've been wasting away on the wrong side of the bar for quite some time. Thank you for reminding me why we started the tavern in the first place. It will miss you."

She blinked away the tears. "It was my pleasure." And she meant it. She sniffed in the wetness and sat up straight. "I have a present for you."

He snapped out of his musing and looked directly at her as if he could suddenly see clearly again. "I already gave them water and food. They are lovely hunting dogs. Thank you."

She frowned, confused. "How did you…?"

He laughed. "As soon as you stepped behind the bar, I asked a friend to stable your horse. Your dogs wouldn't let anyone near it. But all it took was some dried mutton and a fresh bowl of water to get them to change their mind. Since you aren't planning to stay they must be for me."

She smiled. "Nothing ever escapes your notice."

He motioned to his cloudy eyeballs. "Even with my eyes like this I can see when my big sister needs help."

"Thank you Markus. I'm going to need your help one more time."

"Anything. You name it."

She began rattling off supplies that would help her combat the heat of the desert in the middle of the day.

Chapter 67

Halen finally slowed his horse, turned off the road, and Van followed him. He didn't have much choice. Shadow was following Halen while Van was, quite literally, just along for the ride.

Halen stopped and hopped from his horse. He was still digging in the saddlebags when Van caught up and Shadow stopped. Van hopped down and looked around them. The road was so far back, he couldn't see it.

Halen spun around holding the same bamboo container from the day before in his hands.

Van's shoulders fell. "What's on the agenda today? Try to kill Van some more?"

Halen chortled. "Sorry about that. You needed to know what it felt like to use your powers."

Van's mouth gaped. "By trying to kill me?"

"Spinning is like everything else, controlled through emotions. Love and hate are the two most powerful. But since I didn't have time to get you to love me or make you hate me I went with the next best thing. Fear."

"I was frightened for my life all right." Van said with eyebrows drawn, hands on hips, and a frown on his face.

"Precisely. And that was close enough to hate to be useful to draw out your powers."

"So, what? Now I'm supposed to know how to use them?"

"Maybe not consciously. Yesterday your instinct took over and you used everything at your disposal to make me stop."

Van thought about the last thing he remembered before everything went dark. "The crystal around your neck. It was the source of your power. I took it from you. The blood." Van's eyes went wide and he felt a shiver ripple through him. "I almost died."

Halen nodded. "The crystal was designed to focus my powers and counteract this." He pulled aside the edge of his cloak to reveal a pin that looked charred, like it was the sole surviving object of a house fire. "When I was cast out of The Order my crest pin was tarnished. I could no longer use my Spinner powers."

Van frowned. "But what about all that stuff I saw you do? The fire dome that the arrows bounced off? The fireballs you threw at me yesterday?"

Halen lowered his eyes. "I kept your father's crest pin after he died. I have been using that to counteract my banishment. But I lost it. Madam Ryes loaned me her enchanted crystal necklace to restore my powers while I train you. It is a very powerful charm. Enough that it can give those without powers magical abilities. But in your hands—it was too much for you to handle without years of proper training. I highly suggest you don't grab for it again."

Van remembered seeing his blood seep out of every pore along his arm and shivered. "I won't. I promise."

Halen smiled. "Good. Yesterday was all about activating your powers. Today, we learn how to control them."

Halen sat on the ground and crossed his legs. He motioned for Van to join him. Van sat down, struggling to fold his legs the same way. When that didn't work he sat up on his knees. They immediately started to cramp up on the hard ground and he shifted his weight onto one thigh with his legs curled along one side of him.

Halen watched him with growing curiosity and finally raised an eyebrow when Van stopped fidgeting. "Comfortable?" he asked.

"Not really. Is it important to be comfortable to perform magic?"

"Not at all. But I am curious as to why you never learned how to do something as simple as sit on the ground?" Halen said as he uncorked the bamboo container.

Van gave him a cold look. "We're civilized where I come from. We have couches and chairs everywhere. We even carry portable chairs for camping."

Halen shook his head as he poured a few ounces of water onto the desert floor. It was so ravenous for moisture the barren ground soaked it in immediately. He pointed at the darkened patch of sand. "Extract the water from the ground."

Van looked at him. "How do I do that?"

"Concentrate on the concept that there is water there and will it back to the surface."

Van's eyebrows knitted together as he stared at the damp spot on the ground. He thought about water, the ocean, the molecules that made up water, and everything else he could think of regarding water. How was he supposed to think about calling water up from the ground?

He glanced up at Halen who was watching him intently. Halen's eyes shifted briefly to the ground and then back up at Van. Van understood the request and refocused on the spot on the ground. It was getting fainter as the growing heat of the day dried the dirt quickly.

Van stared at the same spot wishing for water to burst forth for ten minutes. When the spot completely dried up he shrugged his shoulders. He couldn't even find a faint outline where the water sat before soaking in. He looked up at Halen shaking his head. "I can't."

Halen held out the necklace. "Try using this to focus your thoughts."

Van tried but couldn't reach for the necklace. The memories of the day before rushed back to warn him. His physical reaction at trying to touch the stone was the same as if he tried reaching for a burning flame. The fear came out of nowhere and he couldn't bring himself to extend his arm toward it.

Halen grabbed Van's wrist and twisted it, squeezing harder until Van winced and opened his hand. Halen dropped the necklace into his palm. It pulsed faintly in time to Van's heartbeat. Then it started pulsing faster in direct response to Van's increasing heart rate.

"Easy, Van. You can control this."

Van looked at him, his face white as a freshly laundered sheet. "I thought you said I shouldn't be touching this thing?"

"Certainly not when you are angry and out of control. But I only have a day to get you ready for The Gauntlet. I know I told you there are no shortcuts for Spinner training but this will get us closer to how you need to feel far more quickly than conventional training methods. It won't kill you. I won't let it." He closed Van's fingers around the crystal and then curled the strap tied to the end of the necklace around his fingers. "I am right here, Van. If I see that you are going too far down the rabbit hole I will pull the crystal out of your grip. Trust me."

Van stared at his closed hand. He couldn't see the crystal, or its light through his tightly compacted fingers, but he could feel it vibrating against his palm like it was an echo of his heart. He tore his eyes from the heartbeat pulsating in his closed fist and looked at Halen, imploring him to not make him use the crystal again.

Halen placed a reassuring hand over Van's closed fist. "Your father trusted your training to me. I need you to trust me too. You are nervous. You need to be relaxed if you are to learn to control the elements. The first thing I want you to do is focus on your heartbeat. See how it races?"

Van nodded.

Halen looked deeply into his eyes. "Slow it down."

Van looked at his hand. His world tunneled until it was just him and the thrumming of his heart. He focused on it and wished it would slow down. His hand expanded to fill his vision like he was a camera swooping into it. The texture of his skin became more defined as he got closer. It became pitted and craggy, his hairs growing until they were as tall as trees in a barren landscape. He felt like a bird flying over a flat desert between limbless trees. The pores enlarged and he slowed down next to one and peered into it. It looked like an enormous bottomless pit. Then he suddenly dropped into it. He closed his eyes and cried out sharply as if he tumbled over the edge of a cliff.

Halen gripped his arm. Van sensed Halen's hand on him, but it felt like it was the memory of it happening rather than taking place at that same moment. "Let it happen," Halen uttered quietly, his voice sounding like it echoed down a long tunnel to reach Van's ears. "Keep going."

Van didn't recognize the environment around him until he realized he was inside his body. His vision adjusted, showing him his veins, muscles, and bones. And then he flew around, passing through the barriers of internal organs and blood vessels like they were holograms, until he was floating over his spine. He watched the electrical impulses of his spinal cord shooting back and forth as they transmitted messages between the brain and the rest of his body.

He focused on the steady rhythm of his heart, his vision shifting until he was a tiny speck staring at a twenty-story version of his heart beating above him. He heard the swelling of his lungs and watched as they expanded and then released the air they absorbed. They started slowing down as he focused on taking measured breaths.

Then his heart rate slowed until it was beating gently, his panic from earlier subsiding. A sense of calm washed over him as he realized he did it. He slowed his heart rate and calmed himself down by taking control of the impulses along his central nervous system.

The view shot backwards rapidly and everything around him shrunk quickly as he returned to the view from his natural eyes. Their focused sharpened and he found himself looking at a smiling Halen. "Did you see it?" Halen asked, breathlessly.

Sweat broke out over Van's whole body. "What just happened?"

"Your mind's eye beheld that which your physical eyes cannot see."

Van looked at him, his hands shaking and his lips trembling. "Is that how you see the world when you—spin?"

Halen laughed. "No. Once you are used to controlling the power you no longer need to visually imagine being there to control the elements as if they were physical objects. It also gets a lot easier if you don't take the time to do that. But you are starting out. You will learn to stop using that crutch in time."

"Before The Gauntlet?"

Halen shook his head. "I would be surprised if you did. It may take a few weeks of practice for your brain to stop assigning imagery to what your spinning is accomplishing." Halen's face fell and the sparkle of excitement dimmed from his eyes as he looked away.

"What is it?" Van asked.

Halen shook whatever was bothering him off and he rolled his shoulders before smiling at Van. "We need to work on getting the water out of the ground."

Van looked down at the spot where Halen poured the water. It was bone dry. "There's no more water."

"I'm not talking about the water you can see. Use your abilities to pull it from where it is no longer visible."

"How can I find it if I can't see it?"

Halen smiled "Use your mind's eye to find it."

Van focused on the spot in the ground where he remembered the water pooled before it absorbed into the parched earth. He stared for a long time until his eyes dried out to match the dirt they studied. It was no use. Without the beating of his heart to guide him, he couldn't do it. He blinked to bring moisture to his eyes and then gave a sorrowful look to Halen. "I can't."

"Of course you can. Close your eyes. Don't look for the water. Just know it's there."

Van let out a sigh and closed his eyes.

"Imagine you are shrinking again like you did when you controlled your heartbeat. But this time drop into the ground," Halen prompted.

Van thought about the spot on the ground. He imagined the dirt and then his mind's eye kicked in, the grains of sand expanding into boulders the size of houses. But they didn't stop there. He watched in wonder as he passed between the gaps of the boulders that were now the size of mountains. The space grew dark and he noticed a small river flowing downward between the mountains. The water expanded and blew apart, becoming individual blobs of crystal-clear balls of liquid.

He thought about sending them up to the surface. The blobs shimmered and then suddenly shifted direction to roll back up the sides of the vertical mountains.

"You're doing it, Van," he heard Halen's voice echo to him from the distance. Van stayed where he was until air was the only thing in the spaces between the mountains. His stomach flipped as he swooped backwards out of the ground. He opened his eyes and thought he was going to be sick from the sudden velocity change. His head swirled and then the world settled.

Halen was smiling wide. Van looked down and saw a puddle of water twice the size of what Halen originally poured.

"It looks like you found some more water while you were down there. Good job, Van."

Van smiled at him but Halen's smile faded sending Van's forehead wrinkling in confusion. "What's the matter?"

"You won't have the luxury of taking hours to do that in The Gauntlet. You will have to learn how to do it immediately. And while someone is using magic against you."

It was then Van noticed the sun wasn't just above the mountain peaks in the distance, like it was when he started, but instantly moved to the highest point in the sky. How long was he sitting there? His leg muscles immediately cramped, confirming they'd remained in the same position for far too long.

He tried to stand but his feet were both asleep and he flopped to one side. Halen stood up and helped Van to rise, supporting him under the arms as if he were an invalid.

Once Van was steady on his feet Halen let go and took a step backward and clasped his hands together, a big smile spreading across his face. "Congratulations, Van. You have done in a matter of hours what takes most apprentices months to accomplish." His smile faded. "But now you must do in half a day what took everyone, even me, years to perfect."

A flame erupted next to Van. He jumped back and stared in shock at the torch that ignited, followed by several more in rapid succession until they completely surrounded Van in burning flame. It was then he noticed that the crystal was missing from his hand. He glared at Halen, who was beaming at him with a mischievous smirk, the glowing crystal sitting firmly around his neck.

Chapter 68

The sun was just touching the crest of the mountains in the distance when Eddie crawled out from under the brightly colored wagon. He was covered in dry dirt with a cut across his cheek just under his right eye that was already scabbing over. He stood and dusted off his pants, creating a small area of soil-free clothing but creating a cloud of fine powdery particulates in the air around him.

"Thanks Buff," he said. "You can lower it now."

Buff lowered the wagon until it rested on the wheel Eddie modified with a gear and pulley system that would translate the forward turning motion of the wheel into a sideways sweeping action.

Eddie checked the connections and grinned with satisfaction. It was crudely cobbled together and his high school auto shop teacher would have shaken his head in disgust at such an inelegant apparatus. But Eddie was proud of what he accomplished with such rudimentary resources at his disposal.

He was repairing and designing simple solutions for people up and down the half-mile caravan for the better part of the day. He was actually having fun and whatever kept him from choking on the dust of an entire caravan was cheerfully welcomed.

A line started not soon after word got around that he fixed the stovepipe that was ejecting black soot into the cooking wagon. He repaired that with some oilcloth, which the cook assured him was waterproof, and several loops of twine. It successfully stopped smoke from filling the wagon and even earned Eddie a privately cooked lunch. It was the best meal he could ever remember having. The cook was actually good and could make more than tasteless beans and scrumptious pancakes.

After an entire day of fixing peoples' smaller problems he was about to unveil his pièce de résistance. His greatest achievement to date, well of the day anyway, which would ensure nobody would ever have to follow behind the caravan to sweep away their tracks again.

He held his hand out toward Buff. "The final broom please."

Buff handed him the broom and he strapped it to the plank of wood next to the four other brooms already connected to the splintered panel someone donated from a previous wagon's broken running board. It seemed these people never threw anything away but instead re-purposed everything to fit a new need when it was no longer fit for its original function. They were a group of people after Eddie's own heart. And besides, the board didn't need to be strong to serve his purposes. A light touch was needed for his invention to work.

He took a step back and reviewed his handiwork. He looked at Buff with a big smile on his face. "Let's take her out for a spin."

Buff looked visibly shaken. "Spin?" he said in alarm. Eddie saw Buff's fists tighten, his knuckles whitening quickly. What was Buff's problem?

Eddie frowned slightly, worried he might have broken some unwritten Traveler's rule. Then he remembered the term used for magic casters and he understood Buff's misunderstanding.

Eddie laughed. "No. Not that kind of spin. The wheels spin when the wagon is moving. That's what I meant."

Buff let out a quick breath.

He looked visibly relieved and Eddie noticed Buff's hands were quivering. Eddie stored that little tidbit of information away for later. Buff seemed to be afraid of the concept of magic and was even more worried about magic users. Now that he thought about it, he noticed that Buff behaved differently around Van once he learned Van was a Spinner. He watched Van warily after the rumors spread around the caravan that Van removed all the blood from his body using his magical abilities. A few even believed Van died in the desert the night before and was now a walking zombie.

Buff motioned to the driver who snapped the reins to get the horses moving. The horses tossed their heads and whinnied in insubordination. With night fast approaching they were hesitant to leave the camp. They knew what it meant when the caravan formed the evenly spaced concentric circles around a large central fire, like it was the bullseye of a massive target. They should have been released to graze with the rest of the horses. Instead they were being asked to leave the safety of the camp and venture into the terrifying darkness.

The driver understood exactly how they felt. "Come on darlings. We won't go far. We'll return quickly and then you can relax for the night."

As if they understood him they started pulling the wagon down the road. Eddie watched the brooms intently as they started swishing back and forth across the road behind the wagon. Buff walked behind the wagon and inspected the road.

He looked at Eddie with a renewed sense of respect. "It works," he said incredulously.

Eddie laughed and wrapped an arm around Buff's shoulders. To his surprise Buff didn't pull away but let it happen. "Of course it works," Eddie said. "I am the great inventor, Eddie of–" He looked at Buff, his eyebrows knitting. "I just realized. I'm not in Kansas anymore, Toto."

Buff reacted suddenly. He shrugged Eddie's arm off his shoulder, glaring at him, all previous signs of admiration gone. "What did you call me?" he said.

Eddie smiled disarmingly. "Relax, dude. It's from a movie."

Buff's forehead was wrinkled as he glowered at Eddie, his shoulders bunching as if ready to take a swing. "Why would you call me that?"

Eddie's heart was pounding so hard he was sure it was going to crack a rib. With white rimmed eyes he stammered, "I'm sorry. I didn't mean any offense. Dude is another term of man where I come from."

"And where you come from?" Buff growled. "Is it also customary to call someone by the name of making?"

It was Eddie's turn to be confused. He drew his eyebrows together, "Making what?"

Buff glared at him for a long moment. Eddie could see Buff was trying to figure out how he could pummel Eddie to a fine pulp without getting in trouble with Madam Ryes.

Eddie decided he didn't need an explanation. He put his hands up. "Whatever I said, I'm sorry. Really. I am."

He watched as Buff worked through the emotions and his hands slowly relaxed. Only then was Eddie able to slowly let out the breath he held. He would have to be careful what he said to Buff in the future. But he needed to confirm something he noticed earlier that morning so he risked one more thing with Buff. Eddie glanced past him and acted like he recognized someone. "Is that Van?"

Buff's face whitened and his torso spun around.

"Or maybe not," Eddie said shaking his head. "Too short."

Buff looked back at him and narrowed his eyes, a low growl

rumbling deep in his chest. Buff might have guessed what Eddie just confirmed, but he wasn't going to give Buff any time to make the full connection. The trick, Eddie knew all too well, was not using Buff's newly developed fear of Van until just the right moment. Using people's fears against them was something Eddie was excellent at. He only did it when absolutely necessary, and since Buff and Madam Ryes were technically holding them hostage, Buff was fair game. He quickly redirected the focus of attention back to the sweeping wagon. "I can work on some improvements to my design if you wish and make a couple more that we can mount along the caravan so the last wagon doesn't have to work so hard."

Buff's face softened and he nodded his head, watching the wagon turn around down the road and return to the Traveler camp.

Eddie smiled warmly and ran to catch up with the wagon to inspect that everything survived the first test. He noticed his hands were shaking slightly as he unhooked the brooms. He survived his first real test with Buff. He didn't know how far he should push it just yet but he knew he would be testing it further in anticipation of their escape.

Chapter 69

Van swayed uneasily in his saddle as he and Halen rode directly toward the bright orange spot on the darkening horizon. The sun went down only minutes before but the ground was dimming quickly. Halen was certain the fire he was following was the right one. They started the exercises close to where the caravan was expected to stop for the night.

He pulled his tattered and singed cloak tighter around him. The gaping holes with scorched edges did little to keep out the cool air of the desert night. His cloak started out relatively new and clean. But Halen was relentless with his training methods. Methods that involved a lot of fire.

Van spent most of the day running in circles within the dust-built dome to stay away from yet another shooting fireball. He knew he didn't look like he was successful in avoiding most of them but he managed to escape his training only slightly charred.

The training worked. He quickly learned to manipulate the element of water without needing to imagine himself near it or shrunk down to the size of a molecule. Halen taught him how to focus his energy while remaining in the real world. Before they finished the final round of training, which was what Halen kept insisting his ruthless attacks were called, Van found he could even pull water directly from the air if he concentrated hard enough.

But the one thing he didn't know was how that would help him fight off someone who was actually trying to kill him. As brutal as Halen's assaults were, he wasn't technically trying to harm Van; much. And despite "going easy" on him Halen still bested him every time.

How was Van expected to compete in The Gauntlet by tomorrow? Madam Ryes couldn't possibly expect him to win could she? Even if he was from the most powerful family of Spinners he only received two days of training. And he spent most of that time in a mini coma after the first lesson.

He looked at his tattered clothing and charred skin. His second lesson wasn't much better than the first. But for some reason Halen nodded approvingly and said he was as ready as he would ever be in the time allotted.

A sudden thought sent a chill up Van's spine. Halen mentioned he was banned from training anyone to be a Spinner. And then Madam Ryes forced him to train Van. But was he really training Van properly?

None of the past two days felt like any kind of real training, seeing as how he spent most of it unconscious or half dead. Van certainly didn't feel like he knew how to spin the elements. He felt more like a preschool kid with his first set of crayons. Coloring inside the lines just wasn't going to happen. Sure, by the end of the day he could move water through the air and splatter it against a scraggly tree trunk. But it was hardly effective against anything but a stationary target. And even then all he accomplished was getting his target wet. It was not a weapon. Not by any stretch of the imagination.

He said as much to Halen who gave him a sideways glance as they were mounting their horses for the short ride back to camp. "I have not taught you how to use your power as a weapon. Only to activate it. It would take far more time than we have to teach you how to best a foe with your Spinner abilities. You won't be here that long."

When Van asked him what he meant by that Halen clicked his tongue to get the attention of his horse and galloped away. Van followed, but kept his distance as he thought about what was expected of him tomorrow.

Halen assured him The Gauntlet was a points awarding contest. He wouldn't have to worry about doing more than getting his opponent wet to score enough points to win. Van practiced moving water around all day. He could certainly do that. But could he do it on demand, while under stress. He still didn't know why she was insistent on entering him into a contest when he was so ill-prepared to compete. What was her end game?

A flame shot past his face knocking him sharply from his thoughts. He glared at Halen who only pointed to the growing flame of the camp up ahead. As they reached the Travelers' caravan the smells of cooking assaulted his nose. It seemed the preferred night meal was beans and rice.

A chill ran up Van's spine and he got the distinct feeling that someone was watching him. But not from the warm direction of the circled caravan. He glanced into the darkness of the empty wasteland unable to shake the sensation that cold eyes were spying on him.

Chapter 70

Under cover of darkness Talia lay on her stomach in the brush. She held the spyglass to her eye and watched as Van entered the Travelers' camp. She located the caravan by midday and was shadowing it just out of sight of the spotters who maintained vigilant watch and scrutinized the horizon for approaching bandits.

As soon as the caravan stopped for the night she tied her horse to a small tree, left a bowl of clean water, and then scuttled closer to the camp on her belly to observe and learn.

She immediately noticed the camp was not as organized as most Traveler camps. They seemed less concerned about security. That didn't bode well. Talia swung her enchanted spyglass to find Madam Ryes. She could see the evidence of magic swirling around the matriarch. She obviously possessed a charm. For what Talia wasn't sure but sneaking up on a caravan that employed magic was going to be difficult.

Why would Madam Ryes bother using magic to keep the caravan safe? Many non-magical caravans stayed safe by keeping a well-organized camp. It didn't make sense. Unless the magic was for some other purpose. As Talia peered through the telescope, she noted more than one color around Madam Ryes. That meant she kept multiple charms on her person. No doubt something that could be directed at a potential attacker.

With Madam Ryes able to respond to any attack with a magical one of her own made things much trickier for Talia if she wanted to extract Van and Halen from the camp with minimal opposition.

She peered through the telescope and watched as Madam Ryes spoke with Halen while Van stood nearby. Halen turned over an exceptionally powerful charm to Madam Ryes right before she motioned to a wagon. After a few verbal exchanges Van reluctantly entered the wagon and the light inside went out quickly. She obviously wanted her warrior rested for The Gauntlet tomorrow.

Talia witnessed The Gauntlet in action on previous visits. It was always touted as a battle of skills. But more often than not it ended in death for one of the contestants. There was no doubt in her mind about Van's chances in the arena. Even if he was a young Spinner, he was unskilled and would be going up against some of the best wizards who were deemed too unfit, psychologically, to join the Wizard's Order, but still trained their extensive power outside the limitations of rules.

Talia was about to sweep her spyglass around the camp to see if she could determine the best way to sneak in unnoticed when she suddenly felt a presence behind her. Her senses heightened as she continued to sweep the spyglass around, not wanting to alert the intruder she was aware of the presence. Though it looked like she was using her spyglass, she was no longer looking at the camp and was instead listening to the distinct sounds of someone approaching her from behind.

The temperature of the desert around her suddenly dropped several degrees and she could see mist carried on her ragged breath. That told her exactly who was sneaking up behind her and she cursed silently under her breath as she felt every muscle tense in fear.

If it were anyone else Talia could turn this around and make some demands of her own. As it was all she could do was remain perfectly still and hope she survived contact. If Talia lived through the next few seconds it would only be because the creature who crept up on her allowed it.

"What are you doing?" a soft feminine voice whispered in her ear from only an inch away.

Talia closed her eyes and swallowed hard. She had no choice but to tell the truth. Anything less would be detected immediately. "I am watching the Spinners."

"Why?" the voice asked so softly it was as if it came carried in on the wind.

Talia kept her eyes closed. Even if she looked toward the voice she knew she could never see who spoke the words. "I'm going to rescue them," she said.

"Why?"

There was no malice in the woman's voice, only curiosity. Talia hoped the conversation would remain that casual. She kept counting the seconds she was still alive. It seemed the creature was not here for Talia, but only passing by and was attracted by the enchanted items in Talia's possession. That still didn't make her any less dangerous, Talia reminded herself as she very slowly tried to relax her tensed and cramping shoulders. Her heart pounded heavily against the ground where she lay.

"They can help me with something."

"Ahh. Your lover."

"Yes."

"Why are you taking them tonight?"

"I can't let the young Spinner enter The Gauntlet. They will kill him."

"What makes you think that?"

"Surely someone like you understands the darkness that lies in men's hearts."

The soft voice chuckled. "True. But then…" The voice suddenly changed pitch and seemed to be distracted by something else. "What is she doing?"

Silence filled the space around Talia and the temperature slowly rose a few degrees. She waited for her heart to steady before she ventured a look around, using her peripheral vision to check for someone who could never be seen when observed directly.

Talia was alone.

And then, for a brief moment, she wasn't.

The air around her chilled a split second before a light touch on her temple sent the world spiraling instantly into darkness.

Chapter 71

Van was drifting off to sleep, exhausted from his day of training when he thought he heard the flare of a match's flame. He opened his eyes as a candle flared to life. He saw the back of a woman with long dark hair lighting one candle after another and positioning them to ensure that no shadows fell on the walls. Each candle's light overlapped the light from the others around it until there were no shadows left inside the wagon.

The woman turned around and smiled at him. It was Maura. He sat up quickly. "What are you–?" Van started to say but he stopped when she placed a finger to her lips and sat down on the edge of the bed. "I have given this a lot of thought and I can't go through with it."

Van was never more confused and the deep creases on his forehead reflected that. "Go through with what?"

She held up a small canvas bag and looked at him, the smile gone from her face. "I need you to close your eyes. And no matter what happens do not open them."

"Why?" he asked quietly.

"I need you to keep your eyes closed no matter what you hear or feel."

He thought about her request and felt compelled to answer her honestly. "I don't know if I can do that," he said.

She looked at him for a moment. "Very well." She stood and ripped a section from the bottom of her dress. She held up the long swatch of cloth, her face devoid of emotion. "Do you trust me?"

What kind of question was that? Van didn't know how else to respond. "Sure. What is this Mau…"

She slapped her hand over his mouth. "Don't speak my name out loud. She will hear you."

He looked around, but they were the only ones in the wagon. "Who?"

She leaned forward and looked him deeply in the eyes. "Do you trust me?"

For reasons he couldn't explain, and despite being unable to remember the night they met, he felt he could. He nodded and she tied the cloth around his head, crafting it into a blindfold to cover his eyes. The material was thick and he couldn't see through it. But he could see the light cast by the flames of the candles along the edges of the fabric below his eyes. "What are you doing?" he asked.

"Shh," she responded and then the weight on the bed shifted as she moved closer to him. "This might hurt a little."

It suddenly felt like Buff punched him in the chest. He cried out as the pain increased and his body felt as if it were expanding like a balloon filled to the bursting point with air. Then the pain suddenly subsided and he flopped to the bed gasping for air and feeling like he'd been kicked down a flight of stairs.

The windows suddenly slammed open and a gust of wind blew the candles out. The darkness around the edges of the blindfold was complete.

"Maura!" a woman's voice demanded.

Van heard the strike of a match followed by the sound of a hand striking a face. He cringed with the sound of the loud slap as if it was his face that was smacked.

He heard Maura sobbing softly. "Please, Mother. He is a Spinner. He needs it. He has to know when to restrain himself. He has to care about others."

He couldn't see a thing. He reached up carefully and pulled back the blindfold. With the edge of the fabric pulled up, he saw a dark shape against the moonlight spilling in from the windows. But when he looked at it, it faded away. Maura was on the floor holding a hand to her face and glaring up at the open window as if talking to someone. When Van looked away again he thought he saw someone standing by the window in his peripheral vision.

"I gave Madam Ryes my word," the woman said. "It cannot be broken."

Maura looked up defiantly at the transparent image of the woman standing over her. "No, Mother, you owed her a favor. She should be doing things for you, not the other way around!"

"Hold your tongue, child."

"No, Mother. I have—feelings for Van."

The woman's laughter crawled up and down Van's spine. "You? And him? It could never be!"

"And why not?" Maura snapped back. "Love doesn't follow the rules. He wants an equal."

Had Maura just said she loved him? His heart fluttered as he realized he might feel the same way about her. Even after only talking for the one night, something about her told him she was his destiny. The one he was waiting for. He knew from the first moment their eyes met.

"Ohhhh, I see. You want him to care about you." The shadow woman placed the emphasis on "you" and it suddenly made Van very angry. This mother was suggesting her daughter didn't deserve his care. But he did care and he felt beyond the shadow of a doubt that Maura deserved it.

Then the mother's next words chilled him to the bone. "You are making a mistake, Maura. If he has his free will, and he finds out what you are, you will lose him forever. You know that."

"I don't know that. And you don't know that!" Maura shot back defiantly.

Van, keeping his peripheral vision focused on Maura's mother, watched as the shadow drifted closer to her and reached out a hand to touch her face. Shadows dripped from her outstretched arm like a darkened mist. "I know it all too well, my child."

"Let him keep it, Mother. He's different. You'll see."

"They are all same. You will come to see that in time. I'm afraid your actions force us to leave sooner than I planned."

"But mother!" Maura protested.

Her mother shook her head. "We are leaving! Tonight! End of discussion!"

Maura slumped on the floor; defeated.

The shadow stood to her full height. "Maybe it's my fault. We were with this caravan for too long. Contact with mortals has affected your judgment. As for him…"

The shadow suddenly turned toward Van. He dropped the blindfold back into place in surprise. The afterimage of what he saw for the briefest of moments burned into his retinas. The face was one of untainted beauty. But he couldn't shake the feeling he just glimpsed into the eyes of pure evil. If this was Maura's mother, what was Maura? Could he love something that wasn't human? His eyes opened wider when somewhere deep inside him answered "yes".

He felt the mother's presence loom over him and the room grew colder. He felt her icy breath on him as she spoke quietly. "Maybe he is deserving. Maybe he isn't. But if you want him to have it back he must earn it."

Excruciating pain exploded suddenly in Van's chest and it felt like his very soul was being torn from his body.

Chapter 72

Van jerked awake and tumbled out of bed. He hit the hardwood floor drenched in sweat and clutched at his chest. He looked around in a panic but found himself alone in the wagon. The sun already brightened the sky but wasn't fully risen yet.

Van looked down at his chest and clawed his shirt up hurriedly to inspect his skin. Everything was as it should be. No big scar indicating he had been cut into during the night. But the memory was still fresh in his mind. The pain was all too real. It felt like he'd undergone open heart surgery without anesthesia. No. Not surgery like he knew it. More like someone just plain ripped his heart out of his ribcage with bare hands.

A loud pounding made his head snap so hard toward the door it wrenched his neck. "Who is it?" he stammered. The door opened and Buff poked his head in. He looked around and then focused on Van still on the floor. He turned his torso back to the door. "He's alone," he said and then backed out of the door.

Madam Ryes stepped into the wagon as Buff closed the door behind her. She looked down at Van. "Trouble sleeping?"

Van looked around and then pushed himself up with the edge of the bed. "A nightmare," he said rubbing at his chest. "I'm okay now."

She smiled. "I just wanted to let you know we will be taking you into The Grease right after breakfast."

"You never did tell me what The Grease was."

"It's a town in the middle of the badlands. Despite the fact that nearly everyone in town is a murderer or a thief it is one of the safest places to live in Midguard. Dameron, the biggest warlord in the badlands, keeps the peace with a heavy hand. I wanted to warn you not to get into any fights while we're there."

"Other than the fight you signed me up for?" he mumbled sarcastically.

She smiled shrewdly at him and waggled a finger in the air. "There are very few rules where we are going. But one of them is no unauthorized fights in The Grease."

Why would Van get into a fight? He'd never been in a fight in his entire life. Why start now? Eddie always talked them out of any impending fights throughout junior high and high school. If she really didn't want him to get into any fights he would need Eddie around. "Is Eddie coming with us?"

She raised an eyebrow questioningly. "Do you want him there to see you win?"

"Yes. But—you think I'm going to win?"

"Halen discussed your training results with me. From what he told me you are more than capable of winning The Gauntlet. I know The Gauntlet sounds scary, but don't worry, it's really just a test of skill. And Halen tells me your raw skill is well beyond the training of an apprentice of a couple years. Given enough time you might become the best Spinner in all the realms."

"But you didn't know that when you entered me in the contest."

She shrugged. "Then I would be betting against you," she added with a smirk before her smile faded. "But to answer your question, no. Eddie will stay here."

"Why?"

"To give you and Halen incentive to return."

Van shook his head. "I gave you my word I would return. Isn't that enough?"

She laughed, tossing her head back. "Please. Your word isn't worth the air it is carried on. Get ready to travel. Your first bout is just after lunch."

"I can't fight right after lunch!" Van said rapidly, hoping he found a way out of the magic battle. "I might get a cramp."

"Don't worry," she said. "You won't be eating lunch. And as for breakfast I'm afraid you'll be skipping that too."

She spun around and opened the door. She paused after going down the first step and looked back. "And don't think about throwing the match. Such actions will not be tolerated. That brings me to another hard and fast rule in The Grease. No cheating."

She shut the door to leave Van alone with his thoughts in the wagon. His chest still felt tight. The memory of his vivid dream still making his whole upper body throb. He felt his heart pounding against his ribs and breathed a sigh of relief. His heart wasn't ripped from his chest after all. If it was gone it wouldn't be beating so hard while he considered the outcome of going toe-to-toe with a magic user who knew what they were doing. One thing was for certain, he didn't think Madam Reyes wanted him to win despite what she said. If she did she wouldn't be starving him right before a major battle.

Chapter 73

Talia's head lolled to the side and she jerked awake. Her horse nuzzled her again, pushing her out of her groggy state. She blinked at the bright sun that was a whole hand's span above the mountain ridge.

The Night Maiden knocked her out cold with a touch but left her otherwise unharmed. Most parents kept the chilling stories of the Night Maiden alive to keep their children from sneaking out of the house after dark. Those same parents laughed about how ridiculous the legend was. It was not possible for someone who was fabled to have been present at or near the beginning of creation to still be alive after countless eons. But it did a great job keeping the kids safely in bed at night.

But Talia knew better and she believed the tales were true. And that was why she was still alive in the morning. She knew not to try to look directly at the Night Maiden. It was a sure way to go to sleep and never awake again.

She vigorously rubbed her horse's muzzle. "Thanks for letting me sleep in. Now help me up." She clung to his halter as he pulled her to her feet. She dusted off her front and looked across the desert at the space were the caravan circled for the night.

Her heart skipped a beat. The caravan was still there, save for one of the wagons that left while she was asleep. She wondered who left the caravan on their own in the middle of the badlands but she didn't have time to contemplate it further before she noticed dust plumes rising up in columns behind three large fast-moving objects headed her way. A clear indicator that a spotter noticed her lying in the sand and several armed men were heading out to see who was irresponsible enough to try to spy on their caravan.

She raised her telescope and focused on the riders and her heart stopped. They weren't men on horseback. Her telescope enlarged the objects, enabling her to see clearly what was coming her way.

Destiny Hounds!

Their coal-black fur, and the fire flaring from the sides of their mouths with each exhaled breath were unmistakable. She saw the blazing red eyes of the lead hound shift as it looked right at her.

She pulled away the scope to see they were still just specks below the line of the horizon. But they drank her scent in and could see her. Even at this distance.

She stuffed the spyglass into the pouch on her belt and jumped into the saddle. She spun her horse around and jabbed her heels hard to get him galloping as fast as he could go.

Destiny Hounds were so named because when they were sent after you your fate was sealed. Nobody, as far as Talia could recall, ever escaped Destiny Hounds. They always hunted in packs of three and were not indigenous to Midguard. Some enterprising fellow brought them over from Magerealm and sold them as the perfect protection. It was bad enough that a fully grown hound stood over four feet tall, boasted razor-sharp claws, and was built more like a bull than a dog. But they used more than their physical prowess when taking down their prey. They also used magic to defeat their quarry.

What was the caravan doing with such expensive baleful creatures? She leaned forward and low in the saddle, urging her horse ever faster. She glanced back and wasn't surprised to see the Destiny Hounds were gaining on her. Once they locked onto a target they never abandoned the pursuit until their kill was evenly divided between them.

She couldn't outrun them and their only weakness was water. But the badlands was notorious for its lack of liquid in any form. The hounds would be on her in less than five minutes and she was surrounded by miles and miles of the optimum setting for Destiny Hounds to take her down without breaking a sweat.

Maybe the hunt was easy for them but she was already out of breath despite her horse doing all the running. Genius was one percent inspiration and ninety-nine percent perspiration. She already felt the perspiration. All she needed was that one percent of inspiration. If she took time to think maybe she could alter her fate and be the first to not let a pack of vicious beasts decide how her life should end.

A frantic tweeting brought her attention to her right. "Walter!" she exclaimed when she saw the yellow canary flying alongside her. He circled her quickly, trying to get her to stop. "I can't," she screamed and pointed behind her. "Look!"

Walter swooshed back and forth, his tiny clawed feet snatching at the horse's ears, making him falter and slow down. Was Walter still so upset with her that he wanted her dead? "What are you doing Walter?"

Walter circled her again, urging her with repeated tweets to slow down. She glanced back. The hounds were close enough she could see their burning eyes fixated on her. She wasn't going to get away by running. And it seemed Walter had devised a plan in that tiny bird brain of his.

She pulled up on the reins and her horse complied, skidding to a full stop in the sand. Walter then landed on the net gun and twittered excitedly. She reached for the net gun and he flew away, landing on the ground a few feet away.

She looked down at him. "You want me to shoot you with the net gun?"

Walter tweeted and hopped back and forth.

"Okay," she said and took aim, ignoring the eager shrieks from the hounds as they approached their prey who smartly decided to give up.

She squeezed the trigger and Walter flinched as the net enveloped him. He immediately expanded to his human form and glanced around before settling his loving gaze on Talia and smiled. "You keep going. I'll hold them back as long as I can."

She was shaking her head, a tear rolling down one cheek. "I can't let you sacrifice yourself for me. I won't lose you again!"

Walter laughed, but Talia detected a nervous note beneath it. "I'm not sacrificing anything! I'll keep them here. When you are far enough away I will throw off the net and fly like the wind to catch up with you."

She hesitated. She didn't want to leave him alone to carry out such a poorly constructed plan. But he wasn't going to let her stay.

"Go!" he yelled. "I'll be fine. These are dogs. I'm only afraid of cats."

Just past Walter she could see the hounds slowing down in confusion. They weren't used to prey giving up and they were apprehensive about approaching too quickly. The scent of magic on Walter distracted them and they directed their attention fully on him, ignoring her completely.

"Go!" he said again. "I'll be right behind you. I promise."

She hopped onto her horse and took off at a dead run, glancing back to see the Destiny Hounds circling Walter and snapping at him.

Chapter 74

Van clung to Halen as they rode into town on the same horse. Once they were inside the gate Halen hopped off and led the horse through the center of town. They'd only traversed a few yards into town before people started taking notice of Van. They stopped what they were doing and watched as he rode by. He leaned forward in the saddle and lowered his head alongside the same side Halen walked. "Why are they looking at me like that?"

"They know you are here for The Gauntlet," Halen replied. "For now, you're just a mild curiosity. But if you do well in The Gauntlet today you will become a celebrity. Try not to let it get to your head."

"Do you think I have a chance?"

"Like I told Madam Ryes your raw talent is rarely matched by someone after years of training. I don't know how but you seem to naturally know how to think like a magician."

"I used to pretend I was Harry. Eddie was Ron. But we never found our Hermione."

"Were they great wizards?"

"Kind of. They were characters in a popular book and movie series. They certainly sparked the imaginations of millions of kids around the world. Everyone wanted to be the boy who lived; even me." Van's smile became a mix of excitement and sudden realization. "I guess I am now."

"Well," Halen said. "Whatever it was it worked for you. You stand a good chance at winning The Gauntlet in the first two rounds."

Van shuddered involuntarily. "Two rounds?"

"The winner is the one who obtains the best score in two out of three sessions. I have heard about the Spinner you are scheduled to fight. He is a little imbalanced, mentally, but he knows how to fight against a Spinner with excellent training. Fortunately for you you've only got two lessons. And neither of those went very well. You should be unpredictable enough to throw him off his game. Maybe even enough to win it and not have to go for a third round."

Van sat up in the saddle and stared blankly in front of him, not really seeing the city roll slowly by. It took several attempts to swallow his heart back down. It seemed to stick in his throat and refused to return to where it belonged. He wasn't expecting to fight more than once. Especially if he won. He certainly didn't want to endure three battles if it came to that.

Someone hollered from inside the darkness of the blacksmith shop as he passed by. "Be victorious, son of Veren."

Van's back went erect and he felt that the eyes on him were filled more with wonder instead of judgment. He wasn't being paraded before them as a joke. He was being paraded through town as a contender. A potential hero. The son of a great man. More than ever he was determined to win. To honor his father. If it was a show everyone wanted he would give it to them.

Chapter 75

Halen led the horse to the arena in silence. He sensed the confidence building in Van as more and more people offered their support and well wishes. That was dangerous. If Van got too cocky he would make mistakes that might cost him the match. Possibly even his life if he made the wrong decisions. Madam Ryes again carried the crystal that granted Halen his powers during the training. If Van got into trouble in the arena there was nothing Halen could do but watch and pray.

They finally arrived. He was surprised to see the entrance line stretched around the outer fence. From his vantage point most of the seats were already full.

"Oh boy," Halen said quietly to himself. So much for keeping a low profile. What had they gotten themselves into?

Chapter 76

Walter kept the Destiny Hounds entertained while he waited for Talia to ride out of sight. As soon as he couldn't see her any longer he stood up straight and glared at the lead hound.

"Beal flow," he said using the same accent he heard Madam Ryes using. The hounds looked at each other in bewilderment. "Beal flow!" he demanded again.

All three hounds immediately sat down, the fire spewing from their mouths diminishing. A thrill shot up Walter's spine. It worked! He looked in the direction of the circled wagons. He couldn't see anything from this distance but knew a Destiny Hound could view anything in the caravan as if it were standing only a few feet away. Their sight was not limited by distance or darkness, only obstructions like forests, mountains, or the curvature of the earth.

Walter focused on the words he'd heard Madam Ryes use before and spoke them now hoping they were correct.

The Destiny Hounds jumped to their feet and took off across the desert, following his command as they raced back to the caravan.

Walter let out the breath he cautiously held and threw off the net. He shifted into a canary so quickly he took to the air without his bird feet ever touching the ground.

Chapter 77

Madam Ryes was walking around her camp looking for Buff when she heard the spotter standing on top of the Destiny Hound wagon call out. "Three coming back!"

Madam Ryes stood to one side as the hounds raced into the caravan camp and up the ramp that took them inside their green, windowless enclosure on wheels. The spotter lowered the door into place and everyone in the camp breathed a joint sigh of relief. Even though the hounds were supposedly under Madam Ryes' command, they were still wild beasts. Nobody ever really controlled them and, the entire time they were outside their cage, no one was truly safe.

Their return meant that whoever was in the desert watching the caravan was by now a bloody pulp. Whatever remained after the hounds had their fill was being fought over by buzzards. She smiled to herself. Hers was the safest caravan in all the badlands even though she rarely let the hounds out of their box. Just knowing the Ryes Caravan was protected by deadly magical creatures kept most everyone from even attempting a raid.

The rest who didn't believe the stories found out firsthand how true they were.

She walked around the caravan, people greeting her as she passed by. She responded with the slightest nod of her head and kept walking until she finally found Buff leaning against a wagon doing absolutely nothing. She glanced around surprised to see him alone. "Where is Eddie?"

He shrugged, which was not easy for him to do as he possessed no neck to speak of. "Fixing various things around the caravan."

"Why aren't you with him?"

"That guy is like a butterfly in a hurricane. He doesn't finish one project before he has some inspiration for fixing another. I'm surprised he has been able to finish anything what with how quickly he moves from one area of the camp to another without any rhyme or reason. But I must admit he's getting a lot things repaired throughout the caravan. We haven't been this operational since right before Todd got himself killed up north."

The memory of their journey along the northern route two summers previously made her shiver involuntarily. Madam Ryes, the stone-hearted leader of a band of ruthless mercenaries, who proved time and again she was not afraid of anything, discovered a few things even she was unwilling to do during that fateful summer jaunt. And taking her caravan anywhere near the northern route again was one of them.

She let go of the memory and fixed her gaze on Buff. "I want you at the arena before they start the third round. Once the young Spinner dies you are to kill Halen. Make it look like an accident if you can."

Buff's face wrinkled in deep concentration. "What if the boy wins the third round?"

"If Jonas doesn't fulfill his end of the bargain kill all three of them."

Buff nodded. "Yes, ma'am. What about Eddie?"

She thought for a moment. "He has proven himself extremely useful. We'll keep him around until he isn't. Find him and tell him to report to me at lunchtime. I want to prepare him for the bad news of his friend's untimely death before word spreads over from town."

Buff nodded and stomped off, his entire upper torso swiveling back and forth as he looked for his charge.

Chapter 78

Eddie held his breath as he watched Madam Ryes' boots head away. He was quietly repairing the axle of the wagon Buff leaned against when she walked up.

He heard everything.

They were going to kill Halen.

And Van!

And him!

He needed to get away and warn the others. But how? There wasn't time for a plan. The how didn't matter. Just do it, he silently told himself.

He mentally ticked off the items on his escape and rescue checklist.

Find a horse, make his way to a town he was unfamiliar with, locate Van and Halen, and then escape the most bloodthirsty woman he ever had the displeasure to meet.

Easy peasy, he reminded himself. He was Fast Eddie. If anyone could do all of that, he could.

He scurried out from under the wagon and stood up, wiping his hands on his pants. He ended up adding to the dust on his palms rather than removing it.

He spun around and slammed into Buff's barrel chest. Buff grabbed him by the upper arms with meaty hands and lifted him off his feet, squeezing the breath out of him. Buff frowned. "How much of that did you hear?"

Eddie smiled uneasily. "I didn't hear anything," he said and instantly regretted letting go of any oxygen as he couldn't suck any fresh air in while Buff held him in the vise grip that tightened with each breath he released.

Buff's frown lines along the edges of his eyes deepened. "You shouldn't eavesdrop on other people's conversations. It's rude."

"You're crushing me," Eddie wheezed.

Buff let him go and Eddie collapsed to his knees. There was barely time to gasp for air before Buff grabbed him by the collar and dragged him through the caravan to Madam Ryes' wagon.

He knocked once, not waiting for an answer before he opened the door and tossed Eddie onto the raised floor of the wagon. Buff climbed the steps and closed the door. He picked Eddie up again and dropped him unceremoniously into a chair. Eddie noted it was the same chair he first occupied when he and Van were captured by Madam Ryes after coming down the mountain. They had come full circle. Only, Eddie didn't think he would live long enough to walk back out the door this time.

Chapter 79

Walter whirled silently through the sky. He followed the Destiny Hounds back to make sure his command to return home was interpreted correctly. He was about ready to return to Talia when he saw Eddie being manhandled by Buff and thrown into Madam Ryes' private wagon.

That couldn't mean anything good for Eddie. And by extension, Van and his trainer. Walter watched Van training from the safety of a branch in a nearby tree. He liked what he saw and knew that if anyone could help him reverse the curse that kept him a bird, it was this young Spinner. He was imbued with the ability and none of the training that might prevent him from helping on principal. Nor was he encumbered with the numerous rules of The Order. Most spells could only be undone by the one who cast it. But there were legends from a thousand years ago of a powerful Spinner who could break the spells of other Spinners and Charmers.

Walter clung to the legend as if it were precedence that it was possible. For that reason alone he couldn't let anything happen to the Spinner or his friends. Walter reminded himself he was more than a bird. He was a man imbued with courage and honor who was only enchanted to look like a bird.

Chapter 80

Eddie sat in the single-room wagon and did his best to avoid eye contact with Buff. Not an easy task in such a confined space. He could only look at all the glowing or swirling liquids in glass bottles for so long before his eyes found Buff's again. Buff, however, never took his eyes off of Eddie.

Eddie admonished himself for being so stupid and not looking around before climbing out from under the wagon. So much for his plan to sneak away and save Van. In fact his plan had only lasted a grand total of five seconds.

He remembered turning thirteen and moving in with the foster family he spent the rest of his young life with. He entered junior high during the middle of the school year. He'd made that same move many times before and knew what to expect. The new kid was always the latest target for bullies who the other kids became desensitized to. Or the bullies became bored with them. Either way, the new kid was always the one to suffer.

But he was only there a week when an even newer kid arrived. Unlike Eddie, the new kid was better looking and moved to their small town in the middle of Kansas all the way from San Francisco. He was instantly popular with the girls, much to the consternation of the boys who had set their sights on them since fifth grade.

When the new boy wasn't interested in becoming a popular kid by following what the other popular kids were doing he quickly became a target for the bullies. It was then that Eddie stepped in and protected him. The newer kid's name was Van and, unlike the rest of the kids in their school, they were the only two who didn't have a father. It was something that bonded them instantly and they became fast friends.

Shunned by everyone else at the school they could always count on each other to bail the other one out of trouble. But now Van was in trouble and there was nothing Eddie could do about it.

The door opened and Madam Ryes stepped inside and jumped slightly when she saw her wagon was already occupied. She glared at Buff. "What is this?"

Buff hooked a thumb in Eddie's direction. "He overheard our

conversation."

She looked at Eddie and let out a big sigh. "Unfortunate," she said and then looked at Buff. "Take him out into the desert. I want his bones picked clean by the buzzards and sun-bleached long before anyone discovers him."

This was Eddie's only chance to change his fate and he took it. He jumped up and grabbed a bottle of glowing electric-blue liquid off the shelf and held it aloft. "If you come near me I will break this on the floor!" he said, trying to let more confidence reflect in his voice than he felt.

Buff froze and Madam Ryes narrowed her eyes at him. "You don't want to be doing that, boy."

Eddie felt bolstered by their apparent fear and held the bottle higher. "Let me go, or I swear, I'll kill all of us—right here—right now."

Buff looked to Madam Ryes for what he should be doing. It seemed he couldn't think for himself and could only do what he was told.

Unfortunately, based on the cold and calculating look in her eyes, Eddie could tell Madam Ryes was more than capable of thinking for herself. But was she thinking two moves ahead like a chess player? Eddie may only be a lowly pawn but he had forced the queen of the caravan into check with only a knight to defend her. He realized his consideration of who they were as chess pieces did not denote a proper endgame scenario, but it was the first thing that came to his mind since, in this caravan, the matriarch was the one in charge. Not a king but a queen.

Madam Ryes smiled, the corners of her mouth turning up slightly. "You want to play rough? I can play rough. I may enjoy giving orders and letting everyone else do the work but I don't mind getting my hands dirty when it calls for it."

A brightening glow emanated from under her shirt just below the collar right before Eddie's stomach flipped repeatedly. He felt like he was falling and his arms flailed around as he lifted off the floor. He looked in a panic around him as everything in the room floated up, including the furniture, Buff, and Madam Ryes. As they floated into the air a glowing crystal necklace floated up from under her collar and into view. Her eyes glowed along with the crystal and she looked at him with a hatred more evil than he could have ever imagined.

"Kill him now, Buff," she hissed.

Eddie swam with his legs and arms but he was floating in the middle of the wagon interior and was out of reach of every surface. With nothing to push off from he was trapped in midair with nowhere to go. Even if he was able to launch himself off a wall or floor where could he go? Buff's wide chest filled up half the width of the wagon. His arms stretching out to either side left Eddie with nowhere to escape.

Madam Ryes floated back down to the floor and, using her feet for stability and leverage, she pushed Buff toward Eddie. Buff floated in slow motion toward Eddie, his lips splitting into an ever widening evil grin as the space between them grew smaller. Eddie flailed pointlessly in midair. There was nothing he could do.

Wait! There was one thing he could still do. He could make good on his threat.

"I'm so sorry, Van," he whispered silently to himself and tossed the glass vial as hard as he could at the closest solid surface.

Chapter 81

Walter clenched his neck muscles, locking his head in place. He focused on keeping the sharpest part of his beak on point as he folded his wings against the side of his body and let gravity take over to increase his speed. What he was planning resulted in the death of thousands of birds every year.

He streaked toward his target, the bright sky reflected in the crystal-clear surface. Right before he impacted, he closed his eyes and prayed Talia would forgive him for even attempting something so risky.

Chapter 82

Madam Ryes watched calmly as the glass vial spun toward the wall. She reached out to it with her mind, empowered by the crystal around her neck, and it started to slow until it revolved in place, not impacting with anything but just hanging in the air.

"Did you really think I was going to let you do something so foolish?" Madam Ryes seethed. How could this little twerp even think he could defy her?

Buff was drifting closer and reached out for Eddie with his ham-sized fists. Eddie floated helplessly in space and waited for the inevitable.

The window shattered and something small and yellow shot into the interior and began swooping around the inside of the wagon, dive-bombing Buff's face repeatedly. Buff covered his face with one hand while swiping at his hair with the other. All the while screaming in terror. It appeared Buff had an irrational fear of birds. This was a side of him rarely seen by anyone.

Madam Ryes held her hand up and mentally snatched at the empty space in front of her, focusing on what was attacking Buff. A glowing apparition of her hand shot from her fingertips and grabbed the swift yellow streak out of the air. The ghostly hand disappeared, along with the yellow bird, and then Madam Ryes glared at the tiny bird closed in her actual fist. To her surprise she thought she recognized it. "Walter?"

The canary pecked at her fingers, drawing tiny droplets of blood, so she squeezed him tighter. He tweeted in agony and his head turned in every direction at once. She could crush the life from him if she wanted. This was what she was used to. Absolute power. And thanks to the crystal around her neck she commanded the power of a Spinner when she wanted or removed it to hide from the Watchers.

Madam Ryes grinned at him, his life literally in her hands. "Don't think I won't end your miserable little existence right now."

The door to the wagon burst open and a cloaked figure stood at the threshold, raised a large-barreled gun, and fired it point blank at Madam Ryes. She raised her hand to destroy the intruder with magic bolts of fire when a net engulfed her and nothing happened.

Actually, something did happen.

Eddie and Buff, along with all the furniture floating in the room, crashed to the floor. Also, and rather unexpectedly, the bird in her hand expanded into a full-grown man. She couldn't keep hold of him as he expanded and jerked her hand away instinctively when she found he was completely naked. He snatched the crystal necklace before she could react and tossed it out between the loops of the net.

The figure stepped fully into the wagon and pulled back the hood of the cloak. Madam Ryes was surprised to see it was a woman who smiled at her in satisfaction. The woman shifted her focus to the man inside the net with her. "Good job, Walter."

Walter smiled back. "Where did you come from?"

"I was sure the Destiny Hounds were going to eat you so I turned around as soon as I was out of sight. I saw you crash through the window and figured you might need some help."

The anger welled up inside Madam Ryes. "Do not think I will let you get away with this."

The woman looked at her. "Actually, not only are you going to let me, you're going to help me."

A groan from behind Madam Ryes drew the woman's attention and she raised a small crossbow, no larger than the palm of her hand, and shot Buff in the neck with a dart. He slapped at his neck, removed the dart, and stared at it in confusion. Then his eyes rolled up into the back of his head and he collapsed to the floor unconscious; drool trickling out the side of his slack mouth.

Eddie picked himself up from among the overturned furniture, looked at the woman, and his face brightened. "Talia!"

Madam Ryes' head snapped to look at the woman. This was Talia? The famed huntress? What was she doing in the badlands? Then she looked at Eddie and it all made sense. She looked back at Talia and smiled. "Are you here to complete your contract?" she asked.

Talia glared at her.

Eddie circled around a sleeping Buff then made his way past her and the naked man trapped under the net with Madam Ryes. As he passed, she looked at Eddie, a growing smile of satisfaction spreading across her face. "The huntress isn't here to save you. She plans to kill you."

Talia jabbed the end of the net gun into her side, bruising a rib. "That's enough," Talia spat.

Madam Ryes rubbed at her side and enjoyed the look of confusion on Eddie's face as she spoke. "She was hired to kill you and your friend."

Eddie looked at Talia, a wariness spreading across his face. "What is she talking about?"

Talia shook her head. "I'm not going to kill you. Or Van."

Eddie's face shifted back and forth between Talia and Madam Ryes. She could see the indecision in his eyes. This was exactly the opening she needed. "If you—" was all she got out. Talia moved so fast, she was a blur as she smacked the butt of her net gun across Madam Ryes face and coaxed her to instant slumber.

Chapter 83

Eddie watched Talia clock Madam Ryes across the face. She crumpled to the floor like a puppet with its strings suddenly cut. He looked at Talia, unsure of what was going on. "What was she talking about?"

Talia closed her eyes and took a deep breath before opening them again and locking him with her mesmerizing stare. "I took a contract to kill a boy and a Spinner. But I never planned on completing the contract. Not once I found out who the boy was."

"Van?" Eddie offered.

She nodded. "Yes. His family is the most powerful of all Spinner lines. I decided to help him instead of kill him in the hope that he would return the favor."

He barely heard her after she said "kill him" as he suddenly remembered what Madam Ryes said to Buff. He looked at Talia in a panic. "They are going to kill Van!"

Talia visibly reacted. "What! Where?"

"In the arena. The guy he's fighting has been told to kill him during the final round."

Talia glanced out at the sky. "They should be finishing the second round about now. Only if there is a tie will they go for a third round. We'd better go."

Eddie was hopping back and forth on his feet, wanting to run to save Van. "She said Van would die in the third round. I think she fixed the fight. I can almost guarantee you they are tied up and going for that third round."

Talia nodded and lifted the edge of the net. The naked man crawled out and shifted back into a bird. He flew up and landed on her shoulder. She turned her head sharply to look at him. "Get to the arena. Watch over Van. If they take him anywhere, I want to know it."

Walter tweeted his confirmation, flew out the door, and took off into the sky with a high-pitched battle cry.

Eddie's head was still spinning from everything that just happened. As opposed to a few minutes before he felt they actually had a chance to save Van. But only if they could get there before his opponent killed him. He looked at Talia. "Should we steal some horses?"

Talia smiled. "That's not a bad idea but we wouldn't get two feet without someone stopping us."

"Then what do we do?"

"Simple. We make someone give them to us."

Eddie frowned. The one thing he would never get used to was how everyone only said part of what they meant. Talia pointed to the shelf where Eddie had grabbed the vial of blue liquid from for his final option play. "Find the one that looks dark orange, almost brown."

Eddie stepped around Buff and grabbed a vial from the shelf and held it up. "This one?"

Talia nodded and took it from him as he stepped back over the hulking body of Buff. She looked at Eddie. "What I'm going to ask of you sounds a little extreme, but it's the only way."

She uncorked the vial and took a sip of the liquid. He noticed she kept it in her mouth as she bent down and kissed Madam Ryes on the lips. This was getting really weird, Eddie thought right before Talia started to glow. She became so bright he shielded his eyes with a hand. When the light died down he froze in place. Madam Ryes was standing in front of him smiling. He looked down, but Talia was now inside the net. He looked back up at Madam Ryes. "Wha—?"

"Don't worry, Eddie. It's me, Talia. This potion swaps bodies for a short while. Drink a little bit into your mouth. Don't swallow it and kiss the big guy to swap."

Eddie took the vial but never took his eyes off Madam Ryes/Talia. "You want me to kiss—him? On the mouth?"

"The liquid will spread across both your lips and the exchange will take place. It's the only way. Just remember, don't swallow any of it."

Eddie looked down at the sleeping hulk and then back to Madam Ryes/Talia. "Are you sure there's no other way?"

She shook her head. "Just do it. If we want to get away from the caravan alive we have to do it as them."

Eddie sipped the liquid. It tasted sweet and smooth on his tongue, like honey mixed with rose water. He held it in his mouth and Talia took the vial from him, corking it again. "Hurry up," she said and motioned for him to kiss another man on the lips.

Never in a million years, thought Eddie as he bent down, would he had ever expected his life depended on kissing a man. Especially one as ugly and smelly as Buff. He stared without blinking at the face of the sleeping giant as he got closer and closer. He puckered his lips and his eyes twitched but refused to close completely as he readied to kiss the man on the lips and let the liquid spread between them.

Suddenly Buff's eyes popped open and went extremely wide right before Eddie was about to touch his lips. Eddie jerked back and accidentally swallowed the concoction when he sat up abruptly. It burned going down and warmed comfortably in his stomach before stuffing his brain full of cotton.

Then the world collapsed in on itself.

Chapter 84

Talia, looking like Madam Ryes, stood her ground as Buff stood up while Eddie fell unconscious, collapsing unceremoniously to land on his face with a soft thud. Buff's face wrinkled with a puzzled expression as he glanced from Eddie to her and back again to Eddie. "What's going on?"

She motioned to the net that held Madam Ryes, looking like Talia, nestled in it. "I caught the huntress. A lot of help you were."

Buff squinted at the net and then at Eddie lying face down in front of him. "Was he trying to kiss me?"

Talia frowned. "Of course not."

The woman in the net started to stir. Talia kicked her across the face and she was out like a candle snuffed with damp fingers. She looked at Buff. "We need to get to the arena. I want to watch the Spinner die myself. Ready the wagon for travel."

She started to leave and he pointed at Eddie. "What about him?"

She considered her options for a moment and then gave Buff a look that said she fully expected her orders to be carried out. "Bring him along. Van needs to see that his friend is okay or he might become suspicious."

Buff stumbled to his feet and wavered slightly, still suffering from the after effects of the sleeping dart. "I don't know if we can make it there in time."

"Get the two horses and hitch them to this wagon but saddle up the fastest horse in the caravan for me. I want to be there personally to see his final breath."

Chapter 85

Van fell against the wall of the arena as fresh blood trickled down his nose from the brutal attack. His hair was matted and covered in mud. His clothes were torn and his skin looked like he spent the past hour rolling around in a blacksmith's coal pile.

He ducked as a clod of dirt slammed into the wall right where his head was positioned only a moment before. He circled his hands quickly and pushed them at his opponent, an obviously better trained Spinner named Jonas.

Jonas casually waved his hand to the side and the earth rose up to block the water flying at him. He then pushed down in front of him and the ground cracked under Van's feet.

Van sidestepped to keep from falling into the newly formed ditch as dirt refilled the hole, leaving an ugly scar in the arena floor.

Van turned just as dust exploded all around him. He was blinded and flailing his arms wildly, trying to regain the advantage he so enjoyed during the previous round.

Jonas must have been playing with him during that first round. Van won it so decisively, nearly everyone in the crowd trampled each other to be the first to change their bets for the remaining two bouts.

During the break Halen told him that Jonas was just playing with him. But Van felt powerful as he commanded the water like an expert magician and scored his points quickly.

This second round wasn't going as well and he didn't feel as confident about winning. He ducked and rolled to the side to avoid another pile of dirt launched at him. He popped to his feet in a crouch and spun his hands quickly, pulling water from the air directly above Jonas and releasing with a push to the floor.

Jonas heard the crowd's excitement swell and looked up in time to dive to the side, getting just his feet wet which only granted his opponent a partial score. But Van anticipated this and jerked a hand up quickly, drawing mud up with the water residing in the ground under his opponent. Jonas, jumping sideways to avoid the water from above, was powerless to do anything about the mud and water rising up under him and he became covered in grime as he hit the ground and the final scoring bell rang.

Van collapsed to the ground and caught his breath as the final scores were tallied. A hush fell over the crowd and Van looked up as the announcer stepped out onto the platform and gripped the lapels of his overcoat as he addressed the spectators. "Ladies and gentleman," he started and then paused to allow for the roar of laughter to die down. "We have seen some of the best spinning from our contestants here today. One in particular, Van, son of Veren who is fabled to have sacrificed himself at the gate of Dragon's Claw to keep the forces of Aeron from invading our great world."

This generated a litany of boos from the crowd. The announcer raised his hands, silently demanding for quiet and surprisingly getting it. "I know, I know. We are confined to the badlands as long as law and stability are the order of the day." He pointed an accusing finger at Van as he looked across the large crowd that filled every available seat of the arena. "And if not for this child's father's selfish and misguided deed we would be helping spread chaos across the realm." More booing emanated from the stands but the announcer continued and the crowd fell silent again quickly.

"I would like to say that the sins of the father are to be placed on the son, but sadly, even in the badlands, that is not something I can do and still consider myself a reasonable man." A few spectators in the back booed, but most stayed quiet as they awaited him to continue.

"But I can punish him for the sins of his own making." He looked down at Van. "You used the element of your opponent to defeat him rather than your own element. If you had hit him with water right before the last scoring bell, you would be victor over both matches. But you included earth, which is your opponent's element, and the final strike is invalid. I have no choice but to award victory of this match to Jonas. Now, shake hands."

Van looked over at Jonas. He was covered in mud and still lying on his side, but the smile across his face said everything. The look in his eyes confirmed to Van he was planning something, sending Van's heart racing in dread. Jonas slowly got up and walked over to Van and helped him to his feet. Van held his hand out but Jonas swatted it away and gave Van a big hug. Oohs and aahs from the crowd gave everyone in attendance the warm fuzzies. But Jonas didn't want Van to experience that same feeling. Jonas leaned his mouth close to Van's ear as they hugged.

"I'm going to kill you in the final round. I hope you've made peace with your gods. You are going to meet them real soon. Besides, I should be giving my fans what they really came here to see. Spinner blood."

Jonas released Van and stepped backward, smiled, and then raised his hands to the crowd. The stands erupted into chaos, everyone screaming and stamping their feet, threatening to vibrate the arena into rubble. Jonas soaked in the admiration and winked at Van.

In that moment Van knew he didn't want to enter the ring again with someone who not only wanted to kill him but could do it without ever laying a physical hand on him.

He looked up at the announcer. "I wish to withdraw."

A hush fell over the crowd and the announcer looked at him from the platform suspended a dozen feet above the sand-covered arena floor. "Say that again."

Van stood erect and tried to give off an air of confidence. "I wish to withdraw from the fight."

This elicited loud boos from the audience.

The announcer looked down at him, his forehead wrinkled in confusion. "You can't withdraw. The bets have already been placed."

Van pointed at Jonas who glared at him, obviously upset about being robbed of the chance to carry out his threat. "He is clearly the better Spinner. With the few hours of training I have I can't possibly beat him. Just give him the reward and let's call it a day, okay?"

The announcer looked at the crowd. You could hear a feather land on a flannel pillow from ten paces away. It fell quiet before when the announcer demanded it. But this was absolute silence. The only thing that cut through the stillness was a baby's sudden cry that was immediately stifled. Van looked up into the stands. Who was so callous as to bring a baby to a blood sport event? Now, more than ever, Van didn't want to subject a child to the brutality that his opponent promised.

The announcer tilted his head as he thought about what Van said.

Jonas yelled up at him. "You can't possibly be thinking about this! I deserve the reward because I won it! Not because some Spinner wannabe coward hands it to me."

The crowd applauded in agreement. The announcer held his hands up and the crowds calmed down. "Calm down everyone. I have—"

Another man came up behind the announcer to interrupt him and whispered in his ear. He nodded and then addressed the crowd. "It is the judgment of the officials that Van is a flight risk. So in accordance with the bylaws of The Gauntlet, the third round will begin immediately."

Van couldn't believe his ears. He looked at Jonas who was dragging his thumb slowly across his neck in the international symbol of throat slitting.

Van scanned the steel bar door that led from the contestant waiting area to the arena and saw Halen standing against it. Van ran over to him. "Do something! You have to get me out of here."

Halen looked at him like a parent looked at a child with his hand in the cookie jar. "You can't refuse once you've been entered into The Gauntlet. And certainly not after two rounds."

Van clung to the bars of the door like he was a prisoner in a jail cell.

"Jonas said he's going to kill me in the final round. Can he do that?"

Halen looked past him at Jonas who watched them with a grin plastered on his grimy face. Halen let out a quick breath. "Just remember everything I taught you and you can win this."

"No I can't. You saw how easily he went after me in the second round. I'm not ready."

Okay," Halen said quickly and reached into his bag. "Poke your hands through the bars."

Van pushed them between the bars.

"No," Halen said and pushed one hand back. "Between the same two bars."

Van shoved his hands through as Halen removed an apple from his bag along with a short length of twine. He took two bites out of it, one from each side, and placed it between his wrists. He inspected it and then took a second bite from one side and did it again, clamping the apple between his wrists. He held it up for Van to see. "I want you to hold the apple between your wrists like this."

He placed the apple between Van's wrists and wrapped the twine around several times, locking everything into place. Halen studied it intently. "Try to pull your hands apart." Van tried but they were tied tightly and the apple stayed put.

Halen nodded. "Now you're ready."

Van's eyes bugged out and his heart sped up furiously. "How does this make me ready?"

Halen looked him directly in the eyes. "Listen carefully. I positioned your hands to the optimum spacing for maximum power. Do you really believe that Jonas plans to kill you?"

Van nodded, pressing himself against the closely spaced bars as if he could squeeze between them to pop out of the arena and escape.

Halen kept his gaze steady and locked onto Van's eyes. "Then don't give him the chance. Give it all you've got. Land your scores on him and finish the round as quickly as possible. He can't make it look like an accident after the final scoring bell so you have to win and win fast."

Van knew his expression went far beyond bewilderment and Halen picked up on that. He looked around conspiratorially and then moved in close, whispering. "Curl your fingers slightly right before you feel the release. That will create a spin on the magic and, if done right, can disable your opponent."

"I thought the spinning was how we moved our hands."

"That's what we want everyone to believe. The spin happens invisibly at the magic level. It's what gives our magic the power it needs to incapacitate—or kill—our enemies."

Van looked at his hands bound together with the apple wedged between his wrists. "Will it kill him?"

Halen's serious look let Van know what he was about to say before he said it. "If done correctly. You, however, have almost no training. You should only be able to knock him out. Unless you're lucky."

Van shook his head vehemently. "I don't want to be lucky. I don't want to kill anyone."

Halen placed his hands on Van's and looked at him like a father looked at his son. Or maybe a master looked at his apprentice, Van thought.

"It's either you or him," Halen stated matter-of-factly.

The starting bell rang, its echo drowned out by the thunderous mob of spectators who elbowed each other as word spread the third and final fight had begun. This time the bouncers at the main door were unsuccessful in keeping the unticketed population from flooding into the arena. It seemed this was to be the fight of the century and everyone wanted to say they were there when it took place. It was so crowded that people spilled into the aisles and everyone, to the individual, seemed intent on causing the whole building to collapse under their rhythmically stomping feet.

Van was about to ask Halen for some words of encouragement when the crowd swelled with excitement, their collective voices rising in anticipation. He spun around with barely enough time to register the thick dust cloud zooming across the ground at him.

Chapter 86

Talia rode forward in her saddle, pushing her horse to greater speeds. Behind her Buff followed with Madam Ryes' wagon. It didn't take much to convince everyone she was Madam Ryes. She looked exactly like her and everyone was so afraid of the matriarch that they never once questioned her unexpected demands.

It was why she was able to take a horse and tell Buff to bring the wagon, with its two prisoners inside, to The Grease. She claimed she wanted to be there personally to see the death order carried out on Van.

But the reason Talia was riding as fast as she could was to stop that order from being carried out. Madam Ryes held a respectable position among those with power in the badlands and Talia hoped to use that influence to stop the contest before it was too late.

She slapped the reins back and forth, using them like a whip across her horse's ribs to urge it to go just a little faster.

Chapter 87

Van hit the ground hard and rolled violently, tossed around like a rag doll by the swirling dirt tornado.

He lifted his head and looked at Jonas who was preparing another storm. He could see the wind whipping around the arena along with the dirt. For the first two fights, Jonas only used the earth as his weapon. But now he seemed to be spinning the air as well. How was he spinning two elements at the same time? Was that even possible?

A tornado swirling full of dirt clods and tiny rocks angled straight for him. Van jumped to his feet and ran awkwardly. His hands were still tied tightly in front of him and he felt like he was in handcuffs. He stopped at the steel-barred door where Halen was watching the fight. He grabbed the bars and held tightly as the tornado tried to rip him free and throw him across the arena. The wind died down and he looked at Halen. "Is he using two elements?"

Halen nodded. "It's subtle, but it looks that way. That shouldn't be possible. There hasn't been somebody with that much control over the gift in ages," he said and then scanned the crowd. "Somebody has to be helping him. I'll find out who and stop them. You keep doing what you are doing. And try to score some points while you're at it."

Halen disappeared down the hallway without looking back.

A rock slammed into Van's spine and he arched back and cried out. It felt like his spine snapped in half as the first scoring bell rang.

Jonas scored the first point. There were still a minimum of four bells to go before the match could be called and a victor named. The first to score five points against their opponent was decided the winner. And Jonas was now one point in with Van still on the defensive and running for his life. Jonas had made it clear Van wouldn't survive all five bells.

He gasped for air as he tried to recover from the impact. Before he had the chance to regain his senses another rock slammed into his side, knocking him off his feet. He wrenched his shoulder as he landed, unable to position his arms properly while tied together. It seemed Halen's great plan only handicapped Van. Another rock grazed his head. The impact was not enough to render him unconscious since the rock ricocheted off his skull at an oblique angle. But it still sent stars swirling in his vision.

He hit the ground facedown and dust lifted all around him as he sucked in choking air. He coughed roughly and then his view of the world tunneled as he looked through the growing haze at what was happening. Jonas dug up a massive boulder that was nearly twice his size from under the arena. It floated in front of him, slowly rotating in place as he focused on keeping its massive bulk airborne.

Jonas made eye contact with Van and smirked. He was fulfilling his promise. Jonas' evil grin cut through to Van's soul and he knew, beyond a shadow of a doubt, that this was the end.

Chapter 88

Talia reached the arena and jumped from her horse, not bothering to tether it to anything. "Madam Ryes," the doorman said in surprise as she ran to the entrance and he opened it for her without demanding a ticket.

She ran inside and took the stairs two at a time to get to the lower observation deck. The crowds were thick and she elbowed her way past everyone to get a spot at the front where she could see down into the arena. Her heart stopped as she saw what sent the crowd into a frenzy.

Her mouth opened slightly as the shadow of the massive boulder cast a gloom over the arena floor as it moved slowly through the air until it was directly over Van.

She glanced around in a panic, looking for someone, anyone, who would listen to her, to Madam Ryes, and stop this madness before it was too late. When she found no one, she screamed at the top of her lungs to stop the fight. But no one heard her over the roar of the crowd that drowned her out as they chanted in unison for the spilling of Spinner blood.

Chapter 89

Halen scanned the crowd, looking for whoever was spinning air to assist Jonas, when he glanced into the arena and saw the massive boulder flying high into the air. His eyes grew wide in disbelief and, for the first time in his life, he felt completely helpless. His entire body vibrated with the impact when the massive stone dropped suddenly onto Van, smashing him flat.

"No!" he whispered breathlessly.

His knees gave way and he faltered, grabbing the shoulder of a nearby spectator for balance before he collapsed. The spectator shrugged him off as he and everyone else in the arena stood to cheer the final killing blow of the tournament.

Halen stumbled over to the inner wall and looked down into the arena. The boulder had landed directly on top of Van. There was no way anyone could have survived the crushing weight. He felt sick to his stomach and looked up into the sky above the open arena. "I'm so sorry Veren," he said barely above a whisper. "I should have trained him like you asked. I resisted because of the banishment. I should have realized, like you always reminded me, some things are more important than the rules." He looked back down into the arena and could see the sand darkening around the edges of the boulder as Van's blood seeped into the earth. "I'm sorry, Van. I failed you when you needed me the most."

He looked up and saw Madam Ryes standing on the other side of the arena looking at him. In that moment his rage boiled over and he knew he would never follow a rule of The Order again. If he could rewind time and bring Van back from the dead he would train him properly. But Madam Ryes, the woman across from him, took that choice away from him. He glanced around, looking for a source of flame so he could exact his revenge on the one who finally ended the Maclean line of Spinners forever. It was time to end the Ryes line of Travelers as well. Then he remembered he no longer held Veren's crest pin; nor the crystal. He was powerless to carry out his vengeance. He leaned forward on the fence and wished it was him inside the arena instead of Van.

Chapter 90

Talia blinked away the tears as she watched the announcer step out onto the platform that extended a short way over the arena. He raised his arms and the crowd quickly grew silent. He waited until he was certain everyone could hear him as he gazed around the crowd. "The judges noticed that one of you was helping Jonas. An air Spinner was giving an extra boost to the contestant. While this usually results in disqualification Jonas has let his emotions get the better of him and he has accidentally killed poor young Van. So I have no choice but to announce Jonas Corliss today's victor."

Jonas raised his arms and the crowd went wild. He welcomed the attention and waved his hands, extracting a more energetic reaction from the crowd that obviously loved him.

Suddenly he stepped wrong and nearly fell to the ground as he stumbled on the softening dirt. His foot sunk into a fast developing puddle of mud. He pulled it out with a sucking sound and stared incredulously at the forming puddle of water bubbling up from below the surface. The puddle suddenly exploded upward and ejected a large mud-covered worm onto the arena floor.

The crowd fell completely still and Talia wiped away the tears to get a clearer look at what was happening below. Nothing like this ever took place in the arena before. As far as anyone knew giant underground worms didn't even exist.

The worm gasped audibly and sucked in air. Then parts of the worm split from the rest, shaking off the mud. It wasn't a worm after all. It was a man. But not just any man.

It was Van!

Van rolled to his feet and stood up slowly, his eyes fixated on Jonas who was taking slow backward steps away from him.

Without taking his eyes off Jonas, Van raised his hands and twisted them back and forth quickly. Cries of shock and surprise from the spectators erupted all around the arena. Talia looked around and watched in disbelief as ale rose into the air from every mug in the audience. From all around the auditorium globs of floating ale formed into a massive liquid ball, rotating above the center of the arena and swirling around in a mixture of golden brown hues.

Jonas saw it too and started to turn to run but Van was faster. He pushed his hands forward and the massive liquid boulder slammed onto Jonas. But it didn't break apart on impact. Instead Jonas was encapsulated in the massive ball of frothy brew. Van lifted it back up into the air with Jonas inside of it flailing around in a panic and holding his breath.

The crowd was stunned to absolute silence. The only sound was that of Jonas's sloshing around as he tried to escape his watery trap. Bubbles escaped his nose and floated up to break through the surface of the big bubble of liquor.

Jonas' eyes went wide and he blew the last of his air out through his mouth and then began to struggle violently as he started drowning.

"Van!" someone yelled from the stands. Talia looked across the arena and saw Halen looking down at Van, sadness filling his eyes as he shook his head slowly. Van tore his eyes away from Halen and looked up at his dying victim.

He seemed to be contemplating letting Jonas die and then suddenly released his hands. The ball of ale lost all cohesion and dropped to the arena floor in a massive splash. Jonas hit the ground with a shattering impact that sent one of his leg bones protruding through his pants. He would have screamed out in pain if he contained more than just ale in his lungs. Instead he sputtered and vomited ale before sprawling out on his side and wheezing.

Van collapsed to his knees and then looked up at Halen. Tears filled his eyes despite the crowd growing wilder than before, chanting his name over and over and over.

Chapter 91

Van, sitting on his knees in the mud, twisted his hands around until the twine loosened. He popped the apple out from between his wrists and pulled the twine away, tossing it to one side. He looked at the muddy hole in the arena floor and remembered the huge rock falling on him. Somehow his subconscious brain knew what was coming and took over where his training was lacking.

He drew water up from below the earth and caused the ground to become as viscous as quicksand. Without thinking about it he held his breath when the boulder landed on him. But rather than crushing him to death it pushed him deeper into the soft mud. Unable to see or breathe he used the water to soften the dirt in front of him while controlling the wet mud behind him to push himself forward through the ground until he was clear of the boulder and then he guided himself back to the surface.

It all happened automatically. He wasn't directly conscious of what he was doing except for wanting to live. His subconscious took over the rest and made it happen. His subconscious was still very much in charge when he nearly drowned Jonas using all the beer he sensed in the arena.

But then Halen's voice cut through the noise of his addled brain and reminded him that he wasn't a murderer. Though at that moment he didn't seem to care much one way or the other.

He let Jonas go and then all the energy and rage evacuated his system, leaving him drained and a little worried for what he'd almost done. Less than a week before he and Eddie set out on a fun road trip. In so short a time Van went from just another college-bound freshman hopeful to a mighty wizard who was able, and willing apparently, to take a human life.

Van knew this was not the kind of life he wanted. He should be starting college and leading a normal life doing whatever he got his degree in. He was still undeclared but everyone told him that was normal. College was all about finding out who you really were. He still had a couple years to figure it out and make his decision before he was required to declare the major that would set him on his life path.

If he made it out of the arena alive he would follow Halen to Devil's Claw and return to where he belonged. He didn't belong here. This world was not for him. He didn't care that he was from a long line of wizards and he might be the most powerful one of them all. He didn't like the lack of emotion he was experiencing. He didn't like not being in control.

He watched Jonas whimpering in shock at the bone protruding from his leg. No. Van was not the one who'd done that. Something else—something primal—had taken over and almost killed another human being. Van was not in control and, if Halen hadn't stopped him, who knew what he would have done? Van never wanted to be that out of control again. One way to guarantee that was to return home where his magic could never work. Technology would suppress it and he would become normal again. Was being normal even a choice for him anymore?

Above him the announcer listened as the messenger whispered in his ear. He nodded and then raised his arms. It was not necessary as the crowd already waited in silence to hear what he was about to say. "In light of the new circumstances the judges have re-evaluated their ruling. Van Maclean is the victor of today's Gauntlet."

There was a moment of hushed silence followed by a loud string of unintelligible curses as someone in the upper row tore his betting tickets to shreds and tossed them in the air. This was followed by an exclaimed, "woo hoo!" as someone else realized his fortunes just changed for the better.

The crowd was a mix of excitement and regret as men came through the steel-barred door and pulled Jonas to his feet. He screamed in pain and then passed out. The men carried him out like a limp sack of potatoes.

Halen rushed through the door and grabbed Van's arm. "We have to go before those who lost a lot of money make it out of the stands."

Van let Halen help him up. "Where are we going?"

"Madam Ryes is already here. She can get us out."

He led Van through the contestant cells and then tossed a cloak over him to cover his head to hide his identity from casual glances as they joined the crowd that spilled through the front doors and into the city proper.

Chapter 92

Talia was stuck in the mob that slowly poured like molasses out of the arena. She finally made it out and saw Buff with Madam Ryes' wagon sitting off to one side. She scrambled through the throng of people and finally to the edge of the wagon. She looked up at him. "Buff. We need to leave as soon as we find Halen and Van."

Buff looked down at her and then his forehead wrinkled. "Who are you?"

Talia touched her face and realized the liquefied daisy dust had already worn off and she looked like her old self. Which also meant...

The door to the wagon erupted open and Madam Ryes flew down the steps, landing in a small cloud of dust that formed around her boots. She glanced over and spotted Talia. She raised her hands and pushed them at Talia. When nothing happened she felt around her neck. Her head shot up and Talia smiled as she held up the crystal. "Looking for this?" she said and blended in with the crowd that surged behind her. She heard Madam Ryes' voice rise several pitches as she screamed for Buff to go after her.

Talia circled around to the rear of the wagon while Buff, standing a good head and a half taller than most of the people in the shifting crowd, headed away from her. Madam Ryes was standing tall in the front driver's seat and scanning the crowd, straining to see which way Talia went. Buff looked back at her and shrugged. She pointed in a random direction and he headed off, pushing the throngs of people easily out of his way.

Talia was already opening the door to the wagon when she heard moaning from inside. Eddie was just waking up. Something suddenly moved in quickly behind her and forced her into the wagon. She sprawled to the floor and spun around, ready to strike back when she recognized Halen. And trailing him was Van looking worse for wear.

Halen looked at her in surprise. "Talia? Is this Madam Ryes' wagon?"

She nodded. "I—borrowed it."

He glanced around quickly and then ran over to the back wall and lifted the mirror out of its wall supports, standing it up on end. Halen slid the mirror into a notch built into the floor and rested the top of the mirror against a brightly colored ceiling decoration as if this was how the mirror should have been displayed all along.

He then started digging through drawers and pulling contents from cabinets.

"What are you looking for?" Eddie asked.

"Madam Ryes has an enchanted crystal necklace."

Talia held up the object she had also—borrowed—from around Madam Ryes' neck. "You mean this one?"

His eyes lit up and he held his hand out. She handed him the necklace and it started glowing immediately. He looked up at Talia. "Have you ever traveled through a looking glass?"

She shook her head and he frowned as he responded. "It will be disorienting to say the least. It's usually the worst for someone when it's their first time but I have no choice. I need you to go through first and be prepared to help Van and Eddie once they pass through. It will be hardest on them since they have not lived with magic as long as we have."

"I can't do any magic," she said.

"How old are you?" he replied unexpectedly.

Her heart stopped. "How old do I look?"

"You look like magic courses through your veins to keep you younger than your years. It should be enough to lessen the effects of travel." He glanced at Eddie who was sitting up and holding his head. "It will be the hardest on him. At least Van is a Spinner. But Eddie?"

Eddie shook the cobwebs from his head. "What about Eddie?" he asked.

Talia helped him to his feet. "Do you believe in magic?"

He frowned, confused by her question. "I always did. But not like I've seen in the past few days."

"Well you're about to experience some first hand and it's not going to be easy."

"Why? What are we doing?"

"We're going home," Halen said and then faced the mirror, swirling his hands around. The reflection faded away and Talia saw the walls of a much larger room through the looking glass. "I'm taking us directly to the Western Basilica," he added.

Talia suddenly felt dread fill her veins with ice. She grabbed Halen's arm. "We can't go there."

"It's the safest place for us," Halen replied.

She shook her head. "No it's not. I was hired by a Spinner from the Western Basilica to kill you and Van."

Halen stopped spinning and the mirror went dark for a moment before returning to reflecting the interior of the wagon. He stared at her, dumfounded. "What? Who?"

"I never got his name."

"Did you see what he looked like?"

"No. We spoke through Skrahyers. I don't even know what his voice sounds like."

"Then how do you know it was a Spinner?"

"My Skrahyer said the one she communicated with lives in the Western Basilica."

Halen's frown lines deepened. "Skrahyers aren't able to know who they communicate with. They are only a conduit for those speaking through them."

Talia shrugged. "I found one who could. Now I won't take a job where I can't learn as much about the source as possible."

Halen sighed heavily and looked at Van who was still in a dazed state and not listening to a word they said. If they were about to ask him to jump off a cliff he probably would.

"Okay," Halen said. "I know a place in the city south of the castle. I will take us there. The boys can spend a little time to recover from the looking glass transfer and then I have someone who will bring us in safely."

Talia crossed her arms. The past few days made her wary of handing her fate over to yet another stranger. "Is he trustworthy?"

Halen smiled. "I trust him with my life."

"Can you trust him with all our lives? Because that's what you're doing."

Halen turned away and began to swirl his hands, activating the traveling mirror again. "He is one of my oldest friends in The Order. He was there for me when everyone else turned their backs. He was the one who told me Van crossed over into Midguard and sent me to save him. He is my only ally. I don't know what I would do if I couldn't trust him."

The mirror shimmered and then showed a small, dark, room. Halen finished and held his hands still. "The looking glass will close a few seconds after I go through, so I have to be the last one. You go first, Talia. Then help the boys once they cross over."

She nodded.

An explosion rocked the wagon. The door ruptured inward and bombarded the small interior with splintered shards of wood. A few pieces pinged off the mirror but thankfully none of them cracked it. The image on the mirror shimmered as the mirror wobbled from multiple impacts. It sharpened again as Halen focused on keeping the portal open. Buff's hulking presence filled the charred doorway behind them.

"Time to go!" Talia hollered and shoved Van and Eddie into the mirror. They disappeared with a shimmer and appeared in the room reflected in its surface. Buff growled deeply as he looked at Talia with murder in his eyes and started climbing up into the wagon.

Halen kept his attention on the mirror to keep the portal active. "Go through! Now!"

"Keep Van safe," Talia shouted. "I'll find you again," she said as she shoved Halen forward. He appeared in the reflection next to a confused Van and a disoriented Eddie on the other side.

She glanced around and picked up a chunk of the door lying at her feet, raising it over her head. She smiled weakly. "You each owe me big for this. Don't worry. I always collect."

She ignored the cries coming from the mirror begging her to reconsider her plan as she brought the pointy chunk down hard. Pieces of silver-coated glass shards rained down around her feet, trapping her in the wagon with an enraged enemy.

She spun around and crouched, readying herself for Buff's explosive attack telegraphed by his tightening shoulder muscles. "Come on, big boy," she hissed through gritted teeth, her bold grin widening. "Let's do this!"

Chapter 93

Van sat on the bed in the second story room of the abandoned house they found themselves in after passing through the mirror. They all watched in horror as Talia smashed the mirror before crossing over. The last thing they saw was Buff behind her; with only one thing on his mind.

Halen told him that she was a huntress and could take care of herself but Van could tell Halen counted himself among those who didn't believe what he said either. What they did agree on was that she kept Madam Ryes from coming after them by destroying the traveling mirror.

Van watched out the window. He calmed himself by observing the waves crashing against the rocky beach. He thought he recognized the scene spreading out before him but that was not possible. He'd never been in Midguard before so how could he recognize where he was?

He barely recognized himself, he thought as his memory called up the scene at The Gauntlet where he was drowning his opponent in midair.

The door opened behind him. In the reflection of the window pane Van watched Eddie walk in and flop down on the other bed in the room. It was not so much a bed as it was a bunch of straw stuffed into a mattress and thrown into the corner, something Halen called a paillasse. Van received the only real bed in the room so Eddie's was hastily assembled with readily available ingredients and dropped in a corner of the floor.

Eddie leaned against the wall and tucked his hands behind his head as he looked over at Van. "I hear we get to go home tomorrow."

Van continued to look out the window. He didn't feel like talking and just wanted to quietly reflect on what he had almost done. He didn't understand why he couldn't feel regret or remorse about it. It wasn't like him.

Eddie shifted uncomfortably on the paillasse. "Of all the things I thought might happen on the road trip to our new bachelor pad, this never even made the list of possibilities."

Van remained silent. For some reason, whenever he didn't feel like talking that was when Eddie wanted to talk the most. "My favorite part was meeting the sisters. Harmony and Maura. I noticed their wagon gone when I was going around fixing things. They left in the middle of the night without even saying goodbye. I would have thought I would be broken up about it more." He shrugged. "I guess it was like one of those summer camp crushes. Didn't mean much to either of us."

Van stared out at the window. His chest still experienced phantom pains with the memory of the dream. Or did something actually happen? Maura said she loved him. He wanted to feel more but he couldn't. Maybe Eddie was right. It was just this world's version of a summer camp crush and now it was time to move on. But he was having a hard time moving on from what happened in The Gauntlet.

Eddie sensed his distance. "Do you want to talk about anything?" he asked.

Van realized he did. He looked over at his closest friend, speaking barely above a whisper. "I almost killed that guy in The Gauntlet."

Eddie nodded and his face went introspective. "Halen told me about that. Wish I'd been there to see it."

"No you don't." Van shot back.

Eddie sat up. He grimaced and leaned to one side, patting down the mattress to flatten out a lump. He settled back on it and smiled. "That's better. Look, Van, Halen explained to me that the magic in you is not something you have automatic control over. You have to learn how to handle it."

Van remembered how it simply took over and did what it needed to keep him alive. "I don't think I can."

Eddie chuckled. "Don't say that, Van. For as long as I've known you, you never shied away from learning something new. You were the first one to jump from the high dive. And you didn't lose your swim trunks like we all worried about. You conquered everything you set your mind to. You can conquer this too."

Van's eyes darkened. "When I use my power I don't feel like I'm in control."

Eddie frowned. "What do you mean?"

"In The Gauntlet something took over me and it was like I was just watching it all happen. I would never have stopped if Halen didn't call out to me. And for a brief moment I didn't think I would stop. Or could stop. But then it just let go on its own."

"What are you trying to say, Van?"

"I wasn't in control, Eddie. And I didn't feel anything while it was happening."

"So it didn't hurt?" suggested Eddie.

Van shook his head. "Not like that. I mean inside. I knew I didn't want to hurt anyone but I didn't care when I was hurting that guy in The Gauntlet. I wasn't angry. I wasn't sad. I know I should feel regret for almost drowning him." Van looked at Eddie. "But I don't. And I don't know why."

Eddie looked at him thoughtfully. "I feel it too, Van. For better or worse this place has changed us. When Halen said we were going home I didn't feel as excited as I thought I would be. I should be happy or at least nervous about returning home. But I don't feel anything. We aren't the same naïve snot-nosed kids driving to a college town with our whole lives ahead of us. We've seen too much to just go back to that."

Van nodded. "That's true. Now that I know I have this—power—inside me, how can I go back to living a normal life?"

"Are you saying you want to stay?" Eddie asked. Van was slightly startled by the question and he lowered his head, thinking for a long time about what it implied. Eddie, thankfully, remained quiet and let Van think for once. He finally raised his head. "No. I don't belong here. What about you?"

Eddie shrugged noncommittally. "I kinda like it here. I could stay for the rest of my life. But it wouldn't be any fun without you around. I go wherever you go, chief."

Van smiled back. "Thanks for sticking by me, Eddie."

"Are you kidding? When we get back home all we will have is each other. Nobody, and I do mean nobody, is going to believe any of this. In fact, I think we should keep what happened here under our hats or we'll be committed to an insane asylum faster than you could say I'm not crazy."

Van smiled wider. "You got that right. I lived through it and I barely believe it myself."

Eddie snapped his fingers. "Oh, right. Halen wanted me to see if you would meet him outside."

Van's forehead wrinkled questioningly. "Why?"

Eddie shrugged. "I don't know."

Van looked out the window and suddenly realized why it looked familiar. He stood up quickly and left the room without saying a word to Eddie. Halen could confirm what he just figured out.

Chapter 94

Van found Halen standing in the dark along the edge of the cliff overlooking the ocean and talking to a young boy. He handed a note to the young boy who then ran off without giving Van so much as a glance.

Van approached slowly and Halen looked out over the water. "Do you recognize this place?" Halen asked.

Van looked along the coastline sparkling in the moonlight. "It looks like San Francisco. But it can't be. I thought I was in Midguard."

Halen nodded. "All three realms have the same geological foundation. The continents, rivers, land features, they are all the same between the realms. What is different is the impact that magic and technology have on shaping the world."

Van spun around and it was then he recognized the mountains that circled the bay. It was San Francisco without the glut of tall buildings. A massive castle stood where the downtown of San Francisco should have been. Halen noticed where he was looking.

"The Western Basilica was built around the gate at Devil's Claw to protect it."

"From Aeron," Van said suddenly.

Halen nodded but looked at him quizzically. "Who told you?"

Van shrugged. "The announcer at The Gauntlet mentioned my father stopped Aeron from getting here with his army."

Halen nodded and then his face grew somber. "I'm afraid that Aeron will get through the next time. But that is not your concern. This is not your fight."

"But if he gets through won't he be moving on to take over my world?"

"That is his plan. But what he doesn't know—can't even begin to understand—is how far technology has advanced in your world. His magic would be useless. I'm sure it will come as a big shock to him but Techrealm is safe from his advances no matter what he tries. He might influence little things here and there but he could never use full magic there. Midguard will take some time for him to conquer but it will eventually fall to him as his army grows. He will recruit his growing army from the badlands. He will then become unstoppable fairly quickly."

Van thought about the people he and Eddie met as they made their way through Midguard. "Why are you trying to save this place? Everyone around here is already miserable. How much worse could it get?"

Halen turned to him. His eyebrows knit together and a frown wrinkling the rest of his forehead. "You haven't seen the best Midguard has to offer."

"There's more?"

Halen's frown shifted to a wistful smile and his eyes lost focus as they looked upon memories. "There's the verdant gardens of the far east. The sprawling metropolises of the old country. Even the limitless jungles south of the equator with a variety of life unmatched anywhere in the three realms." His eyes focused again on Van. "There is much worth saving in Midguard. Your father understood that better than anyone. Unfortunately you didn't get to see the best places and the wonderful people there. But a lot has to change if we hope to defend the realm successfully against the likes of Aeron. If we do manage to push him back, millions will die in his conquest of this world."

Van thought hard about his next question and finally decided he needed to know the answer. "If I stayed would you train me?"

Halen smiled. "Of course. But one man won't make a difference in the fight against evil. You would most likely die. That is not the best way to win this war. It is better if you return home to where you belong. Where you will be safe."

Van looked at his hands. Hands that almost killed someone. "Maybe you're right," he said.

Halen smiled and placed an arm around Van's shoulders. "But I am glad to have been given the chance to meet you. You have become a fine young man. Your father would have been proud."

Van smiled. "Thanks, Halen. That means a lot to me." Van said though he didn't feel much of the pride he knew he should.

Halen clapped his hands together. They echoed loudly in the silence of the night. "You need to get some rest. I sent a messenger to my friend in The Order. He will guide us safely to the gate. And then you go home. Go ahead and get some rest. The worst is behind us."

Chapter 95

Calen held the dagger against the young boy's neck, a trickle of blood forming along the edge of the sharpened blade. The boy's eyes were wide with fear.

"Do not lie to me again, boy," Calen growled. "Who gave you this letter?"

The boy shivered, causing the blade to slice deeper into his skin. "I swear. He told me his name was Halen."

Calen held the letter up. "Who else knows he asked you to give me this?"

"Nobody," the boy squeaked.

Calen pulled away the blade and shoved the boy away from him. "If you tell anyone about this your grandchildren's grandchildren will wish you kept your mouth shut. Now go."

The boy dashed from the room without looking back. Calen unspooled the message from someone who was supposed to be dead.

"Calen," the message began in Halen's handwriting. Calen would recognize that stylistic capital letter C anywhere. "I am in Bay City at the place where we used to play as children. I have the package and await your instructions on when and where to deliver. Always yours, Halen."

Calen crumpled the parchment letter in his fist. Halen was close. And he brought the young Spinner with him. How could this be? Halen was dead. The Skrahyer confirmed it. It was his blood at the hunters' camp.

The hunters!

Calen cursed himself. He killed them before talking with them. He should have verified they actually killed Halen before he dispatched them. But he had very little time to act and the Skrahyer already confirmed it. Halen was dead.

He suddenly glanced at the reports on his desk from the Watchers. They identified Spinner magic being used in the badlands the day before. But that was on the other side of the Ridge Mountain Range from where they found Halen's blood and Veren's old crest pin. Halen would never have let go of that pin if he was alive. Everything added up to him being dead. Everything except the letter he just received written in Halen's own hand.

He thought about using the candle to ask Aeron how he should proceed but he knew what was needed of him. And Aeron would undoubtedly reward his initiative if he took care of this on his own.

Calen pulled on the string yellowed with age around his neck. It was stained by years of living so close to his skin. He removed the key that hung from the knot at the bottom and crossed the room to a locked cabinet. Once unlocked, he pulled on the handle. The doors moaned from neglect and disuse. He hadn't opened this cabinet in years. He never needed to before now.

He reached in and removed a dagger secured tightly in its sheath. Calen had commissioned this dagger from the Forge of the Twin Dwarves. Upon completion he ordered them imprisoned in the southern continent before taking the dagger to a powerful witch in Midguard. At his request she cursed it. She assured him that whenever it was removed from its sheath it would kill someone before returning to its casing. Its first confirmed kill was the old witch herself. He placed the dagger in its sheath and never removed it again. As far as he knew her dried blood still clung to the intricate etchings on the side of the double-edged blade.

He inspected the sheathed dagger and then tucked it deeply into his cloak. He must get to Halen before daybreak. Before Bay City woke up and there would be witnesses placing him in the city.

He smiled to himself as he felt the weight of the blade in his interior pocket. It was time to see if the curse was still active. Even if it was not the blade still held the blood of a bona fide witch. Blood, even decades old, that could kill a man once mingled with his own. His smile widened as he remembered the witch's blood would do far worse to Halen before it killed him and he would plead for the sweet release of death.

Calen opened his door slowly stopping each time it creaked. He peeked into the hallway. It was clear and he closed the door just as painstakingly slow before he disappeared into the night. He was so eager to conclude his nefarious task that he failed to notice the shadow following him out of the Western Basilica and into the dark countryside.

Chapter 96

Halen sat alone in the living room. The owner of the house abandoned it long ago leaving only a few candles that they used to hold back the darkness of the empty house. Van and Eddie were settled in their room upstairs, though Halen very much doubted they were getting any sleep.

Halen remembered the look in Van's eyes when his powers acted on their own, nearly killing in the process. Halen remembered experiencing those same feelings when he was apprenticed to Van's father.

Veren was very patient with him and helped him work through the feelings of helplessness. But he remembered feeling like an observer when something inside him took over and spun the elements without any input from him. Veren taught him how to control the magic. Taught him how to control the monster living alongside his spirit in the same body.

But Van didn't have years of training to learn how to govern his ability in a controlled environment before releasing the beast inside him. He received only the barest of instruction and then been thrown into an encounter; forced to use his powers or die trying. And the power residing inside him wasn't about to let him die.

Van's powers were unlike anything Halen ever witnessed before or even heard sung about by the traveling bards. Not even the legends of powerful Spinners from times long ago came close to what Halen saw Van accomplish in the arena.

Was the prophecy true? Could Van be the one written about so long ago? If so was Halen dooming two realms because he was unwilling to defy the commands of The Order? No. He was willing to defy their orders. But Van didn't want to continue his training. That much was evident despite his question. He was too afraid of what he could do. His power was raw and unrestrained. It frightened him. Halen could see it in his eyes. Halen wanted to tell him that it frightened all of them in the beginning. Learning that there was a part of them that was separate from them but at the same time inseparable from them. That knowledge was all part of their training.

But Van wasn't an apprentice in the Wizard's Order.

And Halen was not his master.

A light knock on the glass pane of the window brought Halen out of his quiet reflection. His eyes refocused and he saw the face of his one remaining friend in Midguard looking in at him.

Chapter 97

"Van?"

Van's eyes popped open and he sat up. Halen was holding a candle that illuminated his face, the wax rolling down one side and pooling around the holder.

"Is it morning already?" Van half-heartedly stifled a yawn and wiped away the sleep from his eyes. A glance out the window told him it was still dark.

"Not yet," whispered Halen. "We are traveling under the cover of night. It will be safer."

Eddie sat up in the corner. "Is it time to go home?" he asked bulging his eyes and stretching his face to force himself to wake up faster.

"That it is, Eddie," Halen responded and headed out the door. Van followed him with Eddie right behind. They stepped out into the cool air, a slight breeze threatening to extinguish the candle. Halen finished the job and blew the flame out. They met up with another cloaked figure standing several feet away from the house along the edge of the road.

Halen clasped hands with the cloaked man and then turned to Van and Eddie. "This is Calen. He will get us to the gate safely."

Calen smiled at Van. "So you are Veren's boy?"

Van's face warmed as he blushed. "So I've been told."

Calen nodded. "Nice to meet you. Let's get you home."

Van followed several steps behind Halen and his friend. Eddie fell alongside him as they walked. "Well this is exciting. Sneaking around in the middle of the night on a secret mission to get us home."

Van shot him a look that lost its impact in the darkness that shrouded them. The moon was low in the sky and deep shadows filled every available space the moonlight couldn't reach. Van thought he saw a shape move in the darkness. He focused his attention on the spot but couldn't see anything as they continued to walk closer to the sounds of crashing waves.

Up ahead Halen and Calen stopped short. Halen's voice rose in agitation, enough that Van could hear it over the waves' rhythmic thrashing of the rocky shore. "We are going the wrong way!"

In the faint moonlight a flash drew Van's eye to focus on Halen and his friend. And then suddenly both Spinners became embroiled in a struggle over a dagger raised above their heads.

Van and Eddie were stunned to silence as the men spun in a tight circle grunting from the effort as they fought for control of the dagger. The dagger flashed downward and Halen doubled over; collapsing to the ground.

"Halen!" Van screamed and then turned his attention on Calen who stood over Halen's body with the dagger in his hand. He glanced up at Van with a murderous look in his eye that was clearly visible even in the faint moonlight.

Van's fists clenched and he took a step backward as Calen approached, the dagger flashing in his hand in the stark moonlight.

"You can't run from me, boy," Calen said. "Aeron wants you dead. And dead you shall be!"

Van looked at Halen who lie motionless along the edge of the cliff. The crashing water against the rocks below echoed up loudly in the still of the night. Waves! Water!

As he looked at Halen's still form on the ground a small amount of rage built up inside him and he felt something else take over. He decided not to resist and let it happen. Van glared at Calen, held his hands in front of him, and curled them into a ball.

Calen saw what he was doing and laughed. "What do you think you're going to do? Use spinning against me? You have no training!"

"I don't need training," Van said through clenched teeth. "I just have to let go."

Van was suddenly far away from his body as if watching from the distance. He watched as he pulled his hands back and the ocean swept up over the edge of the cliff and slammed into Calen, knocking him to the ground.

The dagger skittered across the ground but Van didn't care. He was focused on lifting Calen high into the air held in the massive rippling sphere of ocean. Calen clawed at the water around him as he blew bubbles. He wasn't given the chance to take a breath before being engulfed in water so he was quickly running out of air.

Van held his hands in position as he watched the man who killed

Halen drown. This time Halen wasn't around to talk him out of killing. He didn't know if he would or not. It didn't matter what he would do. He wasn't in control. His instincts took over. Van wondered if his instinct were always so bloodthirsty or if awakening the magic within him changed him.

Inside the sloshing ball of water suspended in the air the cloaked man struggled to swim. But Van kept pushing him back into the center so that he would never feel the comfort of breathable air again.

"Stop!" a voice yelled from the side. Van looked over at Eddie but the voice had been pitched higher than his by several octaves. Besides, Eddie was looking away from him in the direction the sound came from. Van peered into the darkness where Eddie was looking as a young woman stepped out into the open from the nearby stand of trees. "Please. Let him go."

From the recesses of his mind Van recognized the voice. It was stronger than what he remembered but there was a hint of familiarity that he couldn't shake.

She took another step forward. "Please, Van. Don't do this."

The water around the cloaked man shimmered slightly as Van reacted to his name being used by the stranger with the familiar voice. But his other self, his more powerful self, was still focused on exacting revenge for Halen's death and added more water from the ocean below to the wave suspended in the air. Calen was weakening as he struggled to hold onto his final breath.

"The Van I knew wasn't a killer," the girl said.

Van looked over at her, confusion filling his face. He finally placed the voice. "Nina?" he asked incredulously.

Her face lit up. "Yes, Van. It's me, Nina."

His forehead wrinkled deeply as he struggled to comprehend this new information. "What are you doing here?"

"I'm an apprentice, Van." She pointed up at the man floating in the wave of water. "I'm his apprentice. Please let him go."

"He killed Halen," Van replied.

"I know it looks like that. Let him go and we can find out what's going on. If you kill him we will never know."

Van regarded the cloaked figure floating in the water and barely moving. A few bubbles escaped the man's lips and then his mouth opened, filling with water. Van released his magical grip on the wave and everything came crashing to the ground.

Van felt so weak once he was fully in control again. Eddie was right there to keep him from collapsing to the ground. "I got you, buddy."

Van could barely stand, but he was aware of Nina rushing over to the man who attacked Halen. "Calen," she yelled. "Can you hear me?"

Eddie hefted Van up and supported him under the shoulder but it was no use. The world was fading away. He used too much of his energy to suspend the wave with his victim inside of it. He struggled to stay awake but exhaustion won out and his vision slowly tunneled to absolute darkness.

Chapter 98

Van's eyes fluttered open. He sat up to find himself in bed in a large stone room. His memory of how he got there was incoherent. Through the open window he could see that it was either early morning or late afternoon.

"You're awake," a soft voice said behind him. He turned and winced as his head felt like it spun much faster than was physically possible. He closed his eyes until the room stopped whirling around him.

He finally opened his eyes to find himself looking at Nina. She smiled at him. "How do you feel?"

He ran a rough tongue across bone-dry teeth. "Like I've been lying in the desert for a hundred years."

She lifted the glass of water from the bedside table and helped him drink it without spilling. "You are a Water Spinner, Van. You dehydrate yourself when you use your power."

He swallowed the water greedily, spilling some down the front of his shirt despite how careful Nina was being. When the glass was empty she turned to fill it from the pitcher of crystal-clear water on the same table.

He watched her, his mind trying to reconcile the young woman before him as the girl he once knew.

"How did you get here?" he asked.

She turned back to him and held out the glass. He took it and drank it all again.

"Lance is here too," she said.

He spit out the water in his mouth in surprise. "You're both here? Why? How?"

Nina laughed and dabbed at him with a towel. "We're Spinners. Just like you."

His mouth hung open. Nina and Lance were Spinners? The memories of their three families being so close when they were young suddenly made sense. But one thing burned in his memory. He refocused his eyes and looked at her. "How come you never returned my calls or emails?"

Her eyes darkened and the corners of her mouth turned down. "I couldn't."

"Why not?"

Her breathing increased rapidly and he could hear her inhale and exhale sharply as the emotions of seeing him again brought back the guilt of her broken promise. "I wanted to. And I thought about you every day. But a week after you left Lance and I were sent here. It is prohibited to communicate with anyone in Techrealm. Please believe me that if I could have…"

She let the words fade to silence. He understood. He'd been in this world long enough to know she was telling the truth.

"Halen?" was all he needed to say to ask the only other question in his mind.

"I'm okay." Halen's voice echoed strongly from the doorway. Van whipped his head around and then closed his eyes until the room stopped spinning again. When he opened them again Halen was already standing beside the bed. He smiled at Nina. "Thanks to the fast thinking of Nina here, help came quickly and I am doing much better. I will have a scar and it will take some time before I fully recover from the poisoning effects of the witch's blood mixing with my own but I am fine."

Van looked at Nina. "What about…?"

She smiled sadly but it was Halen who answered. "You didn't kill him, Van. And thanks to your quick thinking we have routed a supporter of Aeron from within The Order." He looked at Nina. "I can't imagine the setback he has caused to The Order by working from within to weaken it." He looked back at Van. "Thanks to you he was forced to reveal himself. I don't know if there is enough time to undo the damage he has done but at least we have a chance to recover. Slim as it may be."

"We will correct the mistakes made by Calen," a deep voice bellowed from the doorway. "But you, Halen, are not part of it."

Halen and Nina turned, stepping aside so Van could see who entered through the door. He was an older man, his greying hair bobbing in the air as he approached the bed. The man smiled down at Van. "My name is Falen. I am the High Master Spinner of the Wizard's Order."

Van's heart beat faster. According to Halen this was the man who banished him from The Order and decreed that Van would never receive training as a Spinner.

"Mr. Falen," Van began.

"Just Falen," he interrupted. "And I know what you are going to say. But as far as The Order is concerned there are no special circumstances. My original decree is to be enforced," he glanced at Halen. "Despite the fact it has been disregarded as of late."

"He didn't have a choice," Van blurted.

Falen looked at him. Van cringed away from that look. It terrified him to his very core. "We always have a choice. It is because of Halen's continually poor decision making skills that I cannot rescind my ruling. He is a disruptive force. And that is not something The Order can allow among its ranks."

"What will happen to him?" Nina asked.

"That is not your concern, child."

"Don't worry about me," Halen added. "I'll go back to living quietly in the outer reaches of Midguard."

Falen turned on him. "And now that I have recovered Veren's crest pin, you will be unable to continue using your Spinner abilities."

Halen lowered his eyes. "Yes, sir."

Falen looked back at Van, no caring reflected in his eyes. "The gate is being prepared for your return to Techrealm. You will be back in your world within the hour." He spun around and was about to leave when Halen stepped in front of him. "Can I have a few minutes alone with Van?"

Falen glanced at Van and then back to Halen. "I guess you can't do any more harm."

Falen left and Halen looked at Nina. "I would like to speak with Van alone."

Nina nodded and left the room, closing the door after her.

As soon as they were alone Halen slipped the crystal from around his neck and held it out to Van. "If you ever change your mind about wanting to be trained this will give your power a boost in Techrealm and you can return to Midguard."

Van stared at the necklace like it was a snake ready to bite him if he reached for it. "I don't belong here. And you heard Falen. I'm not wanted here. Why would I come back?"

Halen's eyes locked on his. "I know you feel that way now. But I'm giving you the option to change your mind. All you have to do is submerge yourself in a large body of water and think about coming here. The crystal will focus your power and you will rise from the water in Midguard."

Van stared at the crystal as it slowly rotated at the end of the string. "How do you know I can do that?"

"Because you've done it before."

Van remembered the crash. Eddie's car landed in a river and then they crawled out of a lake. "I did that?"

"The crash was caused by Calen when he tried to kill you. He confessed that much. But your power triggered and brought you and Eddie to Midguard to keep you safe."

Van laughed apprehensively, remembering everything that happened to him since the crash. "Coming here was not what I should have done if I wanted to stay safe."

"But you did it, Van. You and Eddie are alive. If you had stayed in Techrealm you would both be dead by now. Calen would have made sure of it. He couldn't use magic against you here. It would have been noticed by the Watchers immediately. The Spinner part of you knew that. Knew exactly where you would be safest."

Van slumped in the bed. "That's the problem. I'm not in control when the—power—takes over."

Halen smiled. "I will train you like your father trained me. You can be my apprentice. Even if for just a little while." He moved the crystal closer to Van. "I will be here for when you decide you are ready to learn to control that which lives deep inside you."

Van looked at Halen with alarm. "What about the decree?"

Halen shrugged. "I will train you deep inside the deadlands. No one will ever know."

Van frowned. "That doesn't sound like a nice place."

"It's not so bad. Not as dry as the badlands. It's a little more humid with plenty of forests to hide in. But the use of magic within its boundaries is hard to detect by the Watchers. I can safely train you there with no one the wiser. Take the crystal. Even if you never use it to return it will remind you of who you really are."

Van finally took the necklace and slipped it over his head. "Thank you, Halen. For everything."

Halen's eyes sparkled. "No. Thank you, Van. For reminding me of who I really am."

The door opened suddenly and men in cloaks, their hoods casting deep shadows across their faces, entered the room. Van instinctively tucked the crystal under the collar of his shirt and out of sight.

"Is it time?" Halen asked one of the cloaked figures.

He nodded.

Halen turned back to Van. "Let's go." He helped Van to his feet and supported him as they headed across the Western Basilica toward the gate that would take him back to his world.

Chapter 99

Van was surprised to see that the gate was nothing more than a large circular stone platform with symbols and words in a strange language carved along the surface of the outer edge. Eddie was already standing on the platform, bouncing nervously on the balls of his feet. Halen helped Van step up onto the raised dais and then Eddie took over, supporting Van as they moved to the center of the gate.

Van looked at Eddie. "I can stand on my own."

Eddie smiled and slowly let go before taking a step back. Van stood tall and looked down at the cloaked men gathered around in front of the platform. Falen stepped through the crowd. He looked up at Van and Eddie. "Let me take this opportunity to thank the both of you for finding Aeron's spy in The Order. I have known for some time that there might be someone working for him inside our ranks. But I was never able to find out who. Goodbye Van, son of Veren. Goodbye Eddie, son of none."

Van looked at Eddie. Eddie shrugged and smirked. "I told him I was a foster kid and never knew my biological father."

The world shimmered around them and suddenly they weren't standing on the large stone. They were instead standing in the middle of the road among tall buildings. Van expected a bigger light show, or at least a lengthy chanting of the men gathered around the round stone. It happened so quickly he wasn't entirely sure anything had taken place at all until a car honked behind them, making he and Eddie jump in surprise.

"Get outta the road, you idiots!" a cab driver hollered out his window and honked again. Eddie grinned at Van. "Home, sweet, home," he said as they rushed for the sidewalk. All around them people talked loudly on cell phones as they crowded past them. There was even the obligatory barking dog in the distance.

Van and Eddie looked at each other. Eddie pointed past him at a phone booth. A rare sight but thankfully they still existed. "Time to call your mom?"

Van looked at the activity around him. "I guess so," he said while already missing the tranquil countryside of Midguard.

Chapter 100

Van took a deep breath and stepped through the office door of the student counselor at his college.

The last few days went by in a blur. Van and Eddie had appeared in the middle of downtown San Francisco. In the exact same spot the gate was situated in Midguard. They made a collect call to his mother which resulted in two plane tickets bound for home the same day. Despite his mother's insistence he take a break, especially after learning the truth about his father, Van decided he needed to get on with the life he was meant to live.

The counselor's nameplate on his desk told everyone who walked in that his name was Dennis Neese. He looked over the rim of his glasses at Van while still filling out something on a handwritten report. He motioned to the chair in front of his desk with the pen in his hand. "Close the door and have a seat, Mr. Maclean."

Van did as asked and sat down to wait for Neese to finish his very important work. Neese took his sweet time filling out boxes on the page, most likely to let Van know who was in charge. When he finished he clicked the pen with his thumb three times and pushed the report to the side before smiling coolly at Van. "Mr. Maclean. You missed the first week of classes and you still wish to attend the rest of the semester?"

Van nodded. "Yes, sir. As my mother explained on the—"

Neese held a finger in the air, silencing Van as he slid a pad of yellow notepad paper in front of him and scanned it. "Yes. Your mother phoned my office to inform us that you experienced car trouble and that is why you were late for the start of the semester."

Van nodded again enthusiastically. "Right, I—"

The finger went in the air again and silenced Van abruptly. Neese studied him for a beat. Then he removed his glasses, folded the temples closed, unfolded them, and then folded them again before placing the glasses neatly on the edge of his desk. He adjusted their orientation three times before he was satisfied. He then leaned forward to let Van know that what he was about to say was extremely important.

"College is your introduction to the adult world, Mr. Maclean. You are here to learn responsibility and—"

"Right—"

The finger popped up, silencing Van for a third time.

"Do not interrupt me again, Mr. Maclean. I am an educator and it is my responsibility to educate you on how things work in the real world. Your fantasy life is over. Other people will no longer bend over backwards to make sure everything goes your way. College is the time to find out who you really are." He glanced down at the legal pad before looking back at Van. "I checked the distance from your hometown to the college. The trip should have only taken a couple of days." He paused for several seconds testing to see if Van would interrupt him again. Van sat there in silence, patiently waiting for him to continue. Well, outwardly patient. His insides were ready to explode as his leg bounced steadily, shaking the entire floor. Neese ignored it and continued.

"Yet your mother didn't call us until nearly three days after classes began. That is well after the time when you should have contacted admissions yourself if you wished to remain enrolled. Your seats for each class were given away. There just is no place for you right now. There is nothing I can do for you this semester, but I have you all set for the winter session. I even moved the tuition you paid, so you won't be losing anything but time. I'm sorry but that is the best I can do for you."

Without giving Van a chance to debate the issue, he glanced at the clock. "I have another scheduled appointment. Is there anything else, Mr. Maclean?"

Van shook his head and stood to go.

"Mr. Maclean," Neese started and then waited to continue until Van was giving him his full attention. "All the studies suggest that you lose skills when they're not utilized. I wouldn't want you to struggle next semester so I highly suggest checking out the nearby community colleges. Enroll in some classes. Keep up your studying skills. Am I making myself clear?"

"Of course, sir. Thank you."

Neese picked up his pencil and jabbed it at Van as he spoke. "It doesn't have to be anything related to your projected major. In fact, take this time to do something you wouldn't normally have considered.

Is there something you're interested in learning while you wait for the next semester to begin?"

The crystal around his neck seemed to grow heavier as he thought about it. He suddenly broke out into a wide smile. "You know what? There is something I could study."

Neese nodded. "Excellent. We'll see you next semester then?"

Van turned away. "Yeah," he said quietly as he touched his shirt where the crystal hung. "Next semester."

Chapter 101

Eddie stared at the thin cable that went from a computer mounted on a metal stand with wheels to the plug just under the dashboard of the car he was supposed to be repairing. He shook his head with a slight chuckle. Cars were becoming nothing more than computers on wheels just like the actual computer on wheels he used to diagnose car troubles. He stared at the rows of numbers and graphical bar charts on the monitor that were supposed to be telling him more than he could ever want to know about the minutiae of the car's operation. Things were just getting too complicated. Even now, the recalls had started rolling out after hackers proved they could take control of a car's brakes and steering remotely over the Internet while it was screaming down the highway at seventy miles an hour.

He missed the simplicity of cars built fifty years before he was even born. No, he thought to himself, what he really missed was the simplicity of the mechanics in Midguard. There he was a superstar. Here he was three decades out of date despite not even being that old.

He sensed the presence of someone else in the garage. He looked up from the green monochrome monitor and his face lit up. "Van!"

Van walked to him quickly and looked around. "Are we alone?"

Eddie glanced around. "Yeah. The boss is at lunch and this garage doesn't get much traffic anyway. Why?"

Van took a deep breath. "I'm going back."

Eddie's heart skipped a beat and then went into overdrive. "You don't mean…"

Van nodded. "I want to learn to control this—power—running through me. Besides, they won't let me finish out this semester. I have to wait a few months for the next one. I thought, why not wait it out in Midguard?"

Eddie pushed the computer cart away. It rolled easily on its wheels until the cable pulled taught and stopped it. "What are we waiting for?"

Van grinned. "We just need a large body of water."

Eddie hooked a thumb over his shoulder. "There's a water tower out back. Do you think that's enough?"

Van's eyes sparkled. "There's only one way to find out."

Other Books by the Author

A is for Apprentice (Fantasy)

Oliver Twist: Victorian Vampire (Fantasy Horror)

A Tale of Two Cities with Dragons (Fantasy)

Shade Infinity (Science Fiction Thriller)

Peacekeepers X-Alpha Series (Thriller)
    Inherit the Throne
    The Warrior's Code

Steampunk OZ Series (Science Fiction Novellas)
    Forgotten Girl
    The Legacy's World
    Emerald Shadow
    The Future's Destiny
    The Dangerous Captive
    Missing Legacy
    Shadow of History
    The Edge of the Hunter

Fugue: The Cure (Science Fiction Short Story)

Jason and the Chrononauts (Kid's Adventure)

Be the first to know about Steve DeWinter's next book. Follow the URL below to subscribe for free today!

http://bit.ly/BookReleaseBulletin